Harvest

A Josh Ingram Novel

t.g. brown

Book layout by www.ebooklaunch.com

Paperback ISBN 978-1-928029-02-1
ebook ISBN 978-1-928029-03-8

Visit my website at www.thrillerreads.com

Also by t.g. brown

O'Henry
(A Josh Ingram Novel)

For Lucas, Jasmine, and Jotie

Prologue

R oy liked it when Edna sat with him on the veranda, taking turns sipping on their lemonade, their rocking chairs almost touching, wood creaking on wood. It was enough for him, being there, sharing the moment, listening to the crickets and watching the bordering tamaracks fade into the darkening sky.

She wasn't the girl he'd met in high school, lithe and agile, fairy-like, where the slightest breeze might swirl her into the air as though she was an untethered feather. Now tipping the scales at 290 pounds, the nightly docking of her cheeks of burden had become a drawn-out ordeal, filled with huffs and puffs and grunts, and always ending with a long wooden groan as the cherry wood accepted its fate. And as he had done in all the evenings before, Roy looked away as though something had caught his attention. Of course, he knew that she knew, but that didn't matter. The alternative would make her uncomfortable, and he wouldn't have that, not for the world.

He'd never paid much attention to how she'd blossomed over the years. In his eyes, she was still the same girl he'd fallen for so many years ago. He loved everything about her. The way the corner of her mouth raised when she greeted him.

Her thoughtful, often infectious laughter that erupted when he told one of his lame jokes, and there were plenty of those. He loved the way she helped others when darkness or depression slipped under the door. And most of all, he loved being there, comforting her, knowing he made a difference in her life. It was enough and always would be.

The night air was cool and a chill had worked its way into his shoulders. The vest he'd bought at the thrift shop was doing little to keep him warm. Then again, it only cost a couple of bucks, and if truth be told, he did kind of like it, blue made him look younger—at least Edna thought so.

He sniffed the air then turned his head and took a deep, long breath. Smoke from the nearby campground had found its way to the porch, bringing with it images of Italian sausages over an open fire, bratwurst smothered in mustard, sprinkled with sauerkraut and onion, or just plain old wieners sizzling away—didn't matter much, 'cause it smelled so good.

Then, as though it had a strict schedule to keep, the evening breeze picked up its pace; its faint breath chilling his skinny, spotted arms. He glanced over at Edna. She never seemed to notice the cold. In fact, he was pretty sure she liked it, so he kept his mouth shut and was content to sit there at her side.

It was moments like these when he'd take account of his life, adding the good and the bad, hoping the needle would tip in his favor, revealing he was indeed a good man. And yet, regardless of the outcome, he would always find himself wondering what it would've been like, how it would've all turned out, had he not thrown his duffle bag in the back of his brother's pickup that gray, bleak, winter morning. But that was a lifetime ago. He'd done his patriotic duty and there was no going back; and besides, he and Edna had become great friends over the years, and he would not trade that.

"You think it's natural for a boy to spend so much time on his own?" Edna asked.

Roy glanced over at Edna, giving her a questioning look. "He's been here, what? A week? He's gettin' his bearings that's all, most natural thing in the world. A boy's got to learn about his environment and think things through. Normal as cowboy boots and belt buckles if you ask me. Solitude, it be good for the mind."

"I suppose if you say so," Edna said, putting down her lemonade. Then she shook her head. "No Roy, I wish it were true. I wish it was like you said, but he's just not right. He's a troubled boy."

"Now, Edna," Roy said, a worried look on his face. "You're gonna get your blood pressure goin' and that'll do you no good. You know that'd be a fact . . . besides, his daddy should be coming for him soon. So you've got to calm yourself."

"Well, *Roy*." Edna's tone sharpened. "Sometimes, it's just not so easy to do, now is it?" She took a sip of lemonade and dabbed the corners of her eyes with a tissue.

Roy said nothing.

"Oh Roy, it's just, well, I caught him this morning with one of the puppies. Daisy, you know, the runt, the black one, got that dab of white paint on her nose and those ridiculous floppy ears."

Roy smiled. "Sure, I think I know the one."

"Well, this morning, I saw him standing over by the corner of the barn; you know the corner with the rain barrel." Edna sighed. "The thing is, he had something in the barrel, and I could hear it splashing around some. I knew something wasn't right, so I hurried over as best I could, and there was Daisy trying to catch her breath, her little white nose barely out of the water, her eyes big and wide as silver dollars. I guess he must've heard me coming up from behind, because he turned; and when he did—*well,* he had this grin on his face. . . . I swear to God! If I hadn't shown up—"

"*Edna,* the boy wouldn't do such a thing, he's your grandson for mercy sakes. What'd make you think such a thing?"

Edna let out a rattled breath and turned to him. "Roy, you know very well, why . . ."

Roy reached over and patted Edna's arm. "Come now old girl; his momma, she's been dead for some time now; she's long gone, she's never coming back . . ."

Edna pulled her shawl up around her massive shoulders and sat back. "I suppose you're right, and I know I shouldn't be thinking this way. But it's . . . it's just that, this morning, when I looked into that boy's eyes. Well, and I know it's going to sound crazy." She sighed again, grabbing hold of Roy's withered arm and gave it a squeeze. "But when I looked into those eyes of his, I swear to God, I could see his momma staring back at me."

Chapter 1

A s the sun descended below the treetops, its granular light filtering through the bare bones of the forest, smudges of tawny brown and hues of rusty orange crept across the white-planked siding, shading the board edges to a firebrick red, giving the church porch the color and pallor of a hot oven.

Father Paul knelt in front of the double doors and picked up an eight-foot long two-by-four, straddling it across the brass handles, nudging it this way and that until he was sure a fine balance had been achieved. *Mmm, maybe one more tap . . . Yeah, that'll do it.*

Satisfied, he turned his face to the late day sun, letting the warmth penetrate his eyelids, his world now blood-red and comforting. *Oh, I really must remember this moment. Certain times in one's life must be held close, nurtured, savored for another day—defining moments—moments that make the man.* He looked around and smirked. *Yeah, I'll remember.*

He turned to Alvin Oates, an elder from the brethren, who was flat on his ass, cross-legged, not more than five feet away. *And I hope you'll remember too, my son.*

The cocoon of twilight, the crumbling final moments of the day, and the short walk into darkness and all the possibilities that came with it, brought a level of joy he could never fully explain. It was as though he was an artist, stroking and dabbing at the canvas, the thick oily pigments binding with the cotton fibers, seeping in, forging a tangible connection with the world surrounding him. *Maybe that's it—I'm an artist . . .* He shook his head and smiled. He knew better.

The fragrance of fresh-cut pine rising from the two-by-four caught his attention, bringing with it a sense of calm, wrapping him in a cloak of tranquility and warmth. He looked up. "You do love me, don't you, Lord?" he whispered, as a tremble trickled up his throat, morphing into a chuckle. "Yes, of course. I know you do."

He scanned the area one last time, unbuttoning his black overcoat with his gloved hands.

It was a good vantage point. The church sat at the top of a grass-covered knoll, maybe five miles out of town, the grounds encircled by a dense stand of aspen and birch. The only access was by way of a quarter-mile of dirt road, grass grown thick between its tracks, curving its way through the woods before arriving at the mouth of the church parking lot. Three older model sedans, all gray and dull, were parked next to the walkway. At the far end of the lot sat a rusty, light-green, three-quarter ton flatbed with the words *GOD THE REDEEMER* stenciled in brown letters across the driver's-side door. As Father Paul read the words aloud, a grin cut the corner of his mouth. He could feel God's presence.

A piano melody accompanied by a small chorus erupted from inside the church, breaking his concentration. They were old voices, soothing voices, the kind he'd listened to as a child, the kind that filled the church every Sunday morning. It made him think of old hymnals, padded kneelers, worn wooden pews—happier times. A smile had almost surfaced when he realized he'd heard the tune before, many times in fact. Yet, for some unfathomable reason, he couldn't quite place it.

And yet there it was, plain as day, the hymnal splayed before him, the words scrolling across the page; low hanging words, words that he should be able to reach out and grasp.

He pondered the tune, shifting his jaw to one side. He couldn't explain why forgetting the name to a song, or anything else for that matter, was so very annoying. Still, as he watched those illusive little letters prance about at the worn fringes of his mind, smiling at him, taunting him— *well*, they really pissed him off. He knew they shouldn't, but yeah, they did.

A familiar ache was working its way across his back muscles, wrapping around his shoulder blades, making them tight and sorer by the second . . .

It's not that he liked to dilly-dally. *No*, of course not, on the contrary. But he had allowed himself to be diverted from the task at hand, and there was always a price to pay for such a petty indulgence. Still, the nagging voice in his head wouldn't let up, reminding him his once infallible memory was, well . . . not so infallible anymore.

"Enough of this," he muttered under his breath, reaching his gloved hand into the duffle bag next to him and pulling out a yellow cordless drill. He replaced the drill bit with a screwdriver attachment, then squeezed the drill's trigger a couple of times. The sharp whine of the electric motor brought with it a clarity and focus he found exhilarating.

Alvin turned his head toward the sound.

Father Paul nodded. "Time to carry out God's will. Are you ready, my son?"

Alvin's mouth twitched, his eyes shifting back-and-forth, making him look like a confused child.

Father Paul squeezed the trigger once more, satisfying himself it was operating as it should, then drove three four inch screws through the two-by-four and into the right door jamb. Duck-walking across the porch to the other side of the double doors he drove in another set of screws, sealing the door shut. *Unbelievable. It's right there on the tip of my tongue.* He tried humming a few bars, but still nothing would come.

He knew it was not the end of the world—it just bugged him, bugged him a lot. *The name will come—course it will, most likely when I'm in the tub tonight, popping to the surface like a bar of soap. Yes, a good soak will help. Always does.*

He looked at Alvin. *Mmm, maybe he'd know?* He considered the man for a moment, then shook his head. There would be no help there. A true-blue follower, Alvin, but not particularly gifted. Shrugging his shoulders, he resigned himself to the fact that it would just have to wait and turned his attention back to the task at hand. "Rise and shine brother. Time to saddle up."

Alvin got to his feet. He was a tall man, narrow at the shoulders, long faced, with a big, lopsided smile. The other men all seemed to like Brother Alvin, for he offended no one and no one bothered him.

Father Paul watched with interest as Alvin tried his best to act calm. Absolute obedience was all he'd ever asked of his followers. Sensing the attention, Alvin shifted his eyes away.

Such innocence, Father Paul thought, and made a mental note of how much he loved the man.

While he preferred to work alone, Alvin had been useful in the past, at times even instrumental in a successful outcome. More importantly, he knew Alvin could be trusted. For no one was more dedicated to him and his doctrines than Brother Alvin.

Father Paul cocked his head, sensing an uneasy intensity brewing. "What is it my son, you seem distracted?"

"It's, it's just that . . ." Alvin's voice trailed off and a thin, taut grin parted his lips. "I don't know, but this being a church and all . . ." He lowered his head and began rubbing the sole of his boot on the porch deck, then looked up. "Father, will God be mad at us?"

Father Paul frowned. "Did not God send us here my son?" The tone of his voice soft and understanding.

Alvin bowed his head again, looking ashamed, his gaze now focused on his fingernails as he picked at the raw, red cuticles.

"Brother Alvin, we are all God's children. We are here today to do his bidding, so that we may experience his promised miracle." Then in a paternal tone, he asked, "Are you questioning God's will, my son?"

"No . . . no, of course not, forgive me Father. It's just that, sometimes, I don't know, I just need to hear you tell me."

"I am here for you Alvin and always will be, you must know that."

Alvin's facial muscles relaxed, the skin below his eyes sagging.

"Shall we?" Father Paul asked, a hint of excitement in his voice.

"Yeah, I guess so . . ."

Father Paul reached back into the duffle bag and withdrew two, pump-action 12-gauge shotguns, handing one to Alvin.

Jacking a slug into the chamber, Father Paul jumped down off the front steps and worked his way around to a side window across from the pulpit and peered in. Under his breath, he said, "*Ohhh* . . . but aren't you a pleasant surprise, Mrs. Hudson. And, you look so very pretty this evening."

Myrna Hudson was sitting at an upright piano pounding out the hymn, body erect, shoulders drawn back, her gray hair tied in a neat bun. Two men stood next to the piano, both close to her vintage, both wearing faded green-and-yellow checked plaid shirts. They sang at her side, glowing in spirit, comrades in faith.

The song felt so very familiar, and yet he still couldn't quite place it. And while he knew he should know it, he also knew such matters would have to be delved into at a more appropriate time. A few seconds later, he saw Alvin poke his head up, peering in through a window on the other side of the church, a worried look on his droopy face.

Their eyes met, and Alvin gave a weak thumbs-up signal just as the singing inside the church came to a lull . . .

Father Paul counted down. "Three, two, one," then raised his shotgun and, with the tip of the barrel, tapped out a single pane of the lattice window.

The old timers stopped, turning their heads in the direction of the breaking glass. Father Paul squeezed off the first shot, and a tremendous boom filled the church, rattling the windowpanes. A split second later, the slug pierced the taller man's forehead, exiting the back of his skull and spraying out gobs of gray brain matter and a fine, bright red mist.

Alvin fired, catching the other man in the shoulder, swinging him around on his heels as Father Paul planted a single round into the man's chest, throwing him backwards onto the floor.

Father Paul's heart raced as he shifted his gaze to the piano. He raised an eyebrow and grinned, his voice calm and reassuring as he asked, *"Myrna . . .* are you hiding from me?"

He looked down, and his grin broadened. The hem of her paisley dress was poking out from behind the piano. The thought of her curled up like a small child, as though hidden and somehow invisible, touched him in an unexpected way. Looking over he saw Alvin's big head still framed by the side window, and he waved him off.

Alvin's face seemed to droop more, then his head dropped out of sight and he made his way around to the front of the church to stand guard.

Father Paul withdrew his shotgun from the window and jogged to the back of the church. Climbing a short flight of stairs, he kicked in the side door and walked straight over to the piano. The room smelled odd, like old hymnals and lemon oil, with more than a trace of burnt sulfur. He stopped to study the exposed section of Myrna's dress. Rectangular, maybe six inches in length, it bore a teardrop tapestry of purple and orange on a dark blue background. *Cotton,* he guessed.

"Myrna." His voice was soft and controlled. "Do you remember me? I must say, I remember you."

She didn't respond with words, only a snotty sniffle.

He stared down at the fabric. "Don't be afraid, Mrs. Hudson. Please, come out from behind there. I know the floor must be so terribly uncomfortable. Our bones do hurt us more as we age, don't they? And it is such a *very* hard floor . . . *ohh my . . .*"

Again, Myrna did not reply.

"Mrs. Hudson, I am talking to you." The timber of his voice strengthened, then a moment later turned almost musical. "*Come out, come out, from wherever you are.* Now! If you don't mind."

The sound of Myrna's breathing grew louder, as did her weeping, until at last she slid out from behind the piano. She was on her knees with one hand held out in front of her face. "I . . . I don't know you . . ." she whispered, her face wet with tears. "Please, just leave me alone."

"You don't remember me, do you?"

Myrna looked down at the floor and said nothing, her body bent over, trembling, arms crossed over her chest.

"I know it has been such a long time Mrs. Hudson, but I want you to think. I want you to think way back to the days when life was simple, and all one had to do was believe in the future. Back to those early days when anything was possible. To the days when a young woman was found dead in her lover's apartment, her throat slit ear to ear."

Myrna's body went rigid.

Father Paul ran his tongue along the edge of his front teeth. "You *do* remember Mrs. Hudson. Don't you?"

She looked up, her eyes widening. "Oh my God, it's you."

"Well done, Mrs. Hudson. I knew you'd remember."

She looked to the ceiling as though asking for help, but there would be no help, no one to come to her rescue, no one to calm her fears. She dropped her gaze to him, hands over her face, her body quivering as she cried.

What an odd thing to do, Father Paul thought. "Really, Mrs. Hudson, whatever is wrong with you? I mean, can't you feel him? He's here with us now, watching you, watching me."

Her crying quieted as she tried to decipher what he'd said, then she started up again, louder than before.

"Oh, Mrs. Hudson, please don't be that way," he pleaded, taking a step forward and placing his hand on her head. He flinched as her warm, moist scalp touched his skin. "Now, now, dear, you shouldn't get yourself all worked up. I know it has been such a long journey for both of us. But now, a new journey begins for you." With those words, he straightened his back and cleared his throat. "As I stand here before you, Mrs. Hudson, I offer to you my sincere thanks. For your sacrifice is but another stitch that shall bring God's glorious miracle into focus. Praise be the Lord!"

Myrna's trembling increased, her body shaking as she tucked her head down, pressing her chin to her chest.

Father Paul stepped around behind her, raised his shotgun in the air, and brought the butt down hard against the back of her head, crushing her skull and severing her spinal cord. She dropped instantly, rolling onto her side, her jaw slack, her body and legs gently twitching. A few seconds later, she stopped moving altogether.

Father Paul put his boot on her shoulder and flipped her onto her back, causing her head to roll sideways. Her eyes, now dull and unfocused, stared off into some distant place she'd never find.

Kneeling down, he withdrew his hunting knife from its sheath and positioned it over her belly. With a steady hand he inserted the tip of the blade into her dress, cutting the fabric from stomach to chin. In one motion he ripped the fabric back, exposing a lace bra and her pale, powdery flesh that somehow reminded him of bleached white flour. A gold chain hung down the side of her neck, a pendant dangled below her left ear. He pinched the chain with his fingers and brought the pendant closer. *A crucifix, how interesting.*

With his index finger and thumb, he began counting her ribs, starting from just below her collarbone. Satisfied with the location, he repositioned the steel tip of the knife. Pressing down, the blade dimpled her milky skin until a red dot pooled around its razor sharp tip.

14

Chapter 2

P arish Road 9 snaked through the depths of Louisiana bayou country. It wasn't somewhere you'd want engine trouble. Few used it, preferring the straight lanes of Highway 32 that got you where you were going in half the time. But there was something to be said for cruising a backcountry road in an old pickup with the windows down. Josh loved his '63 Chevy Step-Side, even though she'd just died, her passenger-side wheels resting in a patch of sweet clover and alligator weed that all but smothered her hubcaps.

Josh tapped his fingers on the steering wheel and turned to Eddie. "Twice in one month? You'd think I'd learn, wouldn't you boy?" Eddie was riding shotgun, sprawled out on his side, his big head pressed against the passenger door. He half-turned his sad, chocolate lab face toward Josh, his droopy yellow eyes somewhat puzzled by his buddy's words. But since none of them included walk, treat, or ball, it couldn't have been that important. Leaning his head back against the door, he exhaled in a long slow puff, ballooning his slack lower lip, exposing his teeth and pink gums.

Mary had told Josh she was finishing up unloading supplies for Crawlies, then she'd be right out. He looked at his watch and frowned—*she should've made it here by now.*

The last time the oil pump died he'd spent the better part of an afternoon cleaning it and had done a pretty good job, or at least he'd thought so. Mary wasn't so kind, telling him straight out he was wishful thinking and should get a new one. He'd tried to argue the point with her, but she'd hear none of it, finishing off by telling him he was truly full of shit. The part that annoyed him the most was, his best friend was usually right.

It was mid-morning, the Louisiana sun was hot and the truck's cab was beginning to smell like an old canvas tent sprinkled with engine oil. And yet to Josh, it was an agreeable scent, reminding him of long summer days. Of cornfields and high-top black sneakers left untied, flies peppered on yellow strips hanging in loose coils from the ceiling of his uncle's gas station. Of heat vapors rising off of the gas pumps, and car tires crunching on the hard packed gravel. Of the sound of the noon train passing in the distance, its steel wheels clacking, the flat metallic notes fading away as it rolled out of sight. Most of all, it reminded him of how good a frosted cola felt in his hand, and how the fizz burned his throat. He looked over at Eddie.

Eddie rolled his eye sideways and saw Josh watching him. A second later, the 115-pound lab was sitting upright, his tongue hanging out the side of his mouth, his crazed eyes saying—*guess what? I got this great idea . . .*

Josh reached over and held Eddie's big head in his hands, kissed his forehead, and then pushed the passenger door open. The big dog squirmed around on the bench seat, his long tail whacking Josh in the face as he jumped out, hightailing it into the bush. Another great adventure had begun.

~ ~ ~

Close to thirty minutes later, Mary finally arrived in her late model Pathfinder, a toolbox in one hand and a brown paper bag in the other. She was short in stature, arguably over five-foot-one, lean, and had the gait of a lumberjack. Her hair was kept short, cut just below her ears, her black, smoky eyes separated by a generous nose.

Josh's sandals were sticking out from under the pickup as she walked up.

"You're one lucky dipstick, you know that? Arnold says there aren't too many oil pumps left in the whole state for an old shitbox like yours. Said you should upgrade a few decades, better chance you'll get what you want, when you need it. He thinks you're, ah . . ." Her voice took on a sugary sweet tone. *"Challenged.* But, don't be worrying your massive cranium about it, I set him straight."

"Yeah, I bet you did." Josh stopped what he was doing and poked his head out from under the wheel well. "I kinda like things to stay the same. Simpler that way."

"Sure you do, numbnuts. Could do it too, if you could make the world stand still," she said, her eyes now brimming with expectation.

Ahh man, here it comes, he thought. He wormed himself from under the truck and got to his feet, trying to rub a kink out of his neck. As he paused to consider what she'd said, a rather large bead of sweat gathered on the tip of his nose.

"Okay Mary. What's going on?"

She looked up into the sky. *"Nothing. . . .* Nothing at all."

"Bullshit—nothing," he said, using his sleeve to wipe the sweat from his nose.

She lowered her gaze and smirked.

"C'mon Mary, spill it."

She reached into the paper bag and pulled out an oil pump, handing it to him. "*She* called."

"She?"

"Yeah. 'She' called, you know '*her*'. The FBI."

"Ohhh . . ." he said, guilt hitting him hard, wrenching tight in his gut. He knew this day would come, it had to. It's not like it was something that could be avoided. Still, he had forced it deep into his subconscious, willing it into submission, convincing himself he could somehow control how the events would unfold. But now, she'd made the call.

It had been a full year since he'd last seen Rachael. He'd done the right thing, or at least that's what he'd been telling himself, waiting until he'd calmed down and sorted things out. *Right . . .* The fact of the matter was, it was all a load of crap. He was in the wrong and he knew it. "So, what'd she say?"

"Well, we talked about the weather, you know, and how it was cold way up there in New York City without you. How she missed the sight of your big butt when the sun hits it just right. And how the dew forms on your lower lip when you're in heat."

"Yeah, yeah," he said, trying not to react, as it would only bring on more.

Mary looked around. "Where's Eddie? I thought he was with you this morning?"

"Out for a run. So, you gonna tell me?"

Mary's eyes grew tired and she took a breath. "She says there's been some action in Lancaster County, Minnesota, outside of Lynchfield. Something ugly went down, I could tell from her voice. Didn't want to tell me about it though. *Need to know* and all that—you know how she is. . . . Said it happened day before yesterday. Wants you to call her."

18

Josh swallowed hard. "Yeah, okay." He could tell Mary was agitated; the subject of Rachael never sat well with her. "Thanks for bringing me the pump."

Mary's gaze hardened and she replied in an aloof tone, "You're welcome."

After a moment of silence, Josh asked, "Any chance you can you stick around? I might need a hand."

Mary didn't respond, acting as if she might've seen Eddie in the bushes.

Josh continued. "Lancaster County? Your parents were from around there, right?"

Mary looked back at him. "Not far off. About 10 miles east of the county line, a town called Meadow, outside of Lynchfield. Well, not really a town, more like a hamlet. Never did know the difference, still don't."

"Huh, I think I remember you telling me about it. So, when exactly did you leave the Meadow?"

"*Leave the Meadow* . . . ? Jesus, Josh, you make me sound like a lost heifer."

Josh raised an eyebrow. "Yeah, okay. So, when did you step out . . . I mean . . . move on?"

"I got out when I was thirteen. That's when I went to live with my grandparents in Nevada. Spent my summers in Meadow though." She thought for a moment before asking, "Why, what's it to you?" Then her eyes lit up. "*What?* You want me to tag along?"

"What makes you think I'm even interested in getting involved?"

Mary gave him a knowing look. "Because, *she* called you."

Chapter 3

S enator Doris Parker sat at her computer, gazing out the front window of her cabin. She'd been trying to find a comfortable position, rocking her ass from cheek to cheek every few minutes, but it wasn't working. Her doctor, an early thirty-something, had told her in his detached, I-don't-really-care-about-you tone, 'Arthritis in the lower spine comes with age.'

Well no shit, asshole! Tell me something I don't know. Bloody doctors. Maybe I won't pay your bill. Then I bet we'd see some real concern.

She pushed her chair away from her computer and winced. "*Ow . . . !* Damnit! Why didn't I pack those bloody pills?"

She knew it really wasn't that big of a deal, all she had to do was go to town and pick some up. But it had snowed overnight and the road would be such a mess, and she hated driving when it was slippery. She turned and looked at George, stretched out on the couch by the fireplace. He was fast asleep; his one arm dangling down. *Maybe I'll have him fetch them, do the old fart good to get off his lazy butt, circulate some of that cholesterol around.*

Then her thoughts turned to what was really bothering her. All morning she'd been struggling to come up with a suitable title for her memoirs. Of course, she knew getting antsy about it wouldn't help. It would come, just breathe and relax, she told herself. Let it come naturally, organically as they would say, whoever the hell *they* are? *What a crock! Nothing comes naturally—if you want it, you fight for it.*

She was glad to be finished with her memoirs. No more mulling over her past—pissing and moaning as to who said what and when and to whom. *Give me a break,* she thought, *most of my colleagues would just as soon sell their mothers. Well, okay, maybe their mother-in-law, to a dockside brothel if they figured it would move them up a notch on the polls.*

She lit a cigarette and took a long draw. It wasn't her second or third smoke of the day, but it was still passable. *I mean really, what kind of person forces themselves out in the public spotlight, only to get dumped on, day in and day out? No one normal that's for sure.* She took another draw and tapped the beginnings of an ash into an ashtray shaped like a tiny green baseball glove.

Having been a duly elected senator, her agent thought she should be able to come up with a better title than '*My Life, and the Sociopaths I Ate Lunch With*'. Her editor and agent thought she was kidding—she was not. A grin began to curl at the corner of her mouth as she recalled the look on their faces when a glint, not much more than a twinkle in the woods, caught her eye. She put down her cigarette, sat forward and slowly scanned the forest, but there was nothing unusual, just frozen trees and fresh white snow.

Another minute passed before she gave up, concluding that, whatever it was, if indeed there was anything, was gone now. She took another sip of her coffee, followed by a long pull on her smoke. *My frigging memoir, I wonder if anyone will ever really understand my time in this world.* She looked down at George. *He gets me though. Oh Lord, how that poor man put up with my incessant wailing all these years, I'll never know.* She watched his swollen belly rise and fall with each breath, the dying embers of the fire dancing on his glasses. *Got to get him out for a long, long walk. I'm not going to be facing retirement alone.*

The night snowfall had produced flakes the size of sand dollars, coating the veranda's railings with a thick layer of down. Doris stepped off the porch and headed for the woodpile, her new winter boots squeaking and squawking on the fresh blanket of snow.

A total of three, maybe four inches had accumulated, covering the ground and giving rise to a subterranean world of leaves and twigs. A world, mapped out in lines of red and orange and black, each color frozen just beneath the ivory surface like brittle varicose veins.

Originally, she'd thought George had gone overboard ordering an extra cord of wood, but now with the early onset of winter, it didn't seem like such a bad idea. Especially since they'd decided to spend more time at the cabin this year, away from all the noise and hubbub—ease themselves into retirement, proper like. Not that she would admit he was right, the man's ego could already fill a football stadium.

Without warning a finger of ice ran down her spine and she shivered. *"God,* it's cold," she muttered, tugging the collar of her coat tight about her neck, attempting to lock in the heat. She didn't want to admit it, but the cold was more bothersome now that she was well into her sixth decade. She found it hard to accept nature was giving up on her, and yet she'd be damned if she would grow old gracefully. It was not in her genes to be a wuss.

Another shiver ran through her, stronger than before, blanketing her skin in gooseflesh. She stopped and looked around. *Faulty thermostat; a sure, early warning sign,* she told herself. *Next time George, you old goat, you're going for the wood.*

Her boots continued to creak and croak as she threaded her way through the birch forest.

The snow was easier to walk on than she'd expected, curling on the tips of her boots, rolling into miniature balls and branching off, creating drunken trails on the forest floor.

A few weeks from now this trip isn't going to be so easy, she thought. *A crust will form and each step will have to be punched through. And the tip of my boot could catch and I could fall.* Doris huffed. *Oh for Christ's sake, would you listen to me? How, pathetic . . . Okay that's it! I am NOT growing old—and that's that.*

She walked on, telling herself to calm down as she dragged George's latest project behind her. It baffled her, how a man of his stature could be so proud of such a simple contraption. It was essentially no more than a large apple box fitted onto a child's sleigh. He had picked it up at a rummage sale the week before, and when he showed it to her, you'd thought he'd discovered the Northwest Passage.

He had tried to convince her the sleigh would be large enough to haul a full evening's firewood. She had her doubts about that, and even doubted the sleigh would last the winter—her George may be a complicated man, but he was not a handyman.

She knelt down in front of the woodpile, untied a corner of the dark-blue tarp covering it, and peeled it back. She tossed piece after piece of the cut and dried birch into the apple box, then tied the tarp back down and turned toward the cabin. All the while Father Paul, not more than fifty feet away, lay on the ground with the crosshairs zeroed in on her neck.

A distinct puff broke the still air and a split second later a tranquilizer dart pierced her cheek below the right eye. Doris grimaced, swatting at it as if she were shooing an insect, then took a few steps sideways, wobbling from foot to foot as a thin stream of blood began to leak down her cheek. She took a step forward, staggered, and collapsed onto the ground.

Father Paul trotted over and knelt, dropping his duffle bag down beside her, then fished out four lengths of rope, steel pegs, and a claw hammer. He pulled her spread-eagle, tying her wrists and ankles to the pegs, pounding each peg in place with the hammer. A lab experiment, mounted for dissection.

He raised his head; the forest had gone quiet. Everything was still, peaceful, like an iced-over pond. *It's so beautiful,* he thought. *Almost too much so.* He loved the country, particularly the woods. The air was so pure and clean.

It was at moments such as this that he could feel 'his' presence. God was at his side.

This is so perfect, he thought, raising his hunting knife to his lips and kissing the blade. He took one last, deep breath then lowered his gaze to Doris and began slicing off the buttons of her winter jacket, peeling it wide open, an angel in the snow. Carefully, he inserted the tip of the knife into her fisherman's sweater and cut straight up from her crotch to her neck, revealing the elastic top of her gray panties, her pinkish-white flesh, and her almond-colored bra. He ran his fingers along her collarbone, the warmth of the tender curve giving him pause.

He watched her ribcage expand and contract, then leaned in close and whispered in her ear. "Mrs. Parker. You must believe, I am no longer angry with you. God has shown me how to forgive." He straightened up and a kindhearted look crossed his face. "Yes, it's true. I have forgiven you." Then, with his index finger and thumb, he counted her ribs, starting from just below her collarbone.

Chapter 4

J osh rolled his pickup into his usual parking spot behind the Tackle Shop, a small store situated on the boardwalk in the center of Hidden Bay Marina; a u-shaped marina he'd bought for back taxes ten years ago.

To call the Tackle Shop a store was generous, as its exterior resembled four outhouses sewn end-to-end and maybe twice as deep. All that was missing was a half-moon cut at either end. Inside, there was a long, wide counter protected from the weather by a two-foot overhang of the roof.

Lily, the store's sole employee, wore the mantle of manager with pride, which to some could seem somewhat out of place given the daily roll call.

Josh opened the passenger door and Eddie hopped out, wagging his tail as he sniffed at the ground. He began pawing the dirt, then raised his head as though he'd heard something and darted off to check it out.

Josh climbed the steps on the south side of the store and walked over to the counter. There was something for everyone in the store, which was rather remarkable given the cramped quarters. Josh had concluded it came down to Lily knowing what her regulars liked and stocking the store accordingly. There were two brands of each product, be it milk, cheese, canned soup, coffee, cigars, ice cream, batteries, plastic gas cans, flashlights, candles, or motor oil. Lily liked to say: *The customer has got to have a choice, so you got to give it to them.*

A short wooden peninsula jutted out from the boardwalk directly in front of the store. On the peninsula were two pumps, one gas and one diesel. A line of old tires had been nailed along the peninsula's edge, providing protection for the boats while filling up.

Lily always ensured there was a decent supply of bait in the freezer, placed strategically against the north wall of the store where it was cooler and would escape the sun for most of the day.

Josh had first met Lily the day he'd bought the marina, and after a few minutes of getting to know her, he decided to keep her on and had never once regretted it. But she was nudging up against her seventy-first birthday and that was a worry. The last few years her arthritis had gotten worse and her stoop more pronounced. And although she'd never complained about the pain, he could see it in her eyes when she thought he wasn't looking.

And she had no one to fall back on, no one to turn to when her health finally failed. Her husband and daughter had both died in a car crash years ago. Her husband had stopped off at a local watering hole for 'a few' before he'd gone to pick up their daughter, Beth, at the airport. On the way home he ran a red light.

Beth's two-year old son, Tyler, had been staying with Lily while she'd gone to Seattle for a job interview. Tyler moved in permanently after the accident.

Lily and Tyler shared a basement suite in town. He was in the eighth grade and walked to school. She drove her old jalopy the mile and a half out to the marina every morning. And while they'd both adapted and seemed to be doing okay, Josh knew it wouldn't be too many years before Tyler would strike out on his own, and then what? The thought of Lily one day living out her retirement alone had been gnawing at him for some time, and he hoped he'd come up with the solution.

The blueprints were drawn and permits approved to build a small cabin on the marina boardwalk, roughly halfway between his place and the store, enough separation so she'd have her privacy, but close enough if she needed help. There, he figured she could live out her old age rent-free and eat at Crawlies whenever she liked. The contractor was arranged, and work was set to begin after Christmas. Now all he had to do was tell her and hope she wouldn't take it the wrong way. Lily was an independent woman.

He knew she'd likely put up a fight, so he figured he'd get the construction underway and later, when it was close to being finished, he'd break the news to her. He hoped she would go along with it; she had to, it was his only plan.

"How's business, Lily?" he asked.

"Fair-to-middling I'd say. . . . Johnson in slip 12 got a thorn up his butt again, still wants slip 17. Believes that slip is more sheltered than his. Says, he needs 17 'cause his boat is so much newer than Marco's. Told me he's not going to wait any longer, wants them switched, and wants me to tell Marco, pronto. And as always, he informed me that maybe I wasn't appreciative of how *important* he is. What he means to the marina, what his name had done for us."

"And . . . ?"

"So, I looked him square in the eye and told him I knew exactly what he had—was a personal problem."

"What'd he say?"

"Did what he always does. Put on that pouty look of his and walked away like he had a full load in his pants. Chicken shit, that's what he is . . ."

Josh had to grin.

"So, Josh, when is *eleven* coming out?"

Eleven was Josh's latest novel of his Detective Vincent Callaghan series. He'd penned the first Callaghan Novel shortly after being released from the Vandenberg Psychiatric Hospital of Massachusetts and moving down to the marina. Writing was supposed to help with the healing process in dealing with his wife's death. And while it did little for that, the book was well received, the series now translated into over a dozen languages.

"Soon," he said. "Scheduled for release at the end of the month."

"Well, good, 'cause I'm getting tired of waiting. And, for that matter, why aren't you writing two books a year, like some other authors?"

Josh stifled a grin. "Because I like fishing too much."

Lily smiled.

"Tyler around?" Josh asked. "I've got something for him."

"He's over at your place . . . but it's been a bad day, Josh. Those girls been picking on him again." She took a breath. "I don't know, maybe if you . . . ?"

"Sure, I'll have a talk with him. But you know he's going to be okay."

Lily didn't respond.

"Ah Lily, it'll work itself out, you'll see."

Lily craned her head up, staring directly at him, scrunching her face until it looked like a very large prune, her razor thin, almost purple lips revealing a hint of a smile. All of which he knew, was her way of saying, thanks.

Josh headed toward his place and saw Tyler sitting on the dock across from his front door. He had a line in the water, and his legs were hanging over the side of the boardwalk. Eddie was flopped out next to him lying on his back, his tongue hanging out—a big, lazy smile on his lab face.

"Hey Mr. I," Tyler said, his voice cracking as a teenager's does.

"Hey Tyler, what's up? Catching anything?"

"Nah, not much Mr. I. Not even a nibble."

Josh dumped his jacket on the chair by the front door and sat down beside Tyler. Eddie squirmed, maneuvering his head in between the two of them. A true Eddie move, making sure he got his fair share of the attention. Josh wrapped his arm around Eddie's huge neck and rubbed his head a few times before letting go.

"Lily says there's been some trouble at school again."

Tyler shrugged.

"You want me to have a word with them for you?"

Tyler looked over. "Nah, Mr. I. Won't do no good. They'd just be meaner the next time."

"Hmm, then what're we going to do, Tyler . . . ? Hey! I got it. *Maybe* we should send Lily over, give 'em all a good scare?"

Tyler started to giggle. "Yeah, okay, that sounds like a pretty good idea to me." Then he glanced at Josh, a serious look now on his face. "You know Lily's old, don't yeah, Mr. I?"

"You're right, I kinda forgot," Josh said.

"Mr. I, you don't have to worry about me, it's all right," Tyler said. "I know I'm a little slower than most of 'em. But I don't think they really mean what they say. Gran says when they get older, they'll know I'm not so different. That's what she says, anyhow."

"I think your Grandma's a smart woman."

Tyler smiled.

Josh placed his hand on Tyler's shoulder. "You're a good person, Tyler. You know that's right? Right?"

"Yeah, sure, I guess so."

"Oh, and hey, I almost forgot, I got something for you. Thought of you the second I saw it." Josh got to his feet, went inside and came out a few seconds later holding a brown plastic tubular container measuring about five-feet long and three inches in diameter.

"What's that?" Tyler asked, now standing.

"Open it and find out." Josh handed him the tube.

Tyler removed a green plastic cap from one end of the tube and pulled out two long bamboo rods. His face brightened.

"A nine-footer, Portuguese cork handle—fast action," Josh said. "Thought you and me, we'd go fishing sometime?"

"You bet Mr. I! *Hey,* you ain't blowing wind up my skirt, are ya?"

Josh grinned. "Lily teach you that?"

"Um, well . . . not really. Yesterday, she and a customer were laughing and she said it to him."

Josh said nothing and watched Tyler admire his new rod.

Tyler turned to Josh. "Thanks Mr. I. This is so cool."

"Glad you like it."

Tyler gave Josh a quick hug, then asked, "Is it okay if I show it to Gran?"

Josh nodded and watched as Tyler ran down the boardwalk to the Tackle Shop. Then he turned and entered his place with Eddie at his heels, and was immediately met with the lingering scent of leather and saltwater, tinged with cigar smoke. He cracked open a couple of windows before noticing the light flashing on his answering machine. He took a closer look—one new message. Figuring it was Rachael, he decided he'd hit the shower first, then make some coffee, pour a shot of brandy and try to figure out what he was going to say to her.

He cranked the shower temperature up until he could barely stand it, letting the heat penetrate his back and shoulders. And while the water was doing its thing for his muscles, it was doing jack shit for what he was going to say to Rachael. A good ten minutes passed and still nothing had come to him, so he hopped out, got dressed, and went downstairs.

He pressed his head back into his leather chair trying to will a clever thought to the surface, anything to diffuse the situation and lessen the tension. But it wasn't working and he knew why. It was his own damn fault. He should've called her, and he didn't, plain and simple.

The ball had been placed in his court when he'd last seen her. At the time, he'd convinced himself he needed to come to terms with the circumstances surrounding his wife's death, and once he'd done that, he'd be ready to move on. But the dreams still came to him late at night, the chill of the root cellar, the earthy scent of dirt and potatoes filling his nostrils, his wife's vacant eyes staring back at him, dead pools of lost hope. And even though he had extracted his revenge on the monster, bludgeoning the killer's skull to a pulp; it was the knowledge he'd been unable to free himself in time and forced to watch his wife suffocate that continued to hound him. It was a wound that would not heal.

He remembered his last words to Rachael. He'd told her that he needed to go back to the marina and work out what he was to do with the rest of his life. *That was a full year ago. Unbelievable.* "I am such an asshole."

Eddie raised his head, checking out his buddy, then flopped back down, his neck laying across Josh's toes. A minute later, Eddie was snoring away, a long drawn out rumble somewhere off in the distance, a lion's throaty purr. Josh shifted his toes, absorbing the heat, and listened to his old friend lying there at peace with the world. *Yeah, so why can't I feel that way?* He closed his eyes and let out a long breath. He knew exactly why—she'd called first.

He reached over and hit play.

"Josh, Rachael here, something's come up. Call me, okay? Please? I hate these damn machines . . . look, just call, all right?"

Hearing her voice again after nearly a year caused a dull ache to form in his guts. *Way to go, bonehead,* he thought.

He picked up the phone and dialed her number.

Chapter 5

Crawlies Pub was located at one end of the u-shaped marina. Josh's home, or 'shack' as his friends called it, was located at the other end.

A number of years ago, Josh had coaxed Mary to come out of her forced early retirement, offering her a fifty percent interest in Crawlies on one condition: she manage it.

She'd had a reputation as a hard-ass detective that would bend and often break the rules to get the job done, not hesitating to stomp on her superiors' egos if she thought they'd stepped out of line. And while her high conviction rate was envied by her peers, her complete lack of tolerance for authority figures and her unorthodox methods greased her early retirement package and she was let go.

Josh had first met her in Detroit. She'd been working on a serial murder case that had crossed state lines, and he'd been called in as lead profiler for the FBI. They'd been friends ever since.

Thanksgiving was less than a week away, and Mary had been busy getting Crawlies ready. As Josh climbed the stairs to the pub, a light sensor tripped and a spotlight came on, illuminating a large scarecrow. It was standing by the front door dressed in black, wearing a tattered coat with tails, calf-length trousers, and holding a seven-foot high scythe. *Inviting,* he thought. *I think she's truly captured the meaning of Thanksgiving this year.*

Softening the scene was an assortment of pumpkins, some butternut squash, and a few bright yellow gourds, set in piles around the porch, plus, two large, 100-pound burlap sacks, one filled with wheat and the other with barley. The top of each bag was rolled back a few inches and a small halogen bulb had been positioned above, casting a bright white light onto the coarse grains.

Once inside, Josh was greeted with the sound of Harmony Joe, a one-man variety show, strumming an acoustic guitar and singing a slow rendition of, "Mr. Bojangles". Mary had been experimenting with the entertainment in an attempt to pull customers in during the November shoulder season. About half of Crawlies business came from tourists, and in November there were barely enough new faces each day to man a Ping-Pong table. Mary had happily informed Josh business was up twelve percent year over year, and the bar had been two-thirds full for the afternoon shift, so maybe she was onto something.

Mary tapped a red ale and handed it him. "So? Did you call her?"

Josh avoided the question, looking over at the card table. The cousins, Jacob Milner and Gerald Pampas, were in their usual chairs playing a warm-up hand. They had operated old man Milner's shrimp boat ever since graduating from high school. Anwar Nasser, who'd arrived in America as a refugee some twenty years ago, was seated next to Little Bob, the afternoon shift bartender.

"Hey, don't get me wrong. There's no mystery here," Mary said, her voice rising. "Rachael and I don't exactly go to the same beauty parlor, but a call, Josh? You'd think, well, it might be a good idea?"

"Yeah, course I called her, but she sounded different. Something's changed."

"Hah, big surprise, dickhead. Comes with the territory, you being such a . . ." She stopped, looking like she was reconsidering what she was about to say, then said, "A woman can't wait forever, you know."

Josh raised an eyebrow and shrugged.

"When're you heading out?"

"First thing in the morning, taking an early flight to Chicago, then transferring to Syracuse."

"Syracuse?" Mary asked. "She told me it went down in Lancaster County."

"Yeah, that too, but she wants me to stop by the Finger Lakes District first, wants to show me something— another killing."

"She say what happened?"

"Nope, not with the Finger Lakes case. She did say that in Minnesota some old timers got clipped in a church. Says there's more to it, but she wants to wait to fill me in."

"You think the two are connected? I mean the lakes and the church."

"Don't know. Maybe? We'll see."

Mary hesitated, then said, "Hey, as you know, I'm from around Lancaster County. If you'd like some help?"

Josh turned to her. "Let me get a handle on what's going on first. See what's up."

Mary studied Josh for a long moment. "Finger Lakes you say? I don't know big fella. Don't think you're gonna like it up there. It can get cold this time of year. Colder than an unsatisfied woman's stare."

"I wouldn't know," Josh replied, with a wry smile.

"Oh, you got that right big boy, you wouldn't know."

A grin tugged at the corners of his mouth as he took a long draw on his beer.

Mary glanced in the direction of the card table. "Go on, get over there. Get your fill, the boys have been asking about you."

He nodded and walked over to the card table.

Anwar was playing solitaire and looked up as Josh sat down. The cousins were debating which was better, river or deep-sea fishing, and Little Bob was trying to dig a bug out of his nose, or so he said.

"Mary says you're going to do another job with the FBI," Anwar said, his accent thick, his vowels and consonants sticking to the roof of his mouth like he'd swallowed a great dollop of honey. "Says your girl called. Says she needs you, needs her big *lawg*."

Gerald Pampas, one of the cousins, spoke up, "Anwar? Get real man. It's lug, not *lawg*."

"That is what I said, "Lawg."

The cousins glanced at each other, exchanging a knowing look.

"Hey, you can call it what you like, lug or lawg, but we're just friends, okay?" Josh said, and immediately regretted it.

Little Bob's eyes lit up. "I can hear it now. '*Ohhh Joshy, you big lawg, are we still friends?*'"

Anwar started to chuckle, and a second later the others joined in. Josh shook his head and had to smile.

~ ~ ~

They'd finished their third hand and were tossing the cards to the center of the table when Mary placed a mug of Irish coffee in front of Josh. "This'll help ease the pain."

Josh looked up. "Thanks, Mary." He took a long, slow sip, drawing in the heady aroma, and wondered what had changed with Rachael.

Chapter 6

J ack's Steakhouse and Grill was located on the corner of Main Street and Lever Avenue. It had replaced a boutique distillery that once boasted high-end and highly sought-after spirits. The distillery went under when the local economy tanked in '08, and was now a popular watering hole; its patrons hip, its beer cheap. The outer walls consisted of dark-brown oak beams and planked siding painted black. Two heavy mahogany doors the color of cinnamon, adorned with polished brass handles and hinges, stood guard at the bar's entrance.

Inside, the air was thick with human sweat, whiskey, and the need for release. The moist air coated the plate glass windows, droplets coalescing, consuming each other, swelling to translucent pearls before slithering down to shallow pools on the sill. The glass, streaked blue and green by the marquee's flickering neon lights, distorted the cars and pickups as they jockeyed for lanes in the late evening traffic. Pedestrians trudged by the window, clutching their coats about their necks as they tried to keep dry under their dripping umbrellas, their bodies stretching and curving as they entered and exited the scene.

It was another bitter November downpour, second one of the day. But it was Friday, and Lana was glad to be done for the week, her mind zoning out, drifting and growing numb. She was thoroughly content to just sit by the window and stare out at the traffic lights shimmering on the wet pavement. She'd felt tired all day, but now, after the first few draws of her beer and listening to her best friend, Beatrice, tell about all the dumb things her boss did that day, she began to feel herself come around. Friday night's embrace was finally taking hold.

It wasn't long before she found herself drifting again, not paying much attention to what her friend was going on about, clipping a word here and there out of the air, so she could nod at the right moment and appear attentive. She was clearly on the outer threads of the conversation, basking in the end of the week glow when she felt Beatrice give her a light tap on her shin.

"Don't look now, but you have an admirer," Beatrice said.

Lana gave Beatrice a thin smile. "*Really?* I just wanna veg out, okay? He's gotta be looking at you, right?"

"Yeah, um . . . not a chance," Beatrice whispered. "*Oh God.* I think he's coming over . . . Yup. He is at that."

Lana didn't want it to be obvious, but looked anyway, expecting to give him the 'I'm-not-in-the-market' stare. But as the man made his way over, she immediately felt an attraction. He was tall, rawboned and lean, had broad shoulders and a warm, confident, boyish smile that made her stomach tingle. She took another long draw on her beer, watching as he approached, all the while thinking Beatrice had got it wrong, that he'd walk right past them and out the door. Then without warning, an unsettling feeling began to press down on her, and her gaze slid across the room to another man. He was sitting at the end of the bar, holding a pint of ale to his lips, his eyes fixed on her, his face devoid of emotion. She felt a chill run across her shoulders and tried to look away, to pull away from his gaze.

"I think you two have the best table in the place. Mind if I join you?" the man asked.

Lana barely heard the words, straining to break away from the other man's gaze. Then her heartbeat slowed and a calm came over her, her breath all but a dying whisper in her chest.

Beatrice tapped Lana's shin again, harder this time.

"What?" Lana said, taking in a gulp of air, her focus now on the man standing before them. "Oh, yeah right. I think we could allow that." She glanced back at the bar, hoping the other man would be looking in another direction, but he wasn't—he was gone.

Lana hesitated for a second then looked up. The man smiled at both of them, then turned and asked if he could borrow a chair from the neighboring table. He sat down, nodded to Beatrice then reached out to shake Lana's hand. "Hi, I'm Jessie, and I know this is going to sound odd, but it's like, it's . . . Do I know you?"

Lana and Beatrice shared a knowing look, and a rush of pink ran up Jessie's neck as he started to chuckle. *"Ohh no . . .* Please forgive me, I mean, how lame was that? Please. Would you allow me to start over?"

Lana half-smiled and nodded, then felt another chill. She turned to the window and rubbed the wet surface with the palm of her hand. A cluster of teenagers were slowly moving past the bus stop across the street, laughing and poking at each other, oblivious to the rain. As they cleared away, she noticed water gushing out a gutter spout of the library. It was flooding across the sidewalk, running over a sodden newspaper, loosely folded and lying next to the bus stop. A man was sitting on the bus stop bench, looking down at the sidewalk, his hair soaked, his black coat buttoned to his chin. He looked up and his eyes locked on her. She gasped.

"Lana, you all right?" Beatrice asked, glancing at Jessie, giving him the 'I'm-so-sorry' look. "Lana!"

Lana turned away from the window. "What? Oh, yeah, sure. I . . ." She looked at them both. "I, I am *so* sorry. It's nice to meet you. Jessie is it?" she asked, willing herself not to turn and look out the window.

Chapter 7

Last call had arrived, and for Lana it had come far too soon. She couldn't remember when she'd had such a great evening, and was amazed at how things could so quickly change. The creepy man was now a distant memory. One minute, she was fully intending on calling it an early night, already prioritizing her next day's 'to do list', and deciding that when she got home, she'd curl up on the couch and catch up on her favorite TV shows she'd been meaning to watch. But now . . . now, she was seriously considering letting Jessie walk her home.

Beatrice had bowed out hours ago, saying she had to get up early and take her grandmother to church—each of them knowing full-well Lana would call her in the morning and report in, giving her all the details. Lana watched Jessie take care of the bill, and couldn't help but think what a nice guy he was and how badly she didn't want the evening to end.

The rain had stopped hours ago, but the streets were still glistening. Had it been July, the summer night air would have dried the pavement, but this was November and the streets were wet and dark . . .

Looking out the window, Lana decided to accept Jessie's offer to walk her home. She lived a few blocks from the bar, not so far that she would feel obligated to invite him in. But it was still an option, if she wanted to. They walked north along Main Street for a block, took a left past The First Baptist Church, then an immediate right down Regent Street to her townhouse, an end unit of a row house complex. She'd fallen in love with the place the first time she saw it. It reminded her of a Brooklyn Brownstone she'd seen on her one and only trip to New York.

They stopped on the sidewalk in front of her place.

"I had a wonderful time tonight," she said.

"Me too," Jessie replied, smiling. "Hey um, I . . . I don't know, but are you hungry? I know a place that'll still deliver. You okay with Chinese?"

She wanted to ask him in, but something felt wrong. Maybe it was her mother's voice telling her to be careful—a woman alone with a man she'd just met. She sighed, her mother was probably right, and as she'd always made a point of listening to her gut, she decided it would be better to wait. After all, she really had known him for only a few hours. *Let's see how you look in the light of day,* she thought. She was about to ask about his plans for Sunday when she noticed a tall man in a black overcoat standing across the street, partly hidden by the shadow of a tree. His collar was turned up and he appeared to be talking on the phone.

Ah, just stop it, she thought. *The guy from the bar's got you spooked, that's all it is.*

The man in the black coat ended his phone call, turned, and walked away.

Lana shivered.

"Are you all right?" Jessie asked.

"What? Oh No, I'm . . . What were we talking about?"

"Chinese, we could order in?"

"Ahh . . . yeah, sure. Chinese, sounds perfect."

Chapter 8

T he GPS indicated an hour and thirty-four minute drive to the Finger Lakes National Forest. Josh had picked up a four-shot Cafe Americano at the Syracuse Hancock International Airport before heading out, and could still feel the effects percolating in his blood as he approached Hanes Creek, a town of 1,546, sitting at the edge of the national forest.

His blood sugar had fallen off a cliff about five miles back, and he knew the shakes weren't far behind, so he stepped on the gas while keeping a lookout for state troopers.

A long curve in the road straightened out just as a narrow bridge came into view, its iron painted bright yellow. On the other side was his destination, Lone Pine Bar and Grill, a roadside diner with faded, gray cedar siding and two big windows facing out onto the river. The lights were on inside, and the parking lot was less than half full. At the far end of the lot there was a fresh pile of snow that had started to melt. Josh scanned the area, but couldn't see any sign of a government-issued vehicle, and began to wonder if maybe she hadn't come.

As he angle parked out front, he caught a whiff of burnt grease and bacon, and his stomach stirred. He walked up to the restaurant door, then stopped and took a moment to run his hand through his hair, knowing full well it wouldn't do a bit of good. His hair was tortured by a number of cowlicks that gave him the perpetual look of a man who had just crawled out of bed. That, and the fact that his nose had been broken more than once, gave him a rather unsettling, hawkish vibe. At six feet two inches and 210 pounds, he could have been described as intimidating, if not for his broad, gentle smile.

Entering the diner, he immediately saw Rachael at the far end of a long line of booths. He took a deep breath. *Ah man! I should've called . . . I am such an idiot.* As he walked past the cashier Rachael looked up, and when their eyes met a sharp ache formed in his chest, and he tried to smile.

Rachael wasn't alone. A man was sitting across from her, and as Josh got closer, the man came into focus. He was an older guy with gray, thinning hair, his skin ruddy and bunched up at the back of his neck. Rachael slipped off the bench seat and stood up. The man followed suit, getting halfway up before dropping back down.

Rachael looked terrific. She was lean like a runner and had an intensity about her that could knock any man off balance. As he looked into her fiery gray-green eyes, he found himself dumbfounded and just stood there . . .

"Josh, how are you?" Her tone was crisp and guarded.

He blinked. "What? Yeah, I'm okay. It's, great to see you, Rachael." He tried to swallow, but his mouth was dry.

"The drive out, okay?" she asked, her tone still brisk and businesslike.

"Ah, yeah sure, the highway was dry." *Something's way off* . . .

Rachael turned to the man on the bench seat. "Josh, this is, Bart Tindleton, he's the local medical examiner from the county office. Bart's here to give us his preliminary report. Our own ME is, as we speak, out in the field. We'll be meeting up with her a little later."

Josh nodded to Tindleton, then turned his attention back to Rachael. "Cecilia Bloom?" The thought of Cecilia made him grin.

"Ohh. I see you still remember her," Rachael replied, her eyes cold.

Tindleton shot a side-glance at Rachael, then took a sip of his tea.

Josh tried to recover with a full smile, which came off more like he was in pain. "So, how is Cecilia?"

"Doing great, just great. She actually asked about you the other day."

Then he saw it. An engagement ring on Rachael's finger. He tried to swallow again, harder this time, before raising his eyes to hers. "Seems, you've been busy."

Rachael's face darkened. "Let's get down to business," she said, sitting back down on the bench.

The waitress arrived to take their orders. Josh settled for a bagel and a small glass of milk—his appetite had faded.

Taking a large gulp of his tea, Tindleton opened his satchel and took out a file. "Sorry, but I've got a lot on my plate today." He flipped open his report. "There's really not much to say. Doris Parker, age 66, died as the result of a stab wound to her thoracic cavity. The knife used had to have been quite large in order to reach the incision depth.

My guess is a hunting knife, big game, one of those with the coarse teeth on the backside of the blade. And that would be consistent with the tearing at the outer edge of the wound. I calculate the deceased had been dead for less than two hours before her husband discovered her—"

Rachael cut in. "Apparently, the husband heard coyotes howling. He went to investigate, and that's when he found the victim, his wife, being fought over by them."

"You say less than two hours?" Josh asked.

"Correct," Tindleton said. "The tearing from the coyotes' incisors were consistent with that of a fresh corpse. Had she been on the ground for over, say, four hours, rigor would have produced subtle, but distinguishable changes to the tear patterns. Her liver temperature confirmed the time of death." He gulped down the last of his tea. "There is one other thing, quite strange really. A piece of her was missing."

"A piece?" Josh asked.

"A rib, her fifth thoracic to be precise. Very odd, really. In truth, I've never come across anything like this before. No other rib—only the fifth. And it wasn't the work of a coyote either, not unless the beast had opposable thumbs and carried a very sharp knife." He turned back to Rachael. "Look, I really have to be going. Would you mind handing this off to your medical examiner? I've already had a word with her and she'll be looking for it."

Rachael took the file. Then Tindleton rose and gestured like he was tipping an imaginary hat, and made his way out of the restaurant.

"So the victim is Parker? *Senator* Parker?" Josh asked.

"Retired Senator, stepped down last spring."

Josh thought for a second. "And the husband, what do we have on him?"

"Retired judge, almost ten years her senior. Second marriages for the both of them."

Rachael glanced at Josh. "Always the hubby, right? Well, not this time. As a matter of fact, he's the one who . . ." Her voice trailed off.

Josh saw she wasn't going to finish her sentence and decided to let it go.

Rachael checked her watch. "We should get going. If we hurry we should be able to catch Cecilia before she has to return to the city. Oh, and I lost my ride. I got dropped off, so we'll need to take yours."

~ ~ ~

The ten-mile trip out to the cabin had all the gaiety of a funeral procession. Josh didn't know why, but he couldn't stop glancing at the ring. And each time he did, his heart sank deeper. If that wasn't enough, Forest Route 29 was rough and the rental, a four-door sedan, kept sliding sideways on the snow and slush, scraping its bottom every few hundred yards, making their progress feel like an eternity. About fifteen minutes had elapsed when Rachael finally broke the silence.

"So, are you going to ask?"

"Hey, it's none of my business. Is it?" he replied, the sharp edge of his tone catching him off guard. "Sorry, Rachael, I shouldn't have snapped at you. I am, I'm happy for you. Really, I am. You deserve only the best. So, when's the big day?"

"Next month, just before Christmas." She turned to him. "A *year* Josh, and not a word?"

Josh hit the brakes and slowed the car, edging past a fallen tree. He said nothing.

"What was I supposed to think?" She continued.

A broken branch scraped along the side of the rental, and still he remained silent.

"Damn it, Josh! You could have called." A layer of pain coated her words.

"Hey, you're right, okay? And I know I should have called."

"So. Why didn't you?" she asked . . . then sighed. "Oh, don't bother—"

"I, I don't know. I guess I wanted to get my head straight, and then, well, it was . . . too late."

Rachael shook her head. "You are such an asshole."

What could he say? She was right.

Silence filled the car again, and some time passed before he asked, "So, how is Kingsley taking it, about me coming back on board?"

"Are you on board?" she snapped. "How do you think he took it?"

"Bet he tried like hell to stop it."

Rachael cracked a wry smile. "Well, that he did, but someone wanted you on the file, this being so *high profile* and all. Seems you still have believers."

"And you, do you want me on board?" he asked, and thought he saw a glimpse of despair on her face.

She didn't respond.

A few seconds later, the cabin came into view.

Josh pulled in between a gray SUV and another four-door sedan and killed the engine.

Rachael unbuckled her seat belt. "Let's see what Cecilia's got."

They'd trudged twenty yards into the forest through the snow when Josh saw the top of a yellow forensics tent, its flaps drawn and tied back with black bows. Cecilia Bloom was kneeling by the victim, measuring the puncture wound and jotting down figures into a black notebook. She lifted her head as they approached and gave a big, bucktoothed smile. "Josh Ingram, my love, where have you been all my life?"

"Under a rock, apparently," he said, glancing at Rachael while tapping snow off his shoes.

Cecilia raised an eyebrow. "Oh, I see. I take it you didn't know about, Thomas?"

"Something like that."

"So, anything new?" Rachael asked Cecilia, passing her Tindleton's preliminary report.

"Right—that," Cecilia replied. "Yeah, there is one important thing. Keep Fumble Fingers Tindleton away from my work. I don't want to see him within a mile of this body, or any other body for that matter. More goddamn contamination on it than a cowboy's shorts in a bull riding competition. The man's an imbecile."

"Anything else?" Rachael asked.

"Yeah, he did get one thing right. The fifth thoracic was removed, and it wasn't an animal that did it. Whoever did the deed was good with a knife, and I'm guessing to some degree had a rudimentary knowledge of anatomy."

"Medical training?" Josh asked.

"Could be, but it wasn't a scalpel if that's what you're thinking. The final cuts around the bone were clean, just not that precise. Someone with a medical background wouldn't hurt, mind you, but a good butcher could do the job."

"Anything else?" Josh asked.

"No, not with me. CSI completed its work this morning. Samples, lab work, etc. are on their way back to the city for further analysis."

Josh turned to Rachael. "So, why's the body still here?"

"You'll have to ask him," Rachael said, pointing at the cabin.

"The husband—the judge?"

"Yep."

"What'd you say the judge's name was?"

"I didn't. But his name is George Higgins."

"Huh," Josh replied, a look of recognition crossing his face.

"He's expecting us," Rachael said. "Shall we?"

~ ~ ~

The cabin smelled of stale air and wood smoke. Judge Higgins was sitting on the couch poking at the dead embers in the fireplace with a crooked stick, its end burnt black. He stood and turned as Josh and Rachael entered.

"Judge Higgins, I'm so sorry for your loss," Josh said, reaching out to shake the judge's hand.

"Thank you for coming, Josh," the judge said with familiarity and nodded to Rachael.

Rachael glanced at Josh then back at the judge.

The judge opened a sideboard cabinet and took out a bottle of brandy, offering them both a drink. Rachael declined, Josh accepted. "I wasn't sure you would come, Josh. I knew you'd worked on the O'Henry file of course, but that was, what? Close to a year ago, maybe more.

Thought maybe you'd gone back into retirement." The judge cleared his throat. "Anyway, thank you for coming."

"Well, you'd have to thank Rachael for that."

The judge considered Rachael as he took a sip of his brandy before saying, "Josh you never knew my Doris. She is . . . *ah hell* . . . was a good woman." The judge's voice turned hard. "She didn't deserve this . . ." He half-raised his hand, shaking his head. "But then again, nobody does."

He went on to talk about his wife, her political career and personal life. When he had finished, he grabbed the brandy bottle and poured another shot for himself and another for Josh.

"Has there been any recent indication of trouble, anyone threatening your wife?" Rachael asked. "Perhaps someone from the political arena, a falling out with a friend, a disgruntled staff member, someone she'd let go before she retired?"

The judge shook his head. "Her staff all loved her. She was one of a kind. A straight shooter, no nonsense with that woman. No, I can't think of anyone." He took another pull on his brandy. "Mind you, if you turned back the clock a couple of decades, there could've been some wanting to get even, Doris being a DA back then. But no, I don't think so, there's never been any real trouble from her past. I'd know if there was, because that woman could talk the ear off a cob of corn," he said, his voice growing weak, his eyes moist.

He turned to Josh. "Josh, I specifically requested you be part of the investigation. And I have to tell you, I got a fair bit of resistance in the process, mostly from that Kingsley fellow. No love there I take it?" He raised an eyebrow. "But I wanted you onboard. I wanted your skill set on the team."

Josh didn't respond.

"Well, you're here now, so there's no need for me to blather on, but thank you for coming. And thank you, Rachael, for making it happen."

Josh shot a glance at Rachael and took another sip of brandy. Then he put down his glass and asked if he could use the washroom.

When he'd left the room, Rachael turned to the judge. "If you don't mind, how is it you and . . . ?" she asked, tilting her head in the direction of the washroom.

"Yes, of course," the judge replied, then paused for a moment, his face grim. "It was some time ago. I was presiding over a case involving a child prostitution ring. The perps brought the children in from Romania and had set up shop in the Lower East Side. It was a disgusting case, as you can well imagine. But, we had them dead to rights. They were going down, the ringleaders all staring at life in prison, which was essentially a death sentence. No sympathy for that sort, particularly in the penal system." He looked in the direction of the washroom. "Josh, he'd done an exemplary job of tying everything tight, no loose ends—those animals were finished.

"There were a total of three defendants in all, a father and his two middle-aged sons. I can still remember the three of them at the arraignment, their smiling, smug faces, carrying on as though none of it applied to them. It wasn't until later, a few days before the trial date, that I understood why. That's when everything went to hell. The physical evidence vanished, and a day later the two key eyewitnesses backed off and refused to testify. There was no longer a case, we had *nothing*. We had to let them walk. Sad as it is to say, and my contention remains steadfast, the defendants had to have had ties to certain members of the force." The judge took a large gulp of his brandy before continuing. "It was the most gut-wrenching case dismissal of my life, knowing full well what lay in store for those children." He glanced at Rachael, then stared out the window. "A week later, all three of the ring leaders were found dead, each with a single bullet in the back of his head. Execution style."

The toilet flushed, and Rachael looked in the direction of the sound, then back at the judge. "Are you saying?"

The judge turned to Rachael. "Hey. I'm not saying anything, and I'm not condoning that sort of thing, but there are some lines worth crossing."

"So . . . if Doris's killer ever gets to trial, you want to ensure justice will be served."

The judge's face soured again as he turned back to the window. "And served cold."

Chapter 9

In late November the sun drops early in Minnesota, and for Father Paul that was a blessing, for the dark made everything a little easier. He glanced at his watch. *She'll be leaving her office soon,* he thought. *Be here in twenty minutes, give or take.*

Even though he'd checked to make sure the neighbor was not at home and knew Lana lived on her own, he pressed the front door bell with his gloved hand. Life can be full of surprises, and he hated surprises. He waited for another few seconds, then rang again. There was nothing, no footsteps padding down the hallway, no light coming on inside, no one calling out, 'I'll be right there.'

How wonderful, he thought, tightening his grip on his duffle bag as he skirted around to the backyard, climbed the porch steps and walked up to the kitchen window.

As he'd expected the silver clasp at the base of the windowsill was locked. He tapped on the screen covering the window with his finger and almost grinned. Then he unzipped the duffle bag and withdrew a flat-head screwdriver, jamming it in between the wood and the screen, popping it off. He laid the screen against the side of the house, then reached back into the duffle bag and withdrew a yellow cordless drill. He checked the tension on the chuck, ensuring the drill bit was tight and would not fail.

In a matter of seconds the drill punched through the pane, creating a neat round hole the diameter of a roofer's nail. Reaching into his coat pocket, he retrieved a short length of coat hanger wire. He ran his fingers along the wire to its slightly curved end, made a minor adjustment to the angle, and then proceeded to thread it through the hole until the tip caught on the clasp. With the palm of his hand, he pushed on the wire, and the clasp clicked open.

The window was old, and its frame had obviously shed its skin a number of times. The last coat of paint was blue. *Rather like that of a robin's egg,* he thought and smiled. It was his favorite color. He pulled up on the window and it protested, emanating a long painful squeak before coming to a full stop, two thirds of the way up.

He ran his fingers along the frame and could feel where the wood had swelled. He leaned in for a closer look and saw a series of skid marks where the window had stopped on previous attempts. He considered the size of the opening for a moment and figured it would be a tight fit, but it would do.

He edged his shoulders in first, twisting and slipping through, then dragged the rest of his torso across the opening, crawling over the kitchen sink and dropping to the floor. He got to his feet and went to the backdoor and unlocked it. If things went south, a quick exit was always a good idea.

He brushed himself off and was taking in the surroundings when a tingle of excitement ran through him. He was alone, standing in Lana's private world, a world where she felt safe. He remembered how happy she looked the week before, the two young lovers enjoying the thrill of a fresh romance. He glanced around. *And your choices are so right,* he thought. The moss-colored walls and chestnut-brown wood floor seemed to give the room warmth and a kind of bohemian feel. Then he noticed a white porcelain vase on the kitchen table, filled with freshly cut flowers. *From your new beau, no doubt? How sweet. Yes, I think I could live here.*

He walked over to an oil painting hanging on the kitchen wall. It was of a cattle shed on a farmer's field, round bales of hay dotting the landscape, the late-day sun flooding the stubble field with light. He slowly ran his hand down the frame's edge and a wave of pleasure washed over him. *Oh, you do have such good taste.* Then another wave hit, causing his stomach to cramp and a muffled squeal rose in his throat. He ran to the kitchen sink and splashed his face with cold water, then turned his head and muttered, "This is *so* right."

He pondered what life would be like, waiting for her to come home from work, her purse in one hand, her briefcase in the other, a tired look on her face. She would give him a light peck on his cheek as she walked through the door. *"Dinner's ready,"* he'd say. *"How was your day?"* But she'd been hard at it all day, and wouldn't like to talk about it. She'd want to relax, and yes, to eat. Basic human needs first and foremost . . .

"What was that?" he whispered, hearing the front door open. *You're early.* He looked around and his heart began to thump in his chest. *But . . . but I'm not ready for you.*

Then came the sound of her kicking off her shoes and opening the entryway closet.

Quickly slipping off his shoes, he picked them up, and dropped them out the window onto his duffle bag. He pulled down on the window, carefully, so as not to make a sound. Then he left the kitchen, turned right, and padded up the stairs.

The sound of keys hitting the kitchen table sent a thrill through him, and he almost missed the top step, grabbing the handrail to steady himself. He moved down the hallway and entered a bedroom. It was a relatively large room with an en suite. *Your bedroom my dear, how very nice . . . Oh, oh, is that you?* He could hear her footsteps coming down the hall.

He slipped into the closet, closing the folding doors in front of him, his nose almost touching the loose-fitting slats, gaps of a good quarter inch between them. It was unlikely she would see him, because the closet was dark, but he'd certainly see her.

She entered the room, tossed her purse on the bed, and went straight for the shower.

After setting the temperature, she returned to the bedroom and began undressing. She was slightly taller than he'd thought, five eight, or maybe even nine. Her auburn hair did seem on the longish side, given the shape of her face, but no matter, she was still quite stunning.

She unbuttoned her blouse and tossed it on the bed, then reached behind her and unzipped her skirt, stepping out of it and folding it once lengthwise, before carefully laying it next to her blouse. His breathing picked up a beat as he watched her. She unclasped her bra and dropped it on the bed, then stepped out of her panties and carried them into the bathroom, tossing them into a wicker basket. Then she stepped into the shower.

He waited for close to a minute, making sure she was well into her routine, before leaving the closet and heading downstairs to the kitchen and out the back door.

When he reached his truck, he lowered the tailgate, retrieved a pine crate from the deck and set it on the ground, then circled around to the cab and got his 9mm from the glove box.

Once back in the kitchen he put the crate down on the floor and removed the lid, then darted back upstairs, taking the steps two at a time, stopping at the doorway for a second to listen. He was relieved to hear the shower was still running, and was halfway across the room when he came to a halt. *What's that? She's humming something?* He didn't recognize the song, but it was a happy tune. He listened for another few seconds—then he heard the water slow, and the pipes pound in the walls. He slipped in behind the en suite door and tried his best to slow his breathing.

The shower door clunked once as it opened and once more as it closed. Peering through the crack between the inside edge of the door and the doorjamb, he watched her towel dry her hair and then her body. *You're so very special, I almost wish . . .*

She hung her towel on a wooden peg and walked through the doorway, then stopped in her tracks, her body rigid. "Who, who's there?" she whispered. "Is . . . is someone there?" She took a step forward, turned, and her eyes opened wide. She was about to scream when he pressed the cold gun muzzle to her forehead. Then he raised his finger to his lips and said, "Now, close your eyes."

Chapter 10

F ather Paul stepped up to the edge of the forest, sweating and breathing hard. He was standing at the top of a low-lying cliff, looking down at the camp below, watching his followers scurry about, tending to their morning routines.

The camp had been set up at the base of an abandoned fieldstone watermill, nestled alongside a wooded ravine. It consisted of eight large canvas-topped wagons that served as living quarters for the senior members of the troupe, plus two green tents, each capable of housing up to ten members, and a ninth wagon made entirely of wood.

The canvas-topped wagons were fashioned after the Sheep Wagons of Wyoming, only larger, their sides mushroomed out to provide additional living space. Inside, there were bunk beds for the children, a compact cast iron wood stove, shelving, and storage cupboards for food and supplies. The parents slept in a loft above, accessed by a pull-down ladder. Every inch of space accounted for and utilized.

Each wagon had been painted its own distinctive color: red, yellow, gray, pink, orange, purple, brown, blue, and white. The ninth—the white wagon—served as both Father Paul's meditation chamber and his living quarters.

The senior members' wagons and the two green tents all faced into a large, circus-like tent that provided a common area used for group dining, worship services, and general day-to-day activities, including socializing. It also sheltered the troupe from the weather, giving them a sense of seclusion and security. Father Paul's wagon sat twenty yards away from the big tent, isolated and alone.

Father Paul was still breathing hard, trying to catch his breath. He wiped a layer of sweat off of his chin with the back of his hand and saw a smudge of blood on his cuff. He considered it for a second before turning his attention back to the camp. The last vestiges of mist had finally burnt off, and the colored wagons, and the big tent with the watermill standing tall in the background had all come into focus. "It's all so beautiful," he said, tears welling in his eyes. Then he looked up. "Now I understand why you led us here."

'God's Troupe' as the followers liked to call themselves, consisted of three distinct rings. The first ring, the outermost ring, was comprised of the children and unmarried teens; they were known as the Life Blood, the future of the troupe. Their duties were to beg and steal on the streets of nearby towns and return to the camp each night with their loot. The middle ring housed the parents, known as the Sustainers. Their duties were to lead, feed, clothe, transport, and teach the young, as well as maintain order and discipline within the troupe.

The elders of the troupe, men from the Sustainer circle, posed as handymen and preyed on the surrounding area, offering to do home repairs and renovations, always demanding payment upfront but never completing or even starting the project.

The innermost ring, the Advisory Council, was comprised of five men, chosen by the elders. Each year, one of the elders would step down and a new council member would be chosen by his peers. Not by the women though, there were no voting rights for them.

The Advisors' duties were to organize the troupe, deal with the local town residents and law enforcement, and most importantly research the next location. A poor site choice would cause hardship, and the troupe would suffer. The Advisors reported directly to the troupe's spiritual leader, Father Paul, who, by his own words, had been chosen by God.

Controlling others had been a far easier task than Father Paul had originally thought. Simply give people a place in this world where they believe they belong, where they believe they are special, and they will follow. *And my followers are good and decent people, and for that they shall be rewarded—for they will witness God's miracle and have eternal salvation.*

The foundation of Father Paul's doctrine was simple— all of his commandments were to be followed without question. And yet there was one decree that resonated more than the others. For he, and only he, had the divine right to choose which girl from the Life Blood would be wed to a man from either the Sustainer or the Advisory Circles.

It had been decreed that on a girl's sixteenth birthday she would be wed.

Hanna, daughter to Carl and Angel Hocklander, had blossomed early and was prettier than the other girls, and her youthful energy and innocence had not gone unnoticed.

Father Paul considered Hanna to be quite charming. She had an inquisitive way about her that made her unique.

Always asking about this and that. She was a special girl, one of his favorites, and for that she would be wed to his most loyal follower, Brother Alvin. Alvin was by far the oldest of the troupe, and quite frankly the least handsome, but he was long overdue, and he had earned the right to a fine young bride—and so the reward would be his.

And since Hanna's birthday was next week, he knew he would have to make known his selection soon, although not quite yet. It was never a good idea to tell either the eager groom or the blushing bride too far ahead, as it had proven to cause anxiety amongst the rank and file. He would make the announcement in the next day or two, leaving little time for trouble to brew.

Multiple wives were not only allowed, they were encouraged. Father Paul had long ago proclaimed that it was a man's right, and his justifiable need, to be cared for by more than one woman. This turned out to be a highly popular part of his doctrine, especially for those with the right to vote. Father Paul understood a man's primal urges were a potent drug. And yet for him, the frailties of men were not his concern. He had a higher purpose, a greater calling.

As he watched his followers milling about, busying themselves with their simple chores, a surge of pride rose up within him. The women, both young and old, were dressed in ankle length black dresses, thin red belts tied at the waist, strings of colorful beads draped about their necks, ornate silver bracelets hanging from their thin wrists. *You are all so lovely.*

~ ~ ~

Father Paul entered his meditation chamber, kicked off his boots, and locked the door behind him. He had gutted and refitted the wagon himself. The trailer, stark and frugal, consisted of a plywood floor covered by a simple, brown oval rug. The walls were bare wood, and he slept on a cot not much bigger than his body. Beside the cot stood an oil heater. Against one wall was a small counter with a stainless steel sink and a cupboard overhead.

At the far end of the trailer was his place of worship. A black curtain had been draped down the end wall, and a copy of the Bible sat on a low, wrought iron pedestal facing the curtain. On either side of the pedestal sat a large, white candle shaped like a milk carton. At the base of the pedestal was a crimson cushion fringed with gold tassels. It was there he would kneel to pray and hear God's voice.

The one indulgence he'd allowed himself was the addition of a curtained platform attached to the rear of his trailer, complete with a generator, a hot water tank, and a claw-footed bathtub.

Father Paul stretched out onto his cot and began to daydream about how his life was about to change . . .

Chapter 11

The troupe's tent, made from military grade canvas, stood twenty feet high at its apex and a hundred feet wide at its base. Inside, two women were pegging laundry onto a wire rope strung tight between two large poles, while a man stacked firewood near the tent's front entrance.

Angel Hocklander stood at a butcher-block table holding a knife in her hand as she watched the man stacking wood. A few feet away, a black cauldron bubbled over an open fire. The hearty aroma of smoke, garlic, and boiled meat rose to the ceiling and exited through fan-assisted vents.

Near the center of the tent and piled into a heap was a baby carriage, two guitars, a dartboard, some stacking chairs, a gasoline lawn mower, and parts of a snow blower, plus other sundry junk that would be eventually sorted and sold off or left as a reminder that they had been there.

Angel gripped the knife tight in her hand and began chopping a carrot the size of a small zucchini. Each chop cut through to the table with a sharp knock that resonated in the air. Keeping busy seemed to help lessen her anxieties about many things, but not when it came to her daughter's upcoming wedding day.

She knew she was alone in this matter, isolated, and dare not discuss it with anyone. To do so would be heresy. And without question she could not discuss it with Carl, her husband, as he would never question the good Father's authority. To do so would leave Carl out in the cold, or worse yet, leave him out of any future selection process. No man would risk that.

She'd seen how the men had grown more interested as Hanna's sixteenth birthday grew nearer, leering and whispering. The thought of her daughter being handed over to one of them made her stomach churn. She jabbed the knife into the tabletop, her breath hot with hate, not just for them, but for herself. For how could she claim innocence? Had she not come into the fold of her own free will? She jabbed the knife into the table again. Her daughter would *not* waste her life serving the needs of a man.

"You look troubled my wife," Carl said, as he walked up beside her, his face puzzled by his wife's unruly behavior. "Something bothering you?"

"I'm just tired, my husband," she replied. "The pressure of the wedding day is weighing on me."

"Of course it is. But you need not worry; it will be a beautiful ceremony. And whoever Father chooses for Hanna, he will be the right one. After all, he chose us."

Angel could feel her husband studying her, looking for a tell, a thread of deception. He touched her, and her skin began to crawl. She looked up at him and forced a smile, knowing full well any chance of escape was dependent on her ability to deceive. If he sensed a ripple of discontent, he would report her to the Sustainers and she would be placed into solitude, to pray and ask for forgiveness, to mend her ways. Eventually, she'd be allowed to rejoin the congregation in its day-to-day activities, but not before the blessed event, and certainly *not* before the 'holy bond' had been consummated. After that, only death could break the matrimonial bond—as it had been decreed by Father Paul.

"Come here you little monster," Hanna laughed, chasing Mortimer past the front entrance of the family's wagon. Mortimer had little legs, but he was fast, faster than the other potbelly pigs, and Hanna was losing ground. And yet, she knew she'd never lose sight of him, for his blue bib made him stand out from the rest. Not that the other pigs were allowed to run free, not like her little boy. He'd been born early, and underdeveloped, and the task of bottle-feeding him had been handed to her. Now three months old, Mortimer was no longer in need of the bottle, but that didn't matter. Hanna needed him.

"Come on Mortimer, I'm getting tired," Hanna said, kneeling down on the tent floor. "If you don't come over here, right this minute, I'll not let you sleep with me tonight." Mortimer stuck his nose out from under a gray, weathered stacking chair, his young eyes surveying the situation. He looked as though he was thinking it through, focusing hard, staring at her. Then in the blink of an eye, he lowered his head and trotted over, not a care in the world, and flopped his little body down at her side, pressing his back up against her. Hanna laid her hand on his side and could feel his heart beating.

Mortimer sneezed, then lifted his head and craned his neck to get a better look at her. He stared for a long moment, then lowered his head back down.

A few minutes had passed when Mortimer raised his head again, this time sniffing at the air. He jumped up and ran toward Hanna's mother, looking back to see if Hanna was coming after him. He did an end run around the cauldron, flying out the other side, and squealed as he brushed up against Carl's leg.

"Get that filthy beast out of here!" Carl barked, kicking hard but missing Mortimer. Hanna rushed over and reached down, snatching up Mortimer. Carl grabbed Hanna by the shoulders and shook her. "Listen to me! Pigs, are not for playing with," he said, a scowl on his face. "You put it in the pen with the others, where it belongs. And you do it now!"

Hanna's heart sank, and her anger rose. "I will not!" she cried, straightening herself up and turning to her mother. "Mortimer is one of the family. Isn't he mother?"

Angel glanced over, but said nothing, and continued to stir the stew.

"You'll listen to me," Carl said. "It's time you put away such childish things. You're to be wed in a few days, and a wife has no time for such foolishness."

"Carl," Angel said. "Mortimer is special to Hanna, she's raised him since he was a baby. You have to give her time to adjust."

"Don't coddle the girl, woman. It's time she takes responsibility for her place in the troupe. She's to be a wife, and childish things must go . . ."

"But, my husband," Angel protested. "She's still a child."

"There'll be no more talk. Tomorrow, the pig joins the others." Then he turned to Hanna. "And you'll do it, Hanna, or I'll throw him in the pen myself."

"You'll not touch Mortimer," Hanna cried, as she wrapped him in a towel. "He's my best friend in the whole world, he's kind and playful and sweet." She looked down at Mortimer and stroked his head. "Why can't you see that?" She turned and ran toward the center of the tent with Mortimer held tight in her arms, then dropped to her knees and patted his head, and whispered something into his ear.

"Was that really necessary?" Angel asked. "Isn't life cruel enough without you adding to it?"

"I'll not have you taking that tone with me, woman. Hanna is to be wed, and the pig goes to the pen—end of discussion."

Angel bowed her head and looked away.

Chapter 12

Barney's Tavern seemed like any other Midwestern bar Josh had been in, except tonight the women were exceptional. Across the room and leaning against the jukebox, a couple of healthy felines were pawing at their men, staking their claim, their cowboy boots pivoting on the beer-stained floor.

Mmm, mmm, there is a God, Josh thought, as he drained half his beer. Then he hiccupped, blinking hard a few times, the room threatening to spin. "*Whoa . . .* Man, I gotta slow down," he mumbled to himself, his lower lip gone numb, a strained grin on his face. Then he thought of the ring on Rachael's finger. "*Ah,* ta hell with it . . ." He took another gulp.

"You're handling Rachael's new love interest rather well," Vivian said, sitting across from him in the booth. Vivian was Rachael's second in command at the FBI Special Crimes Unit located on The Lower East Side. She and Charley Gupta, another member of the team who was sitting next to her, had both flown in on the afternoon flight.

"Ya really think so?" Josh replied, his tongue thick as a rubber welcome mat at a coin laundry.

"Maybe we should get some food and coffee in you?" Vivian asked.

"Yeah, that's a good idea," Josh said. "*Hey Charley,* ya hungry? Wha'da ya say, ya wanna eat somethin'? Ya wanna eat some . . . fried chicken, maybe? Wha'da ya think, Charley, how about it—ya want some *chicken?*"

Charley smirked and shoved another French fry in his mouth. Vivian waved over the waitress and ordered the food.

~ ~ ~

Josh had polished off a pound of salt and pepper chicken wings, a large basket of French fries, and a bowl of potato salad when a three-stack of corn-on-the-cob dripping in butter was plopped down in front of him.

Five minutes later, he dropped the last cob on his plate, wiped his chin with a napkin, and looked up with a dopey smile on his face.

"Feeling better?" Vivian asked, raising an eyebrow.

"Not bad. But you know, I sure could use a *drink.*" He winked. "Kidding, just kidding for Christ's sake. Lighten up, Vivian, would ya?" He held both hands up as though he was surrendering.

"*Riiight,*" Vivian replied. "Charley, I don't know about you, but I'm going to turn in."

"Yeah, me too." He turned to Josh. "You coming?"

"Right behind you. You two go on ahead, I'll be there in a minute." He sniffed at his coffee, winced, and took another sip.

As Charley and Vivian were leaving the bar, Sheriff Holly Oleson passed them in the doorway, giving them a nod before striding straight across the room to Josh. She stood at the side of his booth, looked him over, then slipped in across from him.

He was having trouble focusing on her face, so he blinked a couple of times, which seemed to help—sort of. He figured she had to be in her early forties, hard to tell for sure. Her blonde hair was tied in a ponytail and had a natural, youthful shine, the fine lines around her eyes adding a cultured, refined look to her face. On closer inspection, he couldn't help but wonder how she'd gotten into her uniform, concluding the gray fabric had obviously been painted on her well-proportioned body, hugging her curves in all the right places. By the time he clued in to how her high cheekbones underscored her incredible blue eyes, the whole point of the question became pointless.

"The FBI have relaxed their standards," she said, checking him over and smiling, her lips slightly parted.

As he looked into her eyes, a sudden feeling of helplessness washed over him, followed by a prickle of trepidation. It was at that moment a stark revelation hit him, an epiphany of sorts. At least, he thought so. *If the eyes are the windows to the soul, then this broad's gonna eat me alive.* He hiccupped again. "I'm . . . I'm not FBI . . . but thanks for noticing," he said, slurring his words. "I'm Josh—"

"I know who you are, Josh." Her voice was warm and sultry, a tone that belied the petite, pretty woman sitting across from him. She appeared to be studying him, as if she was making her mind up about something, then she shifted in her seat. "Wha'da ya say, we have one for the ditch?"

"*Huh? Where's the bitch?*" he replied, his voice squeaking. He cleared his throat and in a deep voice, grunted, "*Huh?*"

"A nightcap? I need to unwind. You up for it?" she asked, wetting her upper lip with the tip of her tongue.

"Yeah, I guess. Sure, why not?" He wasn't sure if it was such a good idea, his focus being less than perfect. He took another long hard look at her and concluded he'd had worse ideas.

Chapter 13

With his head burrowed deep into a goose down pillow, Josh cracked one eye open, rolling it slowly around in its socket when a ray of sunlight ricocheted off a mirror and walloped him in his retina. *Aaagh . . . ahh man.*

He smacked his lips and frowned. The taste was bad, real bad, like someone had set a camel on fire and stomped it out with his tongue.

Then it dawned on him. He had no idea where he was. With his head still pressed into the pillow, his free eye continued to scan the room. *Where the hell am I? It's not my room. . . . Is it?* It was at that precise moment he took notice of a warm bare ass pressed up against his lower back. *Nope. Not my room.* He reached behind him and ran his hand along a curved hip, and when he cupped a plump breast, a sleepy moan erupted. Whoever it was shifted and rolled over, throwing her arm around him. He bit his lower lip and carefully rolled over and lifted the covers, coming face to face with the sheriff.

All at once the events of the night washed over him, sketchy as they were. He exhaled a forced puff, realizing too late it was a cruel thing to do. Holly scrunched up her nose in response to the sour onslaught, turned her head, and buried her face into her pillow. Josh swallowed, smacking his lips again and shuddered, then slipped out from under the blanket and stood up.

He looked around. *Uh-huh, gotta be her place . . . it's so clean . . . like really clean, like out of a woman's magazine clean.* He was taking in the fresh cut flowers on her nightstand when he realized her decorating prowess was not his immediate concern. Grabbing his pants off the floor, he got one leg on and had the other halfway up before losing his balance and began hopping sideways on one leg. Turning in a tight circle, he fell to the floor with a loud thud. He glanced over at the bed. Holly stirred, but didn't wake.

The spinning hadn't done much for his head, nor had landing on his back, so he decided to stay put and wait for things to settle. A good minute passed before he managed to get his other pant leg pulled up.

Once back on his feet, he wobbled into the bathroom, flipped up the toilet seat and took care of priority one. He washed up, finishing with a splash of cold water on his face, and brushed his teeth with his index finger—which wasn't great, but at least it buried the camel.

He crossed the bedroom floor to the window and peeked out. The first rays of the morning sun were cutting along the neighboring rooftops. Across the street, a stray dog was digging in a tipped over garbage bin, bits and pieces of wrappers, paper plates, and a few red plastic cups were fanned out on the sidewalk like a river delta. He looked down the street and spotted his hotel at the end of the block, the diner's yellow neon sign reading *OPEN*.

He turned back to the sheriff. She had rolled onto her side, her bare leg draped over a pillow. He watched her for a few seconds, then slipped out the back way and quietly closed the screen door behind him.

~ ~ ~

Back in his hotel room he took a long, hot shower, shaved, put on a clean pair of jeans, a light-yellow golf shirt and gray sports coat. He grabbed a bottle of water from the minibar and gulped it down, which immediately brought on a renewed sense of nausea. What he really needed was coffee and lots of it, so he headed down to the hotel's restaurant thinking he might even choke down some breakfast. Vivian and Charley were seated at a table by the front window. They waved him over.

"So, what time did you get in?" Vivian asked, a noticeable smirk on her face.

"Sometime . . ." His words slipping out slow and tentative. "Late, I guess."

Vivian kept her focus on him. "Charley and I will be interviewing members of the congregation today. How about you, what're *you* going to do?"

"Ahh . . ." Josh mumbled. "Yeah, the sheriff and I, we're . . ."

"Yes, go on," Vivian encouraged. "The sheriff and you are . . . ?"

"Yeah right, we're meeting up with Rachael at the church, to go over the crime scene."

Charley made a choking sound and started to chuckle. "Well, that should be interesting."

Josh didn't respond, and took a sip of his coffee.

After breakfast they went their separate ways, Vivian telling Josh to 'be careful out there' and giving him a knowing smile.

Josh grabbed a couple of large coffees to go and was on his way back to the sheriff's place when she rolled up in her

Jeep. He climbed in the passenger side. "Morning Sheriff," he said, and handed her a coffee.

"I take it we're off to meet your boss."

"That's right. Rachael Tanner, she's already at the church. And just so you know, she's not my boss, I am an—"

"Advisor, yeah I got that," she said, with an edge to her words. "You left early?"

"I, I didn't want to wake you."

"*Yeah . . .* you're a considerate guy." She looked straight ahead, and punched the gas, only to come to a lurching stop at the next set of lights. As they waited to make a left off Main Street, the tick-tock, tick-tock of the signal light resonated in the cab like hobnailed boots in a dark alleyway. He wasn't sure why, but he knew something was off . . . way off. *Did I do something wrong? Don't think so. And yet . . . ?*

He started to play back the events of last night in his head. It did kind of seem like a dream. In fact, he couldn't remember much about it other than she was extremely athletic and flexible. He looked over at her and suddenly remembered her straddling him. *Whoa, all that was missing was a lasso in your hand,* he thought. *Then again . . . ? Nah.*

Holly reached across and patted his thigh, giving it a firm squeeze. "Thanks for the coffee, cowboy."

Chapter 14

Yellow crime scene tape had been draped around the church, suspended by iron rods stuck in the ground every twenty feet. The forensic team was wrapping up, refilling their big blue plastic crates, coiled orange extension cords in one crate, spotlights and other equipment in the others.

Josh and Holly ducked under the tape, circled past the front doors sealed tight by a two-by-four, and entered the church through a side door that was hanging on one hinge.

Rachael was standing by an upright piano with her back to them. She was on her cell, and by the tone of the conversation, Josh figured it had to be Kingsley, her boss. Kingsley had never wanted her as part of his team and never let an opportunity pass to let her know it.

Josh watched her as she began to pace back and forth. He'd hoped she would've found a way to reduce her stress level by now. She was like a thoroughbred, high-strung and hard to control, which ultimately meant she was hard on herself. But even with her fist clenched and a scowl on her face, he couldn't believe how beautiful she was.

He knew Kingsley would be upset, livid in fact, because she'd brought him on board. Years ago, he'd caught Kingsley red-handed doing things he shouldn't have been doing, back when they were both lead profilers. But Kingsley was a survivor, a bureaucracy beetle, always skittering into the shadows before the shoe came down, always forming alliances with others of the same ilk, forever contemplating his next move.

Rachael hung up and was staring at the floor as Josh and Holly walked over.

"Another rib taken," Rachael said, still looking down at the dried blood where Myrna once lay. "Fifth thoracic from the left side, cut out clean, carbon copy of the senator's. No apparent mutilation, sexual or otherwise. Just a clean harvesting of the rib." Rachael turned and noticed the sheriff.

Josh was about to speak when Holly stepped forward and shook Rachael's hand, introducing herself.

"Sorry we're running a little late," Holly said.

Rachael nodded and started right in, her focus back on the crime scene. "Three victims. Two were elderly men, both shot. Trajectory of the blood splatter indicates the shots came from the two broken windows, both men considered collateral damage. Myrna Hudson was the primary target, her wounds matching those of Senator Parker." She looked directly at Holly. "What can you tell us about Mrs. Hudson?"

The sheriff cleared her throat. "Myrna, she was pretty well known around town. Her involvement with the church and various charities made her a bit of a celebrity. Never had a run-in with the law. Her family, that is, her brother and sister, moved away years ago. Her parents are long passed. And her husband, Johnny, well he died, um . . . must be two years ago, now. She has one child, Clark, he works over at King of the Hill Burgers." She paused for a moment. "Odd name choice for the restaurant really, since the town's highest hill is no more than eleven feet. Clark, he's got some kind of mental problems, hears voices and such. I have to throw him in the cell every so often, until his meds take over. Word is though, he does make a spectacular burger."

Holly rubbed her thumb on her forehead. "What a horrible waste. Myrna, Harold, and Kyle, they were all good citizens, never a hint of trouble, kept their noses clean, stayed out of other peoples' business." She stopped to ponder what she'd said. "Certainly no more than anyone else, this being a small town and all." She knelt down and touched Myrna's dried blood. "No . . . this is some kind of crazy shit. These folks were vanilla as ice cream, which in my book rides well with me." She frowned. "Shouldn't have happened. Not to them."

"Can you think of any connection Myrna could've had to Senator Doris Parker?" Josh asked.

Holly thought for a second before shaking her head. "Uh-uh. The senator, she wasn't from around here. Nope, I can't think of one."

Josh's face soured. "Well, there's *gotta* be one . . ."

Rachael looked at Josh, surveying him hard for a few seconds before turning to Holly.

"Have to say, he's looking a little rough this morning, like he's been out tomcatting all night."

"I think you're right. Seems a tad shaky in the knees, don't you think?" replied Holly.

Rachael nodded and they both smirked.

Josh just closed his eyes.

Rachael switched to a professional tone. "Sheriff, thanks for bringing him out this morning."

"Hey, anything I can do Agent Tanner. This whole thing has got the town pretty well worked up. Everyone knew the victims of course. Guess what I'm saying is, anything you need, anything at all, you call me."

"Thanks Sheriff," Rachael said, and raised her hand. "Actually, I could use a list of her closest—"

"Already have my deputy working on it. A list of friends and family members, complete with phone numbers and addresses, will be in your hands by day's end."

"Thanks again, Sheriff," Rachael said.

"Not a problem. In fact, I can tell you right now who Myrna's best friend was. Her name is Candice Carter, she and Candice grew up next door to each other, married local boys. Both sang in the church choir and could be seen around town having lunch together. Always been tight those two."

"The bodies?" Josh asked. "Are they still in town?"

"On ice, down at the funeral home," Holly said. "Orville, he's the funeral director, told me this morning he's ready to ship them off to your ME." Holly checked her watch. "Hey, look. I need to head out now. So, I'll see *you* later?"

Josh nodded and from the corner of his eye saw Rachael staring at him.

"Eight o'clock, all right?"

"Yeah, sounds good," Josh said, not wanting to labor the point.

Rachael did a quick double take at Josh and then Holly.

Holly caught the look and studied Josh for a second, then without another word, she turned and left through the side door.

Josh continued to survey the room, taking time to study the two broken windowpanes situated directly across from each other. "Two shooters," he said. "Caught them in a crossfire, had no chance to take cover."

"Yeah, and sealing them in like that was a nice touch, the sons-of-bitches. Took out the two old guys with shotgun slugs . . . could've dropped a train at that range. But not the woman though, they took their time with her . . ."

"Yeah, how decent of them."

Without warning Josh's stomach growled a low gnarly sound that Rachael seemed to pick up on.

"I'm not seeing how the senator fits into this," he said. "And why a single rib from each victim?"

Rachael nodded, then asked, "So, who do you want to visit first? The best friend, or the not-so-right son?"

Josh said nothing.

"Way too early for burgers," she said, watching for his reaction, knowing his weakness for fast food.

Josh shrugged. "Never too early for that, but you're right, the best friend it is."

Chapter 15

The big tent was almost empty, the Lifeblood and Sustainers having been sent out earlier to raise funds for the troupe. All except Angel who was preparing dinner.

The five men that comprised the Advisory Council were congregated at the far end of the tent, sitting on plastic chairs in a half circle around Father Paul.

"Next on the agenda, finances," Father Paul said. "Brother Kerrin, your report."

Kerrin fidgeted with his papers, clearly uncomfortable with the situation.

"Brother Kerrin, if you please."

Kerrin nodded. "Early reports suggest the town is not responding as well as expected. Word is, a few years back another troupe targeted a town called Litton, over in Winston County, some nine miles south of Lynchfield. People apparently still remember it, and are not as quick to dig into their wallets."

"And the law?" Father Paul asked, his voice tightening in his throat.

"Been quiet so far."

"Right. Well, at least that's something."

"Now, turning to the balance sheet." Kerrin continued. "Specifically funds on hand. As of this morning we have $3,424 in the till. I estimate maybe three weeks before that runs out. Having said that, Brother Herald and Brother

Arnold report they are close to securing a sizable renovation deposit. If that comes through, we should be fine for an additional month or so."

Father Paul said in a stern voice, "God helps those that help themselves. Do you believe that, brother Kerrin?"

"Yes Father," Kerrin replied.

Father Paul turned to the group, waiting for their response.

"Yes Father," they muttered in unison.

"The Lord's a listening! Wha'da ya say?"

"Yes! Father! God helps those that help themselves."

"So, what're we going to do?"

"We're going to do God's will!" they cried.

Father Paul smiled. "Yes brothers, we're going to do God's will . . ."

Father Paul turned to Brother John. "Next order of business is the ceremony. I trust everything is in order?"

"The platform will be completed by the end of the week. We'll be wheeling it into the big tent after Friday's sermon. Peter's done a fine job, a beautiful job actually. I think you'll be proud."

"Good . . ." Father Paul turned to Peter. "Thank you, brother."

"That leaves one last item on our agenda," Father Paul said as he ran his finger down his yellow notepad. He looked up and paused, taking in the moment before continuing. The men were focused on him, their eyes eager with anticipation, hungry to know who would be the one, the lucky one.

He wished he could've passed on what he was about to say, as he'd grown fond of Hanna. She had an innocent energy about her that touched him. But it was expected of him to choose. So, he would do his duty, even if pandering to man's baser instincts was less than agreeable to him.

And yet, he knew he couldn't complain, far from it. More than any other tool at his disposal, the power to choose provided him with potent leverage, a leverage that helped keep the pack in line. And like it or not, he did need them, needed their faith, now more than ever if he was to succeed. As he scanned their faces, he sensed their hunger, each of them wanting the young bride.

"Now, I could've waited until after the promised miracle, my brothers. But I confess, I must have your focused attention for the holy event, for it is the power that we as a collective summon from the Lord that ignites the flame."

His gaze passed from face to face, each set of eyes locked on his. "God has spoken, brothers. He has told me who is to have Hanna as his bride."

A palpable hush fell over the men.

Father Paul put his hands together as if in prayer. "It is a truly glorious thing, having a woman to care for you, to bear your children and attend to all your worldly needs . . . *Brother Alvin,* stand and step forward."

The group gasped.

"God has chosen Hanna for you, my son. Care for her and treat her well."

A big lopsided smile crossed Alvin's lips and he bowed his head.

A disgruntled murmur rose up from the others, instantly turning to a chorus of malcontent. Hanna was a prize they had all coveted.

Brother Damian stood up, throwing his chair backward onto the dirt. "This is such bullshit! I was next in line, everyone here knows that to be true. Hanna must be mine! I have earned her!" The others froze and went silent. For no one had ever questioned the Father's judgment.

Father Paul's eyes narrowed, and then he smiled. "Brother Damian, fear not my son, for you have a right to feel pangs of resentment. We are all God's children, trying to find our way. I feel your pain, brother. I understand and respect where you are coming from. So please come, come closer so I can lessen some of that burden you are carrying. It cuts me to the core to know you are troubled, my son. Come. Come stand by me, let us pray together and lessen that ponderous load you are carrying."

Damian looked around for support, but all eyes were staring at the dirt floor. This was uncharted territory. He'd overstepped his bounds, and the others refused to meet his eyes. Damian slowly stepped forward and bowed his head, then dropped to his knees at Father Paul's feet. The father placed one hand on Damian's head, raising the other high into the air. "Lord, we seek your guidance, for one of our flock is in pain. Please Lord, show us the way."

The group began chanting as one. "We pray thee Lord, show us the way."

~ ~ ~

Angel was tending to the cooking, which she found far less disagreeable than having to beg on the streets. All the others, the men, women and children, including Hanna, had left for town and wouldn't be back for a few hours.

Her only company was a couple of rangy dogs. The bigger of the two, a black lab cross, was sprawled out on a tattered oriental rug. The smaller mutt had his head tilted to one side and was scratching his ear with his rear paw.

The stew still needed to simmer for a good hour, so she decided to feed the dogs. Somehow they instinctively knew what she was about to do and both were now sitting at attention waiting patiently for their bowls to be filled.

She took a step back to watch them eat, the larger dog's hind leg lifting sporadically as though it was attached to a string, his eyes glancing over at the other dog's bowl, checking to see how much was left.

She had just finished stirring the stew and was tapping the big spoon on the edge of the pot when she heard a commotion coming from the far end of the tent. Normally, she wouldn't have paid any attention, as Father Paul had decreed women were strictly forbidden to take part in the affairs of the men. But she'd heard her daughter's name and decided to check it out.

Laying the spoon across the edge of the stew pot, she ducked down and made her way across the tent floor to the rummage pile. It wasn't a perfect vantage point, her vision partially obstructed by the spokes of a bicycle wheel. But at least she was hidden and in that she took comfort. She could see Father Paul standing in front of the Advisory Council. He had one hand raised high into the air, and his other hand, his healing hand, was on Brother Damian's head. It was like a picture she'd seen in the bible, exactly where, she couldn't recall.

Without warning, Father Paul's body started to tremble, and the others leaned back as though a strong wind had channeled down upon them. The chanting grew louder, and one of the men fell to the ground, sobbing.

Father Paul's eyes opened, and the chanting came to an abrupt halt, the men's focus now locked on him. Then his eyes rolled back into his head, the whites exposed, wet and glistening. "Hallelujah!" he cried, then looked down and grabbed a clump of Damian's hair, yanking his head back. Reaching inside his robe, he withdrew a large hunting knife, and in one clean motion sliced deep into Damian's neck, its sharp edge seemingly stopped only by the man's backbone. It was a clean, fast stroke, blood pouring from the wound like a tipped can of red paint, running down his neck in rhythmic pulses. "The Lord has taken our brother into his loving arms!" Father Paul cried. "Brother Damian feels pain, no more. *Praise the Lord!*"

With that, the chanting started again, louder than before. "*Praise the Lord . . . praise our father . . .*"

Chapter 16

Candice Carter lived on a quiet street bordering a ravine curved like a lazy S. The homes dated back to the 1920s, most being three-story brick structures with steep roofs, accented by copper that had turned green with age. Maple and oak trees lined both sides of the road, their orphaned leaves, red and yellow, dangled over the sidewalks like forgotten Christmas ornaments.

Carter's house was a brown brick, one and a half story cedar shake roofed home with a large picture window facing onto the street. As they climbed the front steps, Josh saw a woman asleep on an overstuffed armchair in the front room, an open book resting on her belly. Rachael grabbed the knocker and tapped a few times. The woman did not stir, but the book slid an inch down her belly and her hand fell by her side.

Rachael knocked again, louder this time, and the woman's eyes opened. Startled, she blinked a few times, closed her book, then rubbed her face with her hands and raised her chair to the sitting position. She waved, acknowledging that she'd seen them.

A few seconds later, the door opened. The woman was of average height and plump, her silver-white hair cut at her shoulders. She looked tired, but tried to smile. Rachael flashed the woman her ID.

Taking a step back, the woman invited them in, introducing herself as Candice Carter and offering them tea. Josh declined, and Rachael asked for a glass of water.

"Radio says it's going to be a record breaker this year," Candice said. "A warm air mass the size of Wyoming has settled in over the area, a stable air mass, they say. Going to be the warmest Thanksgiving ever." She paused. "Rest of the country, well, not so much. Some parts already got a big dump of snow, I hear. . . . But we're long overdue for some fine, fall weather—so we'll take it." She smiled.

Josh returned her smile.

Candice stared at him for a moment, clearly puzzled. "Excuse me, but do I know you? You look familiar."

Josh spotted one of his books among a pile heaped on the floor and changed the subject. "Nice home you have here."

"Oh, thank you," Candice replied. "I came into some inheritance money a few years back, so I took the plunge."

"We're sorry about your friend, Myrna Hudson," Rachael said. "We understand you two were close."

Candice tilted her head and for a moment appeared lost in thought. "Myrna was a lovely woman. She was a friend, you know, a true friend." She turned to Josh. "I'm going to sorely miss her. Already do . . ."

Rachael gave her a second to finish, then asked, "Mrs. Carter, can you—?"

"Please . . . call me Candice."

"Okay, Candice. Can you think of any reason someone would want to harm Myrna?"

"Oh my, if only you knew how silly that sounds." Tears started to well in her eyes. "Myrna was a cornerstone of this town, people looked up to her. She headed the church choir for goodness sake. . . . Oh, heavens no, she didn't have any enemies—none at all."

"Someone from her past, from work maybe?" Josh pressed.

Candice blew her nose before continuing. "Myrna worked at Peeble's Bakery for close to thirty years. Retired a couple of years back, six months before I did, to be exact. Myrna loved that bakery. 'Everybody goes to Peeble's,' she liked to say. Candice looked hard at Josh and then Rachael. "You must understand, Myrna was a gentle soul."

"Does the name, Doris Parker, ring any bells?" Rachael asked. "Senator Doris Parker."

"Well no, other than she was our senator for many years, of course. Why do you ask?"

"Do you know of any connection between the senator and Myrna? Affiliations, clubs that they once both belonged to?"

Candice shook her head.

"Was Myrna seeing anyone? Even on a part-time basis?" Josh asked.

"Sort of . . . she'd go for dinner with Reginald Tolgerson, that is when he's in town. His friends call him Reggie. He's a nice man."

"Were there problems between them?" Rachael asked. "A spat perhaps. Something go off the rails recently?"

"No, no, of course not. The only rift, if you could call it that, was he wanted to marry her."

Josh raised an eyebrow. "And she didn't?"

"Well, not really. It hasn't been that long since her husband, Johnny, passed. Close to two years now. Anyway, she told me she's got accustomed to being on her own, kind of liked having her own space."

"What about Tolgerson? Does he live nearby?" Rachael asked.

"He does, but that won't do you much good. He's been working in Canada, driving a truck in those darn tar sands. Won't be back until the end of next week. Two weeks in, twelve hours a day, then two weeks off, then the process repeats itself. Been going on a long time now. But the money's good, so he says." She put down her empty teacup. "I expect he'll try to be back in time for the funeral though."

After a few more minutes of questioning, Rachael nodded to Josh, signaling they should head out.

"Sorry I couldn't be of more help," Candice said.

They had just reached the car when Rachael's cell started to chirp. She fished it out of her pocket and answered. "Yes, yes I understand. Yeah, I got it. Next flight. Understood." She hung up and turned to Josh. "Kingsley wants me back in the city. A ticket's waiting for me in Duluth." She checked her watch. "I'll have to leave soon . . ."

"Problems?"

"Yep . . . Kingsley wants me *out*. A few months back he opened an internal review on me and the file is getting thicker as we speak."

"What's he got?"

Rachael sighed. "Allegations of misconduct brought forward by one of his minions, claiming I falsified evidence to get a murder conviction. Not to mention claims of my subverting the chain of command, insubordination, and God knows what else. He wants me out, and who knows, he might get it. He's certainly got the 'old boys club' riled and the pressures mounting."

"Anything I can do?" Josh asked.

She shook her head. "No. I'll be back the day after tomorrow, probably late afternoon. That is, unless Kingsley tries to make his final move on me."

"You think he'd do that? Now, in the middle of an investigation?"

A wry smile crossed her face. "Politics trumps everything, you know that."

"Yeah . . . right. One of the many reasons I'd never come back." A long pause followed. "Oh, and I ah, I forgot to mention, Mary's arriving tomorrow."

Rachael frowned.

"She used to live around here, knows people. Could be of help."

"You sure about this? Bringing her on-board?"

"What?"

"Well, she *is* getting on."

"Actually . . . she's not that much older than me."

Rachael smirked, then pulled out a temporary ID for Mary from her jacket pocket and handed it to Josh.

"Give her a chance, she'll grow on you."

Rachael shrugged. "*Great.* Can't wait to see her again."

Chapter 17

The foot traffic at Duluth International Airport was sparse, so Josh didn't have to look hard to see Mary's five-foot one-inch frame ambling toward him, her head bobbing up and down as though she was walking on uneven ground. He couldn't help but smile. The woman was a force to be reckoned with. He'd never figured out what he liked about her the most, but what he did know was, he would never find a better friend. Then he noticed something was different about her.

As she came into full view he saw what was different. It was her hair; the color was off. As she drew closer he could make out burnt orange streaks running through her raven-black hair. *Christ, she looks like a colorful bird, an oriole maybe. Certainly, a well-fed bird,* he thought. Her hair was a near-perfect globe. *Has a kind of 'jack-o'-lantern verve'.* He grinned. "Lookin' good, Mary. So, what's that on your shoulders?"

"Your left nut," she snarled.

On the long drive back to town Mary was quiet and kept to herself, looking out the side window.

The hillsides were still wet from the previous night's rain, and the fall grass glinted in the mid-morning sun. Trees stripped of foliage dotted the landscape, their thick trunks encircled by leaves piled around them in the shape of a doughnut.

A farmer was standing in a field near the road. He was waving his arms, funneling a small herd of cows through a barbed-wire gate that emptied into yet another field. His rubber boots were slick with dew, and a cigarette was hanging from his lower lip. Mary swallowed and sniffed at the air coming in through the car vents, hoping a nicotine molecule or two would find its way into her blood stream.

"You hungry?" Josh asked.

Mary blinked. "*Famished*. I devoured one of those little packets of nuts they hand out on the plane. I mean *really,* what the hell good does that do for a grown woman? An insult to one's dignity, that's what it is, watching middle-aged adults greedily pinch out the salty little devils, sucking on their fingers like chimps at the zoo. It's embarrassing."

"Finish yours?"

"Damn straight—almost got a pack from the baby next to me—would've too, but the selfish brat's mother got to it first."

They continued another five minutes, and were still about thirty miles out of Lynchfield when Josh spotted a roadside diner and pulled in. A sign above the front window, read: *Elmer's Home Cooking.*

The place was empty, except for a waitress sitting on a stool by the cash register, rubbing her left ankle while she read the paper. In the kitchen, a short-order cook was scraping down the grill with a large putty knife, listening to some talk radio show.

The waitress looked up. "Sit anywhere you like," she said, her voice almost as tired as her makeup.

"No shit," Mary mumbled.

"You're a *happy camper* this morning." Josh grinned, knowing quite well that inane drivel like that would really piss her off. "Feeling well?"

"Peachy," Mary sneered. They took a front booth next to a pay telephone, and before Josh could get his jacket off, the waitress arrived with a pot of coffee and poured them each a cup.

After they ordered breakfast, Josh filled Mary in on the killing of the senator in the Finger Lakes District, then recapped the three killings at the church. The theory being that the two old men were considered collateral damage, and that Myrna Hudson was the primary target.

"Got any ideas?" Mary asked.

"Not a lot. Same killers, but that's about it."

"Leads?"

Josh looked at her. "That's why you're here."

Mary squinted, giving him a hard look.

"What?" he asked. "You couldn't get ahold of anyone?"

"Oh yeah, I did. And aren't I the lucky one?" she said, her tone glib.

"And?"

"I'm just hungry, Josh. Let it rest, okay."

He nodded, knowing full well she couldn't let things brew for long.

Barely a minute had lapsed when Mary said, "Ah, it's just that the only person in this whole damn town that I could find to talk to was Lance Oleson. And . . ." She looked at the clock on the wall. "And, we better eat up fast. We're expected at his house in less than an hour."

Josh frowned. "Lance Oleson? He's related to Sheriff Holly Oleson?"

"What? Yeah, I guess so. He's her older brother. Actually . . . a lot older," Mary said, before asking, "So, Holly's the *sheriff?*"

"She is."

"Huh, that's interesting . . . Last time I saw her, she was just a kid."

Huh is right, Josh thought, trying to remember if Holly had mentioned her brother, Lance, the other night. Then again, he couldn't recall much about the night, so he quit trying. He turned to Mary and could see she still had the remnants of a sour funk clinging to her. "Okay Mary, spill your guts, what's eating you?"

Mary swallowed. "It's just that, well. The summer after I graduated from school, Lance and I. We were, at least *I thought* we were, an item. We dated for I think, was . . . close to a month, then he up and dumped me—the creep. Haven't seen him in thirty years."

"More like thirty-three."

"*Thank you,* for the update."

The waitress arrived back at the table with their food.

After finishing her breakfast and her second cup of coffee, Mary looked to Josh. "You ready?"

~ ~ ~

Lance Oleson's home was a rancher located on the outskirts of Lynchfield. It was small, not much bigger than a single-wide trailer. Its yellow clapboard siding was pale and cracked. Josh pressed the doorbell and a tinny, three-tone chime played from inside. A moment later, the door opened and a tall young man, mid-twenties, with broad shoulders and a tentative smile on his face, opened the door.

"Hi," Josh said. "Is Lance Oleson in?"

"Ah yeah, sure. Just a sec." The young man turned his head and yelled out the open backdoor. "Pa, some people are here to see you!"

No answer.

"Pa!"

"Yeah, yeah? Tell 'em to come around back!"

Josh and Mary circled around the side of the house to the gate, and as Josh opened it, he asked, "So Mary, you and Lance, hey?"

Mary's face soured.

"What?" Josh asked.

"Don't get me wrong, I can't blame everything on him. After all we were just kids, and he seemed like an okay guy at first. Well, I thought so anyway. Later? Not so much."

"And then he dumped you like yesterday's French fries?"

"Yes, Josh, that's the way it happened," she said, and then went silent.

He could tell she expected him to ask what had happened. He said nothing and waited.

After a few seconds she looked at him. "The thing about passion is, at first it burns bright, hot, hotter than a Mexican tin roof. But it's so damn fragile. It can be snuffed out with the wrong turn of a phrase, an ill-timed gesture. And, you know, when it's gone, it's gone."

"And . . . ?"

"And, that's it."

"That doesn't make sense."

"Doesn't have to. I'm a complicated woman."

Josh glanced at her and raised an eyebrow.

Mary met his gaze and smiled.

Chapter 18

L ance was a tall man, bald, with a substantial gut and long, hairy arms. He was standing by the doorway to a tool shed, oiling a door hinge, and perked up as he saw them crossing the lawn. "Mary Kowalski! *Darling*, I can't believe it's you. Biggest mistake I ever made was—"

"Dating me," Mary blurted, stepping up in front of him.

Lance started to laugh. "Now that's what I mean, never was there such a girl in all my life." Then he spread his arms wide open and went in for the hug. Mary just stood there, frozen, like a trapped seal pup waiting for the club, her body enveloped in his embrace, her head barely visible, her gaze fixed on the shed roof—a blank, oxygen-starved look on her face.

Thinking she'd had enough, Josh said, "Lance, we would like to ask you a few questions." He flashed his temporary FBI ID.

Lance released Mary and she took a breath.

"You bet," he said, and looked down at Mary. "Gal-darn-it, Mary, you're working with the F-B-I?"

She nodded, still catching her breath, and gave him *the look.*

Josh cut in before she could respond. "Lance, we're hoping that you might tell us something about Myrna Hudson?"

"Well I knew her, of course. Everybody knew that ol' gal." He stopped and turned to Mary. "You know, I still feel bad about what happened, Mary. I should've never took up with Suzy."

"Suzy?" Josh asked.

"Myrna's baby sister," Lance said. "Suzy was a few years older than me and, well, *you know . . .*"

"More than a few," Mary said.

"Yeah, and again, I am sorry about that, Mary." Lance changed the subject. "But, what happened to Myrna, that just don't seem real. But no, I didn't really know her that well. She was a religious gal, sung in the choir. Me? Hell, I like to hunt and fish and drink beer. Travelled in different social circles, if ya'll get my drift."

"Like a fucking snowplow," Mary mumbled.

Josh looked at Mary, then back to Lance. "What about Senator Parker? Ever come across her?"

"No . . . No, but I saw her on the news, about her being dead and such." Lance was still shaking his head when a loud, crackling screech came from inside the shed. He turned his head toward the noise. "Police frequency, pick it up on my ham radio," he said, then walked into the shed and adjusted the dial.

"Come on in folks, don't be shy. Being a ham is my passion, you see." He looked back at them. "Everyone's got to have a passion, at least that's what my doc says. And this little baby's made me friends all over the world. Reached out as far as Singapore, I have." He stroked the radio's top. "Kind of a fluke really, an *abnormality* they called it. Well, don't just stand there, come on in."

Josh and Mary stepped in through the doorway.

Guts of old radios, motherboards, transistors, resistors, and processors were strewn out along the back counter. A holstered .45 revolver and a green fishing net hung on a pegboard behind the counter. Heaped high and off to one side of the shed were red, blue, and green coils of electrical wire. On the other side were neatly stacked boxes of fire alarms, motion sensors, and carbon monoxide detectors. Pinned on the walls and ceiling were centerfolds of naked women in awkward and less than flattering positions. Mary stared at the pictures for a moment before shifting her sight to Lance.

He held his hands out in front of him with his palms up and said, "What can I say—my boy, he likes the stuff. Quite passionate about it, too." Lance gave Mary a wink and waited for her reaction.

Mary just looked at him.

Lance rolled his eyes. "Yeah, all right, Mary. I've thought of taking them down. But . . . hey, really? Boys will be boys."

Josh could see Mary was about to unload, and jumped in. "Lance, we believe there may be a connection between Myrna Hudson and Senator Parker."

"Yeah. And how's that?"

"We believe it could be the same killer."

"That a fact, no kiddin'?" Lance pursed his lips. "Hmm . . . a connection? No, I can't see one. I mean, Senator Parker, she was a big-wheel, aren't no people like her around here, not from these parts." Then it clicked. "Holy smoke! She's lost a rib too?"

Josh and Mary exchanged glances.

"What . . . ? It's a small town, and Myrna and those two ol' boys, well, everybody knew them." He took a moment to think while he scratched his ass. "But the bad guys, they'll get what's coming to 'em." He scratched again and sighed when he hit the spot. "Funeral's a week from this Saturday, you know. Whole town's turning out."

Josh and Mary said nothing.

Lance knelt down to tie his boots and looked up at Mary. "Mary, I was kinda wondering if, you know, if you were gonna be sticking around for a bit?"

She patted his shoulder a few times while surveying his bald spot. "That's a nice thought, Lance, but I'm thinking I'll be real busy. But I am glad I got to see you again. Maybe we'll see each other around town."

Lance reached into his back pocket and handed Mary a card that read: *River City Alarms, Lance Oleson, President, '24 Hour Service'*. "Call me if you change your mind?"

Mary examined the card, holding it by the edges, and smirked. "There's no river in town, Lance—only Haney Creek, which would be hard pressed to even be called a creek."

"I know that, but I kinda like the sound of River City, and well, you know . . . I have plans, been thinking of expanding, pushing out into Dalton and Clifford Counties. Hire me some staff, maybe even franchise—"

Another squelch on the radio cut the air, and the sheriff's voice came through, her words garbled in static.

"Reception can sometimes be tricky around here," Lance said. "Ordered me a new aerial last week—a great big one—should get here any day. That baby's gonna fix it." He looked to both of them for an indication of interest and got none. He frowned. "But you know, the interference, she's not always so bad, can change a lot. Heck, just twenty minutes ago, the Sheriff, that's my sister Holly, she was coming in fine. Sounded real excited though, said she'd found something. Told her deputy, he should get his ass out there, toot sweet."

"What'd she find?" Josh asked.

"Hell if I know, but she did sound a little choked about it; it being the town's graveyard and such."

"Graveyard?"

"That's what she said."

Josh felt his cell vibrate in his pocket and dug it out. "Hey Sheriff, we're just talking about you. Uh-huh, right, yeah okay." Josh hung up and turned to Lance. "The graveyard, how do we get there?"

Chapter 19

The graveyard had grown since its first guest checked in on May 12, 1849, and had slowly spread up both sides of Cutter's Hollow, impregnating its fertile earth with towering pines. Tombstones blanketed the ground, row upon row, standing erect like hackled fish scales.

Catholics were buried on one side, Protestants and other faiths on the other. The two sections were joined by a narrow, covered bridge crossing a shallow stream, clumps of bulrushes at the water's edge, white fluff protruding like cotton candy.

Gray clouds had moved in. The last shafts of sunlight circulated amongst the graves, slowly moving across the tombstones. Sundials, in a world where time has no meaning.

A fine sprinkling of rain had started to pepper the windshield as Josh took a right off of the highway onto a paved road that led into the cemetery and down to the bridge. On the other side of the bridge he saw Holly's Jeep with a cruiser parked next to it. There was a third vehicle, a late model Ford pickup, parked a short distance away. It was partially hidden by a large pine, and was backed up to what looked like an open grave. A small group was gathered, peering down into the hole, their arms crossed, faces grim.

Josh crossed the bridge and pulled the rental up next to the sheriff's SUV, then killed the engine. He and Mary got out.

Holly turned and saw Josh, giving him a warm smile, then noticed he wasn't alone.

Mary caught the sheriff's questioning look and shifted her gaze from Holly to Josh.

"Sheriff," Josh said. "I'd like you to meet Mary Kowalski, she's my—" He'd barely got the words out as another cruiser rolled up, tooting its arrival, followed by a drawn out whine.

The sheriff looked directly at Mary. "I'm sorry, but did Josh say you were his *aunt?*"

Mary squinted. "That's right, I'm his *aunt*. I don't know how you could possibly think otherwise."

Josh cut in. "Mary's a friend, I've asked her to help out in the investigation. We worked together in Detroit some time ago."

"Oh. Sorry about that, my mistake. I hope you didn't take offense . . ."

Mary was giving Holly her best 'go-screw-yourself' look, when a glint of recognition registered on Holly's face. "Kowalski? *Right,* your family lived in Meadow. Just a minute, you dated my big brother Lance, didn't you?"

"It was a long time ago," Mary replied.

Holly grinned. "You know he still has your picture, and the other two girls he dated, all three of you, pinned to the wall in his bedroom." She paused. "He got married once, but it didn't take. Never had much luck since . . . poor boy. Oh, and hey, sorry again about the aunt thing."

Mary smiled with an, 'un-huh, just keep talking bitch', look in her eye. Then she turned and walked toward the grave.

Holly chuckled. "Appears your friend has anger management issues."

Josh closed his eyes for a second, deciding not to go there, then asked, "So, what's going on here?"

The sheriff looked in the direction of the open grave. "Someone broke into the cemetery last night, dug up the casket, and walked away with it. Simple."

A fine mist was seeping out of the grave, lapping over its lip and covering the immediate ground. As they walked toward the grave, the air grew stale. It was the scent of decay, a familiar odor that Josh had smelled countless times, at countless crime scenes.

A harsh screech cut through the air, followed by a solid bang—metal smashing against metal. Josh turned in the direction of the noise, his face now wet, beads of rain gathering under his chin and dripping onto the grass. He saw a stout, bald-headed man standing by the Ford's tailgate, attaching the locking chain. Then the man lit a cigarette, turned, and walked over, cupping his smoke in his hand in an attempt to keep it dry. "Never have I seen such a thing. Been workin' and livin' here all my life. Stuff like this, never happens around these parts."

"Fred, is the custodian of the cemetery," Holly said. "Fred, this is Josh Ingram and this is, ah, um . . . Mary. They're with the FBI. I'd like you to tell them what you told me."

"Well, like I said Sheriff, there's not much to tell. I mean, why would anyone want to rob a grave? Especially this one." He took a puff and scrunched up his face, then said, "It's just plum loco, digging her up like that. It don't cut mustard with me . . ."

"What're you saying?" Josh asked.

"Well hell. It's like this, no one's ever visited that little girl in all these years, not that I know of. Not since, well, you know."

"No, Fred, I really don't know," Josh said.

Fred sneered. "Since she died of course, *duh.*"

Mary chuckled and asked, "Did anyone see anything? Surveillance cameras?"

"Nah, no witnesses. No one comes here at night, except maybe some drunk kids on a Saturday. Happens sometimes, not often. And we got none of them security cameras neither, if you're wondering; this here is a depository, not too many withdrawals, if you know what I mean."

"So, whose grave was it?" Josh asked.

Fred shot a glance at Holly and continued. "That's the thing. No one's ever showed a lick of interest in her. Sad, her being the only teenager ever murdered in the county, as far as I know." Fred looked down and started to tap his boots together.

"Fred—just get to the point," Holly said.

Fred didn't respond.

"Her name was Megan Truscott," Holly said. "She was murdered in the early nineties by her boyfriend, Lyle Carpenter. She was eighteen, and he was, I think, maybe twenty. The trial went well into the fall, and Carpenter was found guilty. He's been locked away in Zuma Penitentiary ever since. That is, until a year or so back when I heard he was released. Time served."

"Seems all very fresh to you," Mary said with an edge to her voice.

"Good point, Mary," Holly replied. "I'd just finished high school that summer, and my father was the town's sheriff at the time. As I'm sure you can appreciate, it was a big deal at our dinner table. And I got updated every night, whether I wanted it or not."

"Yeah, I get that," Josh said. "But what I don't get is, what are we doing here?"

"This is where it gets interesting. The woman that was murdered in the church, Myrna Hudson, she was one of the eyewitnesses in Lyle Carpenter's trial, and Doris Parker was the DA." Holly shook her head. "It happened such a long time ago. I didn't put it together until I saw the grave—then it clicked."

"Well, holy shit," Mary blurted.

"Nothing holy about it. Carpenter slit his girlfriend's throat and let her bleed out on his kitchen floor. Whole town went into shock. Wanted him lynched, and with good cause if you ask me. But my father had no time for any of that vigilante nonsense and got the situation under control. So, the trial continued to its end."

Josh thought for a second, then asked, "Carpenter, where is he now?"

"Don't know . . . Gone. Dropped off the grid the day he got out. I'm told he hasn't been heard from or seen since."

"What about the other eyewitnesses?" Mary asked. "Any of them still around?"

"The only one I can think of would be Emma Bunny, she lives in town." Holly paused for a moment, then said, "But come to think of it, I'm not so sure she was allowed to testify . . . ? And the other witness, Lana Friedman, she left town years ago." As an afterthought, Holly added, "Oh right, and there was Glenda Bunny, Emma's mother. She was a witness too, but she's been dead for some time—buried right here in this cemetery as a matter of fact."

"Aw man," Josh said.

"What?" Mary asked.

"We'll need to dig her up."

"Who?" Holly asked.

"The mother, Glenda Bunny."

Holly eyed Josh warily.

Josh continued. "We need to make sure she has all her parts. And as for the daughter—she'll need protection for now, at least until we can figure out what's going on."

"I'll have a cruiser parked outside her store this afternoon and later at her home."

"Store?" Josh asked.

"Emma, owns a shop downtown, took it over when her mother passed. It's called *Down the Rabbit Hole*. Sells kids' books, educational stuff, toys, that sort of thing."

"Also, we need to locate Lana Friedman," Josh said. "She'll need protection too."

Holly nodded.

"And I'll need to see the trial records for Carpenter and your father's case files."

Holly regarded Josh for a moment, a frown threatening to surface. "I'll have my deputies get to work on it, have to dig them out of the basement. So . . . *is* there anything else?"

Josh grinned. "No, thanks Sheriff, but I do appreciate your enthusiasm."

Holly half-smiled. "Just happy to be of service." Then her smiled broadened. "I'll call you later, then."

Josh gave a slight nod and pulled out his cell.

Mary looked directly at Josh, narrowing her eyes.

Josh punched in Rachael's number and she picked up on the second ring, sounding tense. She told him she was about to step into the Internal Affairs Division office, so he'd have to be quick. He gave her a thumbnail recap, finishing off with how Lyle Carpenter had dropped off the grid, and the need to find both Carpenter and Lana Friedman. She said she'd get her team working on it but had to go, and hung up.

On their way back to town Mary didn't say a word, staring out the side window. Josh finally spoke up. "About you and Sheriff Holly, you two gonna be all right?"

"Who?" Mary asked.

"The sheriff."

"Actually Josh, I don't know. There's something definitely wrong with that woman."

"Yeah, she's got an aggressive streak, I'll give you that."

"You're unbelievable, you know that?"

He glanced over at her. "How about cutting me some slack, okay?"

"*Whatever . . .* But I'm telling you, that broad gets under my skin something fierce. And frankly, numbnuts, I'm at a loss why you don't see it?"

Josh looked at his watch. "Three o'clock, the daughter's store. You good to go?"

"No Josh, I want to go to the opera." Mary paused, then said, "*Fine*, let's go."

Chapter 20

Josh eased the rental car over to the curb and got out first. A wooden sign painted forest green hung above the store's front door. Written in large yellow letters was the store's name, framed by a daisy chain of tiny orange carrots along its perimeter. The sign read: *DOWN THE RABBIT HOLE.*

Located on the north side of Second Avenue, it was one small shop in a line of similar shops selling curios, novelties, and antiques. The store's front was made up of soft-edged, reddish-brown cedar shakes that gave it a sort of gingerbread vibe. The air was cool, but the late day sun was warm on Josh's back as he stood at the door. He reached out to grab the handle, shaped like a big red ladybug covered with dime-sized black dots. The knob squeaked as he turned it and the door opened.

Inside, the air was soupy, smelling of fresh cut apples, cinnamon, and seasoned potpourri, reminding him of hot apple pie straight from the oven. He drew in a long breath and surveyed the place. The walls were lined with books, large, shiny, colorful books with pictures of castles and elves, trolls and gigantic mushrooms. There were two small round tables, each covered with a white lace tablecloth, both strategically positioned to ensure patrons would have to navigate the store in a serpentine fashion.

At the far end of the room was a coffeepot set on a walnut serving table, its red light on. Cubes of sugar were neatly stacked to one side of the pot, and a small stainless steel jug of milk sat on the other side, tagged with a note: '*Two percent . . . A good read: 100 percent.*'

"I'll be with you in a moment," a woman's voice called from the back. A moment later, a tall, slender woman stepped out from behind a beaded curtain. Her shoulders were drawn back in an almost awkward fashion, but her motions were fluid, her hips swaying, glimpses of thigh revealed through a long slit in her dress. It was a stride most men would find attractive. Women, on the other hand, would just roll their eyes. A big welcoming smile crossed her face. "It *is* you, isn't it?" She reached out to shake his hand. "So good to meet you, Mr. Ingram, my name is Emma Bunny."

Josh shook her hand and turned to Mary. "This is Mary Kowalski, we're working with the FBI."

"So very pleased to meet you, Mary," Emma said, then turned back to Josh. "FBI? You're here because of the murders at the church, aren't you?"

"Yes, we are," Josh said.

"This is just so disturbing, don't you think?" Emma asked, her voice now tinged with excitement. "I mean, I know drama like this happens on the news all the time, but never in a zillion years would you think it could occur here, in our little town. Ours is an oasis of tranquility. We all love each other so, sometimes I get to thinking we're all just God's Little Angels."

Mary glanced at Josh, raising an eyebrow.

"About your store's name. It's an interesting choice," Josh said, attempting to change the focus.

Emma's voice hardened. "The name was my mother's doing, but that was many years ago." She tilted her head from side to side, stretching her neck until it made a knuckle-cracking sound, and then began kneading her shoulder with her hand. "When mother died, I didn't have the heart to change it, you see. But now . . . Believe it or not, I kind of like it. I guess you could say I had to grow into it."

Josh said nothing.

"Do you like my dress?" she asked him. "I got it in Petersburg last month. It wasn't on sale, but I just *had* to have it."

"It's a very nice dress," Josh replied.

"Do you really think that, or are you saying it to be polite?"

"No, I really like it. It brings out the color of your eyes."

"Do you really think so?"

"I do."

Mary rubbed her face with her hand and mumbled something unpleasant.

Emma slowly crossed her long legs, her gaze lingering on Josh a beat too long. "So, what is it I can do for you, *Sugar?*" Her voice was now warm and sensual. "May I call you Sugar?"

Mary cleared her throat and peered at Josh, giving him a look that said, *careful what you wish for.*

"Josh, is fine," he said, forcing a smile. "Emma, we would like to ask you some questions about the trial of Lyle Carpenter, and specifically about your mother."

"Are we talking about my biological mother, or my real mother? My biological mother, you see, well, she died when I was very young."

"Whichever one was at the trial."

"Oh, you mean my real mother."

"That'd be the one."

"Oh my, that was ages ago. Why are you asking about her now?"

"To be honest, we're not exactly sure, we're just trying to connect a few dots."

A puzzled look surfaced on Emma's face.

"But your mother did testify, correct?" Mary pressed.

Emma took a deep breath, acting like she was thinking of what she would say. "Oh, she did that," she said, rising to her feet and walking to the window. She began playing with the curtain cord, wrapping it tight around her index finger. "I was a witness too you know, but they wouldn't call me to the stand. Said it was because of my age."

"And you didn't like that?" Josh asked.

Emma turned and looked at them both, a blank look on her face. "Would you folks like some coffee, or maybe tea? I just made a fresh pot of tea before you arrived, and the coffee is always fresh. I hope you like rose tea? I do, I find it to be so delicate."

Mary went for the tea and Josh the coffee. A minute later, Emma returned with a tray, and they sat at one of the small round tables.

"You are a perceptive man, Josh," Emma said. "A moment ago, you were so right. I've never forgiven them. You see, it's always bothered me that I wasn't allowed to testify. They said I was too young, but I was the closest one to Lyle Carpenter that night, the night he came out of his place, or should I say, the garage?"

"I'm not sure I follow?" Josh said.

114

"You see, my mother and Aunty Myrna . . ." She paused for a second, plopped two lumps of sugar in her cup, and gave it a stir. "Well, like I was saying, my mother and Aunty Myrna, Lana, and me, we were on our way home from the movies that night, walking past Lyle Carpenter's place. He lived up over the gas station on Harper Road, or rather, what used to be a gas station in those days. So, as I was saying, we were walking home, minding our own business, when all of a sudden Lyle came stumbling out onto the street, his shirt soaked red with blood. I can still remember him being such a mess. And his *face* . . . I do declare. It was like he'd seen a ghost."

"Back up a sec. You said Aunty Myrna?" Mary asked.

"Oh. No, not a real aunt you see, but that's what I'd always called her. She was actually Lana's aunt, but we both called her Aunty."

"You said you were the one closest to him?" Josh asked.

"You have to understand, I was seven at the time, and my ball got away from me. It ended up rolling next to one of those big bay doors. I loved that ball. Some things you just grow attached to. Don't you get attached to things, Sugar?"

Josh ignored her question. "So, you got a good look at him?"

"I did. *Oh yes* I did. It was only for a second, before he turned and ran off. But to this very day, I swear, I saw him standing there with a crucifix in his hand, and not some knife as the others have said. But because I was a child, they thought I must've been mistaken, my imagination running wild, like a child's does. Well, as you can imagine, it upset me something terrible, not being allowed to say what I saw."

"And who decided that? Not to put you on the stand?" Mary asked.

"I don't know. I was a kid. No, that's not right." She suddenly looked as though she was about to solve a problem, then her eyes brightened. "Oh, I was a kid all right, of course I was. But later, I heard it was the judge that put the clamper on it, or on me rather."

"The judge, is he from around here?"

"Well, in a manner of speaking he is."

"Which means?" Mary asked, her cheeks turning red, her body ready to pounce.

"There's no need to take that tone with me," Emma said. Then she began rubbing the back of her neck again and closed her eyes. "The judge, he's dead. Trudy, his daughter, who's a good friend of mine, told me about it. Ya know she sprinkled her daddy's ashes at the baseball diamond—the judge loved baseball."

"And what about Lana, did she testify?" Josh asked.

"Oh yes. Lana was older than me. Thirteen . . . I think, yes that's right . . ."

"And she said it was a knife in his hand?"

Emma nodded.

Josh studied Emma for a second, then said, "Look Emma, I'm not sure how to frame this, but there are certain aspects to the murder of Myrna Hudson that are similar to that of Doris Parker."

Emma's eyes widened. "The Senator? She's dead too?" She put her finger to her lips as though she was asking them to keep a secret, and whispered, "I didn't know. I don't have a TV you see. I find all that negative mumbo jumbo, well, it just gives me the worst dreams."

What . . . ? Josh thought, then said, "We have reason to believe Myrna's death and that of the senator may be connected to Lyle Carpenter's trial."

Emma's face turned pale, the blood draining from her cheeks.

Now came the part Josh wasn't looking forward to. "I wish I didn't have to ask you this, but we will need to exhume your mother's body, see if there are any similarities in her death to those of the senator and Myrna."

Emma swirled the remaining tea in her cup, her face expressionless, a glimmer of worry in her eyes. "And I suppose you want my okay?"

"It would allow us to move faster, give us a better chance of catching whoever is behind the killings."

Emma pursed her lips and looked up at the ceiling, her eyes moist. After a long moment, she lowered her gaze. "Yes, yes, you may proceed," she said, and turned to Josh. "Mommy's okay with it."

~ ~ ~

Mary yanked the car door shut and locked it. "That broad's got a gummed spark plug."

"What?"

"Your new friend 'I'm a Bunny', she's not firing on all cylinders."

Josh didn't respond.

Mary went on. "Her elevator's stuck between floors. Not the sharpest—"

"It's *Emma* Bunny," Josh cut in. "But point taken, she's crazier than a two-pecker woodpecker in a pumpkin patch."

Mary turned to him. "That's so stupid!" she snorted. "Where do you come up with stuff like that?"

"It's not stupid."

"Oh . . . Okay then, I guess it's not stupid," Mary replied, giving him a knowing look. He glanced over at her and smiled.

Josh started the car and let the engine idle. A full minute had passed when he finally said, "And yet, why would a kid have said she'd seen a crucifix in Carpenter's hand? Not something a seven year old would come up with."

"She's still seven years old, if you ask me . . ."

Chapter 21

Josh pulled away from the curb and drove a few blocks before coming to a T-intersection. He waited for a tanker truck to pass then made a left onto Sixth Street and headed for the hotel. They had just passed the last set of lights and were coming up to the hotel when his cell began to vibrate. He fished it out.

"You got a pen?" Holly asked in a detached tone. "I have Lana Friedman's address for you."

"That was fast," he said. "Sure, let's have it."

Holly relayed the address and clicked off before he could say anything back to her.

What was that about . . . ? He turned to Mary. "54 Regent Street, Pillar Junction. Ring any bells?"

"Yeah, I know it; it's a town about forty-five minutes from here." She pointed over her shoulder. "That-a-way."

Josh glanced at the gas gauge, then his rearview mirror, then pulled a U-turn and let the hammer down.

~ ~ ~

54 Regent was an end unit of a row of townhouses facing a sparsely treed, vacant lot. The lot's sole distinguishable feature was a rusted '48 Studebaker, its hood popped, its driver and passenger doors missing. A stunted maple had grown through where the car's windshield should've been, its branches spread out like that of a table umbrella.

The row of townhouses on the other hand, looked recently renovated. The windows were clean and sparkling, the roof shingles intact and free of moss, each unit boasting a small patch of manicured lawn out front.

The streetlights were on and the moon was low in the sky as Josh rolled the car up to the curb. They got out, and he handed Mary a pair of latex gloves, then slipped his own on. He told her he'd take the front and she should go around back.

As he stepped up to the door, he saw it was ajar and pushed it open. "FBI, anybody home?" he called out, receiving dead silence in return. He went inside. The place smelled of old wood and furniture oil. He cut through the front room, passing an upright piano set against an inner wall and an easel displaying a half-finished oil painting of two mallards in a slough, then stepped into the kitchen.

Mary was on her hands and knees, examining a set of scuff marks. "They start by the kitchen table and continue to the backdoor. Wooden box would be my guess. Must've been heavy to scrape the wax finish like that."

Josh knelt down. "Looks fresh."

"Yeah, looks like . . ."

They worked their way up to the second floor and entered a large bedroom. On the bed, clothes had been neatly laid out and the bathroom light was on.

Josh sidestepped across the room to the en suite door and edged his shoulder up against the doorframe. On the floor by his foot, he saw a few drops of fresh blood, each drop splattered to the size of a red poker chip. Instinctively he reached into his jacket to where his holster had once been. Then waving to get Mary's attention, he pointed to the blood and then to the bathroom.

Mary nodded.

He slipped into the bathroom.

"Clear!" he called. The room looked normal enough. The mirror was dry, a white towel hung on a wooden peg, and a single toothbrush sat in its cup. He opened the shower door and saw water collected around the drain. He called out, "Shower's been used within the hour."

He walked back into the bedroom. "You know he's taken her alive?"

Mary looked at him and said nothing.

"Which means he has plans for her—" *Without warning, his wife's lifeless eyes were staring back at him, a plastic bag drawn over her head and tied tight about her neck. Water droplets lined the bag, her skin wet and gray as ash.* Josh blinked a couple of times and turned his head away, trying to avoid Mary's gaze.

"Hey, you okay?" Mary asked.

"Yeah, I'm all right . . . I'm fine."

"You sure? 'Cause you don't look fine to me."

Josh forced a smile. "It's okay. Thanks, but I'm good."

"Okay then, Josh," she replied, eyeing him warily.

They checked the other upstairs rooms. One room had a stationary bicycle facing a small TV. The other room had been made into a makeshift office with an opened laptop on a bare wood table. A teacup and saucer sat next to the laptop.

They made their way back down to the kitchen. On the counter sat an answering machine with a red number 1 flashing on its screen. Mary hit the button. The new message was from a man who identified himself as Jessie, wondering why Lana was over an hour late, and that he and Beatrice were already on their second drink. He added that they'd both tried texting her and were beginning to worry. "Hope you're okay," he said. "Call us as soon as you get the message. We've saved a spot for you and there'll be a beer waiting with your name on it. So please hurry and call me. Oh, and in case you've lost my number, it's . . ."

Mary jotted down the number.

Josh was standing by the window over the kitchen sink, pinching at some glass powder that had accumulated below a drill hole. "Looks like he came in through here, likely forced the clasp open with some kind of wire."

"Yeah, okay, but why not just break it?" Mary asked.

"Plans can change, things go wrong, maybe she doesn't show. This way he could come back another time—anytime he liked."

Mary handed Josh the slip of paper with the phone number on it, and he made the call. Jessie answered, sounding concerned, and said that he and Beatrice would stay put and wait for them to arrive, then he gave Josh the address.

Josh punched in Rachael's number on his cell and she picked up on the first ring. "We've located Lana Friedman's home. The forensic team will need to suit up." He gave her the address, and filled her in on the details: the window entry point, the fresh blood splattered on the bedroom floor, the water collected around the shower drain, and that her friends were worried why she'd not shown up at the bar.

Rachael confirmed she'd get the ball rolling, and that she'd be back in Lynchfield tomorrow by late afternoon, but she had to go, Kingsley was on the warpath. Then she hung up.

~ ~ ~

Close to fifteen minutes had passed when Josh and Mary entered the bar. The place seemed quiet for seven o'clock and was maybe half-full, the office crowd already thinning out, the lifers and singles bellied up to the bar, looking to stave off loneliness, if only for a few hours.

It was dark inside, and it took a few seconds for Josh's eyes to adjust. Before he could say anything, Mary nudged his arm and pointed. "In the back."

Josh made the introductions, flashing his temporary ID before he and Mary slid into the booth across from them. Jessie looked to be in his mid-thirties and had a tense almost frightened look on his face. Beatrice was on the plump side with a round and caring face. She looked worried.

"Is Lana okay?" Beatrice asked, the expression on her face saying she thought otherwise. "We've been trying to reach her, she was supposed to be here an hour and a half ago . . ." She glanced at Jessie then back to Josh.

Josh hesitated for a moment before answering. "We're not sure what, if anything, has happened to Lana," he lied. "We're trying to piece it all together. Maybe we could start with how the two of you know Lana?"

"I've been her best friend since high school," Beatrice said. "Oh God, she's not all right is she? I called her office, and her manager who was working late, said he remembered her leaving, said she'd left early which was quite unusual for her."

Josh and Mary remained silent.

Jessie fidgeted in his seat, then said, "Well I, um . . . actually, Lana and I just started dating. Today would have been our first real date. I met her here, last week as a matter of fact."

"Do either of you know anyone who would want to harm Lana?" Mary asked. "An old boyfriend maybe?"

"No, I can't think of anyone," Beatrice said. "Lana's last boyfriend was like, over a year ago. I got the feeling that the chemistry wasn't working. Nothing seriously wrong with the guy, Lana just said there was nothing there. I don't think she's heard from him since. In fact, I know she hasn't, because she tells me everything."

Josh turned to Jessie. "Where were you between three and six o'clock today?"

Jessie's eyes widened. "I . . . I was working out at the gym, then I came here and met up with Beatrice at five-thirty. I've got a few days off. I'm training for a triathlon. A buddy of mine was there too, so I guess he can vouch for me."

Neither Josh nor Mary spoke, keeping their focus on him.

Jessie continued. "Look, there's cameras everywhere at the gym. You can check them if you don't believe me." He paused. *"Ah,* I can't believe I'm talking this way. *Oh God,* I think I'm gonna be sick."

"It's okay," Mary said in a calm voice. "Just take a few deep breaths and drink your water."

Josh allowed Jessie a minute to recover, then asked, "Is there anything that comes to mind for either of you that would suggest Lana was having any kind of trouble in her life?"

They both shook their heads.

Beatrice said, "I don't know if this is important, but the night we met Jessie—there was this guy. Lana said he kept staring at her. I didn't hear about it until the next day, but she told me he gave her the creeps."

"Did she say anything else? What he looked like, anything that stood out about him?" Mary asked.

"No . . . only that he kept staring at her. Like he was seeing right through her. Lana said it really creeped her out."

"Did he say anything to her?" Josh asked.

"I, I don't think so. No. She would've told me." Beatrice looked sideways for a moment, then added, "But, come to think of it . . ." She turned her gaze to Jessie. "The night you walked Lana home. She told me she wasn't sure if she wanted to ask you in, but then she noticed some guy across the street, talking on his phone. She couldn't tell if it was the same guy from the bar, but it spooked her enough to ask you in."

"First I've heard of it," Jessie said.

"What made her think it might be the man from the bar?" Josh asked.

"I don't think there was anything specific, at least she never said anything to me about it."

They all turned to Jessie.

He shook his head. "No, like I said, she never mentioned the guy to me."

Mary asked Beatrice, "You and Lana, you come here often?"

"Most Fridays after work. We have a couple of drinks. Like to unwind a bit before heading home."

"Had Lana seen him here before? The man that gave her the creeps?" Josh asked.

"She didn't say. I don't think so, though."

After another few minutes of questioning, it was clear there would be no further pertinent information coming from either of them. Josh handed them each a card with his number on it and asked them to call him if anything else came to mind.

As they walked out to the car, Mary stopped and bent over. "Aghh shit," she said, grimacing.

Josh turned to her. "What is it? What's wrong?"

"Ah, my friggin' stomach's cramping up, something I ate, I think."

"Are you gonna be all right?"

She straightened up and took a breath. *"Yeah . . .* I'm fine. It'll pass. Let's go."

Chapter 22

Father Paul had insisted that she be placed far from the camp. None of the others were to know of her existence. No one else but Alvin, not until the ceremony.

"Sure like to see him try holding a flashlight and carrying all this stuff," Alvin mumbled to himself, a jug of water in one hand and a tray of food and a flashlight in the other. "Sure as shootin', if I fall, it's gonna go flying. Then what would I tell Father . . . ? Maybe I'd just say *nothin'*. Or that she'd got her food like she's suppose to." He thought about that for a long moment, then shook his head. *No way, he'd know for sure, always does.*

Alvin walked for another five minutes, stepping over roots and fallen trees. *Darnit all, why's this one so important anyway? What makes her so special? Ah to heck with this! I'm gonna put it to him. Gonna tell him straight out: No way am I doing this again. Get someone else to do the dirty work.* Then his foot caught a root and he stumbled, forcing him off the trail, the tray waving in the air. "That's it! I'm not doing this no more . . ." he sputtered.

He turned back to the trail, went another twenty feet, and there it was, the marker. The queen of hearts, pinned to a large chestnut tree. *Yesss! Thank you, Lord,* he thought, as a huge wave of relief washed over him.

He had dug the hole a full fifteen paces north of the tree, because, as he had told Father Paul, '*He'd dug holes before . . . fewer roots to cut that way.*' Even so, it still had taken him the better part of a full day of digging to get it done. But he'd done a good job of hiding her, and he took pride in that, knowing no one could find her 'cept him.

As he paced out the fifteen steps, another thought came to him. *Maybe I should just tear off the card and walk away . . . say I couldn't find her.* This was an entirely new sensation for him, the thought of her life in his hands. And he kinda liked it. *Yeah, I could. And no one could prove nothin'. Serve him right for putting her so far away from camp.* Alvin thought some more, then sighed. *Nah, wouldn't work. Probably just get me in trouble.*

Then his boot kicked up against something solid. He knelt down and brushed away a two-inch layer of leaves and twigs, revealing a square, four-foot chunk of three-quarter inch plywood. He lifted the plywood off the hole and set it off to the side. He could hear her whimpering in the dark, and aimed the flashlight beam into the hole. A split second later, the pungent stench of stale urine hit him, and he grimaced.

Lana was crouched on a bed of straw, eight feet below, a heavy wool blanket wrapped around her. A wooden bucket sat next to her, covered by a ragged piece of cloth draped across its top. She blinked into the light and tried to raise her bound hands, a ball gag in her mouth, her eyes pleading . . .

She tried to speak, to cry out, but her words were muffled. She twisted her crouched body, tugging at her chains attached to a rebar rod driven deep into the clay. Then she screamed into her gag, and began to frantically pull at her shackles, but it was no use. She lowered her head and started to cry.

Alvin watched her for a moment, then set the food and water on the ground, then walked around behind the big tree, returning a few seconds later with an aluminum ladder.

She twisted her torso again and looked up, her blood-shot eyes blinking into the light.

"Time to fill your belly," he said.

Chapter 23

"Y'all sure this couldn't have waited till morning? Twice in one day—*jeez*." Fred said, standing five feet below ground level, his eyes level with Holly's ankles. "The Mrs., she likes me home, watching the television with her in the evening. Got her favorite shows. Says, ain't much enjoyment watchin' 'em without me. Kinda indispensible, I am." Fred was five feet four inches tall, had a potbelly, and a handlebar mustache that partially offset his bald head.

The digging had proceeded quickly, as Fred had said it would, since the grave plot had evidence of *'untoward behavior'* that must have occurred in the last few days.

"Need some help down there?" Josh asked, pointing a large, flathead screwdriver in Mary's direction. "She's not that big, but she's got a strong back and a wonderful work ethic."

Mary glanced at Josh and gave him a pained smile.

"Nah, county won't pay me in full if I have someone else in the hole. But, would y'all mind if I took me a smoke break?"

"Sorry Fred, but we need to move fast on this one," Sheriff Holly said.

Fred eyeballed the three of them and a grin tugged at one corner of his mouth. "This one? Y'all are thinkin' it might have a rib missing too, aren't ya? Just like poor old Myrna?"

No response came from above.

Fred wiped his brow on his shirtsleeve, looking up at them. "Ah heck. It's no secret. Everyone in town's talking about the killings."

Still no response.

"Jeez, lighten up folks, we're just exhuming a corpse. No big deal. Mrs. Bunny's certainly not gonna care." He took a moment before he resumed digging, muttering under his breath, "Navel gazing city slickers, bet y'all check your turds before flushing." He raised his voice. "And why is it you *police* always look like you just shit your—?"

"Fred, how about we dispense with the commentary," Holly growled.

"*Fine*, no problem, just as soon not be talkin' to y'all anyhow." No sooner had the words left his mouth when his shovel tapped on something solid that made a hollow sound. He tapped again and looked up at them. "Knock, knock?"

"*Seriously*, Fred?" Holly asked.

"Well, you guys are no fun at all. Galdarnit, I'm done here. You have my permission to do whatever you have to do." He finished clearing away the dirt from around the casket lid, climbed out of the grave, dusted himself off, and walked away without looking back.

Josh slid into the grave with the screwdriver in hand. It was a simple, black wooden coffin. Using the tip of the screwdriver, he ran it under the lip of the lid until he felt the catch. He pushed against the latch and heard a *click*, then dug his fingernails under the lid's lip, wrenching it upwards and was surprised at how easily it opened. The gasket seal had been tampered with.

Mary moved around to the foot of the grave where a halogen light had been set up, and directed the beam down onto the coffin. Josh fully opened the lid, and was welcomed with the sour stench of rotten eggs. His throat immediately tightened, and for a second he thought he might puke . . .

Inside the casket was a skeleton, remnants of body tissue—dark and leather-like—drawn tight to the facial bones; the flesh around the teeth and nasal cavities eroded, yielding a morbid and toothy grin.

By the shape of the pelvis, Josh could tell it was a woman, but what got his attention was the gaping hole in her ribcage.

Chapter 24

The knock came at Josh's hotel room door at around 2 a.m., an hour after he had fallen into a restless sleep. It wasn't a loud knock, more like a whump, or rather a series of whumps, as though the palm of a hand was doing all the work. But the whumps were persistent and kept coming, slowly slipping into his murky sleep. Three whumps, then two, followed by another set.

As distracting as this late night disrupter was, it wasn't his first concern. No, he had another, more pressing problem, a finite complication that had been daunting him for what felt like an eternity. He knew he should've solved the conundrum by now, but he hadn't, and he really couldn't explain why. It was simple—just use the toilet.

There it was again, louder this time—knuckles on wood. He could feel his thoughts being drawn toward the surface, rising through the fog. A slow, steady, persistent ascent, until at last it breached his consciousness and his left eye opened. *Someone's at the door? Someone's in trouble. Rachael?*

He turned on the bedside light, threw back the sheets, and rolled out. Did a quick check to ensure he hadn't solved his little problem, pulled on his pants and waddled to the door. He looked through the peephole, blinked, and looked again. *Emma Bunny?*

She looked stressed, as if she was in some kind of trouble, her eyes shifting from left to right, then glancing back over her shoulder. And yet, something else about her was off, way off. He watched her for a few more seconds, but couldn't put his finger on it.

He opened the door.

"Emma? Are you okay?"

"I'm all right, Josh." She checked him over. "But, I'm not so sure about you." Her gaze focused on his knees, bent slightly inward.

He half-smiled and told her to take a seat. A minute later, he came out of the bathroom to see her still standing in the middle of the room.

"Feeling better?" she asked.

"Yeah, actually a lot better. So. What's going on?"

Emma went to take a chair and stumbled, lost her balance, and hopped over to the bed to sit down. She looked up at him, her bottom lip protruding. "Seems I've hurt my ankle, Sugar. Would you be a dear and rub it for me?"

"*What?* Yeah. No, no, I don't think so," he said.

She stared up at him, crossing her legs and letting her coat fall open, exposing most of her thigh. "Well then, Sugar, could you at least pour me a drink?" she asked, eyeing the brandy on the coffee table. "I could use a little anesthetic about now." She reached down and began rubbing her ankle with both hands, sliding her hands up her calf, massaging the muscle in long, slow strokes. As she did, she raised her eyes to him. "How about that drink?"

"Yeah, not a chance," he said, his eyes gone cold. "Emma, what the hell's going on? It's the middle of the night."

She gave him another pouty look and got to her feet, poured herself a brandy and then one for him. She held it in her hand for a second before passing it to him, and then sat back down on the bed.

Josh placed the snifter on the coffee table and just looked at her.

Emma eyed him. "You remember, you told me if anything else came to mind, I should give you a call." She let the words hang for a few seconds. "Well, Sugar . . . something's surely been preying on my mind. Been giving me a load of trouble, you see." She gave a long sigh and raised an eyebrow. "It's you, Sugar. I've been thinking about you, you've been occupying my thoughts all night. Tossing and turning, that's all I've been doing. Not healthy for a woman in her prime to ache so, you see. But you know what it's like, don't ya, Sugar? That terrible ache." She grinned. "Well, I just knew I had to do something about it." She slowly stood up, untied the belt to her coat, and let it drop to the floor.

Except for a black lace bra and thong panties, she stood there before him in all her natural wonder. "I'm thinking I can help you sleep, Sugar."

Josh swallowed hard, raising his hand. "Ah, no offense, but I'm sleeping just fine," he lied.

She started to chuckle, placing her hands on her hips. "Well then Sugar, you can help me get some rest."

Suddenly, his cell started to vibrate on the bedside table. Emma reached out and snatched it before he could protest.

She looked at the phone. "Someone called, *Rachael?* Someone you know, Sugar? Maybe I should go ahead and answer it for you?" she asked, an impish smile on her lips.

Josh lunged forward, grabbing her arm, and they tumbled onto the bed, his body on top of hers—the phone still ringing. Emma giggled and squirmed against his weight as he twisted the phone out of her hand. He got off the bed and pointed at her to keep quiet, then took the call.

"Josh, Rachael here. Sorry to call this late, but Kingsley is out of his mind." As she started to bring him up to speed, he noticed Emma had rolled onto her stomach, her legs spread, her G-string all but disappeared. She turned her head toward him, propping it up with one hand, swirling the cognac in the other. She took a long sip, then ran her tongue along her upper lip.

"Josh! Josh! Are you listening to me?" Rachael demanded.

"Uh yeah, ahh, no, no I'm not, but I will—" He hung up. "Look Emma, somehow you've got this all wrong. I'm sure you're a good person, maybe had too much to drink, probably a shitload too much, but . . ." He hesitated. "Look. I hate to be this guy, but I have to ask you to go."

Her smile began to fade, and her eyes tightened as a scowl gathered on her face.

"Now!" he ordered.

She took a deliberate breath, her eyes widening. "So why'd you come on to me, all smiling-like, at my store today? A girl's got feelings too, you know." Another pouty look crossed her face.

He grabbed her coat off the floor and handed it to her. "Not sure where this is all coming from, but I am sorry if I've given you the wrong idea."

She began putting on her coat. "It's her, that *bitch* Holly, isn't it? She say something about me?"

"I don't know what you're talking about."

"Josh, why'd you wanna go listenin' to her anyhow?"

He remained silent.

She sneered at him. "Just what sort of man are you? Turning a girl's head the way you did. And now . . . acting all innocent like. And don't say you didn't, 'cause you did." She paused, pursing her lips. "Uh-huh, I know you did, you and those hungry eyes of yours, roaming all over me. A girl knows when a man wants her." She tapped her finger on the lip of the snifter, a smile lighting up her face, and laughed. "You're a *scaredy-cat*, that's it. Yeah, that's it, isn't it? A real woman comes to your door, and you just about peed yourself—didn't ya, Sugar? Scaredy-cat. Ha! That's what you are." She giggled some more, then stopped. "Well, you've had your chance bucko," she said, her voice deepening. Then she looked to the ceiling, took a deep breath, and bellowed, "I want a real man! Right here, right now!" She turned back to Josh, her upper lip flared. "*Huh*, not some *scaredy-cat*, that's for sure."

It took him the better part of a minute to get her out into the hall. He shut the door and locked it, gave it a few seconds, and then put his ear to the door. At first there was nothing, then he heard the elevator ping and the sound of the doors opening and closing. He looked through the peephole—the hallway was empty. He grabbed the phone off the bed and returned to the door, checking the hallway again just to be sure. "Unreal," he said under his breath. He turned and slid down to the floor, his back pressed up against the door.

He'd just finished punching in Rachael's number when he heard it. *"Josh honey* . . . let me in. You're just confused, Sugar. You don't understand me, that's all."

Chapter 25

The Lancaster County sheriff's office was located dead center of Main Street, tucked in between Kennedy First Financial and the Post Office. A bakery with an added on coffee shop, and a 1960's vintage pool hall, sat directly across the street. Thick maples lined both sides of the road, running north for three blocks before terminating at a set of derelict railway tracks and a boarded-up grain elevator, its roof sagging like a glue horse spine. Beyond the tracks were the 4-H Fairgrounds, a five-acre parcel of land used for community events and the annual Lynchfield Bluegrass Festival. A fire in 2008 had burned down the ground's main barn. It was rebuilt the following year, and painted candy apple red. A quarter-inch thick iron plaque, the dimensions of a cookie sheet, was bolted next to the front door commemorating the Barn Raising of 2009.

Lynchfield's population stood at 7,228, and serviced an additional 5,000 from the surrounding farms and other smaller towns. The population never changed much from year to year, except for Christmas and Thanksgiving Week when the children returned home to catch up with friends and family.

Josh stepped into the sheriff's office and saw Holly talking on the phone in the corner office. She was looking out onto the street, her chair leaned back, her boots resting on the windowsill, ankles crossed.

The main office area was comprised of a small open space with a potbellied stove set close to the inner wall. Off to one side of the stove was a cabinet with a countertop just big enough for the coffee pot and microwave. A locked gun cabinet and a coat rack were on either side of the front window. A small room, presumably for the deputies to share, was next to Holly's office. A much smaller room, not much bigger than a broom closet, sat next to the deputies' office, and was empty except for a folding card table and two black wooden chairs.

From where he was standing, Josh could see into the holding cell at the back. Its outer wall was made of red brick and light was pouring in through a small barred window near the ceiling. The cell door was open, and the cell was empty.

Deputy Hal Rogers, Holly's right hand, came in from outside and set his broom against the front doorjamb. He told Josh his boss had been on the phone for some time, something to do with squatters setting up camp near town, and that she might be awhile, then he showed Josh to the office with the card table.

There was a banker's box on the floor with a thick, plain manila folder on top. A red tag was attached to the box, sticking out from its edge like a deer's ear. It read: Police/Coroner Reports. The folder on top was about an inch thick and stamped with large gray letters: Trial Records.

Josh decided to tackle the preliminary police reports first, then the statements from witnesses, and finish up with the final report and trial records. A couple of hours had passed by the time he closed the manila file. Other than the sheriff's father's signature on virtually every police report, he couldn't find anything noteworthy. It appeared to be a straightforward case. The eyewitnesses had testified they saw a knife in Carpenter's hand, a knife that had his prints on it, its blade smeared with the victim's blood. The coroner's report was equally unremarkable. Essentially, the victim's throat had been cut, carotid arteries severed, and she'd bled out.

Josh leaned back in his chair and crossed his arms. *It doesn't add up,* he thought. *It's not that there's misleading or contradictory information in the reports. That's not it. In fact, they're linear, sequential, and squeaky clean . . . maybe too much so.*

The one item of significance he didn't find was Emma Bunny's claim that it was a crucifix and not a knife in Lyle Carpenter's hand the night he came out of the garage. In fact, neither her name nor the crucifix showed up in any of the records.

He had skipped breakfast, preferring coffee until he was fully awake, and was starting to get hungry. It didn't help that the room's sole window had been left cracked open, allowing the air from the diner down the street to seep in. *Ah man, why does burnt grease haveta always smell so good . . . ?* There were those who would council him to turn away from his culinary decrepitude. Janis, his New York agent, had impressed upon him that '*eating like a Provincial*' belied his image to the public. She left out the part about how it could snuff out her bread and butter ticket and ruin her plans for the seaside cottage she always talked about. But deep down he knew she was right. Wallpapering his arteries with gunk was not a brilliant idea, but he couldn't seem to help himself. Some things are worth it—some things are sacred.

He poked his head into Holly's office. She had her sleeves rolled up, head down, pen to paper, and didn't seem to notice him. Her hair was tied back in a neat ponytail, a few blonde strands hanging down almost touching the paper. She looked up and stretched.

"Morning," she said. "You look rested."

Josh gave a weak smile.

"Any update on Lana Friedman?" she asked.

"Forensic team is on site, databases notified, NCIC," he replied. "Forensics called a half hour ago, got a locator ping on her cell, found it in a hedge next to her driveway. How about you?"

"Bulletins gone out, county hospitals notified. Patrols here and Pillar Junction have her picture, as does the local media, which . . ." She glanced at the clock on the wall. "Should hit the airwaves in about an hour. Deputies Hal and Greta are assisting, checking with the neighbors, but still nothing to report. She's clean, no priors. No gray areas to dig into. She's a *good girl*."

Josh nodded. "I'm about to head over to the diner, grab some lunch. Care to join me?"

Holly didn't answer at first. He could see something else was bothering her. She managed a thin smile and said, "Yeah, sounds like a good idea. Sometimes, I completely forget to eat."

"Hey, you all right?" he asked.

"No, not really, but it's okay. Just some garden-variety wackos have been spotted outside of town. Bob Stapleton, who owns the pool hall, dropped this off." Holly grabbed a small poster off her desk and handed it to Josh. It read: 'Save yourself, the Devil is near.' "He said a woman and a young girl, both wearing long, black dresses, were attaching it to the telephone pole outside his place."

"Save yourself?"

"Who knows? Probably, the world's about to come to an end." She let out a disgruntled puff and shook her head.

Josh waited for her to continue.

"Well, okay, I don't know what their thing is, not with this bunch anyway, but they're freeloaders that's for sure. We had a group of them in Winston County a few years back. The sheriff there asked for our help. It took him the better part of six months to force them out. Thing is, once they get settled, they're like friggin' bedbugs. They get dug in and it's hard as hell to get rid of them." She sighed. "And the worst part is, the bastards like to prey on people's good nature, particularly the elderly—always finding ways to pick their pockets." She put her pen down on her desk. "In Winston, they posed themselves off as handymen—always get the money up front, then do little, if anything in return. And they'll keep coming to town, no doubt about that, women and children, begging on the streets and stealing where they can." Holly stopped. "But hey, it's not your concern. All in a day's work, right?" She rubbed her chin with her hand, then looked directly at him. "Yeah, I'm getting hungry too, let's go."

~ ~ ~

Harriet's Diner was located on the corner of Third Avenue and Main, and had occupied the same spot since it replaced Mel's Hardware in '62. A yellow neon 'Open' sign sat high on the diner's window. Below that, a wooden sign read 6 a.m. to 10 p.m.

It was almost noon, and the place was empty except for two white-haired women seated near the back, playing cards. The air smelled of pulled pork, fried onions, garlic, and stale coffee.

A long line of booths ran down one side of the restaurant, opposite a green linoleum counter. Behind the counter ran a parallel line of soda fountains, and below those were stacks of clean dishes and trays of cream-colored coffee cups. A narrow opening to the kitchen, measuring roughly one-foot-high and six feet long, allowed for the orders to be picked up.

Josh and Holly took a booth by the front door. A moment later a waitress showed up, her hair rolled into a tight bun covered by a net, her faded pink dress matching her faded smile.

"Slow day, Esther?" Holly asked.

Esther grinned. "That's why I feel so secure at night Sheriff, knowing you're standing guard, applying your considerable powers of deduction and keeping us safe." She'd punctuated her sentence with a smirk, then her eyes brightened. "Hey, I know you . . . you're that writer fella, aren't you?"

Josh gave a slight nod.

"My hubby, he's got all your books," she said, slapping her order pad on her thigh. "Well, this is so exciting. Wait'll I tell Sam, that's my hubby." She stopped and looked Josh in the eye. "I have to read to him now, you know. He's not so good at reading these days."

"Josh is assisting the FBI with the investigation of the church murders."

"You're investigating! Oh, this *is* something to write home about . . . Samuel, he's going to be thrilled." A blush of red bled out from her collar and into her cheeks. She fanned herself with her hand. "Sorry, I must sound like a silly school girl."

"Hey, not at all," Josh said. "Always good to hear someone likes my writing."

"Well *thank you* for saying that, Mr. Ingram." She gave Holly a knowing look. "Such a gentleman."

Holly did not respond.

"But you didn't come here to make small talk, now did you, Sheriff? So, what can I get you folks?"

Holly ordered a granola yogurt and berry concoction, dry toast, and an herbal tea. Josh went for a double cheeseburger, loaded, a large order of fries with gravy, and a soda.

When the food arrived, Josh wasted no time digging into the burger.

"That stuff'll kill you, you know."

He stuffed a few fries in his mouth, munched away, swallowed, washing it down with a couple of gulps of pop, and said, *"Ooo yeah . . ."*

Holly smirked. "I like a man who throws caution to the wind."

About halfway through her yogurt, she took a moment to lick the front and back of her spoon before asking, "So, the case files . . . you find anything?"

"Umm," he replied, as he swallowed another mouthful. "That's just it, isn't it—there's nothing. Not a thing. Someone's put a lot of effort into making sure of that. I mean, being orderly and precise, that's one thing, but this borders on, well . . ."

"On what?" Holly asked.

"Obsessive."

Holly chuckled. "That'd be my daddy all right, he was some kind of control freak, everything neat and tidy. I'm sure he'd be turning in his grave if he knew what a mess my files are in. His everything-in-its-place gene wasn't on the shelf when I came along."

Josh watched as she pinched a slice of onion that had dropped from his burger and placed it on the edge of his plate. She looked at him and smiled.

"Went to see Emma Bunny yesterday," he said. "She told me when Carpenter came out onto the street that night, he was holding a crucifix and not a knife."

"Well, Josh, if you've spent more than a few minutes with Emma, you're probably already having doubts?"

"Yeah maybe. But a crucifix? I don't see how a kid would come up with that?"

Holly shrugged. "What can I say? If it's not in the files, then it never existed. My father was nothing if not thorough." She looked down at her spoon and said, "Emma, she has a history you know. Back in high school, she got herself molested. Was never right after that."

Josh gave her a long, hard look, and said nothing.

"It was her senior year, she was your usual drop-dead gorgeous bimbo. Had all the boys walking around with their tongues hanging out. The school's quarterback and I think two others from the team were involved. I mean how cliché is that?"

"So, what happened?"

"Actually, not a lot. Team was having a winning year, looked like we might be heading for the state finals." She shrugged. "Got swept under the rug. Town wanted it to go away. So, it just sort of went away."

"Your daddy okay with that?"

Holly jammed her spoon back into the yogurt container and took another bite.

They sat in silence and finished eating.

"Tell me, what sort of man was your father, other than being a neat freak?" Josh asked with an edge to his voice, hoping to throw her off balance—and saw he'd touched another nerve.

"He was a caring, protective man. A good father. Family always came first," she said, her tone tinged with anger, and then it was gone. "But what about you, what's your father like?"

"He's dead," Josh lied, and watched for her reaction. He could tell she wasn't buying it. But then again, that wasn't his problem. Some subjects should be left off the table. His father had been a successful District Attorney up until the day a death penalty case, his father's first high-profile case from ten years earlier, was overturned due to new DNA evidence exonerating the man. The evidence had turned up a month after the man's execution. His father couldn't deal with it, blaming himself for the death of an innocent man. He fell and never bounced back, sliding onto the street and into the shadows, cutting off all ties with both Josh and his sister.

A few years back, Josh had funded the construction of a group home in his father's neighborhood. With the help of Alice Whitaker, a caseworker with a Catholic nonprofit, his father had taken up part-time residence at the home.

Josh tried to touch base with the group home about once a week, to see how his dad was doing. But each time he went to pick up the phone, a sadness would come over him, and he would have trouble punching in the number. Not because he didn't care, that much he knew. And yet, why was it so difficult to make the call? Had he become callous, deciding his father was lost and beyond all hope? Or was he simply coping, not wanting to revisit the pain of knowing his father lived on the streets? He didn't know the answers, but he knew he'd never give up on his dad.

"Well then, let's leave the dead in the past, shall we?" Holly said, warmth seeping back into her voice. "I take it you're not quite finished with the files?"

"Another couple of hours or so should do it." He felt his cell vibrate. Fishing it out he saw it was Rachael. "Sorry, I need to take this."

Holly nodded.

He put the phone to his ear. "Yeah. Not a problem. Right. I'll call you if something breaks. Okay, sure." He hung up.

"Trouble?"

"No, that was Rachael. She won't be getting in until tomorrow, in the evening, then she wants to meet with me and bring her up to speed."

Holly watched Josh for a moment, and then said, "She's a pretty woman, Rachael."

"Yeah . . . I guess she is." *Where the hell did that come from?* "She's getting married soon. Next month in fact."

A smile crossed Holly's face. "That's okay, Josh. Now you have me."

Josh managed a weak grin.

"Well, if you're finished clogging your arteries, I'd better get back to work, I've got lots to do. . . . And so, we're still on for eight?"

"Oh yeah . . . Hey about that, I'm gonna need to take a rain check. Mary's not feeling well, called me this morning, she was up most of last night. Said she's getting better, but she didn't sound so great. Anyway, she wants to see me. It's to do with a staffing issue back at the marina. One of the waitresses has hired a lawyer and is threatening to sue for wrongful dismissal. After that, I have a few things to take care of and then I'm going to turn in for the night." He knew it was a weak excuse, and felt like an ass for saying it.

"*Fine.* Yes, of course, do what you have to . . ." she said, then she gave him a cold smile and reached out, pinching his cheek—maybe a little too hard.

Chapter 26

The late morning light flooded the sheriff's office, catching bits of fluff and dust particles floating in the air, warming the black, potbellied stove and the wooden handles of the steel bucket sitting next to it.

Josh opened the door and was greeted with the aroma of fresh brewed coffee, sharp and bitter, like the shavings of dark-chocolate.

Holly was sitting at her desk and called out, "I just made another pot, help yourself."

Josh poured himself a coffee then poked his head into her office. She looked stressed and weary, like her day had just turned to shit.

"What's up?" he asked.

Holly pushed her chair back from her desk. "Those lowlifes I was telling you about. Word is they've settled in on the Martin property. A neighbor called it in, said they've already set up camp. *Goddamnit!* Mable Martin, she's gotta be over ninety now." Holly rolled down her sleeves and buttoned her cuffs. "Anyway, I've got to go check it out."

"It's private property, right?"

"Huh? Oh yeah, I wish it was that simple, but no, once they're settled, it'll take a string of court orders and a month of Sundays to squeeze 'em out." She got out of her chair and walked over to Josh, gently placing her hand on his chest. "I missed you last night."

"Yeah, sorry about that . . ."

"Uh-huh," she said, studying him.

"Easy prey, the elderly?" he asked, changing the subject.

"What? Ah, yeah sure, they are that . . . Always go for the weakest in the herd, right?"

Josh said nothing.

"Then they pit the legal system against itself, manipulating it, until they get what they want. And what makes my blood boil is, they're so damn good at it . . ." She walked back to her desk, grabbed a couple of files, and tossed them into her credenza and locked it. "Probably because it's all they do. Perish the thought they would ever have to do an honest day's work."

She paused for a second, then continued. "The neighbor said she'd seen a young man out at Mabel's place a while back, maybe a few weeks before the whole clan showed up. If that's so, it's the same drill as Winston County. First, they send out a fine-looking young man to the farm, says he'll do odd jobs around the property for room and board and maybe a little spending money. Then, after he's worked there for a while and established some trust, he gets the widow to make it formal, getting her to sign a rental agreement or a lease, because *'it'll make him feel better—so he doesn't feel like he's taking advantage'.* Once that's signed, a few days later his loving, extended family shows up."

"And the lease gives them tenants' rights."

"Damn right it does."

Josh hesitated a second before asking, "You going alone?"

Holly shrugged. "Hal and Greta are on highway patrol, but, yeah, I better get out there before someone does something real stupid."

"Then, I'm coming with you."

~ ~ ~

The Jeep Wrangler was white with black trim, had oversized all terrain tires, a power winch on the front, flashers on the roof, and the word SHERIFF stenciled in large black letters covering the doors. Holly was behind the wheel and Josh was riding shotgun.

They followed Highway 14 for close to two miles before turning off onto Route 117, following it for about fifteen minutes before turning off onto a narrow gravel road hugging Willow Creek that brought them to Shepard's Mill.

There was a large, circus-like tent set up in front of the watermill with a number of covered wagons facing into the tent. A couple of kids were dodging in and out between the wagons, laughing and giggling. Two women suddenly appeared from the tent, wearing long black dresses and white skullcaps. They grabbed the children by their hands and pulled them into the tent.

Holly rolled the Jeep up beside a late model pickup parked near the tent entrance, stopping a few feet from a large iron dinner bell bolted to a wooden platform.

Josh took a moment to check out the mill's water-wheel, poking out from behind the tent while Holly answered a radio call from Hal and Greta. From what he could see, the wheel looked in good shape, the trough and the paddles appeared to be undamaged, as did the wheel itself. So much so, he figured it could probably still do a full day's work. The thought of something so ingenious and beautiful being put out to pasture, redundant, and earmarked for the junk pile somehow didn't feel right to him.

They had just stepped out of the Jeep when three men strode over to head them off.

"Sheriff, this here is private property," the largest man said, stepping out in front of the others. "Unless you've got yourself a court order, your business here is finished."

Holly forced a chuckle. "Seriously gentlemen. This is not your property. It belongs to Mabel Martin. So unless you've been invited, in my books you're trespassing."

At that moment, a young man in his early twenties came out of the tent and walked up to the big man, handing him a legal-sized file folder.

"That's for the courts to decide isn't it?" the big man said, showing Holly a copy of a signed lease. "We know our rights, Sheriff."

Holly glanced at the document then back to the man. "Where's Mabel?"

"Said she's not feeling well, doesn't want visitors today. Says she needs her rest."

"We'll see about that," Holly said, and turned toward the house.

The man stepped sideways to block her, planting his feet on the ground, his arms crossed, a smug look on his face. Without hesitation Holly drew her .38, jamming the barrel into the man's crotch, and pulled the hammer back until it—clicked. The man froze.

Josh considered Holly for a few seconds, trying to gauge the level of her intent, then looked at the man. "You'd better back off, before *they* get blown off."

The man must have come to the same conclusion, as he slowly moved out of the way, his face drained of color— now a pallid white mask. The others followed his lead and spread out as they all retreated toward the tent.

Josh whispered to Holly, "Remind me to never piss you off."

Josh and Holly continued to the house, entering through the front door. Mabel was sitting at the kitchen table, a pile of used tissues scattered about the floor. She looked up. "What am I going do, Sheriff?" she asked, her face wet with tears.

"It's all right, Mabel, we'll get rid of them. Might take some time, but we'll show them the door."

Mabel started to sniffle. "I'm a *stupid* old woman, that's what I am. Thought he was a good boy. He'd help me out some . . ." she said, looking to Holly for acknowledgement.

Holly placed her hand on Mabel's shoulder and gave it a pat.

"It's just I, I haven't been doing so good since Arnie died, you know. Thought the young man was going to help me. Stupid! Stupid! Old woman, that's what I am."

"Aww Mable, they tricked you—could've happened to anyone. And like I said, we'll get rid of them, I promise. May take some time, but we'll boot those sons-of-bitches' asses clear into the sunset."

A smile surfaced on Mabel's face, then it soured. "But, there's so many . . . ?"

"Yeah, well, first things first," Holly said. "And the first thing we have to do, is get you out of here. Is there anyone you can call? Someone you can stay with until things settle down?"

"My sister, Edith. She's been trying to get me to come over ever since they arrived."

"Good. You give her a call, and I'll help you pack. If that's okay?"

Mabel blew her nose and gave a weak nod.

Josh said, "Hey, while you two are packing, I'm gonna take a walk down to the mill, have a quick look around."

Josh crossed the lawn to the entrance of the big tent, pulled back the canvas flap and stepped in, then waited a moment for his eyes to adjust. He half expected to see the three men they'd encountered earlier, but they were nowhere in sight.

The air was smoky and seasoned with the scent of the food cooking, smelling of onions, garlic, and rosemary. It smelled better than good, so Josh decided to follow his nose. He saw a woman staring down into a large, black stew pot set in front of one of the covered wagons. She seemed unaware of his presence, standing motionless, a large wooden spoon in her hand. She was maybe forty years of age, pretty in her own way, wearing a black dress that almost touched the dirt floor, her hair tucked under a white skull cap.

The stew was gently bubbling, the embers beneath the pot flickering from red to black, and back again.

"That smells awfully good," Josh said, startling the woman.

Angel turned to him then averted her gaze. There was fear in her eyes, and her hand trembled as she wiped an errant curl of hair from her face. "You, you shouldn't be here," she said, still looking down. "The men, they don't take to strangers."

Josh glanced around. "The only person I see, is you."

Angel didn't respond.

"So, what're you cooking?" Josh asked. "'Cause I gotta tell you, it's killing me. It smells so good."

"Please sir, I don't want you to get into any trouble. You must—"

At that moment, Josh heard a squeal and a pig not much bigger than a toaster ran out from under the covered wagon, a chunk of red cloth the size of a handkerchief in its mouth. A second later a young girl, a teenager, came from around the side of the trailer, chasing after it.

"Mortimer. Give it back! That's mine, you'll make it dirty . . ." the girl cried out.

"Hanna," Angel said in a hushed voice, "stop your yelling this instant, you know better—you'll wake your father."

Hanna stopped, took notice of Josh, then picked up the pig, tapping its nose with her finger. She said something to it and smiled. Then she looked up at Josh. "You like pigs, mister?"

He grinned. "As a matter of fact, I do. So, what's her name?"

"It's a he, and his name is, Mortimer."

"Oh, of course, well, how do you do, Mortimer?"

Hanna studied Josh for a second, then squinted her eyes and asked, "Are you coming to the Miracle, mister?"

"The what?"

"Hanna, hush your mouth!" Angel blurted. "Strangers are not welcome, you know that."

"Why not, momma? It's exciting. Father Paul won't mind. . . . Don't make sense, why something so special is not—"

"Hush, *not* another word."

"Father Paul?" Josh asked. "Is he the leader here?"

Angel nodded and looked down.

Hanna gave her mother a defiant look and turned back to Josh. "It starts at eight o'clock, mister, this Friday—"

"Hanna . . . !"

"What's all the ruckus?" Carl barked, as he stepped down from the wagon. When he caught sight of Josh, he sneered, "Who are you? You got no business being here, mister." He turned to Angel. "And what do you think you're doing? You are not to be talking to strangers, woman. Father Paul will not be pleased."

"Carl, my husband, I was just telling him he should leave."

Carl was a big man with long greasy hair, barrel-chested and thick at the waist. As he turned back to Josh, his scowl broadened, baring his yellowing teeth. "She told you to go, mister. Best you do as she says."

Josh looked him straight in the eye. "Umm . . . nope. Don't think so. I'm thinking I'm going to stay for a while. Kinda like the atmosphere around here."

"Get your ass outta here!" Carl ordered, picking up a chunk of two-by-four lying by the fire. "Or I'll—"

"Carl! Please, let him be," Angel begged, and turned to Josh. "Please sir, please don't cause trouble."

Carl took a few strides and grabbed Angel by her arm, swinging her around to face him, and slapped her hard across her cheek. "You gonna learn to *shut* that trap of yours, woman." As he raised his arm to strike her again, Josh latched onto it, twisting the big man's arm behind him, forcing him over and pressing him down until his face was hovering over the bubbling stew.

"Now Carl, that's just all messed up," Josh said. "Just what kind of dimwitted thoughts are going through that big, pea-brained head of yours?"

Carl muttered something, groaning in pain. "What was that, Carl? What did you say?" Josh asked, twisting Carl's arm further. Then Josh turned to Angel. "If you're willing to press charges, we can protect you, ma'am?"

Angel looked down at the dirt floor and did not respond.

"A simple nod will do, ma'am. I can make this all go away."

Angel looked up. "No . . . it's not our way. He is my husband."

Josh's eyes narrowed, and he could feel his anger growing. "Carl, I need you to tell your wife you're so very sorry, and that it won't ever happen again. Then tell her you are a loser, a sniveling coward, and you don't deserve her."

"Fuck you, asshole! You're gonna regret this!"

"Oh, I already do, Carl," Josh said, forcing the man's face down to within an inch of the boiling stew.

"Please sir, no more trouble!" Angel pleaded, glancing around as though the others may show up at any second.

Josh looked over at her and could see the panic in her eyes. He hesitated before letting go of her husband, watching as Carl fell backwards onto his ass. Carl immediately dug his heels into the dirt and pushed himself away from the fire. "I'm going to kill you for this!" he snarled.

"No, Carl, you're not. And if I hear you've laid another hand on your wife . . ." Josh took a step and bent down, bringing his face in close, looking directly into Carl's eyes. "I'm going to hurt you, Carl. Hurt you *real* bad." Josh could feel himself losing control, his rage growing unabated.

"Fuck you mister, I gonna—"

Josh grabbed Carl by his hair and pulled him back to the fire, the big man screaming and kicking up dirt. He knotted his fingers into Carl's long hair and pressed his face to the hot coals. He was about to drive his point home when Angel stepped forward. "Please mister, no more. Please, just leave, you must go, now!" she cried, her face wet with tears.

Josh took a breath, trying to clear his mind, and saw the daughter staring at him. *Ah hell,* he thought, and released his grip on Carl, who quickly rolled himself away from the fire. Angel knelt down by her husband, put her hand on his shoulder, and looked up at Josh, fear in her eyes.

"You best remember what I told you," Josh said, staring down at Carl.

Carl didn't answer, only turned his head.

Josh was brushing himself off, making his way back to the tent flaps when he heard Holly calling his name.

Carl scrambled to his feet, picked up the two-by-four, and took a few long strides. He swung the chunk of wood, putting both his weight and shoulder into it, catching Josh across the back. The force of the strike sent Josh tumbling forward, and he landed on his side. Without hesitation, Carl kicked Josh in the lower back, once, then twice. Josh rolled away, evading the third kick, and got to his knees, his mind now flooded with rage; his pain masked by a fresh rush of adrenalin.

Carl went for another kick, but his boot missed its mark, and only grazed Josh's cheek. The force of it threw Carl off-balance, landing him on his back.

Josh got to his feet before Carl could recover and planted one foot on Carl's upper arm, pinning it to the ground. Then in one motion he kicked backward with his heel catching Carl's forearm, forcing it in a direction it was not meant to go, the cartilage snapping like a crisp celery stalk, his forearm now facing the wrong direction. Carl screamed, clutching at his arm, and began rocking himself back and forth.

A few seconds later Holly came running into the tent, her gun drawn, and saw Carl holding his arm and crying. "What the hell is this?"

Josh gave her a knowing look and raised his hand. "The man needed an adjustment, that's all." Then he turned to Carl and pointed his finger. "Remember what I told you."

Chapter 27

The Advisory Council table was round, made of three-quarter inch plywood, and was covered with a black cotton tablecloth. It was an hour before dinner and a special meeting had been called. The remaining four members of the council and Carl watched as Father Paul ran his fingers through his hair.

"That man had no right to rough Carl up like that," one of the council members said. "Breaking his arm and such."

"We can't let something like that slide . . ." said another, the rest of them grunting in agreement.

Father Paul turned and considered Carl for a moment. Carl's arm was in a fresh cast and held in place with a blue sling. "What exactly did you do, Carl? A lawman doesn't just break your arm because you looked at him wrong."

"Nothin' I swear Father. It was just . . . well, he was interfering. Saying we got no right to control our women folk."

"What did you do, Carl?" Father Paul asked, his eyes hard as flint.

Carl glanced down and adjusted the sling, his red and swollen fingers sticking out from the cast.

"All I did was give Angel a taste of my hand. And I . . . I told the prick it was none of his business. We can do as we see fit."

Father Paul said nothing, continuing to stare at Carl.

"A woman needs guidance," Carl protested. "We have the right to make 'em obey—a man has these rights."

"Well now Carl, you have touched on a crucial aspect of our doctrine," Father Paul said. "And I want you all to listen carefully to what I'm about to say." Two of the brothers were whispering to each other. Father Paul slammed his fist down on the table. "Gentlemen, may I have your, attention?" The two men sat up straight and took a breath.

"Good, that's good, because I wouldn't want any miscommunication to come between us. Now gentlemen, our women are God's gift to us, and we must, and I want you to take special note on this aspect; we must all treat them with the utmost respect." He took a moment to survey his followers. "Now brothers, God knows this is not a perfect world; and we all know a woman needs guidance. But gentlemen, in future, should any of you find one of the flock is less than agreeable with her station in life, you are to bring her to my attention, and I will deal with her. I will set her straight, and put the misguided one on the path to righteousness."

"Father," Carl blurted, holding his arm. "What about this?"

Father Paul smiled. "Oh, I do feel your pain, brother. Make no mistake about that, and I understand your predicament. A man does not disrespect another man, and to do so in front of that man's woman, well, that is an unforgivable sin. Brother, you have my word that a just punishment will befall that man, *for he will feel the hand of God upon his shoulders.*" He held his hands up, palms out, and said, "Now, let us all join hands and pray."

Chapter 28

After Josh and Holly dropped Mabel off at her sister's home they swung by the church for a second look, arriving back at the office a few minutes after five.

Holly went straight to her office and closed the door. She told Josh she'd file a report on the incident at the tent, in case there was blowback. Something that neither of them thought was a real threat, since people of that ilk tend to shy away from the law, plus the fact that Josh was simply defending himself. After that, she'd be contacting the sheriff in Winston County to compare notes on the drifters, and see if he'd ever heard of a Father Paul. But more than anything else, she was looking forward to seeing him later, after he'd brought Rachael up to speed.

Josh made a fresh pot of coffee, poured himself a cup, then walked into the closet-size office and took a seat at the card table. He was glad to be alone and able to concentrate, his line of sight settling on the banker's box. *So . . . why do it? It was a simple case—why sanitize it? There was no need.* He took a deep breath and let it out in a puff as he reached down and opened the file box.

~ ~ ~

A couple of hours passed as he poured through the reports again, listing out the salient elements of the case on a pad of paper, drawing lines connecting anything remotely related . . . then turned to doodling in the margin as he tried to come up with something new.

Finally, he leaned backward, wincing as his bruised back pressed against the chair, his hands knitted behind his head and began his recap. There were four eyewitnesses the night Lyle Carpenter emerged from his place: Myrna Hudson, Glenda Bunny and her daughter, Emma, and Lana Friedman, niece to Myrna. And since Myrna Hudson, Doris Parker, and Glenda Bunny are all dead, and since Emma Bunny's account of what happened contradicts what the others have said, and since Lana Friedman is still missing— the well is definitely running dry. Which means, it's time to expand the investigation, he thought, dig deeper into the lives of the other players. Holly's father had cleansed the files, but why? What was he hiding, if he was hiding anything at all? His deputy at the time, Horst Rutland, was noted in the file and still lives close by. As for Lyle Carpenter . . . his trial appears to be at the center of it all. And while Carpenter may have dropped off the radar, a trip to Zuma is worth a shot.

Then there's Lana Friedman. Josh sighed and sat forward. *We've got absolutely nothing, no leads, nothing. She's simply vanished. We need a friggin' break . . . and soon.* He chucked his pencil across the room. *Forensics better find something quick 'cause this guy's not going to keep her around for long.*

He began rubbing his forehead with his fingertips. *And yet, if he'd wanted her dead, he'd cut her on the spot, like the others, like Myrna Hudson and Senator Parker. But he hadn't, so he had plans for her . . . which means she could still be alive.*

He sat there for another half an hour, mulling over the events. The room was quiet except for the humming of the clock above the door. It was a virtual white enamel pie pan, the kind he'd watched as a kid waiting for the recess bell, its red second hand gliding around the black numbers. Then he noticed the time: seven forty-five. *Time to go.*

He deposited the files back into the box, laying the trial folder on top. Closing the office door behind him, he stepped out onto the street.

The sky was black except for the halos crowning the street lamps, forming a line of progressively smaller circles, telescoping into the distance. Josh breathed in the cool night air and smiled, suddenly aware of how much he was looking forward to seeing Rachael, even if she was taken.

Large snowflakes were floating down around him, melting on contact with the sidewalk, leaving behind a carpet of pansy-sized puddles. And while it was a fact that the daytime temperatures were setting record highs and that the sidewalks had retained some of that heat, once the sun dipped below the horizon, the air cooled faster than a politician's smile.

As he continued down the sidewalk, his mind crossed over to the boardwalk back at the marina. He thought of Eddie and wondered how the big mutt was doing. Tyler would take good care of him, he knew that. Just the same, he missed having Eddie at his side. Then he thought of how the ocean smelled of seaweed and salt, and of the pelicans dive bombing and scooping up herring from the cresting waves. And of playing cards with his friends and how it was all so good, so right—hoisting pints and laughing, simply enjoying the state of *being*. He missed it all.

As he crossed Main Street, a muted roar of laughter came from Peterson's Pub. There was a table by the front window, people standing and laughing. A white-haired man at the head of the table was holding a glass of red wine high in the air, basking in the limelight.

Josh had just reached the front door when Rachael appeared, coming around the corner and walked straight into him, knocking her cell out of her hand.

They both reached down to pick up her cell, but she got to it first, and that's when he noticed the backup piece—a small knife—strapped just above her ankle. He recognized the knife, it was wafer-thin and flat, with the dimensions of a credit card. It had a small steel loop on its handle that enabled a quick withdrawal from its sheath. It was considered an effective close quarters weapon, its two-inch razor sharp blade, tiny, but deadly—to be used when all else fails.

He stood up and smiled.

"After you," he said, opening the door.

She grinned, a thin, expectant smile, and slipped in front of him.

The pub was packed, steamy and smelling of beer and perfume. A man with long gray hair tied back in a ponytail sat in the corner, finger picking his acoustic guitar, singing a '60s war protest song. The place was warm and had a comfortable feel to it, the wood-planked walls adding to the relaxed ambience, as did the dim recessed lighting, cocooning the patrons in a tanned glow. The table by the front window had a large yellow helium balloon tied to its centerpiece, the words 'WE'LL MISS YOU' written on it in bold purple letters. The white-haired man was beaming with all the attention, his ruddy face elated, enjoying a final moment in the spotlight.

Scanning the room, Josh noticed a pair of women across the bar, buttoning their coats and slinging their purses over their shoulders. He and Rachael shouldered their way through the crowd and slipped into the booth. A comely waitress with long red hair tied in pigtails, wearing emerald green tights that accentuated her athletic thighs, flashed Josh a smile and said she'd be right over.

"How was your trip?" he asked.

Rachael didn't respond.

"I take it Kingsley's still . . . Kingsley?"

"Yes, he's still a prick, if that's what you mean."

Josh said nothing.

"I met with the review panel, and . . . Well, I don't know what's going to happen, the jury's still out. But regardless of the outcome, he'll keep pushing forward with his agenda to get rid of me. And now, with you in the picture, his indignation is over the top. He hates your guts, and he's on my case for bringing you back on board."

"Sorry to hear that. But, did *you* bring me back? I thought it was Judge Higgins who wanted me on the file?"

Rachael didn't answer.

"Hey, I can step aside if that's what you want?"

Rachael's reaction was unexpected. She reached over and gently placed her hand on his. "I want you to stay."

"Okay." *What's this? You're about to get married . . .* He wanted to give her a hard look, one that said *don't even go there.* But when he took a closer look at the road-weary woman sitting across from him, he gave her an awkward smile. *Man, I don't get women at all.*

"You all right?" she asked.

He tried to smile again. "Yeah, no, I'm good. Let's order a drink and I'll bring you up to speed."

He was halfway through his glass of Shiraz when he began the recap. He told her about how Glenda Bunny's exhumed corpse revealed a missing rib, same as Senator Parker and Myrna Hudson. And how Myrna, Glenda and her daughter Emma, and Lana Friedman, had seen Lyle come out of his home the night of the murder. He explained how Emma was still upset she'd been denied the right to testify at the trial due to her age, and continued to maintain it was a crucifix and not a knife Lyle had in his hand that night. He finished off with the fact that Sheriff Holly Oleson's father was the sheriff at the time of the trial and how all the files and records appear to have been scrubbed.

He went over his run-in with the squatters and his dust-up with Carl, and the late night drama at his hotel room with Emma Bunny.

"Sounds like you've had your hands full, so to speak."

"Sounds like."

"*Hold on,* wasn't that when I called your room and you hung up on me, then called me back?"

He gave her a guilty shrug.

Rachael watched him for a minute, then asked, "So, what's next?"

"We speak to Lyle Carpenter."

"Agreed. Now, we just have to find him. Vivian's getting nowhere, coming up empty handed. Says she's pretty much run out of leads. Carpenter is off the radar. If he's not dead, he's hiding."

"Yeah," Josh said. "But if he is alive, then why hide? He'd served his full sentence."

Neither spoke for a while, then he asked, "And Lana Friedman, any luck with forensics?"

Rachael shook her head. "No, not really, other than it looks like it was her blood on the floor, the DNA from her hair brush matched. Christ, we're really not getting very far, are we?" She paused. "And what's the deal on the files being scrubbed?"

Josh nodded. "That's got a smell to it all right."

"And what's the good Sheriff got to say about that?"

"Apparently, her father can do no wrong."

"And you believe her?"

Josh turned the palms of his hands up. "What can I say, she loved her old man."

Rachael studied Josh for a few seconds, then asked, "How about you and the sheriff? How's that going?" She paused, and a rush of pink ran up her neck. "Sorry, maybe I'm getting ahead of myself." Then she tilted her head, and asked, "Am I, getting ahead of myself?"

"A little."

"*Ohh . . . ?*"

"How about you and Tony?" Josh asked, turning the tables on Rachael. "Your world unfolding as planned?"

"It's Thomas, and actually he wants to come here for Thanksgiving, just for the evening. I told him I thought it was a bad idea, but I think he's going to show up anyway. Says he wants to get away from the city for a few hours— wants to meet the people I work with."

"Great idea . . . be fascinating to meet him," Josh said, not meaning a word of it. He surveyed the room for a moment before coming back to Rachael. "Look, Rachael, maybe we should call it a night. We can meet up in the morning, maybe have breakfast, plan out the day."

Rachael hesitated, then drained the last of her wine and asked, "Walk me home?"

Chapter 29

The cool, damp air of the woods reminded Alvin he should've grabbed his jacket from the truck before heading out. To make matters worse, the sun was on the tail end of the day and he knew the temperature would soon drop. And yet, the truth of the matter was, he was too pumped to care. Each time he thought of his young bride, his mind went into a tizzy, scrambling the thoughts in his head. So much so, he'd barely noticed the branch that had stuck him in the forehead, or the trickle of blood caught in his eyebrow, or the drops on his cheek.

He knew what he was doing was wrong, the wedding still a few days off, but he didn't care. He had to see her. *I am one lucky son-of-a-bitch,* he said to himself, wanting to scream it out so all the world would hear.

Fifty yards farther into the woods she came into view. He stopped and took a moment to enjoy her, his tongue licking the blood at the corner of his mouth, the taste metallic, like wet pennies in the snow.

Hanna was sitting on a fallen oak, straddling it as though she was riding a horse, her dress hitched up and exposing one knee. Alvin watched intently as she leaned sideways, stretching her arm out, reaching down and under the tree.

Unable to resist, he walked up to her. "Hi, Hanna girl, what ya doin'?" he asked, a big smile on his droopy face.

"Nothing much. Just cuttin' me some Oakies," she said, a pairing knife in her hand. Then she did a double take. "What happened to you, Alvin?"

"Oh, that." He wiped the blood off his cheek with his hand. "Got stuck by a branch. Should've watched where I was going."

She continued to stare at him then noticed the silver whistle hanging around his neck.

"*Mmm* girl. I gotta say, them Oakies be one of my favorites. Finest eaten mushrooms they is. Thinkin' I'd like to pick me some." His belly swirled with excitement, forcing him to clench his teeth and keep his face all friendly-like. "You're gettin' to be a big girl, a fully-growed woman, I reckon."

Hanna cocked her head, studying him again, a handful of hair hanging down over one eye, a puzzled look on her face. "You want to pick some, Alvin?"

He didn't respond.

"Hey Alvin, you okay? Got yourself a troubled look. Something not sitting right?"

Alvin half-grinned. "No, I be just fine. It's such a special day, just wanna take it all in."

As he knelt down beside her, her soapy scent sent his mind into a twirl. He tried to focus and keep his thoughts straight, but he couldn't help himself. Her innocent face was so close it made him tremble inside. He gently placed his hand on her shoulder. "So, are ya gettin' excited?"

"About what?" Hanna drew back from him, frowning.

"About the miracle, of course?"

Hanna's frown deepened. "Yeah, I guess . . ."

"Don't sound like you're too excited to me, girl. What's wrong?"

"Ah, nothing."

"Hey, you can tell ol' Alvin."

Hanna shook her head.

"C'mon, something's troubling you, I can tell. You can trust me—I ain't gonna tell no one."

"I don't know. It's . . . it's just, you know, I'm not ready to be wed, Alvin. I got things I want to do, places I want to go, things I want to see. It's just not fair."

"*Oh my* . . . Come here girl. Give ol' Alvin a hug. It's gonna be okay, you'll see."

Hanna turned and wrapped her arms around Alvin, giving him a tight squeeze.

The warmth and feel of her body sent an intoxicating rush through him. He patted his hands on her back and gave her a long squeeze, then let his hands slide down the curves of her body.

Hanna stood up and took a step back, looking him in the eye. "I . . . I'd better be getting back, momma will be looking for me," she said, her lips slightly parted, her body tense.

Alvin thought his heart would explode, and he lunged for her. She took another step back, tightening her grip on the knife.

"You get away from me Alvin, you're acting weird."

"Now, Hanna, don't you be like that. We're friends you and me. I'm not gonna hurt you. You gotta learn to trust me, girl."

"No, you're being too weird, Alvin. And I'm . . . I'm going home now." She held the knife out in front of her and waved it at him.

Alvin's face grew dark, his eyes wild. "What're you doin' with that thing? You better be careful, you might poke me with it."

He took a step toward her, and she swung the knife, nicking his shirt.

"Now, you gotta learn to respect your elders, girl." A grin surfaced on his face. "No, that ain't right. You gotta learn to respect your *husband*."

Hanna's eyes widened, and she cried out, "Get away from me! You freak!"

Alvin lunged again, grabbing her wrist and twisting the knife out of her hand, then smacked her hard across the face with the back of his hand.

Hanna stood there, stunned, a blank expression on her face.

Alvin slid his large hands around her waist and pulled her tight to him. "Relax, girl, you're gonna like what ol' Alvin's got for you . . ."

As he inhaled the fresh scent of her hair, a twig snapped behind him. He craned his neck to look, just as a rock the size of a cannonball hit him on the side of his skull, swinging his face in the opposite direction. A split second later he dropped, landing at Hanna's feet, unconscious.

Angel grabbed her daughter by the shoulders. "Hanna, look at me. Baby! Are you all right?"

Hanna looked at her mother and tears began to flow.

"Baby, I promise you, right here, right now. We're getting out of this place and we're *never* coming back."

Chapter 30

Dinner was running late, and most of the other families had already moved indoors for the night. Hanna sat quietly at the dinner table, her cheek bruised, a black welt over her eye. Carl was sitting across from her, his arm in a sling, brooding. The table was small and sat in front of a short ladder leading into the family wagon. An old, soot covered oil lamp hung above the table, its faint light readily absorbed into the twenty-foot stretch of darkness to the next wagon. Avoiding eye contact with her husband, Angel busied herself, scooping out mashed potatoes from a big aluminum pot, plopping a large dollop onto each plate.

"This wouldn't happen to a married woman," Carl growled. "It's not proper; a woman being alone in the woods, tempting a man like that. Father Paul will want an accounting." He ladled out some beef and mushroom gravy onto his potatoes and continued. "My God, Hanna, Alvin could've been killed. You're absolutely sure you didn't see who hit him?"

Hanna shook her head, staring at her food.

"He's saying you must've. Are you *sure* you didn't see who it was . . . ?"

Angel felt her stomach acid rise in her esophagus, her disgust with her husband now complete. Bad thoughts were

174

flooding in, willing her to act, screaming for her to stick a fork deep into his fat, ugly throat.

Angel swallowed. "Hanna will be wed, week from today, my husband. She'll be fine after that." She gave Hanna a look that said, *do not say a word.*

"Let this be a lesson for you, Hanna," Carl went on. "Not to be giving notions to a man, stirring his needs. A grown man has . . . well, he has desires that must be satisfied. You're very lucky he's to be your husband. A husband can forgive such things."

Angel glanced again at Hanna then raised a half-full jug of ice tea. "Tea, my love?" she asked Carl, tipping the jug in his direction and questioning with her free hand.

"Let this be another lesson for you, Hanna," Carl said, a satisfied tone coating his words. "A good woman such as your mother here always knows how to please her man." He gave Angel a few pats on the rump with his hand. "That's why God created a woman, so she could take care of her man." He stuffed a huge spoonful of potato into his mouth, the dark gravy wetting his lips, then washed it down with a few glugs of ice tea. He hesitated for a second, then gulped down more tea, some of it leaking out of the corners of his mouth and dripping off of his chin. "Now, about that pig. I don't want to hear another word about it. It stays in the pen, where pigs belong."

Hanna's eyes moistened. She put down her spoon and turned to Angel. "Momma?"

"Hush child, your father's right, the pig's got no place in our home."

"But momma—"

"You listen to your mother," Carl said. "Pigs be good for one thing, and one thing only . . ." He stopped in mid-sentence and began to fiddle with his collar, trying to loosen it. *"What the?* What's goin' on here...?" He struggled to get to his feet, one leg sliding sideways on the dirt floor. He grabbed at the table to steady himself. *"Woman?"* He turned to Angel. *"What have you—"* Then both legs gave out and he toppled over, falling face down in the dirt.

"Hanna," Angel said.

Hanna did not respond.

"Hanna!"

Hanna looked at her mother with a vacant stare.

"Quick! We have to hide him. And then we're getting out of here!"

Again, Hanna didn't respond. She simply sat there, looking at her mother.

"Hurry child, I don't know how long he'll stay under."

Hanna pushed herself up from the table, wobbling it a little, and rose from her chair.

Angel grabbed Carl by an armpit, Hanna grabbed the other, and together they dragged him under the trailer as far as they could. They laid a tarp over his exposed legs, piling a few folding chairs on top for good measure.

Angel went into the wagon, grabbed a packed leather bag from under the bed, and climbed back out. She saw Hanna sitting on the ground, her elbows on her knees, her head clasped in her hands. Angel's heart sank. *Oh God, what have I done?*

She grabbed Hanna by the hand and pulled her to her feet. "We have to go. *Now* child."

They headed out, working their way behind the wagons, staying out of sight as they maneuvered around the tent cables and a few 45-gallon drums, dodging electrical wires strung out in every direction, before finally reaching the end wagon. The pigpen was a good hundred feet to their left. Straight ahead were the woods and their freedom.

Suddenly, the large iron bell by the tent's entrance started to clang.

"Hanna, follow me," Angel said.

"But momma? Mortimer, we can't leave him!"

"There's no time, baby."

"No! I won't leave him!"

"I am so sorry baby, but we have to go. Now! They're coming."

"Momma. But I can't."

"Oh Hanna, we'll get help, then we'll come back and get Mortimer, I promise. But baby, we have to go."

A look of resignation registered on Hanna's face as Angel pulled on her arm, jarring her forward. Their first few steps were jumbled and awkward, and Angel almost stumbled. After that a rhythm set in, and they caught their stride. The forest floor was flat and almost free from underbrush. Angel was starting to feel hope trickle in, when the ground dropped from under them, throwing them off balance, sending them tumbling down a shallow embankment. With no time to think, they scrambled up the other side on their hands and knees, twigs tearing at their dresses, their boots slipping and sliding on the rotted leaves. They had just crested the embankment when Angel put out her arm in front of Hanna, bringing them both to a halt.

Angel peered into the trees, trying to get her bearings. She figured they had to be near the edge of the woods and the road would soon appear. With that, she felt a fresh surge of hope and grabbed Hanna's hand, and together they pressed on.

Another few minutes passed and they both were breathing hard and out of breath when an excruciating pain shot through Angel's leg. Her knee had clipped a tree stump, flipping her over, landing her on her back. She grabbed her damaged knee, pulling it toward her chest and willed herself not to scream.

"Momma! Are you okay?" Hanna cried, kneeling down beside her.

"I . . . I'm fine, I'll be all right. Just need a minute." Angel knew she wouldn't be all right, and waiting wasn't an option. So she took a deep breath and tried to straighten her leg. A flash of pain jolted through her and she screamed.

"Momma! What're we going to do? We need to go . . ."

"I know child, I know we do. Help me up."

Hanna latched onto her mother's forearm and pulled Angel to her feet, her one leg frozen and bent at the knee. Angel winced and clenched her teeth, again willing herself not to scream. She wrapped her arm around Hanna's shoulder and was about to take a step when her body went rigid. She turned to Hanna. "Did you hear that?"

"What Momma?" Hanna asked.

"Someone's out there."

A few seconds later, flashlight beams could be seen coming through the trees, circulating on the forest floor.

Angel looked around, searching for a way to escape, praying for a miracle, but there wasn't one—they were coming from every direction.

Chapter 31

With the killings at the church, and the FBI poking around, the man knew the best course of action and the logical choice would be to keep a low profile. He knew it was the right thing do—of course he did. But when the ache was upon him, and his cravings got riled . . . *well,* he had to feed them. What else could he do?

Perched on top of a gently sloping hill, the man had a clear view of the gas station below. He liked the spot, as the surrounding pine trees did a good job of hiding him. It was a safe place, where he could ponder life and all its absurdity, while the thrill of the chase, ever-present, simmered in the back of his mind.

He particularly liked the fact, that once the hunt began, he could simply accelerate down the hill, dovetailing Margaret, what he liked to call his old Crown Vic, onto highway 49. Then, let the party begin.

Friends, at least the few he could count as friends, saw him as a patient, levelheaded man, which was how he saw himself. And up until a few years ago, they would have been right. His first venture had come along by chance, certainly not a planned outing, at a time when his somewhat defective moral compass had lost its way. It was a clumsy ordeal to be sure—way too much risk. But the reward . . . *well,* there was no going back after that.

At times, it bothered him that he'd been such a late-bloomer, this being only his fourth adventure. *If I'd set my mind to it and started earlier, just think what I could've accomplished,* he thought, *how many more there could've been?*

He sniffed at the air and scowled. "You're getting a little funky, Margaret," he muttered, eyeing the wax paper his burger and fries had been wrapped in, now sitting on the passenger seat next to him; the smeared condiments reeking of onions and burnt animal fat. He reached over and grabbed the tainted paper, scrunched it up, and jammed it into a bag stamped *King of the Hill Burgers.* He rolled the top of the bag tight with his fingertips and for a second thought of chucking it out the window, then quickly rejected it. *Can't do that,* he scolded himself. In fact, he loathed those who littered. *Like, who do they think they are? Polluting the world . . . like no one else matters.*

He needed air, needed it bad, so he got out of the car. He sucked in a deep breath. The air was fresh and good and clean. Fall was his favorite time of year and always had been. Then the thought of starting so late in life returned, as things that bothered him tended to do . . .

But as he stood there in silence, looking up and taking in the stars, the delicious scent of fall filling his mind, his late start didn't seem all that important. Maybe it was the season, fall always made him feel alive . . . knowing nature was simply taking a rest, and then another cycle would begin. He rubbed the stubble on his face. "Yeah. I've still got a few good miles left in me." He got back into his car.

He'd found waiting was the hardest part, but knew deep down inside that toughing-it-out was the right thing to do. Waiting for the right moment was a crucial part of the game—*get the risk right, or get caught.* Then, as if on cue, his left leg started to tighten. Tension had gathered in his calf muscle and it was threatening to go into a spasm. He stretched his leg and pounded his heel on the floorboard a few times, shifting his ass around in the seat until he could get a real good stretch. All of which he knew would help, at least for a while. He tapped his watch. *Another half hour and I'm outta here.*

He wasn't entirely sure why, but '*selection*' had proven to be best between ten and midnight. There were still a reasonable number of cars on the road at that time. Most were from out-of-state, stopping and getting gas, which did have a certain rationale to it. The closest major center was 4 to 5 hours away, thus the need for gas. And since most people finished their workday by around five or six o'clock—add 4 to 5 hours driving time, and presto—the ten-until-midnight sweet spot was created. It was a simple formula that had proven to be dependable. He liked that. Things that were dependable.

On his first adventure he'd got lucky, the opportunity simply presented itself and he took it. The others had not been so easy, forcing him to wait long stretches, night after night, killing time in his car. He found listening to the police scanner helped, as did reading his latest novel on his e-reader.

He was about to retrieve his e-reader from the glove box when he caught sight of a two-seater sports car pulling up to pump 8. The car had come in fast and he hadn't gotten a good look, barely a glimpse of the woman inside as the car rolled up to the pump, but it was enough to get his blood flowing.

He zeroed his binoculars in on the car. *Expensive. Probably German.* "Heck, the paint's gotta be worth more than you, Margaret." Then he reached over and patted her dash as if to say he was sorry for having said it. He loved the old gal.

From his vantage point, the outermost set of pumps had always provided the better view. The two-seater was at the last pump island, its black paint shimmering under the overhead fluorescent lights.

Without warning his cell rang, startling him. He reached into his jacket side pocket and fumbled the phone to the floor. *"Shit!"* he growled, reaching down for it and looked at the screen. *Home calling.*

He took the call.

"Hey dad, I'm glad I caught ya. We're out of milk for the morning, can you pick some up?"

"Will do," the man said, in a forced, controlled voice. "Anything else we need?"

"Nope, that's it. Thanks, dad."

"Oh and kid, just so you know, I may be a little late. So don't wait up."

"Sure, love ya, dad."

"Love you too, son." He pressed end call. "Ahh! There she is," he said, just as she stepped inside the store, the door closing behind her. "Damn it." He had again missed his opportunity to get a better look, and glared at his phone as he slipped it back into his pocket.

A couple of minutes later the woman came out with a bottle of water and a tissue box. She seemed young, he thought. Difficult to say from this far away, but given the shape of her body and how her dress clung to her hips, he guessed she was in her mid-to-late twenties. He swallowed. *You'll do just fine . . .*

She got back into her car and started it.

He squeezed the steering wheel until his leather gloves squeaked, his heart thumping against his rib cage. "Now, if you'd just turn my way," he whispered.

She pulled away from the pumps and rolled across the tarmac toward the edge of the highway.

Ohh, please, please, just this one small favor.

She stopped, letting a long string of trucks go by . . .

"A man's dying here, girl! Roll the dice."

Then she turned on her left signal light and headed west onto Highway 49, a paved secondary that connected with I-71 some twenty miles farther down the road. A few seconds later, her two-seater sports car cruised past him.

The man's smile broadened as he turned the key and Margaret came to life. He rolled down the embankment, dovetailing the old boat onto Highway 49. Less than a mile out, he checked the rearview mirror and saw darkness, not a headlight in sight.

He managed to stay a good quarter of a mile behind her. *No rush,* he thought, as he knew precisely where he'd make his move. At the six-mile mark he checked the rearview mirror for the last time and punched the gas. He slid in behind her and hit the flashers, the colored lights bouncing off her car and the surrounding poplars.

The sports car slowed and pulled over.

As he walked up to her window, he couldn't help but notice how good the night air felt on his skin. All the excitement had made him sweaty, and he wasn't particularly fond of that look, thought it made him look needy. And he wanted to look his best.

He tapped his ring on the window and the woman rolled it down.

"Yes Officer?"

"Need to see your license and registration, ma'am."

"Sure, okay, just give me a moment." Her voice had a certain warmth to it, even if it was strained.

He watched her fumble with her purse, her hands digging around in it, until finally she passed the documents through the window.

"Please stay in your car ma'am."

He walked back to his car and pretended to call it in, then returned a minute later.

"I'll need you to step out of the car, ma'am."

"Why? What's wrong officer?"

"Just get out of your car, ma'am," he said, the timber of his voice strengthening.

The car door opened and she stepped out. She was wearing a cotton dress cut at the knees with a short light green sweater that seemed to work well with her blonde hair that fell to her shoulders. She had a concerned look on her face, but was trying to look confident, like she was in control.

His pulse quickened.

"Turn around and place your hands on the car, ma'am."

"*What?* Please, there must be some sort of misunderstanding."

"Hands on the car, now!"

She complied and placed her hands on the car.

He took a step forward. "Now spread your legs."

"Look, you can't—"

"Do it now. I won't ask again."

She spread her legs about six inches and snarled, *"Satisfied?"*

He began patting her down, running his hands along her sides, the sharp edge of her hips sending a savage rush to his core. He glanced up and down the road, then grabbed one of her wrists, wrenching it around behind her, then the other, and cuffed her. She was about to protest, when he grabbed a handful of her hair and slammed her face into the side window, crushing the cartilage in her nose.

Chapter 32

As they approached the entrance to their hotel, Josh stopped at the front door and told Rachael he was going to kick back for a bit, unwind some before calling it a night. He left out the fact he'd agreed to meet up with Holly later, and wondered why. *She's not gonna care one way or the other—so why not tell her?*

Rachael studied him for a long moment before reaching out and touching his face with her fingertips, then leaned forward and kissed him on the cheek. It seemed like a kind gesture, friendly in a way, but brought with it a bag full of mixed feelings. He figured he should say something, anything, to show he understood. To let her know he knew exactly what she was thinking. But before he could perjure himself, she stepped back and said, "See you in the morning?"

"Right," he replied. *Fantastic comeback . . .*

Suddenly, an uneasy feeling struck him, an instinctive squeeze at the back of his neck, as though they were being watched.

"What is it?" Rachael asked.

"I, um . . . not sure," he replied, turning to look. "Probably nothing." He quickly scanned the area, but couldn't see much beyond the lamppost next to the hotel gate. He turned back to her and said, "Goodnight, Rachael."

She gave him a questioning look, then walked into the hotel.

The hotel veranda had two small tables, each fortified with a propane heater. The table on the opposite side of the deck was occupied by a young couple, who were quietly talking and holding hands. He decided to have a drink and sat down at the table next to the front door.

The waitress arrived and he ordered a brandy and coffee, then fished out a cigar from his inside jacket pocket and ran it under his nose. *Thank God for small pleasures,* he thought, as he took in its leathery fragrance, his mind slipping into low gear and drifting back to his marina.

Without warning the heater popped on, followed by a low hum, prying him out of his self-induced torpor, his face and shoulders now basking in the red-grill warmth. A minute later the brandy and coffee arrived. He took a sip of the brandy, followed by a long drag on his cigar, and found himself thinking about Rachael. *She's about to get married to Tony, or whatever the hell his name is, but then she's sending out these signals. That is, if they are signals? But, she's sending something?*

His thoughts continued to loop around in his head before he finally reached the conclusion that he was in fact, an asshole, and a self-indulgent one at that. *Face it, you had your chance and you blew it. Time to move on.*

Ten minutes later the waitress returned with a second snifter and a fresh ashtray.

He took a gulp of brandy and washed it around in his mouth before swallowing, then leaned his head back against the hotel wall and closed his eyes. The propane heater cycled on again, the warmth soothing. He wondered how his dad was making out. Last time he'd spoke to Alice—

who ran the not-for-profit that watched over his father—she had said his father was doing okay, okay for a street person that is. He figured it was too late to call her, she would've gone home by now; he'd make the call tomorrow.

He took another swallow of brandy—and there it was, that feeling he was being watched. He put down his snifter and surveyed the area again, harder this time. There was nothing noteworthy, just a couple of teenagers under a streetlight kicking a tin can back and forth. Then an old flatbed pickup turned at the end of the street, its headlights throwing light on a woman crossing the road. The woman was tall, wearing a long coat, and was pushing a baby carriage. He took another sip and watched as the woman got the front wheels of the carriage onto the curb and continued down the sidewalk. He scanned the area for another minute, but there was nothing. So, he decided to let it go.

He checked his watch. He still had a few minutes to kill, so he turned his attention back to the police reports and trial records. It wasn't what was in them that was getting under his skin, it was what was *not*. They'd been scrubbed clean, but why bother? For an 'open and shut case', a case that some would've called a proverbial slam-dunk? *Bullshit,* there's no such thing, not in a murder trial. Things get messy, grit gets sprinkled in causing all kinds of friction. Conflicting evidence crops up that may or may not get discounted, but it's all there, mixed in with the facts—messy stuff, stuff you expect. Of course, the richer and more prominent you are, the messier the file gets, creating more doubt—and more importantly—reasonable doubt. A simple formula, that'd proven to work well for defense attorneys all over the country. He shook his head. *Nah, the files are way too clean, even for a poor boy. So then why do it? Why clean them? It makes no sense.* But what bothered him the most was that there were no leads to follow. Time was running out for Lana Friedman, if it hadn't already. They needed a break, needed it fast, or she was lost.

He drained the last of the brandy and was contemplating giving Mary a call, to see how she was doing and if she needed anything brought up to her room. He'd retrieved his cell from his jacket pocket when another thought occurred to him.

~ ~ ~

The oiled barrel of the rifle sat perfectly still on the hickory branch. The air was calm, so that would not be a factor, and the lights on the hotel veranda were helping some, providing light for the shooter to zero in on the target. The only sound, other than a tin can off in the distance, was that of a breath being slowly released as the shooter's finger squeezed back on the trigger . . .

Chapter 33

At the same moment the sound reached Josh's eardrum, a searing pain ripped through his thigh, as though a red-hot knitting needle had pierced the muscle. Jolted, he rolled out of his chair onto the deck, yelling at the young couple to get down. They hesitated, then dropped to the floor, the young man pulling the woman under him, covering her body with his.

Crossing the deck on his hands and knees, Josh reached the porch handrail and pressed his back against the post. He turned his body, craning his neck, and peered out onto the street, waiting for the second shot. But there was no second or third shot. Whoever it was—was gone.

Josh glanced over at the young couple. The woman's face was pressed against the man's chest. Then looking down, he saw blood blossoming on his pant leg. He stretched his leg. There was pain, but it was dull and throbbing. Sticking his fingers through the hole in his pants, he ripped the cloth back, exposing a neat, round entry hole, the size of a garden pea. He ran his fingers under his thigh. It felt warm and moist, and then he felt the other hole. He removed his hand, now wet with blood, then got to his feet and yanked the tablecloth off, sending the snifter, coffee cup, and ashtray into the air. He had just tied his leg off when the waitress came out the door. She saw the blood and screamed, her hand covering her face. A second later, the front desk clerk and another staff member came running out the door.

"Call 911," Josh told the clerk, "there's been a shooting." The clerk's eyes opened wide and she ran back inside.

Rachael came storming out the front door and saw the blood. "*Oh God,*" she blurted, then knelt down and inspected his leg. "How bad is it?"

"Went straight through, must've missed the artery. I think the shot came from somewhere over there," he said, pointing to the left, beyond the gate. "But there was no second shot, he's gone."

Rachael glanced down at his leg; the tied tablecloth was turning a deep red. "I'm taking you to the hospital."

He gave her a nod and slung his arm over her shoulder just as Mary came out the door. "Jesus, Josh," Mary said, her hair matted with sweat and clinging to her head. "Are you all right?"

Josh nodded. "Just a scratch, Rachael's taking me to the hospital. I'll be fine." He gave Mary a hard look. "But you, you look like hell. You should get back to bed. I'll see you tomorrow."

"But . . ." Mary said, grabbing a chair to steady herself.

"No buts, I'll see you in the morning. Mary . . . I'll be fine."

She pressed her lips together and stared at him for a second, but didn't argue the point further.

~ ~ ~

When they reached her SUV, Rachael pushed Josh up against it and told him not to move. He was only half-listening, scanning the area as a force of habit, as he knew it was unlikely the shooter would stay around to watch the excitement since there was no crowd to hide in.

Rachael had moved the passenger seat back as far as it would go and was helping Josh in when the sheriff's Jeep and another cruiser pulled up beside them. Holly jumped out and came running.

"Josh, are you okay?" she asked, a worried look on her face.

"Bullet went right through."

"That's not what I asked. Are you all right?" The tension in her voice rose.

Josh shrugged. "Yeah. I'm okay."

"Did you see the shooter?"

He shook his head.

"He's bleeding pretty bad," Rachael said. "I'm taking him to the hospital."

Holly turned to her deputy. "Get the area cordoned off and call forensics."

"Best guess is, the shot came from over there," Josh said, pointing to a tree maybe fifty feet past the gate lamppost. "I'm thinking around those bushes, next to that tree."

Holly gave more instructions to her deputy, and turned back to Josh, and was about to speak when Rachael blurted, "Josh, we have to go . . . right now."

Holly glanced at Rachael then to Josh. "I'll get things started here and meet you at the hospital."

"Okay," he said, then turned and climbed into the Tahoe, wincing as he pulled his leg in and closed the door.

A few seconds later another cruiser arrived, and Deputy Hal Rogers climbed out. Holly lowered her radio, telling him the crime scene team would arrive soon and to keep the media and anyone else behind the tape. She slipped the radio into its holster, then turned and watched the Tahoe exit the parking lot.

192

Chapter 34

A pall of smoke circulated above the brethren, suspended in a lazy current caught under the big tent's canvas, tainting the air with an earthy spice-like aroma. Murmurs of elation rolled out in sporadic waves across the room. The troupe's expectant gaze never straying far from their savior's door.

The evening sermon was cherished, even ached for, for it was the daily nourishment that only their father could provide. And tonight was special, for one of their own had broken the sacred bond.

And yet, no matter how much they longed for the ceremony to begin, how much their souls yearned for his words, they dared not disturb him. To do so was unthinkable.

Father Paul lay flat on his back, studying his reflection in a small pink hand mirror, no more than two inches in diameter. He was contemplating the order of events and how they would unfold over the next few days. And even though he knew the agenda by heart, he was having trouble blocking out the troupe's energy. He could feel their desire seeping through the cracks of the trailer walls, like night crawlers, penetrating his thoughts, distorting reality and clouding his mind. "You must remain calm. They mean you no harm," he whispered, holding the mirror close, his one eye staring back at him. "Yes . . . it's all right. Just let go, embrace them, accept their love for they give you strength, the power you so desperately need—the power to create . . ."

Then he thought of how his followers brightened each time he told them of the miracle to come. How their belief in him was pure and resolute. "You see, they do love me," he murmured. "You have nothing to fear." He looked away, his gaze coming to rest on the braided rug lying in the middle of the floor. "And yet, what if they are not ready? They might not understand." He put down the mirror and looked up. "But they will understand, won't they . . . ? Oh yes, of course they will. Once they bear witness; they will understand, they will truly believe in their coming salvation."

The voices were getting louder, more enthusiastic now—the time for the evening sermon was almost upon him.

He swung his bare legs out of bed, shivering as he dropped his feet to the cold floor. He slipped on his flip-flops and stood up. Stretching out his arms, he began pacing the length of the trailer, his nightshirt unbuttoned, his arms swinging at his sides.

He liked to pace, for it allowed him time to think, and he particularly liked the night, when the shadows climbed the big tent walls. Suddenly, a high-pitched scream came from outside, breaking his concentration. One of the faithful has succumbed to God's will. Immediately the others joined in, and the pitch of emotion climbed higher, the swell of passion palpable, swirling around him.

He stopped and slowly turned his head toward the commotion, his high, angular cheekbones cutting his profile, his skin stretched tight on his neck. He craned his neck further and further until he was looking over his shoulder, the corner of his eye moist and oily, his black pupil dilated. "Oh yes, I'm coming for you."

He opened the cupboard door above the sink and retrieved a purple silk cloth, trimmed with golden lace tassels knotted at the ends. He placed the cloth on the floor next to the rug, and then rolled the braided carpet into the shape of a large cigar. Beneath the carpet were two narrow rectangular doors, recessed into the floor. He slipped his fingers through the embedded brass handles of the door closest to him, pulling it out of its resting place and set it against the trailer wall.

Inside the cavity was a gray box, measuring not much more than six feet in length, two feet wide and a foot high. The box was partially covered with a thick, dark-blue felt blanket. On the blanket lay a small bouquet of chicken feathers, soft and white, the quills tied together with a single strand of green speaker wire.

He knelt down and picked up the bouquet, stroking the feathers before raising the bouquet to his mouth, clenching a single quill between his front teeth. Taking great care, he drew back the felt blanket in precise, one-foot increments, folding the cloth and smoothing out the edges as he went. He set the blanket to the side and gently placed the bouquet of feathers onto the cloth, as though at any second they might turn to ash. Near the head of the box were two red candles shaped like bricks, each with a long white wick. Next to the candles sat an ornate silver treasure chest the size of a shoebox.

He spread the silk cloth onto the floor, set the chest on the cloth, and placed a candle at either side. He struck a wooden match against the side of the chest and lit the candles; the sour scent of sulfur flooding his nasal passages. Then with his thumbs, he released the two clasps on the chest, each making a single distinct *clack* as it let go. As he opened the lid, a spasm of pleasure ran through him. He pounded the floor with a clenched fist and cried out: *"What exquisite torment this is!"* Without warning, the collective roar of the congregation broke through, chanting, *"Father . . . Father . . . Father."*

He carefully reached into the chest and slipped his hands around two grayish-white ribs, grasping one in each hand, their surface smooth and comforting.

He forced himself to focus on Doris Parker and Myrna Hudson, and of the harvesting, and how innocent they looked; so still and peaceful, their gaping wounds smiling back at him. The chanting went on. *"Father . . . Father."*

But you were not innocent, were you? No, not by a long shot—not then, not now—but there will be redemption. His grip tightened, his knuckles blanching, his cartilage pressing out against his skin, white and bulbous. He raised the ribs above his head, his arms fully extended, and could feel his heart beating in his chest.

Without warning, another belly rush hit him and he buckled over. He closed his eyes, and said in a trembling voice, *"It's happening."* With his arms stretched out again, and his hands clenched tight, another surge of raw energy struck, and he cried out, "I feel you, Lord!"

The troupe wailed in response, for the connection had been made—the divine connection—God's love was there among them, tangible and real.

He held the ribs high above his head for almost a minute, then lowered his arms and returned the ribs to the chest, closing the top with a clack, clack.

He picked up the bouquet of feathers, and in long, fluid strokes waved them over the gray box, sweeping with his hand in a slow, circular motion, spiraling toward the ceiling, brushing away any and all foul spirits that might be lingering on the surface. Pushing them back to the netherworld.

Satisfied all the impurities were gone, he removed the lid and peered inside. A tender ache filled his chest. "You are so lovely, my dear," he whispered, and then rolled onto his back and gazed up at the ceiling. Tears trickled from his eyes, and as he wiped them away with the heels of his hands, he chuckled. "So, tell me again. What's the first thing you'd like to do? Oh, no . . . no—no don't tell me." His voice was suddenly giddy with excitement. "You want me to hold you in my arms, don't you?" A pause. *"What?* Oh, yes you do. You told me so, remember?" His voice sounded strained for a second, then softened. "And I will my love, you'll see . . ."

Then he rolled onto his side and reached into the box. And with the tips of his fingers, he gently stroked her dry, gray cheekbones . . .

Chapter 35

Lynchfield General Hospital consisted of a two-story main building with a wing on either side. A circular driveway was out front, its center island readied for winter; the soil turned and the shrubs wrapped in burlap.

The ER was quiet, all the chairs in the waiting area empty. The admitting clerk sat behind a glass partition, her head down, reading a paperback novel.

Josh had almost made it to the clerk when an ER nurse came around the corner and cut him off. She told him the sheriff had called ahead, and led him straight into one of the examination rooms.

The nurse took his vital signs then helped him off with his clothes and into his gown, then tied a new tourniquet, all the while asking him about his pain and medical history, then said, "The attending physician will be with you in a minute." She turned and left the room.

The doctor was taking longer than expected. Josh could hear Rachael on the other side of the curtain, quietly talking on her cell. He couldn't tell exactly what was being said, but his name was being used, and it wasn't a happy conversation. His heart sunk at the thought of her being under the thumb of Kingsley, constantly having to deal with all his bullshit, and knew, something had to give . . .

As he eyed the transfusion equipment, the red crash cart tucked away at the side of the room, the monitors and oxygen mounted on the wall, he was reminded of how hospitals often deliver bad news, and of the sadness and sorrow of those left behind.

The aching in his leg had gotten worse, and he was thinking of loosening the tourniquet, when the curtain drew back and the doctor, wearing a white lab coat with a stethoscope draped around her neck, appeared. She was a small woman, standing less than five feet tall, fragile, sparrow-like, her brown hair cut above the collar. She looked tired; the skin under her eyes puffed and tinted the color of nicotine. She studied him for a moment and smiled. It was a warm, knowing smile—it was then he knew he was in good hands.

It didn't take long for her to clean and stitch up the wound, apply the dressing and give him a shot of broad-spectrum antibiotics. "You're lucky the bullet missed the femoral. Had it not done so, you'd not be sitting here."

Josh nodded.

"Here's a prescription for codeine. It'll help you with the pain, but you shouldn't be driving." She went over the antibiotics regimen with him and advised him of warning signs to watch out for. She then told him if he should take a turn for the worse he was to come back to the hospital. Then, she walked out.

Rachael drew back the curtain and looked him over, her gaze coming to a rest on the bandaged area. "You know, an inch or two higher and you'd be singing in a higher key." He could tell she was trying to sound casual, but he knew she was worried.

"Hey, nothing to worry about. A quick stop at the pharmacy then I'm good to go." He stood up and put his clothes back on, his pant leg torn and stained with blood.

She glanced at him then looked away, followed by an awkward pause that seemed to linger.

Josh let out a breath, then said, "Wha'da ya say we get out of here?"

Chapter 36

By the time they arrived back at the hotel, the local forensic team was in full swing collecting and labeling evidence, and had begun work on sketching the scene. Halogen lights had been strategically set up around the front of the hotel, yielding a stark, harsh atmosphere that set Josh's teeth on edge, reminding him of the countless scenes he'd attended as a profiler.

They ducked under the yellow crime scene tape and made their way over to the sheriff, who was talking with a member of the CSI team.

Holly turned and saw Josh limping toward her and smiled. "That was quick. Good to see you're okay."

"Yeah, got lucky," he said. "Bullet was a small caliber, missed the bone and artery—went clear through. Gonna smart for a while, but I got these." He held up two pill bottles and gave them a shake, then asked, "Have we found the bullet?"

"Yep, but won't do us much good. Hit a nail in the wall, flattened it out like a pancake. Won't be getting much from that. But because of its mass, I'd say it's probably a .22, maybe a .22 long." She held up a small evidence bag and passed it to Josh. He examined it for a second and handed it back, nodding his concurrence.

"Josh, was very lucky," Rachael said, her tone edgy and unsettled.

"Well, don't you worry, agent," Holly said. "I'll take good care of *our* boy."

"*Right*," Rachael said. "So, where exactly are we at?"

Holly turned her back to Rachael, directing her attention to Josh. "You were correct about the perp's location. We found a couple of boot prints by the shrubs next to the hickory tree. We're doing the plaster casts now." She pointed to where a couple of techs were busy preparing the casts.

"The casing?" Josh asked.

"Not yet . . . combing the area as we speak," Holly said, her back still to Rachael. "And I know the answer, Josh, at least I think I do, but is there anyone who—?"

"Look, Josh." Rachael spoke up. "I can see I'm not needed here, so I'll catch you in the morning." She turned and walked toward the hotel. Without looking back, she said, "Good night, Sheriff."

Holly watched Rachael as she climbed the steps and walked inside the hotel. "Your boss seems to take a personal interest in you, Josh. If I didn't know better—"

"Sheriff!" one of the techs called out from under the hickory tree. "Found it, found the casing!"

Holly paused to consider what the tech had said, then replied, "Good work."

They walked over to the tree and the crime scene guy handed Holly a pencil with the casing stuck on its end, the brass tilted to one side like a top hat.

"A .22 long," Josh said.

Holly nodded, then turned to the tech and handed the pencil back. "Get this off to ballistics and put a rush on it. . . . Okay Josh, so tell me, any idea who's got it in for you?"

Josh shrugged. "Don't know. Not around here, anyway."

"Your getting shot kind of contradicts that statement. How about from that camp of lowlifes?"

"Thought about it, but don't think so. The guy I dealt with would be in no shape to do much, and the others . . . ? Nah, killing in cold-blood takes a special breed." He sighed, letting out a long breath.

With the adrenaline rush subsided and his frontal lobes marinated in a combination of pharmaceutical goo and the residual brandy still left in his blood stream, he was finding it tough to stay alert. "Holly, I think I'm gonna call it a night."

She sized him up for a second. "Okay, but you'll stay with me tonight." Her tone suggesting it was not up for discussion. "In case of complications," she added.

"Ah, sure. Thanks, but I'll be okay. I won't be sleeping well anyway, probably thrash about all night, keep us both awake." It was another lame excuse, and he could see she wasn't taking it well. "C'mon, I'll be all right."

"Yeah . . . no, it's not all right," she said, almost sneering. "All right, have it your way. But I'm posting a deputy at the hotel tonight."

"Not necessary," he said. "The perp won't be trying again, not for a while, not with the hornets all riled."

"Just the same, the deputy will be there."

~ ~ ~

Back in his hotel room, Josh poured himself a brandy, downing it in one gulp when his cell rang.

"You doing okay?" Mary asked.

"Yeah, a couple of stitches, that's all. How about you?"

"Actually, I'm feeling better. The last purge seemed to clean me out. Should be ready to roll in the morning." She paused. "Can I bring you anything? Anything you need?"

Josh smiled. "No, I'm good. How about you? You need anything? Some chicken soup, a glass of warm goat's milk perhaps?"

He could hear her laugh. "A good night's sleep is all I need," she said. "Be ready to go in the morning."

"Good to hear. Good night Mary."

"Night, Josh."

Chapter 37

Incense pots the size of grapefruits dotted the tent floor, spewing out steady streams of smoke. The wavering cords nurtured the cloud above, feeding it and keeping it alive. The pungent aroma, a brew of pine needle and cedar, circulated among the ragged rows of the faithful, their eager faces turned toward Father Paul, chanting, "Father. Father."

Carl and Hanna sat in the front row a few feet apart. Tears welled in Hanna's eyes as she watched the spectacle unfold.

Father Paul was standing on a stage, his black robe reaching down to the wooden surface. A thick gold chain with a large golden cross, hung from his neck. He was staring up into the tent canopy, the hood of his robe flat on his back, his arms stretched out to the heavens. He lowered his hands and brought his line of sight down to the troupe, and they all fell silent.

A long moment passed, then in a thundering voice, Father Paul shouted, "We seek thee oh LORD for your divine guidance, for one of our flock has strayed! We are troubled oh Lord, for without loyalty there can be no trust—no bond with you Lord, our savior. Without loyalty, the bond that ties our imperfect souls to you becomes weak, and we are tempted by sin.

"For without loyalty, we cannot enter paradise! We cannot be with you. Oh Lord! Show us the way—we beg of you."

The chanting started again, "Father. Father."

Father Paul closed his eyes. He could feel their want, their need, for they were his children.

Then he opened his eyes and they fell silent.

"We seek thee oh LORD, for only your mercy will save the lost one. We beg of you, make her whole again so she may experience your love and enter your divine kingdom. We ask for forgiveness of her sins—redeem her, make her whole again, we beg of you!"

"Father. Father," the troupe chanted, its pitch rising.

Father Paul nodded to Alvin, who was standing near the back wall of the tent. Angel was at his side, her wrists tied to her waist with a thick white rope. Alvin grabbed her by the arm and started walking her down the aisle toward the stage. Angel grimaced, favoring her one leg, making their progress slow while the troupe continued chanting . . .

"Yes, bring the lost one to me," Father Paul commanded.

Angel stepped onto the stage, bowed her head and started to cry. Alvin sneered and kicked the back of her legs, causing her to fall to her knees. Angel cried out in pain, then raised her head to Father Paul and whispered, "Please, please have mercy . . ."

Father Paul placed his hand on her head, raised his other hand high in the air, and shouted, "Only through cleansing, can glorious redemption be achieved and everlasting life entered into."

"Praise be our Father!" the troupe called out.

Father Paul looked down upon the troupe. "And I shall deliver her, our cleansed one, into God's loving arms, where she will be freed from the evils of temptation, free to love God for all eternity."

Alvin dragged Angel to her feet, keeping one hand on her shoulder and the other on her lower back. Together, he and Father Paul guided her off the stage, through the crowd and out into the night air, the troupe following at their heels.

At the doorway to his meditation trailer, Father Paul stopped, lifted Angel's chin with his hand, and kissed her on her forehead. He turned to the crowd. "And our sister shall be saved! Glory to God!"

"Glory to God!" the troupe cried in unison.

Angel and Father Paul entered the trailer and the door closed, all while the brethren chanted, "Praise the Lord. Praise our Father."

Hanna closed her eyes and wept . . .

~ ~ ~

The chanting had endured for close to two hours when the door finally opened and Father Paul stepped out of his trailer. He spread his arms and called upon Hanna to come forward and pay her respects to her mother.

Hanna entered the trailer and a minute later re-emerged, her face moist with fresh tears, holding her mother's neatly folded clothes in her hands. She made her way through the troupe, entered the big tent and fell to her knees.

One by one the faithful entered the meditation chamber to bear witness. And once inside, they saw Angel had indeed been delivered to the house of the Lord, for she was gone.

Chapter 38

With his hunched shoulders, thinning gray hair in full retreat and clearly crossing over to the losing team, Hollister Hardwick didn't look his full six feet, three inches. He had a pained expression on his face, born from an unforgiving ulcer that forced him to eat bland foods, what he considered 'cardboard fodder'. But what was really annoying him today was that his allergies were threatening an encore performance. For him, winter couldn't come soon enough. He'd been sitting on a bench, cooling his heels outside the sheriff's office, for close to an hour when Josh and Mary arrived.

"By the way you're walking, I'd say you'd be Josh Ingram," Hollister said. "Name's Hollister Hardwick, retired Marshall."

"Glad to meet you, Marshall," Josh said, and turned to Mary. "This is Mary Kowalski, she's assisting on the investigation with the church murders."

Hollister seemed to perk up upon seeing Mary. The color now back in her cheeks, her eyes bright and looking healthy again.

"Marshall," Mary said, shaking his hand.

"Just Hollister, as I said. I'm retired. Pulled the plug a few years back." He grabbed the door handle. "Shall we go inside? Sheriff Holly's not in, in fact you just missed her. But I sure could use a cup of Joe about now."

They went inside. Josh poured their coffees from the fresh pot on the counter, and they each took a seat by the potbellied stove.

Josh spoke first. "Sheriff Holly said you're investigating a shooting that occurred some time ago. A cold case, and the perp you're looking for could be the same one who shot me?"

"Victim was shot once in the thigh, just like you," Hollister replied. "But he bled out before anyone could find him, poor bastard."

Josh said nothing.

Mary asked, "How'd you find out so fast? About Josh, I mean?"

"The sheriff, she's as efficient as she is pretty. Sent me photos of the casing, knowing I'd be on it like a raccoon on pork rind. Plus, I still have a few friends on the force."

"You said, 'just like me'?" Josh asked.

"The markings on your .22 casing are a perfect match to the file I've been working on."

"Yeah? So, how old is your file?"

"About seven years, give or take. But it's the same gun all right."

"Fuck me," Josh muttered.

"Someone trying to. That's for sure, son."

"So, you're retired?" Mary asked, her eyes questioning. "Ahh—you're a *dick?*"

"My ex certainly thinks so, but no, just helping out an old friend. It was her son who was killed. The boy's mother has got a backbone of iron. Determined as hell that the murderer be brought to justice."

Josh straightened his leg and winced. "So, what've you dug up so far on the other shooting?"

Hollister pursed his lips and shrugged. "Not much. Got bugger all to be precise, 'cept the casing came from a '63 Winchester, 1st production year, 1933. Not many of those puppies still kicking around, mostly locked up in collectors' closets or museums. Perp never left much behind, seems to be a tidy fella."

"Motive?" Josh asked.

"That's the thing, doesn't appear to be one. Nothing I've been able to come up with. Could've chalked it up to a random act of unkindness, that is, until today. Now, with you getting shot by the same gun . . ." He reached into the inside pocket of his leather jacket and handed Josh two casing pictures, one from each shooting.

"Whereabouts did the son get shot?" Josh asked as he opened the envelope.

Hollister walked over to the state map thumbtacked to the wall. "It occurred here," he said, pointing to a spot on the map. "About twenty miles northwest, just across the county line."

"The killer's from around here then," Josh said.

"Kinda looks that way. Here, or somewhere close-by. Of course, there could be other conclusions, but I can't think of one, unless you believe in coincidences." He paused for a moment and frowned. "But no, I like to run with variables I can see right out in front of me. I'm betting the killer lives close-by."

"Any details as to how the perp goes about it? Anything peculiar?" Mary asked.

"No. Only that he uses the Winchester." He took a moment before continuing. "Of course, with Josh here being shot by the same gun, there could be more victims."

They all remained silent for a moment.

"Yeah. Okay," Mary said. "But if the shooter is local, why take a shot at Josh? He's not from around here."

Hollister didn't reply.

Josh handed the pictures back to Hollister, and asked, "So, what's the backstory on your client's son?"

"Not much to tell. Good kid, good-looking, good family. He was on his way home from university for the Christmas break. Was about to graduate from medical school, I understand. He'd stopped in at Cherry's Bar, that's near Campbell Falls, fifteen minutes west of here. Well the owner, Cherry, she said she remembered him because he was, and I quote, 'a strapping hunk of beef jerky'. Not too sure exactly what that means, but I know I ain't got it." He glanced at Mary. "Cherry told me he was with a girl that night, but she was tending bar and didn't get a good look at her."

"Did any of the waitresses see her, the girl he was with?" Mary asked.

"A couple did, and no they couldn't describe her, it being Saturday night. Told me Saturdays they get run off their feet. I have to say, I know this to be true—spent a few nights there myself."

"But they remembered him?" Josh asked.

"You got it. All did, the ones I talked to anyway. Seemed to focus on how handsome he was."

"Cherry still around?" Mary asked.

"I'm sure she is. Why, you thinking of heading that way?"

Mary glanced at Josh. "Why not? I'm not needed much around here at the moment, and it'd feel good to be doing something useful for a few hours, something I could maybe sink my teeth into."

Josh shrugged. "Yeah sure, why not? See what you can find."

Hardwick turned to Mary. "Mary, you mind if I come along?"

Chapter 39

Cherry's Bar stood out against the Minnesota skyline like a Siberian Yurt. Its near-round shape, white clapboard siding, and octagonal roof sporting a rooster weathervane had all the charm and warmth of smallpox blister.

Three late model pickups were parked in a row near the middle of the parking lot, the lunch hour sun glinting off their windshields. Near the bar's entrance was a white supply van with mud splattered across its side, partially covering red stenciled letters that read: *Loo's Country Fresh Chicken.* At the far end of the lot sat a lime-green Gremlin with a golf ball stuck on the tip of its aerial, its front driver's-side tire flat.

Inside, a multicolored jukebox with gold trim was playing a hurtin' cowboy ballad. The air smelled of burnt onions, refried beans, stale beer, and decades of nicotine soaked walls. A scrawny bald kid, his foot resting on the edge of a white wooden stage, was busy tuning his electric guitar. A forty-something plump woman with long, stringy black hair had her belly pressed up against the bar and was licking the salt off the rim of a martini glass as Mary and Hollister walked in. Her beady eyes followed them as they made their way over to a booth by the front window.

They sat down, and when a waitress came by they each ordered a pint of ale.

"So, I take it you know Cherry?" Mary asked.

"Yeah, I suppose you could say that."

"Uh-huh. That meaning?"

Hollister smirked. "Cherry and I go back some. She had a thing for me, you see. Still does, I believe."

Mary raised an eyebrow and took a moment to give Hollister the once-over. He wasn't a handsome man, not now anyway, but in his youth he probably wasn't that hard to look at. *Pleasant enough, that's for sure,* she thought, *but definitely not a chick-magnet—more of a 'you're safe with me, I'll take good care of you,' kind of guy.*

Hollister must've sensed Mary was checking him out, as he suddenly seemed to find something interesting about one of the buttons on his shirtsleeve.

By the time the drinks arrived Mary was amazed to find herself still thinking about him. *Huh, I wonder what makes this guy tick?* She was fully prepared to pursue a further moment of reflection when a woman appeared at the table, wearing a name tag that simply read: *Cherry.* The woman looked to be somewhere north of fifty-five, had on a bit too much makeup, big blonde hair, and an arrogant look that made Mary's eyes narrow.

"Hollister Hardwick. What's brought your sorry ass into my little corner of the world?" the woman asked, a vinegar spray bottle in one hand and a roll of paper towels in the other.

Hollister glanced up from his shirtsleeve with a surprised look on his face. "Jesus, Cherry, you could give a man a heart attack, sneaking up on him like that."

"Hollister, the only beat you got is between those big hairy thighs of yours, and I can't say I've sensed a pulse there for some time."

Hollister cleared his throat and glanced at Mary.

Cherry turned to Mary. "Sorry hun, me and H.H. we were sweethearts back in the day. I like to have a little fun with him, meant no harm."

"Hmm. I'm thinking I might've liked to have known *Harry Thighs* in those days myself," Mary said, smiling at Hollister.

"You and half the girls in the county," Cherry said, then started to chuckle.

"Actually," Mary said, "we've come to ask you some questions about Daniel Samson."

Cherry turned to Hollister. "What? Big H not filled you in? He's grilled me on that boy so many times, you could ring the dinner bell." Then in a sweet voice, she added, "Haven't ya darlin'?"

Mary's gaze slid to Hollister then back to Cherry. "I told him I wanted to hear it from you direct, without him mucking up the details with his take on things."

"Well in that case, I'd be happy to tell you what I know, but there's really not that much to tell." She cleared her throat. "You see, we all knew Danny, 'cause he was a local boy. Not to mention the fine hunk of beef he'd grown into. He had all the gals in the county salivating, ready to eat him alive." She tore off a sheet of paper towel and dabbed her forehead and neck. "Godawful thing it was though, him getting killed like that. Well anyway, as I've told Hollister, the last time I saw him was that Saturday night. Now, you gotta understand, this place always has some kind of action going on, but Friday and Saturday nights, it's busier than a 600 pound gorilla's colon in a corn dog eating contest."

"That busy?" Mary asked.

Cherry nodded, then paused to mull things over, and said, "Well, that Saturday night the barkeep, he'd called in sick, so I had to manage on my own—if you can imagine. Didn't even have time to powder my nose. But, a hottie like Danny—yeah sure, I noticed him."

"And he was with someone?"

"Yes, he was. A blonde, as I recall. Didn't see much of her though, other than the back of her head. And, the next time I looked they were gone. What can I say, time flies when the place is a rockin'."

"Did you notice anything unusual about the woman? The clothes she was wearing, shoes, anything at all?"

"No, sorry hun. Like I said, it was busy that night." She hesitated for a moment, as though she was trying to decide if she should say more. "But you might want to call on Francine, she was Danny's girl for the longest time. Come to think of it, she has blonde hair too."

"And you're sure she wasn't the blonde girl in the booth that night?" Hollister asked, his face registering this as new information.

"Oh, heck no. Francine's close to six feet tall, skinny, model like, no mistaking her."

"You know Francine's last name?" Mary asked.

"Sure do. It's Mather, Francine Mather. Lives with her parents, about a quarter-mile south of my place. She went back to school, and I understand she's almost finished her nursing degree over in Parkerville and will be moving out soon. Parents pretty happy about that."

Cherry wrote down the directions on a strip of paper towel and passed it to Mary.

Chapter 40

The road leading to the Mather house was narrow, with long stretches of washboard gravel. Mary eased off on the gas, letting the rental's suspension absorb most of the vibration, and glanced over at Hollister. He was smiling and tapping his thumb on his knee as though he had a tune playing in his head. She wasn't sure what to think of him. He seemed like a decent sort, as far as men went. And it'd been ages since a man, any man for that matter, had shown an interest in her. And if her inkling was on target, maybe, just maybe, he actually did like her, and *that* would take some getting used to. She cranked the wheel and turned onto a dirt driveway, continuing another fifty yards before rolling to a stop in front of a house.

The home, a 1960s vintage rancher, had a covered veranda that ran along its front. There was a red swing set on the front lawn next to a sandbox made from what looked like discarded lumber. Mary stepped out into the afternoon sun and had raised her hand to block the glare when the screen door flung open, slamming hard against the wood siding, and a girl, maybe four years of age, ran down the steps and onto the front lawn.

"You can't catch me, Grandma!" the girl yelled, glancing over her shoulder.

There was no Grandma in sight, but a chicken feeding by the swing set poked its head up, clearly startled, its indignant, orb-like body gone rigid for a second before it took off, making a beeline for under the porch.

A few seconds later a tall, thin, angular woman, the skin on her face tanned and weathered, opened the screen door and took notice of Mary and Hollister. She stopped and stared, her mouth turned down at the edges and asked, "Can I help you?"

"We're with the FBI, and we're looking for Francine Mather," Mary said.

"Yeah, she lives here. This here's her home."

"We were hoping to have a word with her," Hardwick said.

A moment of recognition flickered in the woman's eyes. "Hollister, is that you?" She started to smile, as though she was dredging up an old memory, then the frown returned to her face, and she turned back to Mary. "What'd you want to talk to my daughter about?"

The screen door opened again and an even taller, thin woman, maybe thirty years of age, walked out. She was wearing blue jeans, a pink sweater, white sneakers, and a baseball cap that covered most of her blonde hair.

"Francine," her mother said. "These people are from the FBI and have come to ask you a few questions."

Francine's gaze shifted to Hollister.

"What sort of questions, momma?"

"Heck if I know, we're just getting to it."

"It's about Daniel Samson," Mary said. "There's been another shooting, and we're thinking it could be the same shooter."

Francine considered Mary for a long moment, and then sighed. "Maybe we all should take a seat." She pointed to a round table and four chairs at the end of the veranda. "Would you like some tea? I've made a fresh pot."

Mary and Hollister both accepted.

"Momma, would you bring out the tea? And maybe some of those coconut cookies you made this morning?"

Francine's mother went back inside, returning a minute later with a tray holding a teapot, three cups, and a small stack of cookies. She set the tray down on the table and went out into the yard to play with her granddaughter.

Francine poured the tea, then asked, "Okay. I'm not so sure I understand. What do you mean, you think it's the same shooter?"

"The same gun was used in both shootings," Mary said.

"*Ohh,* I see," Francine said.

"We understand you and Daniel were once an item?"

"Yes, that was some time ago, but you're right, we were. And then he left me."

"For another woman?" Mary asked, and took a sip of her tea.

"Yes, that is correct," Francine said, a crisp tone to her voice.

"Were you aware of anything unusual going on around the time of his death?" Hollister asked.

Francine's face screwed up, the skin around her eyes tightening. "Unusual? Yeah, I guess . . . he'd been screwing that slut, if that's what you mean."

"And I take it you didn't like that?" Hollister asked.

"No, *sir.* I did not."

Mary shot Hollister a questioning look, then asked Francine, "Do you know who he was seeing?"

Francine took a second to respond, gazing out over the yard. "No, but that bitch was the reason he left me. Never did find out who she was, Daniel wouldn't tell me. I tried to get it out of him. Even tried to follow him once. He must've seen me though, because he lost me. Felt pretty stupid about it afterwards. Decided it wasn't worth it, and let it drop."

"Must've hurt bad," Mary said. "Letting him go."

"Yeah, it did. Hurt a lot. But it wasn't a few weeks later when we'd started talking again. He told me he was sorry and wanted to get back together."

"So, he'd broke it off with the other woman?" Hollister asked.

"That's what he told me. He said she took it hard, but he'd made up his mind. Told me he'd never loved a woman like he loved me."

Mary rolled her eyes. "And you bought that load of horseshit?"

Francine bit down on her lip, her eyes welling. "I loved him, and I still do."

Mary looked over at the swing set and pointed. "That's your daughter I take it?"

Francine answered with a half-smile and started fiddling with her wedding ring, rolling it back and forth with her thumb.

"How long have you been married?"

"Going on five years now. Glen, he's a good man."

"Did Daniel ever say anything about the other woman, give you any details?" Hollister asked.

"Just that she pursued him, that he wasn't looking. That it just sort of happened." Francine stuck her jaw out as though she was about to make a declaration. "And I truly believed him . . . that he wasn't looking."

Mary swallowed hard, trying to control an urge to slap Francine upside the head. Then she took a long look at Francine and saw the woman fighting back the tears. "Well shit, Francine. *Love*, it can make a fool of anyone."

Francine raised her eyes to Mary. "Can't it just."

A few more minutes went by, and when it was clear they'd reached a dead end, they finished their tea and said their goodbyes. On their way back to the car, Hollister's cell started to vibrate. He dug it out of his jacket pocket. "Yeah, Hollister. Oh, hi Sis . . . un-huh, yeah, *seriously?* Okay, okay I understand. Sure, okay, I'll be there. Calm down . . . *I said, I'll be there.*" He hung up.

"Trouble?" Mary asked.

"Sister's kid. Got caught with a bag of Ecstasy. Got him in lockup, in Duluth. Said I'd go down and see what I can do."

"Will you be gone long?" Mary asked. Her tone sounded as though she wanted him to stay, and she immediately wished she'd kept her mouth shut. She wasn't in the habit of letting her guard down.

Hollister started to smile. "Maybe a day or two. See how things go." His smile broadened. "So, Mary. You gonna be able to manage without me?"

Mary huffed. *"You asshole."*

Hollister started to laugh.

Chapter 41

Josh spent the early morning hours going back over the case files, hoping to find something, anything, that would lead them to Lana, but came up empty-handed. He reread the notes on Lyle Carpenter, about him being brought up within the 'system', his last set of foster parents having left town a month before the trial began, retiring to Florida. Then he checked online for the quickest route to Zuma Penitentiary, followed by a second unsuccessful attempt at setting up a meeting with retired deputy, Horst Rutland. Each time he'd tried, Rutland's wife said her husband wasn't well and could not be disturbed.

At ten o'clock he tossed the files back into the box and headed out to meet Rachael. They had a late breakfast, then spent the rest of the day chasing down leads, working through the list of people who knew Myrna Hudson. But other than hearing what a fine citizen Myrna was, and how shocked they all were, they'd gotten nowhere.

Rachael was scheduled to take a late conference call with Kingsley. Then she had to touch base with Vivian and Charley, and catch up with the remainder of her team in New York who were working on other files.

Josh returned to the hotel.

~ ~ ~

Josh plunked himself down on his bed and was thinking about what he should do for supper when a call came through on his cell. It was from retired deputy, Horst Rutland's, wife. She said her husband was now awake and alert, but he'd better hurry if he still wanted to see him.

~ ~ ~

Josh slowed the rental and turned off of Main Street, then headed two miles west on Highway 14, then 13 miles straight north on Route 117, passed the squatters' camp, then hung a left and continued another 10 miles or so to the Rutland ranch.

Josh was feeling more alert than he had all day. He'd purposely skipped his last dose of codeine, wanting a clear and focused mind for the meeting with Horst, but kept a couple of pills in his pocket just in case.

A near-full moon, the color of a ripe pumpkin, was rising on the horizon and dominated the sky. Josh rolled the car to a stop on the outer lip of an oiled driveway, a few feet short of the front porch.

The house was a small bungalow in need of repair. The porch listed hard to one side and the clapboard siding was blistered and peeling. A single flower box below the front window was chockfull of weeds, the clover heads hanging over its edge like seasick sailors.

A gray-haired woman, maybe mid-sixties, wearing an apron covered in yellow daisies over a blue denim dress and holding a dirty white rag in her hand, watched from the front door as Josh got out of his car.

She wiped her hands on a clean part of the rag. "You'd be Mr. Ingram, I take it?" she asked, opening the door.

"Yeah. And I'm sorry about the hour."

She half-shrugged. "Been married to Horst most of my life, and a good deal of that time he was a cop. It is what it is. Come on in, he's been expecting you."

Josh climbed the staircase, trying not to wince as the stitches pinched his skin, his thigh still sore and swollen. He forced a tight smile and followed her inside. The place was warm and humid, smelling of spilt piss and rotting cabbage.

"I have to warn you, Horst's not having a lot of fun tonight. Grab a seat, I'll see if he's decent." She disappeared behind a tattered curtain made from a white bedspread.

Josh could hear whispers followed by a hawking sound and then a nose being blown. The woman came out from behind the makeshift curtain with a half-full bedpan in her hands. "He'll see you now."

Josh, trying not to breathe through his nose, drew back the curtain and entered the space. The smell of urine and festering flesh was ripe, causing his throat to tighten. The man before him was gaunt, bald and skeletal. There was an intravenous line draining into his emaciated left arm. In his right hand, he held a red button attached to a white plastic cord that led to an analgesic pump.

"Gotta make this quick," Horst said, his voice straining as he raised the red button a little higher. "Don't know how long I can last. The pain, it's bad . . ."

Josh cleared his throat. "Okay, then I'll get right down to it. I'm hoping you can give me some background on Holly's father when he was the sheriff."

Horst said nothing.

"He *was* the town's sheriff at the time of Lyle Carpenter's trial. Correct?"

"Yeah, what of it?"

"Like I said, I want to get some background on him. Just what kind of cop was he? Was he a good man?

Horst glanced to the side and grimaced, then returned his gaze to Josh. "Son, are any of us . . . *good* men?"

Point taken, Josh thought. "The way I figure it, we're all shades of good and bad. Some shades darker than others. So tell me . . . what shade was he?"

Horst tried to give a wry smile, but it failed to surface. He shifted his weight and sighed. "I hear you've been sniffing around town, checking into the murders up at the church, and the murder of that Senator Parker, so it'd be my guess you're thinking there's a connection to Lyle Carpenter's trial?" Horst raised an expectant eyebrow.

"That's about right."

"Hey, I'm dying, but I ain't stupid." Horst grunted and shifted his weight again, trying to find a comfortable position. "So you'd better get to the point, son, because I'm about done here," he said, placing his thumb on the button.

"It's to do with the case files. They've been scrubbed clean, like, really clean. I don't get it. I mean, why bother? They had three credible eyewitnesses, and the murder weapon with both the perp's prints and the victim's blood on it. Case closed. No need to sanitize."

"You really think that?" Horst asked, his tone bordering on disgust.

"No, actually I don't. And that, Horst, is why I'm here."

"Well, good for you. Um . . . ? Ah hell, whatever your name is," Horst said, his thumb still resting on the button.

"I'm Josh Ingram."

"I know who you are. You being a smartass with me?"

"No, I'm not. So tell me. Why cull the files?"

"Ahh, Christ," Horst said, a pained grin on his face as he turned his head to the window. "Such a green-as-grass deputy I was back then." He paused, then started to cough, a dry rasping hack that seemed to suck all the wind out of him. It took a few seconds for him to recover. "Not that I was young, hell no. I'd got laid off at the factory . . . Holly's daddy, he did me a good turn back then, giving me the job . . . likely 'cause our families go back some. But I was green, there's no denying it. Zippity-do-da-day, couldn't spot a lead if one sat on my face. So really, what the hell did I know?" He tried to laugh, but grimaced instead, and then looked directly at Josh. "But, answer me this. Why is it that I, who didn't have a lick of horse sense, could see the sheriff wasn't acting right . . . being all secretive like? If I saw it back then, then it must've been real, you hear what I'm saying?"

Josh remained silent.

"Well, shit! Holly's daddy, he held onto those files like a teenager with a stack of girly magazines, wouldn't let no one else see'm. I mean, I was just a green deputy back in the day, but I could tell he wasn't thinking straight . . ." Horst twisted his torso and groaned.

"Why do you think he did that, kept the files so close?"

"Don't know for sure. I did ask him, but he just told me it was a big case and he didn't want any screw-ups. Then he told me if he caught me messing around with 'em, I'd be finished, that's for sure."

"But you think there's more to it?"

"Hell yeah. I mean, why be such a prick about it? Didn't have to be, that's how I see it."

Josh thought about it for a second, then asked, "So, what do you think he was hiding?"

"Don't know. Guess, we'll never know. Not now, anyway."

Horst eyeballed Josh. "Hear you've been seeing Holly." His face soured. "You're one lucky son-of-a-bitch her daddy's dead, or he'd been doing you good."

Josh didn't say a word and just stared at the man.

"Now, don't get me wrong, her daddy was a decent cop. But we all got our weaknesses. His was Holly. And after his wife up and left him, he turned all his attention to his little girl."

"And?"

"And she could do no wrong."

"Yeah. So what?"

"So, he'd fix you up good right about now, if he thought you were tapping that fine ass of hers." Another shot of pain hit, he winced and pressed the red button. "Now Holly's brother, that was another story. The sheriff, he never did take to his son."

"And why was that?"

"Don't know, could never make sense of it, them kids coming from the same stock. But the fact of the matter is, I don't think the mother liked her son much either. Hey, don't get me wrong, both of them kids were always a little off. Just like their momma, all three cut from the same cloth. But why both Holly's momma and daddy didn't take to Lance, I don't know."

"What was Holly's mother like?"

"Pretty, just like Holly. She and Holly had left town . . . when Holly was . . ." His voice was tapering off to a whisper. The morphine had taken over. A second later his eyes grew dim and closed.

His wife drew back the curtain. "No sense trying to talk to him now, he's gone for the night."

Chapter 42

The wagon was dark inside as Hanna lay curled up on her bunk bed, knees drawn to her chest. She was thinking about her mother and how much she missed her, wishing she was there by her side—that they could escape together and always be together. Then she thought of Mortimer, of how much she missed him and how good it would be to hold him again.

All that stood in her way was her father. Carl had been drinking heavily all evening, moaning about Angel and how she'd let him down, and had only climbed into bed when the bottle was dry. Now all she had to do was wait for him to drift off.

Close to an hour had gone by when he finally started his usual routine of weak gasps and annoying sputters. It was one of many things she hated about him, things she loathed. But tonight was different. Tonight, it meant freedom.

She carefully slid out of her bunk, sidestepping a metal bucket half-full of water, grabbed her dress and her boots, and tiptoed out of the wagon and down the steps to the tent floor. It was dark, except for a light left on by the entrance flaps of the big tent. The troupe had turned in for the night and the camp was quiet. The air was chill and smelled of burnt wood and wet canvas.

She slipped her dress over her head. It was cold and damp, and she shivered. Then she pulled on her boots, tied them, and headed for the pigpen.

The pen was enclosed by a chicken wire fence. Its gate was constructed with yet more chicken wire attached to a hockey stick with its blade cut off. The stick was connected to a gatepost by two wire loops, one at the bottom and one at the top. Hanna lifted the top loop off first, then pulled the stick out of the bottom loop and swung the gate open.

The pigs were flopped out in the mud, lying on their sides like bloated river rocks. All were asleep except for Clarice, an enormous sow, her snout in the mud, her teats jutting out like engorged pencil erasers that ran down her belly in neat parallel rows.

Clarice raised her head as Hanna stepped into the pen. She blinked once, held her focus on Hanna for no more than a second, then laid her head back down in the mud, her small, pink eyeball peering through a thin slit in her eyelids.

"Mortimer," Hanna whispered. "Mortimer it's me. Come on out, sweetie." She waited for a response, but got none. "Don't be scared. It's me, Hanna. I've come to take you with me."

Again, nothing. Seconds passed, and Hanna began to tremble as the thought of never seeing Mortimer again entered her mind. Then her eye caught movement behind the trough at the far end of the pen. A second later, Mortimer stuck his head out and upon seeing her, squealed and came racing toward her, tripping halfway, plowing his face into the mud, then scrambled to his feet and made the final dash, running into her arms. She cradled him, holding him tight to her chest, and could feel his heart pounding.

She kissed his forehead, over and over, and told him nothing would ever separate them again.

With Mortimer secured in the crook of her arm, she slipped the top loop back over the hockey stick and headed out. From there it was a short sprint to the edge of the camp and into the forest.

She'd gone barely fifty feet into the forest when a sliver of light appeared. As she got closer the light grew stronger and brighter, illuminating the lower branches of a stand of poplars.

She crouched down and duck-walked toward the light. Suddenly, she came to an abrupt halt, jamming her boots into the dirt. She could see two men standing by a 45-gallon drum set near the light. And while she couldn't see either of their faces, she was sure the taller of the two was Father Paul. They were talking about something, but she was too far away. She placed her hand gently over Mortimer's mouth and whispered to him to keep quiet.

As she edged closer, she was able to make out a few of their words, but couldn't connect them to anything that made sense. She crept closer, inching forward on the wet forest floor until she was standing in the shadow of a large maple. She knew she should turn and run, disappear into the woods . . . but something inside her was making her stay.

She peered around the edge of the maple tree. The bark felt rough against her skin, scraping her cheek. There was a single kerosene lamp on the ground, its harsh white light spreading across a carpet of fallen leaves.

Father Paul was wearing long gray underwear that covered most of his body, plus a red winter vest. On his hands were bright yellow gloves, and on his feet were black rubber boots that rode halfway up his calves.

He bent his long frame over, his back to her, his yellow gloves busy at work. She poked her head out a few more inches for a better view, careful to keep within the tree's shadow.

Father Paul was tying off the end of a rolled tarp that was lumpy and bulging at its middle. Once again, Hanna knew she had to get out of there, leave, and never return. She put her lips to Mortimer's ear and whispered, "One more minute, then we're gone for good, I promise."

Without warning, Father Paul turned his head in her direction and she gasped. A leather-like mask was riding high on his forehead. It had large, goggle lens and what appeared to be a small tin can somehow attached to it.

Father Paul continued to scan the area, then stopped—he was looking right at her. Hanna withdrew her head behind the tree, willing herself not to cry out, and held her breath.

A full minute passed before she had the nerve to look again.

Father Paul had returned to his task, his yellow gloves once again working fast, tying up the other end of the tarp. He straightened his back and waved the other man over. As the man came into view, Hanna recognized his clothes, and a second later, recognized him. It was Alvin. He was wearing a simple white dust mask and had his silver whistle around his neck.

Alvin picked up one end of the rolled tarp and Father Paul the other. Together, they carried it to the drum, leaning it up against a tree.

Alvin pried the drum lid off with a crowbar, tossing the lid on the ground next to a collection of glass containers, one the size of a cookie jar, plus two other, smaller jars. Lying next to the containers was a canoe paddle.

Together, the men hoisted the rolled tarp high into the air, and stuck one end into the drum. Hanna could see the tarp was too long for the drum, its one end protruding.

The men made a number of attempts to get the offending portion down into the drum, grunting and cussing as they did, but the tarp was stiff, and wouldn't bend.

"I told you we waited too long!" Alvin cried, panic in his eyes. "It isn't gonna fit, is it?"

Father Paul frowned. "Emotion is the Devil's work, my son. Now calm yourself, and help me take it out."

After pulling the tarp from the drum and setting it down on the ground, Father Paul made a time-out gesture with his gloved hands. He took a step back and placed his hands on his hips, looking as though he was giving the situation his due consideration. Then he turned on his heel and walked back to camp, returning a few minutes later with an axe in his hand—a large, double-headed axe.

Alvin cocked his head, a pained grin crossing his face.

Father Paul walked over to the tarp and set his stance, his legs wide apart. He raised the axe high into the air, pausing for a split second, tightening his grip, then brought the instrument down hard, gravity pulling on his hands, the arc of the blade cutting through the night sky in a blur and sinking deep into the earth. Missing its mark.

Father Paul stood motionless for a second, then pulled the mask off his forehead and scratched at his hairline. Putting the mask back on, he began rolling his shoulders in a slow circular motion, loosening them as though he was a gymnast readying himself for competition. He raised the blade again, and this time brought it down in one clean, fluid stroke, the blade cutting into the tarp and yielding a dull, wet thud. It took a few more full-throttle swings before he'd severed the tarp in two, the axe head now glistening red and dripping.

Hanna's heart thumped against her ribcage as though it might explode.

The men dumped the smaller chunk of the tarp in the barrel first, and it dropped out of sight. The second chunk, the thicker piece, came next. They stuck the wet end in first and tried repositioning it a few times, but it was of no use, it still wouldn't fit.

Father Paul muttered something under his breath and pushed Alvin aside. Then he picked up the axe and turned it upside down, raised the axe head, and began tamping the troublesome piece down into the barrel. Inch by inch the tarp sunk, and had all but disappeared when a small flap fell open, exposing a bloodless, gray hand. The next thrust of the axe crumpled the fingers, and the hand slid out of sight.

Hanna took a step back and was about to turn and run, when Mortimer let out a squeal. She grabbed him tight, holding her hand over his mouth, her mind racing. She had to run, she had to get away, but her legs were frozen and wouldn't move. She closed her eyes. *What if he is looking this way? What if he heard? Oh God, what if he's coming?* She wanted to look, to confirm that he wasn't coming, but she didn't dare, how could she?

She opened her eyes . . .

Chapter 43

Father Paul had returned to the drum and was leaning over it. He had the cookie jar in one hand, and a green garden hose in the other, its end somewhere inside the drum. Hanna could hear water splashing around as he emptied what looked like cotton balls out of the jar and into the drum.

Father Paul turned his head in Hanna's direction. The mask was now covering his face, but she could still see his eyes shifting behind the big lenses. Suddenly, he shook his head and pulled the mask off. He spit on the eyepieces and wiped them on his long underwear, then held the mask out in front of him toward the light and frowned. He tried cleaning them again, then stopped and began pinching at his eyes. He stomped his foot on the ground and gave his head another shake, then quickly put the mask back on and turned his attention back to the barrel.

The barrel sounded as though it was nearly full, the splashing water sound having changed to a quiet gurgle. Alvin handed Father Paul the paddle and he began stirring the solution.

It's now or never, Hanna thought.

With Mortimer still held tight to her chest, she back-tracked through the trees, sprinting across the far end of the parking area, then turned back into the forest, skirting passed a pile of old tires and was clearing the camp perimeter when her foot caught an empty paint can, sending it flying. It bounced twice before hitting a stone, causing a loud, hollow metallic clank. A second later the camp dogs started to bark.

Father Paul, who was shaking out the last of the lye pellets into the drum, turned in the direction of the noise, his goggled eyes scanning the forest, his breath puffing out from the mask in tiny white clouds that rose around his face.

He pointed to Alvin. "Go. Check it out," he said, his voice muffled. "I'll be finished in a minute."

Alvin nodded and headed in the direction of the sound. He was nearing the entrance flaps to the big tent when Carl staggered out.

"I think . . . Hanna's on the run," Carl said, slurring and trying to catch his breath.

Without hesitation, Alvin stuck his whistle in his mouth and blew, the shrill sound filling the camp. One after another, lights were flipped on from within the trailers until they were all lit.

~ ~ ~

A few minutes later, the men had all gathered around Alvin, each looking tired and yet excited. Alvin chose two of the men to go with him. They'd take the camp truck and check the roadway along the property's boundary, and the others would form a line and comb the woods. He told them Hanna was on foot and couldn't get far, but when they did find her, they were to bring her back to Father Paul's meditation trailer.

Chapter 44

The moon slid in and out of the clouds, helping Hanna retrace the path she and her mother had taken. She'd come to the edge of the forest, and was looking down at a narrow, paved road. There was a thin fog moving across the asphalt, slowly swirling over its surface. She slipped down into the ditch and was coming up the other side when headlights from a pickup appeared on her left, approaching fast. She recognized it. It was from the camp. Fear crushed down on her, her breath tightened in her lungs, and her body began to tremble. She knew what would happen if they caught her.

She turned to run in the other direction, but came to a halt. A second vehicle was coming, rounding the corner, its headlights filtering through the trees and mist.

A few seconds later the vehicle, a four-door sedan, pulled up, and stopped a short distance in front of her. The driver killed the engine, but left the lights on. The car door opened, and a tall man stepped out and walked toward her.

The brakes of the pickup squealed as it ground to a stop behind her. She turned to see Alvin and two others in the cab, their stern faces lit by the other vehicle's headlights, their eyes locked on her.

She spun around to face the man who had stepped out of the car.

Chapter 45

Josh switched off the car heater and rolled down the window. He'd been thinking about what the dying deputy had said, *". . . are any of us . . . good men?"* when it dawned on him. He couldn't remember how far he'd driven, or if he'd missed the turnoff. That's when he caught sight of a woman standing in the road with her back to him. He hit the brakes and came to a stop.

The young woman turned and looked straight at him. She was captured in the brilliant white headlights, her long black dress and red belt standing out against the night sky, her boots all but covered by the drifting fog. Even at twenty feet, he could see her face was bruised. She looked scared and lost.

Then a pickup, its brakes squealing, rolled up behind her and killed its lights.

Josh got out of the car and walked toward the young woman. She didn't move. She just stood there, trembling, holding what appeared to be a small animal. As he got closer, he did a double take.

"Hanna? Is that you?" he asked, taking note of the black welt over her eye almost closing it off, and the half-moon cut below it, bleeding into her cheekbone.

Hanna looked away just as the doors of the pickup opened.

The three men got out of the truck and walked toward Hanna. The leader had a baseball bat in his hand, and spoke first. "Mister, best you step away from her. She's one of ours."

Josh patted Hanna lightly on the shoulder, and told her to get in the car. Then he turned to the men and sized them up. The leader was maybe six feet tall, narrow at the shoulders, with large meaty hands, a bandage on his head and a scowl on his droopy face. The other two could have been brothers, with their big round heads, potbellies, and steel-toed shitkickers. They got to within five feet of Josh when he raised his hand for them to stop.

"We aim to take what is rightfully ours mister," said Alvin, raising the bat high. "Best you step aside."

Josh smiled, then shook his head. "Gentlemen, you do know this young girl has the right to live in a safe environment? Something in the Constitution about that, if I'm not mistaken."

"The Lord is our Constitution, no law bigger than that," Alvin said, his eyes wild.

Josh sighed. "Now fellas. Make no mistake, you're not taking this young girl with you, so you best tuck your tails between your legs and scamper back into your truck. Better yet, give each other a hand job. I wouldn't want to see you go home empty-handed."

"Fuck you!" Alvin cried, swinging the bat at Josh's head and missing by an inch, the trailing wind brushing his eyes. As Alvin went to swing again, Josh pivoted on his right foot, bringing his other foot around and catching Alvin behind the knees, throwing him onto his back. The force of the kick caused Josh to lose his footing, and he fell to the ground.

The other two men were on Josh before he could get to his feet. He blocked the first boot aimed at his head, but another caught him in the kidneys. He grimaced and rolled away, catching the next boot in his hands and twisting it hard, turning the man's body and flipping him to the ground.

Josh scrambled to his feet as Alvin swung the bat, missing again. Josh caught Alvin with a hard right to his ribcage, forcing him to drop the bat and bend over in pain. Clasping Alvin's head in his hands, Josh brought his knee up fast connecting with Alvin's face, the impact tearing Alvin's head from his grasp. Alvin stumbled back onto his heels, his front teeth gone, blood gushing down over his chin. A second later, he dropped to his knees and fell face-first onto the road.

The other two men moved in on Josh from either side. Josh swung around, pivoting to roundhouse one of the men on the side of his leg, snapping his knee sideways. The distinct crack of cartilage was immediately followed by a piercing scream. The other man threw a wild right, missing his mark. Josh nailed him with a hard elbow to the jaw, followed by an upper cut to the chin, and the man dropped to the road, unconscious.

Josh turned to see Hanna behind the windshield, waiting for him. It was then he noticed a sharp pain in his thigh, and looked down to see a fresh spot of blood on his pants.

Chapter 46

It was close to midnight when Josh arrived back at the sheriff's office. Mary was making her way across the street, and picked up her pace when she saw he wasn't alone.

"Ahh no," Mary said, as she examined Hanna's battered face, taking note of the small pig in her arms. "Where'd you find her?"

"On the road, close to the squatters' camp. A few of them came out to greet me, told me, 'she was theirs' and they wanted her back."

"They do this to her?"

Josh nodded. "Yup, I think so, but she hasn't said a word."

Mary glanced at the blood on his pants. "You taught 'em a lesson, no doubt?"

"I tried. One I think they'll remember."

"Good for you," Mary said, then looked down at the pig and back at Josh.

"Kinda late for you, isn't it?" he asked.

"Ahh, I couldn't sleep. That night of puking has knocked the shit out of my rhythm."

Josh nodded, and noticed Mary's gaze return to Mortimer, and he said, "Hanna's very fond of him. His name is Mortimer."

"Well then, Hanna," Mary said, stroking Mortimer's head. "We'll just have to make your little guy comfortable."

Hanna glanced at Mary and tried to smile.

"And you? Are you okay?" Mary asked Josh, looking at his pant leg.

"Pulled a few stiches. I'm all right."

Mary considered Josh for a moment, then turned to Hanna. "You look cold, dear. What do you say we go inside? I'll find us something hot to drink." She put her arm around Hanna and they went inside.

A deputy was sitting on the edge of a footstool buffing his boots as they entered. He looked up at Josh. "You just missed Holly. There's been a fatality on Highway 49. She'll be gone for a while." Then Hanna came into view. "What happened to her?"

"Long story," Josh said. "The cell empty?"

"Yeah . . . yeah, it is," the deputy said, his focus still on Hanna.

"She'll need to see a doctor," Josh said. "Until then, try to make her comfortable. But no one else sees her. Got it?"

"Got it," the deputy replied.

Mary took Hanna by the hand and led her to the washroom to clean her wounds. When the door closed, Josh turned to the deputy. "You'll have to keep a close eye on her. I don't want her skipping."

"That won't be a problem," the deputy said.

A few minutes later Mary and Hanna came out of the washroom and walked over to the cell door, then Mary said, "Go on in, I'll be with you in a minute." Hanna nodded and walked into the cell.

Mary eyed the coffeepot for a second, then opened the cabinet door and scrounged around some, before finding a few packets of hot chocolate. She poured some milk into a mug, heated it in the microwave, then stirred in the chocolate.

Mary entered the cell.

Hanna put Mortimer on the cot and he immediately ran to the end of the mattress, turned, and ran back, dropping down beside her. Hanna wrapped her hands around the mug but said nothing, her gaze returning to Mortimer.

The deputy laid out a gray wool blanket and a pillow at the head of the cot, fluffed the pillow, and then left the cell.

Mary said, "I'll check in on you later, okay dear? And don't you worry, you'll be safe here."

Hanna looked up and nodded.

~ ~ ~

Josh had almost finished bringing Mary and the deputy up to speed regarding the altercation on the road when the deputy, standing by the window, abruptly asked, "You think they'll be coming for her?"

Josh shook his head. "No, not likely. The town's not in their comfort zone. Like to do their dirty work in a pack, off the grid."

The deputy considered what Josh had told him, then nodded. "The coffee's fresh, help yourself. Oh, and Holly said to give you this." He grabbed a large manila envelope off a chair and handed it to Josh. "Photos of the boot prints I think, at least that's what Holly thought."

Mary poured a coffee for herself and one for Josh, then they went into the back office, each taking a seat at the card table. She ripped opened the envelope with the end of a pencil, and took out two eight-by-eleven photos of the plastered boot prints, a yellow ruler set along the edge of each photo. She passed them to Josh.

He inspected the photos, holding each one up to the light, running his fingertips over them, as though he could feel the tread marks. "Klondike boots."

Mary gave him a wry smile, her upper lip raised. "No shit, Sherlock," she said, eyeing the capital letter K in the center of the sole.

"You're a treasure, you know that."

"Aren't I though."

He set the photos on the table. "Size eleven. That makes the perp close to six feet."

"Well, congratulations. Close to six feet tall and wears boots, you've just described half the men in America."

He paid no attention to her, pointing to the sole of the boot. "Do you see it?"

Mary stared at him skeptically, then leaned in for a closer look.

"There's a shallow impression about an inch above the K, the size of a dime, most likely caused by a bubble during the manufacturing process. That's the boot's fingerprint. Makes it unique."

Mary nodded, as if to say *yeah, I get it.*

Then he said something that seemed to catch her by surprise. "And . . . let's keep this little imperfection between you and me, for now anyway."

"Yeah, okay," Mary replied.

They had finished their coffees and were about to head out when a grin threatened to crack at the corner of Mary's mouth. "The town's shindig is tomorrow night. You going?

I hear 'Mr. Right' is planning to come to town, it being *Thanksgiving.*"

"Who?" Josh asked.

"Rachael's *'fii-ann-ce'*." She grinned. "Actually, I don't think she was that thrilled about him showing up, given what's going on. But she did say that if he shows they might drop by for a few minutes. If there's time, that is."

Josh flinched at the thought of seeing them together. "Maybe. We'll see," he said, his voice tight in his throat. "Not exactly a social call we're on here."

Mary gave a noncommittal nod and took a sip of her coffee.

"But it is Thanksgiving, and I suppose everyone in town will be there. Might be a good opportunity to mingle and ask a few questions. Yeah, I guess I could cut a rug for a few minutes."

"*You?* Cut a rug?" Mary asked, a smirk on her face. "Oh please, the only rug you can cut is on a factory floor. Give me a break, Footloose, I've seen you dance."

"Yeah, okay. But you have to remember, I wasn't up to my, uh . . . usual standard."

"Uh-huh."

"You going?" he asked.

"Wouldn't miss it for the world."

Chapter 47

Josh had an hour to kill before he and Rachael were to see Myrna Hudson's son, Clark, at King of the Hill Burgers. He knew the chances were slim that they'd get much from the meeting, but he also knew a break in a case can come from the most unexpected places.

With a fresh cup of java in hand, and the morning sun on his back, he decided to take a stroll through the downtown core. The clerk at the hotel had told him Main Street was blocked off in preparation for Thanksgiving. She warned him he shouldn't expect a lot, mostly people walking about and visiting with one another. But she did say it could have its moments.

As Josh neared the end of a short block that emptied on to Main Street, he stopped to look in a shop window. The shop was much smaller and older than the others, its frontage made of red brick, its door barely six feet in height and slightly below street level, requiring a step down before entering. Stenciled in a golden arc across the window was *Hank's Fly Fishing Gear*. Along the window edges were dog-eared advertisements offering courses from novice to skilled angler, each with a telephone number circled in red.

He cupped his hands on the glass to get a better view inside. A single light bulb hung from the ceiling, its glow all but absorbed by the unfinished wood walls, giving the place a peaceful feeling. It was a place he could walk into and disappear for a while. He moved his hands a few inches across the glass. In the center of the room were stacks of heavy wool sweaters, racks of dark blue and red plaid shirts, khaki colored vests, taupe jackets, light brown raincoats, and a cluster of pea soup green, chest-high waders. Tucked off to one side, near the front of the store, was a wooden workbench. A tiny spotlight had been left on, illuminating a single fly caught in a vice, its wings a radiant green, its head an iridescent yellow.

As his gaze moved from the rods and reels to the fishing nets hanging on the wall, he began to think about Tyler, hoping he was doing okay. Growing up was tough enough, but for a kid with a disability, adolescence could be just plain ugly. And for a sensitive kid like Tyler, the scars might never fade.

Josh continued down the sidewalk, passing a pawnshop with wire mesh over its window and a billiard hall not yet open for the day before turning the corner to Main Street. On the corner was a 1950's barbershop, complete with a ten-foot-high, red and white barber pole standing by the open front door. Inside were three large brown leather chairs bolted to a black-and-white checkered floor, each chair outfitted with a large, wrought-iron footrest. By the window was a bench, where the 'next-ups' were patiently waiting to be called.

Strung high above Main Street was a large orange banner with black letters on it reading *Happy Thanksgiving*. The day was starting to get warm, and Josh could feel his body heat venting out from his collar. He took off his jacket and slung it over his shoulder.

People were milling about, smiling, taking in the day. Small groups were huddled here and there, talking and laughing. All of this was making him think he should be back at his marina, maybe taking Tyler out for a fishing lesson. Maybe even start his next novel. He could almost feel it, a half-full brandy snifter at his side as he pounded out the first chapter; Eddie flaked out across his feet and snoring like a comatose drunk. *Good thoughts.*

Then his father crossed his mind, and his thoughts soured. *Was he safe? Was he sleeping and eating as he should?* He knew full well that wouldn't be the case. Then he remembered it'd been more than a week since he'd last called in to check on him. He made a mental note to call Alice, underscoring it a few times in his mind, when a man about ten feet away called out, "Hey, buddy!"

Josh glanced over.

"Yeah, you. You're that writer guy, right?" The man stood behind an old suitcase striped dark green and black, the grain of the leather shiny, tough, like that of a snake's skin. The case was stamped with a multitude of travel stickers, some of them peeling off, others heavily scuffed. Lying on top of the suitcase was a juice harp and a hand puppet in the shape of a cow's head.

The man looked to be in his mid to late-thirties, his thick black hair tied back in a ponytail. His face had a few days of growth, but was neatly manicured. He was wearing a tweed sports coat, blue jeans, and hiking boots with turned-down wool socks. He looked happy, fit, even cool, which seemed odd to Josh. He regarded the man for a moment, thinking that if there was such a thing as a Busker Fashion Magazine, this guy would be on the front cover. Then his thoughts shifted back to his dad, and he frowned. His father lived on the street, and he certainly wasn't fit. And he sure the hell wasn't happy.

Josh gave a slight nod to the man as he walked by.

"Whoa, love your work, Amigo."

Josh turned to the man.

"Gotta tell you man, I like your books a lot. In fact, I've read most of 'em."

Josh raised an eyebrow.

"Well, okay, maybe three?"

"Seriously?"

"Okay, *two*, but me and Carlos, we loved 'em both, man."

"Carlos?"

"Carlos is my buddy. We shared 'em. Get 'em at the secondhand shop, around the corner." He pointed down the street and to the right.

"So. You've lived here long?"

"All my life, Amigo."

"In that case, maybe you could help me. I need background information on someone who used to live around here. Her name is Lana Friedman. Any chance you knew her?"

The busker eyed Josh for a moment. "Um . . . sure, I remember Lana. She was a friend of my little sister. She was always hanging around our place, staying for dinner that sort of thing. Nice kid though."

"What can you tell me about her?"

The busker hesitated, then picked up the sock puppet and began to fiddle with it. "Thanksgiving Week, it's a biggy around here. Shops get all dolled up. Main Street is blocked off. A man can do well in an environment such as this."

Josh half-grinned and reached into his breast pocket. Withdrawing his wallet, he took out a twenty and held it out in front of the busker. "All right, what can you tell me?"

The busker took the twenty. "Ahh, not much, man. Maybe? But you know, it was such a long time ago."

"'Tis such a fine day, isn't it?" Josh asked, reaching into his wallet and withdrawing another twenty.

The man sighed and grabbed the twenty. "Yep, an' it's just gettin' started."

A flash of anger registered in Josh's eyes.

"Hey, don't be like that, man." The busker took a step back. "I'm not looking for more cash. No way! I was talking about it being a new day, and it's just gettin' started." He held both hands out in front of him, palms up. "Got my sleeping bag hanging out to dry. Weather's unreal, and I just scarfed me down some waffles, a little toast, and some coffee." He patted his belly. "Life is good, Amigo, if you know where to look."

"So, what can you tell me about Lana?"

"Sorry man, I really can't tell you much. She just grew up, then left town." He furrowed his brow. "For college I think. Yeah I'm pretty sure that's right. But that was years ago. She's history, man."

Josh could see the busker weighing his options, then he went to hand a twenty back. Josh put up his hand. "No, you keep it."

Across the street, a man with a trapper's beard was standing near the Barber Shop. He was holding a banjo and had an opened instrument case at his feet, primed with a few greenbacks. He was wearing a small Mexican sombrero with red stitching along its rim and a way too small vest that sagged from all the collector buttons pinned to it. He tipped his hat in Josh's direction then commenced strumming his banjo, singing loud and full of emotion.

"That's Carlos, my buddy," the busker said. "Been trying to get him to clean up his look some, maybe get a cut and a shave. Definitely some new clothes."

Josh's thoughts were drifting, easing away, soaking up the warm weather.

"What? You don't think he needs a shave? Hey, buddy! I'm talking to you."

"What?" Josh asked, realizing he'd not been listening.

"Oh, I get it. I'm not that interesting, is that it? Is that what you're trying to tell me? Someone in my position in life don't count for much. Big shot writer like you, why bother tuning in, right?"

"Hey, look. You're right, OK? I, I wasn't paying attention . . . I was offside. Sorry about that."

The busker glared at Josh, looking him over, gauging his sincerity. "Yeah okay, I guess," the man said, his smile returning. It was a smile that said everything was cool, and yet his eyes didn't look quite convinced. He looked down the street and pointed. "Okay then. See that pole, next to the barber shop?"

Josh saw it, but didn't answer.

"Know why it has a red and white spiral?"

Josh shook his head.

"Medieval times, baby. Back then barbers didn't just cut hair, they performed surgery on their customers, even pulled their teeth." He watched Josh with a 'you-didn't-know-that, did ya?' look on his face. "And part of a barber's 'full-service deal' was bloodletting, using leeches and such." He gave Josh another 'gotcha' look. "So you know why that pole is red and white?"

Josh raised an eyebrow.

"'Cause they used to wrap the blood soaked bandages around it to dry, that's why." A smug smile crossed the busker's face. "Interesting, yes?"

"Without a doubt," Josh conceded.

"Okay then, this is a good thing. Now we are communicating, Amigo. We are having ourselves a real conversation. . . . So tell me, why are you snooping into Lana's history?"

"I'm assisting the FBI with the investigation of the people killed up at the church."

"What?" The man leaned back. "Lana's got something to do with that?"

"Not really. It's more to do with a trial that took place a long time ago. Lyle Carpenter's trial."

The busker's eyes lit up. "Whoa, haven't thought about that in like, forever. What a fiasco that was."

"Yeah? What makes you say that?"

"Ah man, it was the biggest hoop-de-do this county's ever seen." The busker reached up and adjusted the elastic on his ponytail, giving it a tug. "The whole town got riled. Saw it myself. Mob marching down Main Street, carrying torches like in the movies, the peasants storming the castle kinda thing. Everyone yelling and carrying on, wanting to lynch that poor kid."

"So, you don't think he did it?"

"That boy? No way, he was just some poor white trash they could pin it on."

"Why would you say that?"

"The sheriff, he was a grade-A asshole. Wanted to show results, show what a *big* man he was on the campus.

You know the type. Just another alpha male establishment prick beating his chest."

"So, you knew the sheriff?"

"Nah, didn't *know* him, but knew of him. Mean son-of-a-bitch he was, liked to hurt people. Sadistic like."

"And you know this, because?"

"People talk . . . we all knew." The busker's face scrunched up. "What, you think I'm lying?"

Josh raised his hand to stop him. Being chastised twice by this guy wasn't going to happen. "All right, look. Is there anything specific about the sheriff you recall?"

"Sorry man, I got nothing specific."

"But you don't think Lyle did it, killed his girlfriend?"

"Uh-uh, no way. Like I said, people talk. You know how it is."

"Yeah, and what did they say?"

"Word on the street was, somebody's gotta pay." He shrugged. "Might as well be the poor."

"That's all you got?" Josh asked, studying the busker's face.

The busker looked at him and said nothing.

Josh withdrew another twenty from his wallet. "If anything else comes to mind, I'm staying at the Grand."

The busker snatched the bill out of Josh's hand.

Chapter 48

King of the Hill Burgers sat on a low hill, bordered by a paved parking lot on its east side and a Veterinary Clinic to the west. As they crossed the lot, Rachael turned to Josh. "Ran into the sheriff this morning, said you brought in a teenager late last night from the squatters' camp. Hanna's her name, right?"

Josh nodded.

"Our good sheriff did an end run around me," Rachael said, her voice sounding slightly annoyed. "Bypassed me and called our Minneapolis office direct."

Josh glanced at Rachael.

"Okay, it's not a big deal, but she could've gone through me."

Josh said nothing.

"Well, at least she's already got a call back from Child Protection. A specialist will be here the day after tomorrow, bringing along a child psychologist. . . . And that's a very good thing."

The front door chimed as Josh and Rachael entered the burger joint.

A gray-haired man, his shirtsleeves rolled up, was cleaning off a table. The man looked up as they entered, and Rachael flashed him her ID.

"FBI? What's this about?" The man's tone revealed a less than interested attitude.

"We're looking for Clark Hudson. We understand he works here?"

"Oh yeah. Well, he's not working today, 'cause of his mother, you understand. Been in his room all day. Probably best to let him sleep."

"Yeah sure, we get that," Josh said. "But we'll still need to ask him a few questions."

The gray-haired man pursed his lips, then said, "I don't know if that's a good idea. Clark's, a troubled man, got more than his share of problems. He hears voices and such, you understand." The man tapped his temple with his finger.

"We'll need to speak with him anyway," Rachael said, her patience growing thin.

The man eyed them both. "All right, but don't say I didn't warn you." He pointed to the back, toward a hallway with washroom signs over the entrance. "End of the hall, then take the stairs to the second floor, room 1A, first door on the right. Remember to knock softly. He spooks easy."

Josh and Rachael both nodded and headed down the hallway.

Rachael lightly knocked on the door, and a few seconds later, a short, thin man came to the door. His hair was oily and matted to his scalp. His blue jeans were dirty, but his white T-shirt looked new and clean.

"Who are you?" Clark asked, his voice tight in his throat.

"We're with the FBI. We'd like to talk to you for a minute, Clark, if that's all right?" Rachael asked.

"I don't know," he replied, pausing for a moment to think, then nodded as if it would be all right. "But you'll need to sit over there." He pointed to a couch with a thick sheet of plastic covering it.

As Josh and Rachael sat down on the couch, it let out a series of squeaks, sounding like very large hands wiping steam off a mirror.

Clark grabbed a metal chair and sat directly across from them and asked, "Do you like to read? I do. I've got a very big collection of books." He pointed to the bookshelf next to the couch.

Josh turned to look and saw stacks of comic books, neatly arranged, filling the entire bookcase. "Sure, I like to read, Clark. I like how they take me away to other places."

"Me too . . ." Clark shifted his gaze to his hands, digging his fingernails into his palm. "Because I don't want to be here right now."

"We are very sorry about your mother," Rachael started to say, then realized Clark wasn't listening, his thoughts clearly elsewhere.

"I . . . I didn't know him," Clark murmured.

"Who? Who didn't you know?" Josh asked.

"The man who came in, asking for my mom. Said he was an old friend."

"When did that happen?" Josh asked.

"A few days before . . . it happened."

"Do you think this man may have hurt your mother?"

Clark shrugged. "I don't know."

"What did this man look like?" Rachael asked.

Clark shook his head. "Hard to tell. He had a cap on, and sunglasses. I didn't see much."

"Was he tall, short, thin, fat?" Josh asked.

"Tall, I guess. I don't think he was fat, but I couldn't see much of him, 'cause he was wearing a long coat."

"What did he say to you?"

"Said he was passing through and wanted to say hello to my mom. That they were old friends."

256

"That's it?" Rachael asked. "Did he give you a name?"

Clark frowned. "The man said, my mom's number wasn't in the book, which it isn't, so I gave him her phone number and address." He inspected his palms, then said, "He seemed like a nice guy, but now, I'm not so sure . . . 'cause he looked at me kinda funny when he was leaving. I didn't like that."

"Did he say anything else?" Rachael asked.

"Nope. Didn't even order a burger." Clark turned to Josh. "Mister, do you think he was the killer?"

Josh took a moment, then said, "No, Clark, I don't. The killer doesn't fit your description of him. The killer was short and fat, and walked with a cane."

Rachael looked at Josh, giving him a look that said, *really?*

Clark sighed. "Ohhh, mister, thank you. You don't know what a relief it is, to hear you say that."

After a few more questions it was clear Clark wouldn't be of any further use, so they said their goodbyes.

~ ~ ~

As they walked across the parking lot toward the rental car, Rachael said, "We'll need to check Myrna Hudson's phone records, see if this guy called her."

"Agreed, but if this guy *is* the killer, he's methodical and would've used a burner to make the call."

Rachael nodded. "Yeah, but it's still worth looking into."

They got back into the rental car, and Rachael turned to Josh. "It was a nice thing you did back there."

Josh shrugged. "Some realities are best left in the dark."

Chapter 49

The town's community hall was essentially a big red barn, its hipped roof protruding three feet beyond its sides, affording it the warmth and feel of a country cottage. A very large cottage.

Mary was outside, standing off to one side of the barn's sliding door. A lit cigarette hung from her lower lip, a tall glass of gin and tonic held tight in her hand. She had her phone to her ear and looked like she was having a good time.

Inside the barn, patio lights were crisscrossed overhead, casting their pastel colors onto the dance floor. Two Minnesota state flags had been pinned to the rafters, the yellow and green state seal standing out against the deep blue background. The dance floor smelled of straw, livestock, and perfume.

Bales of hay were stacked three high on the stage providing a backdrop for the band. Two fiddlers were in full-flight, working their magic, cranking out a Virginia reel while couples lined up on both sides of the dance floor, facing each other, alive, and having fun.

Picnic tables skirted the outer edge of the dance floor, and the town's Mayor, one Lester P. Tipple, was sitting at the head table, a large centerpiece of sunflower heads signifying the table's importance. Seated around him were men uniformly clad in gray suits. The bank president, the lawyer, the developer, and their women. The collective veneer of their glowing faces doing little to hide their sticky monetary bond. The mayor's fat pink face glistened with sweat, a cherub-like grin of unhealthy proportions on his lips. He said something and they all laughed. Table number one was having a good time. Josh recognized the scene. He'd seen it before, the inner sanctum and the shady real estate deals that come with it. Some things never change.

"Hey, Ingram!" A thick, distorted voice called out from a far table. It was Lance, Mary's old flame, and it was clear to all those around him that his ship had already set sail. Josh watched him for a few seconds, thinking about walking over, when he saw Holly from the corner of his eye.

Josh turned and waved. Holly saw him and waved back. She was wearing tight fitting blue jeans, cowboy boots, and a checked black-and-yellow lumberjack shirt, tied in a knot at the front. She strolled up to him, placed her hand on his shoulder, raising herself onto her toes and went to whisper in his ear, but nibbled his ear lobe instead. He smiled, taking in her freshly scrubbed scent.

Josh hadn't seen Rachael since he'd arrived. He was starting to wonder if she'd show when he saw her standing by the front door. He glanced around, trying to catch a glimpse of her significant other. Tony, Timmy or Tom, or whoever the hell he was. He couldn't remember the name. Or maybe he chose not to. But in any event, it didn't matter, because he wasn't there. She was alone. Holly grabbed Josh by the forearm and gave it a hard squeeze.

"Care to dance, stranger?" she asked, giving him an 'I'm-gonna-eat-you-alive' smile. She took his hand and led him into the center of the dance floor. It was a fact that she looked great in jeans, and while that thought should've been enough to hold his attention, the thought of Rachael standing alone by the front door wouldn't leave him alone.

Another song was starting, a slow tempo tune. The Minnesota-two-step had begun, an enormous relief to men everywhere. There was a plethora of body contact, and the steps were so simple a drunk orangutan could handle it. Holly moved in close, pressing her body against his, her heat penetrating his clothes, her scent getting stronger. He couldn't figure out what exactly she smelled like. Lavender? Rose perhaps? But whatever it was, it didn't stop his thoughts from returning to Rachael. He turned his head and scanned the room, but couldn't spot her. Maybe she'd seen him and left. *But why would she do that?*

At about the halfway point of the song, he finally caught sight of Rachael standing next to a thick log pole. She was looking straight at him, staring, no expression on her face. Just watching. He was about to wave in her direction when Lance walked up to her. He said something, and she shook her head. Then he tried gesturing with his hands, pointing to the dance floor, a fermented smile on his face. She frowned. He tried again, pointing to the dance floor, and she shook her head again. Defeated, Lance's smile evaporated. He turned and retreated back to his table.

When the song ended, Josh took Holly by the arm and they shouldered their way across the dance floor. As they got closer to Rachael, he felt Holly slide her arm around his waist.

"I see you've met Lance," Josh said. "Holly's brother."

Rachael looked at him with a slightly puzzled look on her face. "I'm sorry? *Oh,* you mean just now."

Josh nodded, and could feel Holly staring at him.

"Yeah. Nice guy," Rachael said, clearly not meaning a word of it.

"So, where's, um, Tony?" Josh asked and saw a flicker of anger flash in Rachael's eyes.

"It's Thomas, and he couldn't make it," she said. "He still might come, but not tonight."

"That's such a shame," Holly said. "I so wanted to meet him. Josh tells me you're engaged. You must be so excited. So, when's the big day?"

Rachael didn't answer. She turned to Josh, and he saw hurt in her eyes. He was trying to think of something to say, something that would lighten the mood when he felt Holly nudge him with her elbow.

"Ah, yeah, can I get you something to drink?" he asked Rachael.

"No thanks. Actually, I'm really quite tired. I have some reports to complete, then I'm going to hit the sack."

"Hey, are you okay?" Josh asked.

Rachael sighed. "Ah, it's okay. It's just that the media's throwing a snit fit, the connection's been made between Senator Parker and the church murders, and they want an update. Kingsley wants me back in New York tomorrow, front and center for the press conference. Word is, the press thinks there's been a 'cover-up'—*imagine that*. And as usual, he wants me to take the heat."

"How long will you be gone?"

"Conference is at noon. I'll catch the afternoon flight, make it back by around six tomorrow . . . but call me if the press show up here before I do. Not likely, but it's possible."

"Yeah okay, but you should know I'm heading for Zuma first thing in the morning. I'll be gone for most of the day, but I should get back about the time you do."

"You're going to Zuma?" Holly asked, slightly startled.

"Yeah. I want to look around, see if I can learn anything. Maybe connect a few dots. Anything that could direct us to Carpenter."

Holly was about to respond when Rachael spoke to Josh. "See you tomorrow, then."

"Good night, Agent Tanner," Holly said, eyeing Josh.

"Yeah, see ya tomorrow, Rachael," Josh replied.

Rachael turned and walked toward the door.

Josh watched as Rachael crossed the floor. She was almost out the door when he sensed Holly staring at him. He turned. "Holly, so what can I get you?"

Holly gave a nonchalant shrug. "Oh, you know, the usual."

"Okay . . ." he said, with absolutely no idea of what she drank.

Holly shot him a hard look.

"Gin and tonic?" he asked.

Holly's eyes narrowed, and she grabbed him by the arm, pulling him back onto the dance floor just as a sad cowboy ballad was getting underway. Josh glanced over his shoulder, hoping to catch a glimpse of Rachael, but she was gone.

Chapter 50

Zuma Penitentiary covered most of Potter's Island, an irregular shaped thirteen-acre lump of Precambrian Shield located a mile off the northwest shore of Lake Superior. On a good day the prison's towering walls and gothic turrets could be seen poking out of the mist. On a bad day it lay hidden, its secrets locked away.

The severing of the umbilical cord took place on August 17, 1899, when Zuma took its first breath, ushering in a new era of jarring intolerance. It was a righteous edifice, capable of cauterizing the wayward spirit, a marvel of human virtue. Without question, that's what the good citizens of Langford County thought—no one else really cared.

Years slipped by, decade after decade sifting through the hourglass, wars won and lost, new lives celebrated and the old mourned. But as the world around Potter's Island evolved, and liberal ideals blossomed at its shoreline, Zuma remained steadfast, its priggish blister of moral superiority resisting any and all attempts at humanity.

Zuma's design was the brainchild of Franklin S. Markus, Minnesota's Governor at the time. Governor Markus, a raging alcoholic, did not believe in coddling the inmates. His election campaign promise, which many believed greased his way into office, read: *"We shall instill*

fear in the hearts of those who would do us harm, so we the
good, decent people of Minnesota, may sleep safe in our beds."

It wasn't until the late 1970s, through intense pressure
brought on by human rights groups calling for Zuma's
closure, that the prison was finally earmarked for
dismantling. And it would have closed had it not been for
the rise of America's War on Drugs and the resulting swell
of incarcerations, bloating the penal system and forcing
Zuma's doors to remain open and its infamous reputation
to grow unabated.

But as times changed, the contrast of how out-of-step
Zuma was with the rest of the world became more
apparent. By the mid-1990s moderation was the theme of
the day, and a new type of warden finally took the reins.
Clarence L. Conway became the eleventh warden of Zuma,
and ushered in a kinder, more humane approach.

Potter's island had one route of accessibility, a twenty-
minute barge ride from the northwest shore of Lake
Superior. There was one round trip per day; food and
supplies were brought in on the 11 o'clock 'morning run',
and garbage was brought out on the 2 p.m. return trip. The
barge, made from welded sheet metal, was dull and gray,
marked with streaks of orange rust down its hull.

Its iron deck carried a small payload, two large, blue
industrial bins, one for supplies, the other for garbage, both
sat at the front of the barge for easy loading and unloading.
A pilot lookout was situated in the center of the barge, and
a six-foot long wooden bench was bolted down at its back.
A corrugated aluminum roof covered the bench, providing
the passengers with at least some protection from the
elements.

Josh was sitting on the bench watching a couple of seagulls as they swooped in and out of the boat's wake, their wings chalk white and luminous in the morning sun. Their chatter punctuating the monotonous chug, chug, chug of the diesel engine.

Progress was slow as the barge plowed forward, the hull smacking against the chop. The larger sprays reached to the back of the barge and sprinkled Josh's face. He didn't mind getting wet. In fact, he welcomed the cold water as it helped offset the incessant rocking motion of the boat, a motion that was taking its toll on his guts. The trip had taken a full twenty minutes, but felt more like an hour. As the barge pulled up along the side of the service pier, the first and only mate tied off the landing cleats with practiced hands, wrapping and pulling the ropes tight. Stepping out on to the dock, Josh was glad the trip had come to its end.

The distance from the pier to the prison entrance was billed as a five-minute stroll. What had been left out was, it was a near-vertical climb that crisscrossed a giant granite outcropping shaped like a huge potato. The steps, chiseled out of the stone face were uneven, making the climb even more difficult. By the time Josh reached the halfway point his damaged leg was giving him trouble, slowing him, and the five-minute stroll became a fifteen-minute slog. By the time he reached the top step he was seriously questioning whether it was worth it.

The entrance to Zuma had been cut into a sheer rock face some thirty feet high. A turret perched high on the wall had two guards inside, their assault rifles zeroed in on Josh's chest.

Josh stepped up to an iron door and peered into one of two CCTV cameras overhead. A second later, a slot in the door slid open and Josh passed his ID through. Then the iron door swung open and a voice coming from a speaker box overhead told him to step inside. He did, and the door closed behind him, followed by the loud metallic sound of a bolt being driven home.

Five minutes later he was surveying the warden's office. A large picture of a ribbon cutting ceremony hung on the wall behind the desk. Service club plaques, with a different warden name inscribed on each, ran along the top edge of the room's walnut wainscoting. A much smaller plaque, commemorating the one hundred and tenth anniversary of the prison, hung below a large portrait of the current governor.

On one corner of the warden's desk sat a framed photograph of a heavyset man and a woman resting against a Jeep, both of them decked out in Great White Hunter garb. Their dark brown leather hiking boots and knee-length khaki shorts were matched by short-sleeved khaki shirts with the obligatory Kenya Park badge sewn above their hearts. The couple's ensemble was topped off with identical Safari Bush Hats.

A bronze cast of a Tyrannosaurus Rex, about eight inches tall, stood on the front of the warden's desk. A silver caption at the reptile's feet read: ADAPT or DIE. Josh heard footsteps coming, and the door opened.

"Mr. Ingram, I'm Warden Clarence Conway. It is so good to meet you." They shook hands. "I must say, this is a pleasure." He paused, then gave his head a shake. "No, no, please. That's such a miserable understatement. I am a big fan of yours. In fact, right this minute your latest novel is on my nightstand, just waiting for me to crack the cover."

"Well, I hope you'll enjoy it, Warden. And please, it's Josh."

The warden was not a tall man, but what he lacked in height he made up for in girth. His body an almost perfect ball, the skin on his face soft, like a giant ripe peach.

"Oh, I'm sure I will," the warden replied, his voice resonating through layers of fatty tissue. He slipped his thumbs under his leather belt and yanked it up, inching it a tad higher on his belly. "You know, I was supposed to have the day off, but I just couldn't pass up the opportunity to meet you." Then he looked directly at Josh and almost frowned. "But you're not here to chitchat, are you? I understand you're interested in one of our previous guests. Specifically, Lyle Carpenter."

"That's correct. I'm working on a case of multiple murders. A common thread each of the victims share is that they were all part of the trial that found Carpenter guilty of killing his girlfriend. I was hoping you could provide some background on Carpenter while he was a guest."

A thin line of pain cut across the warden's eyes, only to be countered by a broad smile. "Since you put it that way, I'd be more than happy to help you. It is troubling to hear his past is not letting him rest." At that moment, the warden's door opened and a young man with tats covering most of his arms and neck walked into the room, pushing a cart carrying a coffee pot and a plate of glazed cinnamon buns. The inmate poured them both a cup, then left the room.

"This is a progressive prison, Josh," the warden said, as he reached for a bun. "Okay, maybe a bit of an oxymoron to call it that, but I do believe we've made some serious progress. Bun?"

"I'll pass, thanks, it's a little too early for me," Josh said, his guts still churning from the boat trip.

The warden shrugged. "Suit yourself." He took a couple of large bites and chomped away, stuffing the residual dough into his mouth with his swollen fingers before realizing Josh was watching him. He grinned, chomped for a few seconds more and washed it down with his coffee, wincing as he swallowed.

The warden cleared his throat. "But let me tell you this, if I didn't think I could make a difference, I would turn in my resignation right this very minute."

Josh said nothing. The warden's words clearly had mileage on them, but he sensed the man believed what he was saying.

"Actually . . . Lyle Carpenter was one of my first projects. I took it on shortly after I arrived here." He stopped and took a long sip of his coffee, then continued. "My biggest regret is that I didn't get here sooner, for that boy suffered more than any one of God's creatures should have to." He took a moment to let the words sink in. "My predecessor, you have to understand, was your typical 'hands off' administrator. It's such a shame how people can be so cruel to one another, don't you think?"

Josh nodded.

The warden grabbed another bun and set it down on a small plate in front of him. He moistened a napkin with the tip of his tongue and rubbed a patch of frosting off his mouth, dabbing it at the corners. "You see, they sent Carpenter here as an adult inmate. Truth be told, he was barely a man." The warden shook his head and sighed. "And a good looking one at that. Well, I guess you can imagine." He stopped again. "No. I don't think anyone could imagine what that boy went through. All prisons have their sadistic element, and Zuma is no exception. But what they did to him . . . I honestly, don't know how he survived."

Josh nodded again, waiting for the warden to go on.

"The first I heard of his predicament was the day he strung himself up from the laundry ceiling. Had the guards not found him when they did, a minute later the story would've ended right then and there. And that's when I decided I had to do something." The warden got out of his chair and waddled to the window, looking out over the prison yard. "First thing I did was lock him in the prison infirmary, give his wounds a chance to heal. It turned out his time in the infirmary lasted far longer than I'd expected. The boy had lost his will to go on. Later, when I decided he was no longer a threat to himself, I had him transferred to solitaire. Of course, there was no justifiable way I could've returned him to the general population. You have to understand, as a good Christian, my conscience would not allow it."

The warden turned to face Josh. "Now, a bright young man sitting in a cell without stimulus, well, that's just another form of torture, isn't it? Being this was my first major command, I was eager to make a difference, to make my mark. A bit naïve I suppose, in hindsight." The warden studied Josh for a moment, clearly trying to gauge his reaction, before he continued. "So, I set Carpenter up with the tools I believed would one day make his re-entry into the general population possible. My approach was twofold. First, I wanted to repair the boy's spiritual soul, provide him with a solid foundation of faith that he could draw upon in time of need. Second, and more from a practical standpoint, I had the cell next to his converted to an exercise room, a training gym of sorts. I wanted to bulk him up, give the boy a chance to defend himself, you understand?"

Josh nodded.

"As it turned out, the hill the boy had to climb was a high one. Now you must understand, Carpenter wasn't stupid, far from it. But he couldn't read or write worth dog shit. So I enlisted a senior inmate, a teacher in his other life, to tutor the boy. To make a long story short, Carpenter did well, warmed up to education like it was his calling. Not only that, the boy took to exercise with the same unbridled enthusiasm as he had for education, converting his youthful frame into a mass of knotted muscle. Which I must say was an impressive site, even in a place like this. But the thing that shocked me the most was how that young man took to the Lord."

Josh raised his eyebrows. "Sounds like a success story . . ."

"One would have thought," the warden said, and let out a long breath. "Over the next few months, we kept a close watch on Carpenter as he assimilated into the general population. At first, we were celebratory in our success, pats on the back all around. All reports coming in were favorable. You see, we had brought a young life back from the brink, and we were damn proud of it.

"But not too long after that, things got messy. One of Carpenter's key tormentors turned up dead. It was a gruesome sight. The man's neck had been snapped, his head cranked around so his corpse was looking backwards. His body stripped bare, genitals cut off and stuffed in his mouth, his lips crudely sewed shut with thick, red rubber bands."

"Rubber bands?" Josh asked.

"Yeah. We figured he got them from the kitchen. You know, the kind that keep vegetables tied." There was a long pause. "Nothing was ever proved as to who had perpetrated the crime, but some things are just known in here.

"As the years went by, Carpenter became more and more reclusive. He started chanting and quoting scripture from the Bible . . . verbatim, mind you. At least that's what I've been told. I even heard he was dabbling in witchcraft. I'm not so sure about that last bit, prison lore I think. But his reputation grew and the others let him be.

"Last time I checked in on him was a few months before his release. I have to say, he'd become almost unrecognizable. It was as though his tortured life had transformed him into some sort of freak. Now, you have to realize, it wasn't his physical presence that had changed so much. In fact, his body had returned to more normal proportions. It was the way he looked at you . . . It was hard to describe really, but it was like he had some kind of power. . . . Okay, okay. I know it sounds nuts, and it wasn't real of course, but it sure felt real."

The warden poured himself another cup of coffee and tilted the pot toward Josh.

Josh held up his hand, indicating he would pass.

"When Carpenter finally got released, I heard there was a small group waiting for him at the gate. Guards reported that they were chanting and carrying on like he was some kind of messiah."

"When did he get out?" Josh asked.

"Going on a year now, I think?" The warden scratched his head. "No, no it was the spring before, yeah, that's right." He ran his finger around the rim of his cup. "In hindsight, his redemption was a colossal failure. Something I try not to think about."

Sensing the warden was about to cut him loose, Josh asked, "Are any of Lyle's roommates still in the system?"

"Yeah . . . one I'm pretty sure." The warden turned to his computer, shifted his belt, and grunted. "My wife says I have to lose a few pounds. I'm thinking she's maybe right?" He waited for a reaction.

Josh remained silent.

The warden gave a shrug and began punching keys. Then he swiveled his chair forty-five degrees and propelled himself across the carpet using the heels of his shoes, like an obese toddler on a tricycle. He opened a file drawer and thumbed through it for close to a minute before pulling out a thick brown file and laying it on his desk.

"Yes, Randolph Gunter. Actually, he's about to get out. End of next month to be exact. He's been here . . . hmm . . . well I guess, most of his adult life. There's a note here that says the guards call him Rudolph on account of his nose. Looks like he bunked with Carpenter ever since he was assimilated back into the general population." The warden paused, then asked, "I take it you'd like to see him?"

"I'm thinking it would be a good idea," Josh replied. "Does he still reside in the same cell? The one he shared with Carpenter."

The warden checked the file again. "Yup, same one." He flipped a few more pages. "Oh, and there's one other person I think you may want to talk to. She completed a series of assessments on Carpenter over the years. The last one occurred about a month before his release. Her name's Katherine Bainbridge. She consults on an 'as needed' basis.

Works out of her home office on shore, close to where the barge docks, or so I'm told." He opened his desk drawer and withdrew a wad of business cards. He began thumbing through them until her card surfaced, then handed it to Josh.

Josh examined the card for a second before slipping it into his pocket.

"Oh . . ." The warden raised his hand, signaling Josh to stay seated. He opened the bottom drawer of the filing cabinet, took out a jar of vapor rub, and passed it over. "I'll have a guard show you the way."

"Yeah, thank you." Josh opened the jar and dabbed a drop of the ointment under each nostril before passing it back. "Warden, by any chance is there a pop machine close by?"

The warden raised an eyebrow. "Yes. In the lunch-room. The guard'll show you."

Chapter 51

J osh held a frosted cola in each hand as he followed the guard. A big man, well over six feet in height, his shoulders were thick as a railroad tie, his neck nearly as wide as his massive head. He was favoring his right leg, as was Josh, both of them walking with a pronounced limp as they made their way through the endless warren of concrete corridors that led to the general population.

With nothing to look at but the back of the clumping hulk in front of him, Josh's attention turned to his surroundings. He figured the concrete slab walls couldn't be more than seven feet high since the guard's head almost touched the overhead flickering fluorescent lights.

As they turned down yet another corridor, a claustrophobic feeling began to creep in, stirring old memories. Josh shifted his gaze to the ceiling corner, attempting to change his focus, and saw a dark hole with black rot spreading out from it. He forced himself to take shallow breaths, trying to stop the sinking feeling from progressing, but it wasn't working. *Gotta reach the other end soon,* he thought, *or as sure as hell, I'm gonna be back in that root cellar . . .*

~ ~ ~

As the final door opened to the general population, the stench of sweat and desperation rolled over Josh in a gush.

He tried his best to concentrate on the vapor rub as he followed the guard up a steel staircase to the second floor.

The cells were built from reinforced concrete. And like the hallways, the cell walls had been painted a light green. Each cell looked to be about nine or ten feet wide and twelve feet long. There was a narrow gray cot on either side of the cell, with a white toilet and a small, round stainless steel sink at the far end. Randolph Gunter was lying on his cot as the guard opened the cell door and Josh entered. The guard remained at the doorway.

Gunter swung his knees off the cot and sat up. "Who the fuck're you?" His voice was thick with a New Yorker accent, his line of sight locked on the two colas Josh was holding. Gunter wasn't a large man, but he had that zero-percent body fat look about him, his muscles clearly defined.

"Shut the hell up, Rudolph" the guard said, jerking his head in the direction of Josh. "He does the asking."

Gunter looked at them both and sneered.

"It's all right," Josh said to the guard, then turned to Gunter. "I'm with the FBI. I need to ask you a few questions about your old cellmate, Lyle Carpenter."

Gunter peered at Josh, then shifted his eyes to the colas.

Josh started to hand Gunter a cola, only to have it snatched out of his hand. The man popped off the cap and chugged down half of it before Josh could say 'you're welcome'.

"I understand you two bunked together for a long stretch."

"Yeah. So, what of it?"

"I'm looking to get some background information on him."

"OK. He one crazy motherfucker, that's what he is."

"How's that?"

"Some kind of loose shit in that mother's head, *bad stuff*, ya hear what I'm saying? Crazy mother, that's what he is. That's what I say."

"I'm told he took to the gospel, fancied himself as a man of the cloth, so to speak?"

Gunter started rocking back and forth on the edge of his bed, his hands grabbing at the mattress. "Hell yeah, call it what you want, but you don't want that crazy mother lying across from ya, night after night."

Josh waited patiently.

"Ever since the day he come back from isolation, that mother'd changed, I'm tellin' ya." Gunter rolled his eyes. "Had himself conversions with the Lord, if ya know what I mean." He took another swig of pop. "Don't get me wrong, we all got to find somewhere to hide, but Lyle, mmm, mmm, damn! He was one gone mother."

"How do you mean?"

Gunter shrugged. "Ah man, he be speaking to the Lord, like, *all the time* . . . I would've shut him up too, but he'd got too big and too crazy. And I didn't want anything he'd be offering coming my way. He must've put on fifty pounds, all pumped up like that. Good for him too, 'cause they left him alone after that. Those that survived, that is." He drained the last of his cola and burped, a long wet one that caused his eyes to water.

Josh handed him the other bottle. "Did you know him before his transformation?"

276

"Nah, but I'd seen him around. . . . Not too surprisn' he turned out the way he did. Such a cherry blossom he was when he arrived . . . you know, a punk."

Josh nodded.

"Young and good looking in a place like this—that's just all fucked up." Gunter shook his head and sighed. "They worked that boy over until I thought he'd die. Went on for months. Sometimes that kind of stuff, she's real bad in here. But for that boy, it was some sick shit."

"I take it no one stepped up."

Gunter grunted in disgust. "What're ya talking at? Stick your chicken neck in where it's not wanted—they gonna light you up . . ."

Josh's brow furrowed. "What?"

Gunter looked directly at Josh and lowered his voice. "Ain't like you see on the TV, no Captain, not here, not in Zuma baby." He lowered his voice some more. "Late at night, that's when it be goin' down and they be coming for ya. . . . Biggest fear there is, they come a knockin' . . . draggin' your sorry ass from your cell, taping your mouth shut and strapping that goddamn pillow over your face, the others all holding you down. And ya can't fight 'em, 'cause there's too many." He paused. "And that's when Smiley comes into the picture. They call him Smiley 'cause he's always got one dopey motherfucker grin on his face. Now Smiley, he really gets off on this shit—he's the one that cuts ya." Gunter held up his pinky finger. "Makes a hole no bigger than the tip of my finger, and then . . ." A pained look crossed Gunter's face. "Then he sticks ya with that electrical cord."

"Ah, what?"

"Pay attention motherfucker. A cord, like a lamp cord, but ain't no lamp attached to it, just a plug on one end and two bare wires on the other end."

Josh said nothing.

"So, as I was saying, he'd shove them wires in through that little hole. Go in maybe an inch, maybe two, I don't know. Then they'd plug that cord in, and *man*, your guts sizzle like a string of links in a deep fryer. And the stink!" Gunter scrunched up his nose. "God almighty himself would haveta leave that room.

"I wouldn't have believed it if I ain't seen it myself, and I'm tellin' ya, ain't nobody gonna risk that. We keep to ourselves, we do."

Josh looked in the direction of the guard, who was now in a deep conversation with another guard. "What about them?"

Gunter lowered his voice. "Those suckers? They be compensated. They be worse than us. Who do you think opens the door and fixes the fuse box, dummy?"

Josh turned to the guard who had brought him there and asked, "Hey Boss, mind if I stretch out?"

The guard smiled and in a deep, gravel voice said, "Live the dream, my man." Then he turned back to the other guard.

"So Gunter, when Lyle spoke to God. Was it like this?" Josh asked, stretching out on the cot and staring up at the ceiling.

"No, the usual way, on his knees, hung over the bed praying. Like a little kid, but a real big kid."

"And, what did they talk about? Lyle and God?"

"Wha'da ya mean?"

"I mean, like a regular conversation? Just two guys hanging out, getting caught up on the day's events? Or was it like, 'Yes sir, yes sir, three bags full sir'."

Gunter sneered. "You're a funny guy. But no, it was more like he was getting instructions. Hell, one night he even went on about doing some kinda *human* sacrifice thing." Gunter stopped and glared at Josh. "Kept my ears to the tracks after that, I did. Didn't want my name coming up. Uh-uh, you'd be not wantin' your name on that mother's list, no Captain."

"What are you saying?"

For a moment, Gunter looked as though he was deciding if he should go further. "Not long after he'd got back, one of those that did'm, the leader I think it was, got his head cranked around till it was looking at the crack of dawn." Gunter took a long swallow of pop. "Then, my boy Lyle. Well, he sliced the dude's junk off and crammed 'em in the dude's mouth, lacing up his lips *ugly-like*, like you see on a goddamn football. Mmm, mmm, that'd be one sick grin on his face, if you ask me. No one bothered my boy after that."

Josh was thinking about what Gunter had said when his eye caught something carved into the wall, barely visible along the edge of the mattress. He took a closer look, pushing down on the mattress and saw some numbers, and read them aloud, "2:21." Then he ran his fingers across them and asked, "What do you make of this?"

"*That . . . ?* Hell if I know."

"But you know about them?"

"Wha'da ya think? Sitting here, in the same rotten shithole, year after year. Course I know every last stinkin' inch of it."

Josh nodded. "So, was it Lyle who put these here?"

"Like I said, don't know, and don't give a fuck."

Bullshit . . . Josh thought, and made a mental note of the numbers.

Chapter 52

Main Street, Appleton was a stub of a street that curved east for seventy-five yards before terminating at the northwestern shore of Lake Superior. A string of tired retail shops lined both sides of the street, including a beauty salon, an art studio, a used bookstore, a food mart, plus a two-bay warehouse housing a coin-operated carwash on one side and the town's art and cultural center on the other. Behind and running parallel to Main Street were a half-dozen clapboard rancher style homes, all in need of repair.

Other than the service and trade workers required to support Zuma's day-to-day operation, the town's population included a small group of artists and writers that had settled there in the late '60s.

At the end of the block, where the land tapered down to the water's edge, stood the last structure. It was a small eatery, aptly named *The Last Stop*. Its cedar shake walls were unpainted, weathered, and blended well with the gray afternoon sky. Emerald green moss, swollen by a chain of late autumn showers, had grown in thick on the roof shingles and lined the outer rim of the gutters.

All of the restaurant's windows faced to the lake, as did its front door. It was dark inside, and Josh couldn't tell for sure if the place was open for business. He tried the handle, the door opened, and he walked inside.

As best he could tell he was the only customer. He took a seat at a table by one of the windows. Not ten seconds had past when a buxom brunette, maybe forty years of age, came out of the kitchen carrying a tray of steaming cinnamon buns smothered in white frosting. She plunked the tray on the counter and yanked out her earphones, clearly startled by his presence.

"Didn't see you come in, love. I'll be right with you." The woman's voice was deep and warm, melodic like a coastal lullaby. Josh had never quite understood why some had the gift to put others at ease, but he knew enough to appreciate it when they crossed his path.

A moment later she showed up at his table, rubbing her hands on her apron. "So, what can I bring you?"

"I could really use a coffee, and I'd love one of those delightful buns."

"Oh, would you now?" She grinned. "Oh, you mean these," she said, pointing at the cinnamon buns. "Sorry love, they be for the warden. He likes my cooking. Whip up a batch every afternoon."

Josh almost smiled.

"Oh yes, I know it is a pity, but they are for him, and it wouldn't be right to tear one of these darlings from their brothers and sisters, now would it?" She grinned again. "Oh, come now, would you look at that face of yours . . ."

Josh raised his nose into the air and inhaled deeply.

The waitress played with her apron string, a smile twitching at the corners of her mouth. "Oh, I suppose one wouldn't hurt, now would it?"

A minute later she returned with a coffee pot and small plate. "You're coming back from Zuma, I take it?" She poured Josh a coffee, then scooped out a bun from the pan and placed it on the plate. The frosting was still fluid, sliding down one side of the bun, a waft of cinnamon in the air. "Napkins are in the canister."

Josh nodded.

"Long drive home?"

He looked up at her.

"Oh love, not many stay around, especially this time of year."

"There is someone in town I'd like to talk to before I head out. Would you happen to know a Katherine Bainbridge?"

"Know her, Kathy, she comes in sometimes twice a day. Loves my coffee, or so she says. Could be she just needs the company."

"You know where I can find her?"

"Sure do," she said, raising an eyebrow. "How's your eyesight?"

Josh didn't respond.

"Turn yourself around and look out the window." She pointed to a bluff some fifty yards away where an orphaned caboose, colored deep red like that of a fresh cut pomegranate, sat on top of a large sand dune. It had three windows, two small and one large, the trim painted hot dog mustard yellow. A black smokestack jutted above the roofline, spewing out gray curls of smoke that stretched out over the lake.

Josh finished off his bun, drained his coffee, and settled the bill. After a quick pit stop in the washroom he headed out, waving goodbye at the door.

Chapter 53

The stitches were starting to pull again as he stepped onto a wooden landing at the top of the sand dune. The caboose, maybe twenty feet away, rested on an abandoned rail spur, its rear wheels butted up against a large pair of black iron backstops. And while Josh couldn't see the shoreline, he could hear the waves lapping below.

The air was musty, with a thread of poplar smoke running through it, smelling like a campfire on a wet morning. A cluster of willow treetops poked up above the edge of the dune, a virtual rat's nest of entangled branches. To the right of the caboose, stood a large crabapple tree.

A patch of bluegrass, neatly trimmed and maybe ten-feet wide, surrounded the caboose. Josh climbed the metal steps to the door and knocked. A folk ballad was coming from inside. He knocked again and the door cracked open. Instantly the ballad grew louder, followed by the unmistakable smell of burning grass.

A gray-haired woman, chunky at the waist and maybe in her mid-fifties, stood before him, the remainder of a lit joint held between her fingertips. She was wearing a loose fitting brown poncho and had a long string of colored beads wrapped around her neck. Her calves were bare, as were her feet.

She sucked hard on the joint, drawing in a number of short puffs, making a *phist, phist, phist* sound. Then, in a squeaking voice, she said, "Sorry for the way I look, but it's my day off, and I like to . . . you know, *kick back*." She gave him a curious stare as she exhaled, letting the smoke out slowly, then blinked a couple of times and grimaced, and began rubbing her eye with the palm of her hand as she tried to pass the roach to him.

He held up his hand. "Ah, not today, thanks. . . . I'm Josh Ingram, and I'm assisting the FBI with an investigation. I'd like to ask you a few questions, if that's all right?" He reached into his jacket and retrieved his temporary ID.

A hint of recognition began working its way across her face as she wet her fingertips with her tongue and snuffed out the roach. "For medicinal purposes, you understand." She blinked her bloodshot eye a few times, then asked, "Are you, Josh Ingram . . . the writer?"

"Ahh, yup."

"Oh, my God," she said, reaching out her hand. "I'm Katherine Bainbridge . . ." A blank look registered on her face for a second, and then she was back. "Sorry about that. Don't you just hate that when it happens? So, ah, where was I . . . ? Oh, yeah, my friends call me Kathy. You can too, if you like."

"Nice to meet you, Kathy."

She eyed him for a moment before continuing. "The warden over at Zuma, he got me hooked on your books a few years back you know. I'm about halfway through the series, kind of a slow reader." Her smile broadened, her pupils big as black marbles.

"Joshua. Can I call you Joshua?"

"Actually, it's Josh."

"Oh, okay then," she said, sounding slightly hurt. "Well now, Josh, don't make me ask again, come on in for heaven's sake. Oh, and I must apologize, the place is such a mess." She paused, her cheeks turning pink. "And, would you look at me. Oh my goodness." She tried fluffing her hair. "I was just about to do my hair." She winked. "But I bet you like the 'lived in look' don't you, a man like you? I'm sensing that, maybe . . . you and me are two peas in a pod?"

"You got me there," he said, giving her a cautious nod as he scanned the room for an untethered straight jacket.

The space felt cramped, but the one large window did seem to brighten the room. He noticed a couple of small built-in bookshelves stuffed full of paperbacks, and was trying to catch a few titles when a teapot began to whistle.

"I'm making a pot of tea, would you like some? We can sit out on the deck if you'd like. I'd be happy to answer your questions there."

"Sure, sounds good."

A narrow door next to a love seat opened to a wood deck that faced the crabapple tree, the ground around it peppered with its shriveled crimson fruit. They each took a seat around a small, round metal table held up by three ostrich shaped legs. Kathy poured the tea.

"So tell me, Josh, what is it you want to know?"

"It's about Lyle Carpenter. I've just come from Zuma, and I understand from the warden you did a number of assessments on Carpenter, including the final assessment before his release?"

Kathy hesitated for a moment and then set the teapot down, then cocked her head to one side and began fiddling with the pot's lid.

"I'd like to get a better understanding of him," Josh said. "Get an idea of what made him tick."

286

Kathy looked up. "Lyle, had such promise, you know. That is, at the start he did, when he first returned to the general population." She got up and padded over to a bench seat on the far end of the deck, lifted the lid, and took out a family-sized bag of sour cream and onion potato chips. She tore open the bag, stuffed a handful of chips in her mouth, then pointed the bag in his direction. "Care for some?" she mumbled, a few chip bits falling off her lip and onto her poncho.

Josh didn't respond.

She shrugged before reaching back into the bag. "At first, we thought we had Lyle on track. That he'd be okay." She pulled her hand out, her gaze now focused on a rather large, perfectly formed chip.

"But he wasn't okay, was he?" Josh snapped, starting to lose his patience.

She sighed, the question jarring her back from the edge of her self-imposed gastronomic nirvana.

"That would be the understatement of the century." She swallowed, clearly wanting to devour the chip. She looked up. "No. It's like something 'clicked' inside of him. But then, we can't be blaming him for that, now can we? I mean, the horrific abuse he went through. Good grief, anyone could go loopy after that—the poor bastard." She fanned herself with her free hand. "You'll have to pardon my language. It's not ladylike to express oneself with *vulgarity* . . . the distillate of the infertile mind." She stuffed the chip into her mouth.

"You sure you don't want some?" She held up the bag.

Josh shook his head.

"*Well*, suit yourself." Then she commenced sucking the salt off her fingers, one digit at a time, making a loud popping sound as she pulled each finger from her mouth.

Eventually, the salt content of her fingers must've dropped to a point where she no longer found any pleasure in them, and she turned her attention back to Josh.

"Lyle was clearly a troubled man. He had a kind of delusional complex, believed he had a special relationship with the Lord Almighty, if you can imagine that. I'm afraid he lived in a world all of his own creation."

"And he was allowed to walk?"

She stared at Josh in disbelief. "He'd served his time. Paid his debt to society. He was free to go." She raised her upper lip, sucking air through her teeth as if trying to dislodge some chip pulp, then said, "But then again, if believing you have a special relationship with the Lord is enough to lock you up, half the people in the world would be behind bars."

Josh raised an eyebrow. "This is a little different, don't you think?"

She pursed her lips and gave another shrug before continuing. "It's strange though. Lyle did have a certain magnetism about him. Now, he was a handsome man and that's a fact. Not like when he first arrived, so I'm told, but still a looker. But there was this thing about him. Hard to explain really. It's like he could draw you in. . . . And I hesitate to say it." She looked directly at Josh. "But it, it was . . . *cult-like.*"

Josh remained silent.

"Well, the way I see it, it's like this. If someone believes in something strong enough, and says it long enough, others will want to believe in it too." She took another sip of tea, washing it around in her mouth, and swallowed.

"After Lyle had recuperated physically from all the horrific abuse he'd endured, the warden kept him separated from the general population for quite a while. But when he did return, he was a changed man. And I'm not saying for the better, that's for sure. Became obsessed with the Bible, quoting scripture as though it was written for him personally. *And the girl he murdered?* Oh, my God, how he'd go on about her and their *forever* love, yadda, yadda, yadda. . . . I gotta be honest with you here. I got seriously tired of listening to that narrative. It's not a fact I'm proud of, mind you. And yet, it was odd of him to talk about her like that. I mean, since he'd slit her throat from ear to ear."

"Did he have any friends or family? Anyone waiting for him?"

"As far as I know, there was only the one person, a woman. She'd decided to champion his cause early on, set an innocent man free, that sort of thing. They wrote back and forth for a number of years. I guess it's not that unusual, really. Lonely woman, good looking guy, set him free and live happily ever after, right?" She gulped down the rest of her tea and began to pick at her front teeth with one of her fingernails, then said, "No, come to think of it, that's not quite right either, Lyle told me it wasn't that sort of relationship he had with the woman. Whatever that means. Then one day, about a year before his release, the woman shows up at Zuma.

"A week later I saw her working at the grocery store. Then, when his release date was finally set, she up and left town. Next time I saw her, she was at the pier waiting for the morning barge to Zuma. There were a few others with her. They'd all come in a van, one of those window types. That's the last I saw of them."

"Did you ever meet this woman?"

"Not really. I mean, I saw her at the grocery store, but she'd never say a word. She seemed awfully shy."

"And . . . ?"

"And nothing."

"So, she never spoke to you? A small town like this, working at the only grocery, and she never uttered a word to you?" Josh's voice was starting to rise.

"Okay, that's not entirely right. She did tell me once to 'be happy' and that, um . . . 'God is watching'. Yeah, that's right. 'God is watching'."

When it was clear the well had run dry, and Kathy was itching to light up again, Josh thanked her for her time and followed her back through the Caboose to the front door.

At the door, she stopped, looking as though she'd forgotten something, and asked, "Could you just hang on for a sec?" She turned and stepped into the kitchen. He could hear her opening and closing drawer after drawer, rifling through them. He took another look at her bookshelf and was surprised to see how varied her interests were, including a wide array of fiction and nonfiction, with a leaning toward true crime. And yet, what stood out the most was an old and apparently well-used Bible.

As he reached for it, Kathy said, "Been in my family for three generations. I'm not particularly religious, which I suspect you may have already figured out. But the thought of that Bible being held in my parents and my grandparent's hands, and how they found peace in its words, kind of makes it special to me. Like a connection with the past, if that makes any sense?"

"Yeah, it does," Josh said, and while he meant it, he was having trouble concentrating on what she was saying. It felt as though he'd missed something. Something that was trying to break through. He couldn't put his finger on it, but it was there, simmering and wanting to surface. A long awkward moment followed, and with no inkling it was about to reveal itself, he passed the Bible back to her.

"Oh, and here's my card," she said. "If the FBI needs some independent consulting, I am available."

Chapter 54

At first, the return trip had seemed shorter. But as Josh pondered the gas gauge needle for the umpteenth time, flatlined on empty, the yellow 'low gas' warning light glowing as bright as it had when it had first come on six miles back, the trip no longer seemed so short. And now that the GPS's 'next gas station'—boarded up and derelict—was disappearing in the rearview mirror, he was having serious doubts he'd make the thirty-one miles to the station down the road.

He peered out the windshield hoping for a sign of civilization, but saw only an endless forest pressing in on both sides of the road. The sky was cloaked in a dull, greasy November twilight, a light he knew would soon fade to black . . .

Ah to hell with it, he thought. Rather than waste time on something he could not control, he turned his mind back to the case.

He knew he'd missed something, some detail, a partially unearthed fragment. He didn't know how important it was, or if in fact it would change anything, but it was there, lurking in the back of his mind.

A few miles farther down the road he was still coming up blank. Whatever it was, whether important or not, had refused to reveal itself. So he changed his focus to what he did know or at least could rationalize. Two of the women who'd played a part in Lyle Carpenter's guilty verdict had been murdered and each had a rib removed. The grave of Glenda Bunny had been dug up, and she too had a rib missing. But what's with the rib? Why bother, when a bullet in the back of the head would do the job? And who scrubbed the files, and why? And where are Lyle Carpenter and Lana Friedman, both of them gone without a trace? Is Carpenter dead? If not, how has he stayed under the radar? Is he the perp . . . ?

If Emma Bunny is correct, and it was a crucifix and not a knife in Carpenter's hand, he has a compelling motive. But then again, Emma's out of her friggin' mind.

Josh took a quick glance at the GPS and shook his head. The next gas station was still seven miles out. As he shifted in his seat to find a more comfortable position, a twinge of pain shot through his thigh. *Yeah, and why take a shot at me? Am I too close to the truth? And the truth about what?* His thoughts were starting to loop when the trees on one side of the road opened up and a set of gas pumps came into view. They were old pumps, two of them, set directly in front of a motel called The Lazy *O*.

The motel was comprised of a dozen units lined up in a row. The clapboard walls were painted white, the windowsills dusty rose. Two American flags were perched on either side of the front office window where a red neon sign, the size of a medium pizza, read: *Vacancy*.

Josh hit the brakes and slowed the rental, turning onto the motel's gravel driveway. As he pulled in alongside the pump island, he noticed there were no cars in front of the rental units, and that the gas pumps were ancient, similar to the ones he'd seen at his uncle's gas station when he was a kid. His stomach sunk . . . *What if they're not working?*

He climbed out of the car, removed the gas cap, and had the fuel nozzle in his hand when an old man came out of the motel waving to him. "I can do that for you, mister." The man jogged over, holding his blue windbreaker tight to his chest with one hand.

The man returned the nozzle to the pump, and then began fighting with his jacket zipper. He glanced at Josh. "They say it's the best patch of weather since '39 . . . but it still feels damn cold to me, especially at night. Wife says it's because of my age." He finally got the zipper free and pulled it up to his chin. He turned the metal flipper down on the side of the pump and it came to life.

As the gas started to pump, Josh felt his tension subside. "Sure am glad you're open for business. Not sure I would've made it to the next stop."

"Hear that a lot," the man said. "Ever since the station up the road shut down." He lowered his voice. "The tanks were leaking underground I hear. Them environmental people came and shut 'em down." The old man shook his head. "I've known Franky half my life, how he's gonna make it now, I don't know. Not much work in these parts."

"Yeah, it must be tough," Josh said.

"It's gotta be . . . Franky says he's doing okay, but I don't know." The old man looked at Josh. "And you should be counting your lucky stars."

"How's that?"

"Tanks near empty. If I'd had a few more before you, you'd be cooling your heels till morning when the new shipment arrives."

"I guess I am lucky," Josh replied, just as a rusted out pickup pulled up and a young girl, a teenager, got out the passenger door.

294

"You're late," the old man said to the girl. "You were to be home two hours ago. Your mother's fit to be tied."

"Come on gramps, I—"

"No. No. You know how she is, worrying herself sick, now go on in and tell her you're sorry."

"But—"

"No buts about it. Go on."

She huffed, then turned on her heel and headed toward the motel.

"Kids these days, they can be a handful," the old man said, smiling, as he watched her go inside. "The Lord, he works in mysterious ways."

"Ahh *sorry . . . ?* Could you say that again?" Josh asked.

The old man hesitated, then repeated, "The Lord, he works in mysterious ways?"

As the old man's words sunk in, Hanna's face flashed before Josh . . . He remembered her holding her pig, Mortimer, and asking him if he liked pigs? Then he remembered her asking if he was coming to the Miracle? And of her mother's stern reaction, telling her to keep quiet—that strangers were not welcome. Then he remembered her telling him that it was this Friday—eight o'clock . . . *eight o'clock, tonight.*

"I need to get into one of your rooms," Josh said.

"Sure thing, there's a bathroom in the office, help yourself."

"What? No, I need to *see* one of your rooms. One of your suites."

The old man hesitated again. "I'm, not so sure about—"

Josh flashed him his FBI ID. "I need to see it, now."

He could see the old man mulling it over, trying to decide what to do. Then the old man clicked the automatic fill lever on the nozzle, grabbed the key ring hanging from his belt, and removed one of the keys, handing it to Josh. "Room 102, two doors down from the office."

Room 102 smelled of dirty rugs and the lingering odor of bathroom cleanser. There was a round table with a brown plastic chair set by the front window. The window curtains, imprinted with pictures of cowboys on horseback were drawn closed. There were two single beds with a nightstand set between them. On the nightstand sat a bedside lamp and an alarm clock flashing a red 12:00. Josh walked over to the stand, opened the top drawer, and withdrew a Bible.

He sat down at the round table and began flipping through the pages. A minute later, he lowered the Bible before taking it up again, working through it, flipping back-and-forth. Finally, he came to a full stop when he reached Genesis 2:21, *the same numbers carved next to Lyle Carpenter's bunk.* Josh read the passage, then read it a second time out loud. *"The LORD God caused the man to fall into a deep sleep. As the man slept, he took one of his—"*

"Hey, mister?" the old man asked, poking his head in the door. "You find what you're looking for? I'd sure like to lock up."

Josh jerked his head in the direction of the old man. "What?"

"I said. Did you find anything?"

"Yeah. A murderer."

Chapter 55

The name *Rooster T's Craft Beer* didn't do much for Mary. She needed a gin and tonic, tall and packed hard with ice. A cowbell tripped as she entered, its hollow clunk announcing her arrival.

The Tiffany pendant lights over the bar cast a weak glow, and it took more than a few seconds for her eyes to adjust. In the back, a few old timers were standing around a pinball machine, its lights flashing, paddles flapping, and numbers rolling. She looked at her watch. 4:09. Her last cigarette had been unkind to her taste buds and her mouth was dry as desert sand. No one was seated at the bar, so she slid herself onto a stool.

"What can I bring you?" The bartender asked as he continued loading the dishwasher, bent over with his back to her. He was muscular, with broad shoulders and had a posterior that Mary was having trouble taking her eyes off.

"You're a musician, aren't you? I can always tell," she said, her line of sight still fixed on his rump. "I'd sure like to hear you play a tune."

"What?" The bartender finished setting the dial on the washer then glanced back at her, catching her in her eye-candy moment.

"Cheeks like that, *hell* I bet you play the clarinet."

The bartender turned fully around and raised an eyebrow. "Only chop sticks. Weak lungs, runs in the family."

Mary snorted and started to laugh.

The bartender chuckled. "So, what're you drinking?"

"G and T packed hard with ice."

"You got it. Name's Bobby T, I own this fine establishment." He eyed her for a second. "Don't believe I've seen you in here before. Pretty much know all my customers."

"Mary Kowalski. Pleased to meet you, Bobby T."

"Likewise." He reached over the bar and shook her hand. "So, what brings you to my corner of the world?"

"I'm helping the Feds with an investigation, the murders up at the church."

"No shit?" he asked, scooping a load of ice into a tall glass, then dumped in a shot of gin followed by a squirt of tonic water.

"I shit you not," she said, pulling her temporary ID from her breast pocket.

Bobby T set her drink on the counter and glanced at the ID. "FBI? No offense, but you don't look like FBI."

"I'll take that as a compliment. But like I said, I'm only helping out."

"Must be exciting?"

"I suppose so," she replied, with a certain lack of enthusiasm.

"C'mon, it has to be." Then his eyes brightened. "So . . . ? Are you getting anywhere? I mean, like—do you have a suspect?"

"Well, Bobby T, I really can't say too much, you understand." She took a long draw on her drink, smacked her lips, and looked him straight in the eye. "Ah, I'm just screwing with you, Bobby T. Truth is, we don't have much. Actually, we got zip—not even one loose thread to pick at. Town's a virtual Mayberry."

"Funny you say that, because I kind of think of it that way myself. Lynchfield's a damn fine place to raise a family. There's just no substitute for small town values, it makes for a strong—"

"Oh God, stop!" Mary said, grimacing. "Let me guess. You're running for mayor? *Not* that there's anything wrong with that."

"Yeah, sorry about that," he said. "Sara, that's my wife, she tells me I have to quit preaching. I got a soft spot for the town, I reckon."

"Who's perfect, right Bobby T?" Mary took another sip.

Bobby T nodded, then the corners of his mouth turned down. "The squatters north of town, you've heard about them I suppose?"

"Yeah. Sheriff's been talking about it."

Bobby poured himself a glass of milk and smiled. "Sheriff Holly, she'll sure as hell boot their asses out of Dodge. She's something else, isn't she?"

"If you say so," Mary replied. "Tell me, did she ever get married? The sheriff that is."

"No, I don't think so."

"Not the type to settle down?"

"I guess." He hesitated, looking somewhat preoccupied. "There's been rumors you know, about her, about Holly. I guess that's not so surprising, this being a small town. But there's been rumors that she's been spotted on the odd, well, *rendezvous*."

"*Rendezvous*? *Ohh*, I do so like a man who speaks French and plays a musical instrument."

"I've got my talents." Bobby grinned.

"Any of these *rendezvous* occur around here?"

He shook his head. "Not that I know of. Guess she don't take a shine to the locals."

"You're not too far from her age. You ever?"

"Heck no. Married my high school sweetheart, year after we graduated. Still hitched and still happy. But back in the day, back when Holly was a senior, I do recall a few tried calling on her. Her daddy though—he was the sheriff back then—he wouldn't allow it, and that's putting it mildly. He had a temper, her old man."

"Yeah? So what happened?"

"Nah, nothing really. But the boys kept their hands off her, if you understand what I'm saying."

"Why? Because the old man would hurt them?"

Bobby smiled. "Something like that."

"Her daddy still around?"

"Nope. He passed . . . must be, I dunno, close to ten years ago now." Bobby T grabbed a damp rag and started wiping the area around the beer taps. "He wasn't well liked, her old man. Word has it, not many showed for the funeral. Heard it was just Holly and one of her father's deputies who came. . . . It does seem awful small now that I think about it, so maybe there were others. People still talk about him from time to time though, him being sheriff and all."

"Her brother, Lance? He didn't attend the funeral?"

"Not sure, maybe? But I don't think he did."

"So, what's her brother like?" Mary asked.

Bobby T avoided the question and continued wiping down the counter area. He finally said, "Odd, I suppose, would be the best way to describe him."

"In what way?"

"I don't know. He's always kept to himself, has a place on the outskirts, comes in maybe once a week to get supplies. That's what I hear, anyway. Weird thing is, when Holly was in high school her brother seemed to take a real interest in anyone who came calling on her. And since he was big and quite a lot older than her, the boys kept their distance. Her daddy was bad enough, but Lance, he liked to mix it up."

Bobby finished with the counter and threw the rag in the sink. "You know, I think there were a few punches that got thrown, and someone got hurt, but that was a long time ago."

"Holly and Lance, they're blood related, right?" Mary asked. "I'm asking, because there's such a difference in their age."

"Yeah, as far as I know they are. Blood related, I mean. Holly was an afterthought, I'm guessin'? Her daddy never remarried after Holly's mom left him, if that's what you mean. As far as I know, he and Lance lived out at the ranch, alone. That is, until Holly came back. Then years later when the old man died, Lance moved out and got his own place at the edge of town. Holly had moved into town sometime before that."

"You said, 'until Holly came back'. What did you mean?"

"The way I heard it, Holly's mother took Holly with her when she left? He paused, looking like he was trying to dredge up an old memory. "Umm, yeah, that's right. I'm pretty sure Holly was gone for a spell . . . then again, I wouldn't stake my life on it, I was just a kid at the time and everything I've heard is secondhand."

Mary nodded. "Any idea how old Holly was when her mother left?"

"Not sure. Quite young, I think."

"She ever come back to town? Holly's mother, I mean."

"Not that I recall. . . . But Holly did of course. Showed up the first day of school, walked right into my seventh grade classroom. I remember, because I had a crush on her the moment I saw her. Hell, all the boys had a crush on her."

"Was her father ever a customer, here?"

"Don't really know . . . He came in only once I think. Searching for Holly. Other than that, he kept to himself, like I said." He paused. "But her daddy, he . . . he had his share of rumors too, spending all his free time out at the ranch, all secretive like."

"What sort of rumors?"

"I don't know. Town gossip, I expect."

Mary waited for him to continue.

"Word was, ladies from out of town would come visiting late at night, that sort of thing. Some say that's why his wife left him. 'Cause he was unfaithful. Others say he had secrets . . . as it was plain *unnatural* for a good looking man in his prime to be squirrelled away like that."

Mary nodded. "So, do you like working here?"

"Must, started out cleaning tables while I was still in school, doing dishes and the like. Went on to waiting tables, then tendering the bar, then got the chance to take it over."

"You buy it from the owner?"

"I did."

"So, who owns Holly's father's ranch now?"

"Um, Holly and Lance, I guess. That's what Doug the UPS guy says. Neither of them live at the ranch, though. Like I said, Lance lives at the edge of town, and she lives 'in town' which I think you already know?"

"Bobby T . . . any chance you could draw me a map, how to get me out to the ranch?"

He grabbed a napkin and drew a simple map, placing an X where the ranch was, then paused for a moment before continuing the line a little farther and placed a second X. "The ranch is easy to get to," he said, pointing his finger at the first X. "But if you end up here." He pointed at the second X. "You've gone to far, that's where the squatters' camp is. It's about eight or nine minutes down the road from the ranch."

Mary nodded, thanked him, and took the map.

Chapter 56

Mary liked to think she could see things before they happened . . . even though it didn't always work out that way. And yet, she figured if Bobby T's directions were accurate, the turnoff for the ranch should be coming up in about a mile or so, likely at the top of the next rise.

She wasn't entirely sure why, maybe it was because the sun was about to dip below the horizon, or maybe it was because the shadows coming off the telephone poles were stretching out across the road like crucifixes, but whatever it was, she was starting to think how nice it would've been if Josh was along for the ride. Not that he was much of a talker, and he certainly could be a complete asshole when he set his mind to it, but he was good company and could make her laugh. And more than anything else, he always had her back.

As she reached the top of the hill she slowed the rental to a near stop and turned into the mouth of a dirt driveway, then followed a wagon trail for fifty yards to a small two-story home with a steep pitched roof.

The house looked tired, its front steps missing a tooth, its roof shingles clawed under like hawk talons, its walls weathered and gray. Along the west side, a fieldstone chimney jutted above the roofline, its stones covered in autumn-red vines that spread across its surface like mold tendrils in a petri dish.

A dry breeze swirled outside the car, peppering sand and grit against the driver's-side window, while bits of debris caught in the rye grass fluttered in the wind. Mary stepped out of the car just as a tumbleweed the size of a beach ball bounced off the door, startling her. "Oh, would ya get real," she muttered, feeling both surprised and a little disappointed at how edgy she was.

She stepped onto the deck of the front porch and noticed all the screens had been punched out. A '50s vintage beer fridge sat unplugged next to the front door. The porch creaked and felt spongy under her shoes. There was no handle on the door, just a latch with a thick twig stuck through it to keep it closed. She reached into her inside jacket pocket and withdrew a pair of latex gloves, slipping them on.

She pulled out the twig and opened the door, running her fingers along the inside wall until she found a switch. A single lamp in the far corner of the room came on, casting an anemic light that petered out long before it reached her. A fieldstone fireplace took up most of the room's far wall. It was flanked by an alcove filled with birch firewood on one side and a set of bronze fireplace tools on the other. A roughly hewn mantle, painted black, ran the length of the fireplace, jutting out from the wall like a lumberjack's mustache.

A string of photos were lined up along the mantle end-to-end, some of them black-and-white, some in color. Mary leaned in for a closer look. They were all snaps of the same man standing next to a variety of dead animals. Picture after picture, he was kneeling, his rifle resting on his thigh, a confident smile on his face. She had to admit, the man had a rugged quality about him and seemed happy, like he was in his element. The photos were all similar, the man kneeling and smiling, and each time looking a little older.

Mary worked her way down the line until she came to the last two photos. The first was of a girl, maybe eight or nine years old, hard to tell, sitting on the man's knee. But this time, she was the one holding the rifle. The last picture was of the same girl, sitting on his knee again, same pose, but there was another person, a young man. He was almost out of focus, off to the side and barely in the frame, his arms crossed, a scowl on his face. She picked up the photo and held it to the light. *That's gotta be Holly,* she thought. *And the young man, aw . . . friggin' Lance.*

She continued to search the place, but really had no clue what she was looking for or if she'd find anything. She knew it was a long shot, but something was off. It was the same feeling that had come over her when she was a detective in Detroit. She couldn't quite place it, but it was there just the same.

Not that the place was that remarkable, far from it. For the most part, the home had the feel of a bachelor's domain. A battered, oversized couch covered with a navy blue cotton blanket took up most of the left wall, while an overstuffed leather chair faced a large box TV, set in the corner of the room.

In the kitchen, it was the same. A small wooden table with a ladder chair at either end sat in the middle of the room. A deep country sink, chipped and stained, its backsplash smeared with a film of grease and mildew, lay nestled under a window. On the table sat a single plate, a coffee cup, and a glass, all placed upside down.

She proceeded down a narrow hallway leading to the backdoor and stopped halfway. There was a picture sitting on a hallway table next to a black, 1960's dial phone. It was a framed color photo of a group of men leaning on the hood of a tow truck, and she was pretty sure one of them matched the picture of the man on the mantle.

A few feet farther down the hall she entered a bathroom on the right. There was a toilet, a sink, and a medicine cabinet. She opened the cabinet to find a half-empty tube of toothpaste, a few condoms, and a spool of dental floss. She raised the blinds and peered out the window. It was starting to get dark. She was about to step away from the window when she caught a glimpse of light coming from the barn on the other side of the yard. Her pulse jumped . . . *Oh, would ya, get a grip.*

She let out a slow breath, then retraced her steps through the house, went out through the front door and crossed the yard.

With her back pressed against the barn wall, her shoulder touching the window frame, she craned her neck and peered in through the window. She didn't expect to see anyone. *Just a light left on*, she thought. And she was right: no one was there.

The space was small, a tack room with a picnic table at its center with two wooden chairs set against one wall. A single light bulb with a pull chain hung from the ceiling. The bulb was coated in an oily grime, filling the room with a gray, dim light. A couple of saddles were pegged to the walls, along with coiled whips, reins, and a posthole auger. In one corner was a large trashcan filled to the brim, overflowing with cardboard, plastic, and a few tin cans.

She tried the door. It opened and she stepped inside.

Next to the window was a coat rack holding two coats, one rain and one winter, each hanging on pegs shaped like a horseshoe. The room smelled of dust, used oil, and a sprinkling of manure. Scattered about the floor were a variety of dead bugs, mostly beetles and wasps, dried out and waiting for the dustbin. Set below the whips was a small wooden door, maybe five feet high and narrow like a linen closet. It had been painted dark green and the paint seemed fresh.

She was about to step out into the open area of the barn when a faint scraping sound broke the silence. She froze. *What was that . . . did that come from below?* The sound seemed familiar, like that of furniture being moved. She could feel her heartbeat in her neck as she waited for it to start up again, confirming that she was indeed not alone. But there was nothing, just a dead calm. A calm disturbed only by the sound of her blood pounding in her ears. A few more seconds passed, then she let out a long, warm breath. *Goddam nerves—that's all—just dumb stupid nerves—end of story.*

Mary opened the door to the stable area, finding a large open space with a dirt floor and a half dozen stalls. All the stalls were empty except one, the last one at the far end. She could see something was inside it. And whatever it was, it was large, seeming to fill most of the stall. It was covered by an old tarp. As she walked toward it, it dawned on her that it must be a car, probably an older model given its size and boxy shape.

She was about to lift the edge of the canvas when her eye caught something on the floor at the back of the stall. It was a three-quarter inch chain, strung through a large O-ring attached to a corner post. And leaning against the post was a hand hook with a wooden handle, used for picking up bales of hay, its tip razor sharp and gleaming.

A dull metallic bang rang out.

She spun around in the direction of the sound. *It's coming from the tack room?* She grabbed the hand hook and crossed the barn floor, back to the tack room. No one was there. She stepped inside and waited. A minute went by, but there was nothing—only the sound of a fly buzzing overhead. Then, there it was, another scrape, and another, coming from below the floorboards. *Shit . . . !* Her mind began to race, calculating her next move, when her attention was once more caught by the small green door. *Ah Christ,* she thought. It was decision time. Getting the hell out of here would be the smart move. She knew that to be a fact. 'Discretion is the better part of valor', and all that bullshit . . . and yet she believed that, once you back off in life and let fear takeover, it's a slippery slope. And, if truth be told, she wasn't one to back off.

As she pulled on the door handle a rusty squeak emanated from the hinges, causing a chill to prickle down her spine. She leaned into the doorway to get a better look and paused. There was music, muffled, barely audible, but definitely coming from below. She leaned farther into the darkness. The air smelled of damp earth, stale like a basement's musty breath. Another chill ran up her neck.

She took a breath and slipped her hand into the doorway, running her fingers along a thin wooden ledge until she touched something that felt familiar. She wrapped her fingers around it, then clicked the flashlight on.

The beam was weak, producing a pale cone of light that made everything grainy like a faded black-and-white picture. She stepped onto a landing that was no more than three-feet by three-feet square. She saw another flashlight farther down the ledge, larger than the one she was holding.

She tried it, but nothing happened. Next to it was a can of rat poison, its lid rusted and bent from repeated openings. Hanging on a spike on the wall was a fly swatter, its yellow plastic surface freckled with bug guts.

The music, while still muffled, sounded vaguely familiar. It had an upbeat, dance rhythm to it, reminding her of that Swedish pop band from the '70s.

"FBI!" she called out. "FBI, who's down there?" She took a breath . . . "FBI, I'm coming down!"

She turned the flashlight toward the staircase, the hand hook still gripped in her other hand, and was thankful her eyes had begun to adjust to the darkness that surrounded her.

About a third of the way down the staircase she stopped and slowly scanned the basement with her flashlight. The clay walls looked like they'd been chiseled out of the ground, hundreds of small, concave chunks removed as though taken out with a pickaxe. The ground was covered with rough-cut planks. Set against one wall was a floor-to-ceiling gray metal shelving unit. The shelves were bare except for the bottom row, lined with canning jars, the contents no longer apparent under a thick layer of dust. At the end of the shelf was a pile of yellowed magazines resting next to a quart of Five-Star motor oil.

In the center of the basement was a large brick furnace. It had a door at its front, measuring two feet by two feet, locked with a heavy padlock.

Mary panned the light across the room, searching for the origin of the music, when her flashlight got tangled in a cobweb. "Fuck off!" she cursed under her breath.

Another scrape—louder this time. She turned in the direction of the noise and could see a soft white glow on the side of the furnace. *Strange,* she thought*, but it . . . it's like, it's coming from below the furnace.*

As she moved closer, the music grew louder. Stepping up to the side of the furnace, she looked down. The weak beam of the flashlight illuminated the top of a small iron door. The door was arched, with heavy rivets punched into it every few inches. A narrow staircase, maybe seven feet long, descended down to the base of the arched door. The space looked cramped, with barely enough room to open the door. The door was slightly ajar, a thin wedge of light pouring out onto the tiny entryway.

No, goddamn way I'm going down there, she told herself. Suddenly, the music stopped and the door began to open, the wedge of light growing and flooding the entryway, spilling out across the bottom step of the staircase onto a gnarled root suspended in the air. A second later, a man began to squeeze out from behind the door, head and shoulders first. He set a kerosene lamp outside the door, followed by a miniature boom box and a shovel. Then he looked up.

The man did a double take. "*Mary?* What the hell are you doing here?" Lance asked, his tone both harsh and startled.

She hesitated, holding the hand hook behind her back. "Uh-uh. The question is, Lance." Her fight-or-flight response had kicked in, leaning hard to the former. "What're *you* doing down there, under the furnace?"

"Alarm tripped. Had to check it out, which I have. And now, I'm asking you again. What're you doing here?"

Remembering his business card, she replied, "You find any burglars down there?"

He didn't respond at first, then asked, "How long have you been here?"

"Long enough, I suppose. *Nice music . . .*"

Lance pressed his lips together and shook his head, then said, "You still haven't told me what you're doing here, Mary."

"It's your father. I've been hearing a lot about him, thought I'd check him out."

"Why?"

"He was the sheriff at the time of Lyle Carpenter's trial. That trial seems to have a connection to the murders at the church, what with Myrna Hudson and Senator Parker having taken part in it. I'm trying to get a full picture of all those involved in the trial." The light from the lantern lit only part of his face, making it difficult for her to tell if he was buying her story.

"Are you alone?" he asked.

Mary didn't respond.

"I'll take that as a yes. What about the other one, your friend?"

A chill touched her shoulder, running into the nape of her neck. "Josh. He's around, trying to get traction, looking for leads—"

"No! Not him. *Hell* no. The FBI skirt he's been seen with. The looker."

"Oh, Rachael. I don't know where she is."

"That's a shame. 'Cause I've been thinking about her some, thinking maybe I'd like to get to know her better." A smile started to form on his thin lips before fading. "So, you find what you're looking for?"

"What?" Mary asked.

"What you're looking for—did you find it?"

"Like I said, your father was in the thick of it, the trial and all, him being sheriff. So I thought I should have a look around, see what he was all about."

"And what *exactly* have you found?" His voice slid hard into sarcasm.

Mary sneered. "Just you, sweetheart."

Lance started to chuckle, leaning back against the furnace, shovel in hand, his gaze falling onto the narrow staircase. Then, as though he'd made a decision, he raised his eyes to her and gave her a smile that seemed almost genuine, but she knew it wasn't.

Mary swallowed, knowing full well he was calculating his next move, when an overwhelming urge to run for the stairs hit her. She clenched her teeth. "Looks like your daddy had a dismal existence if you ask me."

"You didn't know him," Lance replied, his demeanor souring.

Mary forced out a short puff of air, the whole situation was starting to piss her off. "The way I see it, there's not much to know. The old fart liked to kill things. Full stop."

Lance smirked. "Yeah well, I think you'd better be movin' on. So, you be a good little girl now and leave . . . before I forget I once had a sweet spot for you."

She noticed his hand was clutching the shovel, and could tell he was coming to a decision. For once, she wished she'd kept her mouth shut. "Yeah, okay, fine Lance, I'm leaving. Still, what I don't get is, just what are you doing down there?"

"It's no concern of yours—got an arrangement that's all . . ." he blurted, then said, "Just fuck off! Okay, Mary?"

"What're you saying, Lance? Arrangement with who?"

"It's none of your business."

313

Mary just stared at him.

"I'm cleaning up the place, gonna be putting it on the market. Leave it at that, all right?"

"Sure you are, starting with below the furnace?" she sneered.

"That's right, starting here." He threw the shovel back inside the small room, slamming the metal door closed before sliding an iron bar through the clasp, sealing the door shut. "Anything else I can help you with?"

"Piss off, Lance," Mary said, and headed toward the stairs.

"And I wouldn't be coming back here again without a warrant if I was you!" His voice rising. "People can disappear around these parts. You got that*, sweetheart?"*

~ ~ ~

No sooner had she started the rental and dropped it into gear when an old three quarter ton 4-by-4 pulled in behind her, Lance at the wheel, an annoying grin on his face partially caught by the dashboard lights.

The way back to town wasn't far, maybe a ten-minute ride, but with shithead following so close behind, the trip was beginning to feel like it would never end. Then, as Lynchfield came into view, the truck veered off onto a secondary road and dissolved into the night.

Chapter 57

With the Lazy O motel disappearing in his rearview mirror, Josh punched in Rachael's number and got: *'The caller cannot be reached at this time.'*

"Goddamnit!" he growled, then noticed the low battery icon on his cell and put a call through to Holly. She picked up on the second ring.

"Holly, have you seen Rachael and Mary?"

"Not Mary, but Rachael's here. You wanna talk—?"

"Put me on speaker."

Holly set the phone on the counter next to the coffee pot. "You're on."

"Look, I can't get into details now, but the leader of that camp of freeloaders, the squatters' camp, is Lyle Carpenter. He's the killer, I'm sure of it. And I think Emma could be in trouble. And Lana too, if she's still alive, which I think she is."

Holly glanced at Rachael. "Greta checked in five minutes ago, Emma's at home, she's okay, nothing new to report."

"Have Emma brought in and put her in lockup with Hanna. Greta stays with them in the cell—got it?"

Holly didn't respond and walked over to the window.

"Understood," Rachael said, glancing over at Holly.

"Look, there's some kind of ceremony going down at the mill, at eight o'clock tonight. And if I'm right that Lana *is* alive, then she's in serious trouble."

Rachael glanced at her watch. "That gives us barely an hour."

"I'm no more than thirty-five minutes out, heading for the camp now. We'll meet out front at 7:45 and go in together. Look, we don't know how many of his followers are involved, so no heroics. We go in together, got that?"

"Copy that," Rachael said.

Holly turned back from the window. "I'll call Hal, he's out on patrol. Have him meet us there."

"And I think it's time Mary and I each had a gun," Josh said.

"Consider it done," Holly said. "Shotguns work for you?"

"*Perfect* . . . Look, my phone's about to die, so call Mary and get her up to speed, okay?"

"Will do," Rachael said, her words coming through just as his cell died.

Holly looked at Rachael, her lips drawn to a thin line. "We'd better go."

"*Now?*"

"We should get there early, scope it out before Josh arrives."

Rachael wasn't convinced it was such a great idea as someone might spot them, but then again, it wasn't an entirely bad idea. "What about Emma?"

"I'll call Greta on route," Holly snapped. She paused for a second, then in an apologetic tone said, "Maybe you should follow me? I know a back way into the camp."

Chapter 58

Mary continued toward town, turned on the radio, tuned in a country station and tried to forget her encounter with Lance . . . The prick was up to something, she was sure of it, and yet what could she do? That is, if there was anything to do? And maybe there *was* nothing, maybe it was just her imagination running wild. *Bullshit,* she thought.

What bothered her the most was that smug look on his face, like he believed he had power over her, like she was a vulnerable woman. The more she thought about it, the more her guts burned.

She wanted to turn around and head straight back, to find out what he was really up to. But if she did, she'd need a warrant. And even if she could get a hold of Josh or Rachael, the chances of getting one were slim-to-none. All she had was a hunch, no more than a vague feeling, and that wouldn't go far. And she sure as hell couldn't go to Holly, so after another minute of deliberation, she decided to let the warrant go—but not Lance, she couldn't let him go.

By the time she reached the edge of town, she'd made up her mind. She had to know what he was up to. Something wasn't right, she could feel it—she had to go back. And if she did find anything, she'd find a way to get the warrant and then come back and make it stick. It wasn't the first time she'd broken the rules.

She slowed the rental and turned into Triple A Hardware and Building Center. After a few minutes of searching she'd found what she was looking for and walked to the checkout, placing a claw hammer, a flashlight, a packet of latex gloves, and a small can of bear spray on the counter.

A sixtyish man behind the counter, his hair gray and thinning, raised an eyebrow. "Better be careful with that. Sprayed myself once, by accident. Had a reaction to it, had to go to the hospital. Spent the next day at home recovering and couldn't go to work, the boss didn't appreciate that. And make sure you're up wind if you're going to use it or you'll be getting a taste of it yourself. Trust me, you *don't* want that."

"Not likely I'll need it, but thanks for the advice," Mary said.

~ ~ ~

It was shortly after 7 p.m. when Mary turned onto the ranch driveway, rolling to a stop in front of the house. Both the house and barn were dark, except for an outside light left on over the barn's side door.

She opened the car door. The air was calm and cool, but the sky behind the house was alive, pulsing, flashes of lightning branching out, the clouds throbbing with life. "Friggin' late in the year for a storm," she muttered.

And yet, if 'one one-thousand, two one-thousand' was still reliable, she calculated the main part of the thunderhead rolling to the north was a good two miles off. She swung her legs out of the rental and stood up, the claw hammer tucked into her belt, the new flashlight in her hand and the bear spray in her jacket pocket. She slipped on a fresh pair of gloves and had just turned toward the barn when another bolt lit the sky, hissing and striking behind the house—followed by a thunderous boom. *"Ahh, would ya give me a break!"*

She took a deep breath and closed her eyes, telling herself to be calm when her cell went off in her pocket. She fished it out.

"Mary it's Rachael. I just got off a call with Josh, he's coming in from Zuma. He thinks there'll be trouble at the mill tonight. Holly and I will be meeting up with him there, 7:45 sharp, then we'll storm the place together."

Mary looked at her watch. "Yeah, all right. I . . . I have to check on something first, but I'll be there, no problem. So, what's going on?"

"He thinks there could be another killing, tonight at the mill. We'll fill you in when you get there."

Mary hesitated, then said, "I'll be there. 7:45." She hung up just as a large raindrop splattered on her nose, then another hit her cheek, then another . . .

She took a moment to gather her thoughts before resetting her sights on the barn.

The new flashlight helped navigate the yard, but it was doing little to relieve the tension in the back of her neck. She knew there was plenty of time to finish here and make it to the squatters' camp, but that wasn't what was bothering her. Lance was up to something, she could feel it. And whatever it was, it couldn't be good—that, she would bet on.

About halfway across the yard she stopped, suddenly realizing how completely alone she was. The flashlight's beam cut a narrow but diminishing swath in front of her, darkness seeping in all around. She swallowed and reminded herself, *Get in—satisfy yourself, and get the hell out.*

As she approached the side door of the barn, her spirits began to lift. The hooded light, rain dripping off its tin edge, was illuminating a small circle of grass in front of the door. She grabbed the handle, then paused. *Okay, no one's here, but when the alarm trips, 'numbnuts' will be on his way, sure enough. That'd give me at least ten minutes before he arrives, maybe longer if I'm lucky.* She thought about it for a second and shook her head. *Ten minutes, tops.*

She stepped through the side door and listened. No beeping, no countdown, no alarm, nothing. She exhaled and turned her attention to the green door. It was padlocked, as she figured it would be. She pulled the hammer from her waistband. Inserting the claw teeth around the clasp, she levered the hammer against the doorframe and wrenched on it, ripping the clasp free.

As she opened the door a high-pitched beeping pierced the air. *Shit . . . ! Ninety seconds, then the siren's gonna blow.* Her heart throttled up as the beeping pressed down on her eardrums, then as suddenly as it had started—the beeping stopped. She stood there, listening . . . There was nothing, only the distant rumble of the storm.

Her line of sight came to rest on the overflowing trashcan. She considered it for a second, then set the hammer on the picnic table and began digging in the trashcan, tossing out pizza boxes, newspapers, egg cartons, and empty tin cans. She'd almost reached the bottom when she found what she was searching for. A glass pop bottle. She dug some more and bit down on her lip as she snatched up a pickle jar.

She placed the pop bottle inside the pickle jar and said, "Perfect."

She quickly pulled a wooden chair over to the side door and climbed up onto the seat. She cracked the door open a few inches, reached up and carefully placed the jar on the door's top edge, holding it steady until she was sure it would stay put.

She took a second to look at her creation, then glanced at her watch—nine minutes. With the flashlight held tight in her hand, she made her way down the basement staircase.

She crossed the basement floor and came to an abrupt halt, peering down at the narrow stairs leading to the arched furnace door. Without warning, gooseflesh covered her arms and a shiver ran through her core. "Oh, for Christ's sake!" she cursed. "Just get on with it."

The steps were small, steep, and uneven. She stepped off the bottom rung and put her foot on the floor. She pulled on the iron slide bar and it slid back with a clunk, the door cracking open. She glanced at her watch and was about to go inside when a muted *whump* broke the quiet. *What was that? Was it outside?* She couldn't quite place it, so she waited for a second to see if it would repeat itself. Nothing. She glanced again at her watch. "*Shit!*"

She ducked down and slipped in through the doorway, and found herself standing ankle deep in a grayish, white ash. The space was tight, measuring roughly two feet wide, six feet long, and seven feet high. She raised the flashlight, moving the beam across what looked like red brick walls that were now covered in soot. The space smelled dirty like a wet ashtray; the air was making her nose itch and her eyes water.

A faint groan came from behind her and she turned to the iron door. *Did that just move?* Then she felt something crawling on her shoulder. *Oh God, don't be a spider*, she thought. She fumbled with the flashlight, almost dropping it as she brushed whatever it was off her shoulder. She was choking down an urge to scream when the beam of the flashlight lit up a single fly caught in a web not more than six inches from her face. Its tiny body was twitching, its one wing free and frantically flapping as it waited for its dinner guest to arrive. Mary took an uneasy breath and glanced around, checking to see if there were any other guests close by.

Turning in a tight circle on her heels, she could feel her panic grow. *Get in and get out!* she told herself. Then, in the corner she saw a black garbage bag leaning to one side, a thin layer of gray ash coating its lower lip. Beside the bag was a shovel. She recognized it. *The shovel Lance threw in before he closed the door.*

She looked at her watch and calculated she had maybe six minutes, assuming he was on his way. *Ahh. Quit thinking! Finish up and get out.*

She followed the beam of light to the ceiling, but there was no ceiling, at least not what she'd expected, only heavy iron bars that ran its length, each set about four inches apart. She studied the bars and thought she could see something on them. She moved the light around to get a better view and realized it was nothing, not in the physical sense anyway, more like a shadow. And while she couldn't put her finger on it, something in the back of her mind, the primal part of her brain, knew the answer. Looking beyond the bars she saw the furnace chamber with its firebrick walls . . . Suddenly, the answer hit her. *That's no shadow. I'm in a crematorium.*

As that thought sunk in, her need to scream kicked into overdrive. She clenched her teeth and pushed back the urge, then grabbed the shovel and began running it through the ashes, hoping beyond hope that she was wrong, that it was just her imagination. She'd covered a third of the space when the shovel clunked against something solid, not heavy, but solid. She dropped the shovel, and began raking her hand through the ashes. A few seconds later she felt it, running her fingers across a gracefully sloping curve with a pitted surface. Her index finger slipped into a round hole roughly the size of a quarter. She took a breath and pulled the object from the ashes, placing it into the light and saw an eye socket and the upper part of a cheekbone.

Without warning, a smashing sound like that of breaking glass came from above. She froze. "*He's here...*" She quickly slipped out through the arched doorway, climbed the narrow flight of stairs and crossed the planked flooring. She had just arrived at the bottom of the staircase when she heard footsteps directly above. She took a step back and ducked under the staircase, clicking the flashlight off.

The basement door opened, and she could hear Lance mumbling. She had no idea what he was saying, but that didn't matter much because he was on his way down.

Each wooden step groaned as it received the full weight of his body. He had barely come halfway down when he stopped and scanned the basement, his flashlight beam moving in a slow circular motion bringing objects to life: the metal shelving, the carved clay walls, and finally the furnace. "*Ohh Marrrry...* I know you're *down here...*" Lance said, letting out a short chuckle. "I know it's you— ya little twat. And I warned you about comin' back... didn't I?"

Chapter 59

The scent of leather coming off the heel of his cowboy boots could've reminded Mary of many things, of peaceful times, of sharing a brandy with Josh by the fire, of curling up on Crawlie's rooftop deck with a good book and enjoying a smoke—but not tonight, not crouched behind the staircase, staring at the tip of a shotgun barrel.

"Just so you know, Mary. I've always kind of liked you . . . And, about this . . . about, you know—tonight, and what I gotta do, well, you know it's nothing personal, right?" Lance started to laugh, squeezing the handle of the .45 holstered low on his hip. "Don't you just hate that, when some asshole tells you, it's *'Nothing personal.'* Course ya hate it. 'Cause when someone's doing you wrong . . . it's very personal—now ain't it, darling? But hey, doesn't have to be all bad you know, if you wanna play along with me, we could have ourselves a little fun before the big finale. Wha'da ya say, Mary?"

Silence.

"What was that? Cat got your tongue . . . ? Ah, don't matter much, 'cause I really don't give a hoot . . . like 'em younger, anyhow."

Mary looked around beneath the staircase, her mind scrambling, searching for something to beat the motherfucker to death with . . . *Screw this!* she thought, and reached through the opening between the steps, grabbed his ankles and pulled back with everything she had.

Lance cried out, then stumbled and tumbled down the stairs, landing on his back, smacking his head on the wood floor; his shotgun skidding a few feet away from him.

He groaned and rolled onto his belly, then got to his hands and knees and gave his head a shake. He looked confused, still trying to shake off the fall when Mary drop kicked him in the face, snapping his head back. His head remained suspended for a split second, his upper teeth cut through his top lip, then he toppled over onto the floor.

Mary stepped over him and carefully reached down, withdrawing his revolver from its holster, the bear spray pointed at his face. She paused, stuck the gun in her waistband, then turned and ran up the stairs as a long rumble of thunder rolled overhead. Upon reaching the top landing, she grabbed the handrail and sucked in a short breath, only to have it freeze in her lungs. Across the tack room and below the coatrack sat two pair of work boots. The pair that caught her attention had a single word stamped in yellow on the back of each boot: *Zodiac.*

She knelt down in front of the boots, turned one over, and saw stamped into its sole a capital Z set inside a small circle, the tread above the circle, unblemished.

She reached for the other boot and stopped in her tracks, her back rigid, her body motionless. "You're behind me—aren't you?" She wanted to jump up, swing around and spray him in the face. . . . Drawing in a deep breath, she mustered all her courage and willed herself to turn her head, only to be staring at the black hole of a shotgun barrel no more than an inch from her face.

At that moment, everything seemed to slow down, become unreal, like a dream . . . then the acrid scent of gunpowder registered and it was all too real.

Lance stood in the doorway staring down at her, a pained grin on his face, his teeth and upper lip leaking blood.

"Yours . . . ?" she asked, touching the boot.

He nodded and tried to smile. "You'd think . . . wouldn't ya?" He clucked his tongue once and squeezed down on the trigger . . .

Chapter 60

The hollow *click* hung in the air—a misfire. Disbelief flashed in Lance's eyes. He looked down, and went to jack another shell into the chamber when Mary swung the door shut. She heard him stumble, then came a loud boom that shook the wall, jarring a shower of dust from the top of the doorframe.

Mary could still sense the vibration rattling in her chest as she ran across the lawn. It was now raining hard and the ground was soupy, the lawn spotted with puddles. Her left foot slipped on the mud as she pulled the driver's door open. She threw the boot and gun on the passenger seat, slamming the door shut behind her. Wiping her face with her shirtsleeve she dropped the car into gear and punched the gas. The front wheels spun on the slick surface, swerving the car as it made its way to the main road. As she cranked the wheel, turning onto the road, she glanced back to see Lance standing under the hooded light, talking on his cell, his arms waving—his face livid.

A couple of miles out Mary stopped checking her rearview mirror and slowed the car to a more manageable speed. *The road's straight,* she thought, *so where is he? And what was he doing on the phone? And who was he talking to?* Another mile passed before she remembered the boot. She clicked on the overhead light, reached across to the passenger seat and turned the boot over. "Ah, shit!" She slammed the gas pedal to the floor.

Retrieving her phone from her back pocket, she hit dial. It went straight to Josh's voicemail.

"C'mon Josh! Pick up your friggin' phone!" she cried, then tried again and got the same message. She glanced at her watch. *Okay, okay. I'm gonna make it there well ahead of him . . . That is, if he's on time.* She reconsidered. *Ah, Josh. You lied, didn't you, you asshole? You're already there. You're going in alone.*

Chapter 61

Rachael kept the Jeep's taillights in sight, maintaining a distance of a few hundred feet between her and Holly. She could hear thunder off in the distance as she glanced at the speedometer, which was hovering slightly below 60 mph.

About a mile farther down the road, Holly slowed to 40, then 30, then the Jeep's lights went off, popping back on a split second later.

What the . . . ? Rachael thought.

The impact was sudden. The last thing Rachael heard was a deafening crunch of metal on metal. Her head whipped sideways then recoiled, smashing against the window. Then everything went black.

The tow truck had shot out at high speed from a secondary road, T-boning Rachael's Tahoe and forcing it off the road and down a steep embankment. The Tahoe slid sideways for the first fifty-feet before the wheels caught a drainage ditch and flipped, landing on its roof and sliding another twenty yards before hitting a tree and coming to a halt.

The tow truck driver stopped at the edge of the road and peered down at the SUV, watching as one of its wheels still spun. The truck headlights were bright, lighting the forest canopy above the Tahoe. The driver put the truck in park, turned off the engine, but left the lights on.

The embankment had a steep grade, and the driver's boots slipped under him as he made his way down toward the SUV, grabbing at weeds and shrubs in an attempt to slow his descent.

Rachael woke face down in the dirt, lying next to the Tahoe. A horrendous ache pounded in her head as she tried to focus, her thoughts dull and confused. Then a jolt of pain shot through her legs, followed by the realization that her pants were off and an enormous weight was pressing down on her thighs. Her eyes opened wide as a large, calloused hand slid under her panties, cupping her ass and giving it a hard squeeze.

The driver's weight was on the back of her thighs, his breathing forced and erratic. She tried to raise her torso and another shot of pain hit her.

"Get off of me!" She demanded. "I'm FBI, you won't—"

"Shut the fuck up!" The driver yelled, as he fumbled with his belt buckle.

"You won't get away with this!"

He started to chuckle. "Yeah I will, darlin'." He grabbed hold of her panties, tearing them off with one pull. Then he grabbed her hair and yanked her head back toward him, her neck craning until she could almost see his face. Pain radiated from her ribs, and she could barely breathe.

"I've been thinking about you, darlin'. Mmm, mm. Yes, I have . . ."

Thrusting one knee between her legs, then the other, he spread her thighs. With the shifting of his weight, her left leg and arm came loose. She knew she had to move fast, because once he dropped on top of her, all hope was lost.

She raised her calf, and with her free hand pulled the two-inch, wafer-thin knife from its sheath.

Rotating the blade 90 degrees, she plunged it into his thigh and pulled with everything she had, cutting muscle and tendons, hoping to inflict as much damage as possible. The driver screamed and rolled off of her, the knife still lodged in his leg, a thick stream of blood squirting from the long, meaty gash.

Rachael got to her hands and knees, breathing hard, trying to ignore the pain in her ribs. As she started to stand, a hand latched onto her ankle, gripping it tight. She looked back and saw the knife in his other hand. As he raised it, she caught a glimpse of a jagged shard of metal behind him, jutting out from the SUV's frame. In one motion, she kicked back with her leg, her foot punching him in the center of his chest, throwing him backward. A low groan escaped his lips as the tip of the shard poked through his shirt. His chin dropped and his head turned sideways, eyes open and unfocused. Rachael got to her feet, grabbed his hair and jerked his head back. She'd seen him before. It was Holly's brother, Lance. She let his head drop and said, *"Rot in hell . . ."*

She found her pants and put them on, then returned to the SUV hoping to find her cell and spent a frantic minute looking for it. When it was clear the phone was lost, she crawled back out, clawing her way up the embankment toward the headlights. As she reached the top of the slope her mind began to cloud over with pain, forcing her to stop and catch her breath. After a moment she stood up and headed for the tow truck.

The keys were in the ignition. She started the engine, dropped it into gear, and booted it for the camp.

A half-mile down the road, her world faded to black again, her foot easing off on the accelerator as the truck veered to the left and rolled into a shallow ditch, where it stalled . . .

Chapter 62

Holly spotted a space next to a white panel van that was parked by the entrance to the big tent and pulled in. She checked her watch. The ceremony was set to start in thirty minutes. She got out, climbed up onto the front bumper of her Jeep, and scanned the road leading into camp. There was no sign of either Rachael or Josh. And other than the white van and some old pickups next to the squatters' wagons, the parking lot was empty.

Walking past the van she noticed its side door was open. A man was inside, pulling a large empty wooden box toward the door. He was bent over, had a pair of oversized black headphones on his head, and was wearing a stained white T-shirt that failed to cover his protruding belly. He turned his head to look at her. There was a red licorice hanging from the corner of his mouth, and a shallow grin on his lips that quickly turned into a frown.

Ignoring him, Holly continued to the tent entrance, drew back a flap, and was instantly immersed into a sea of chanting and the pungent smell of incense and smoke. It took a moment for her to get her bearings.

Given the congregation's fevered chanting, she figured the commencement of the ceremony would start on time, if not sooner. And whoever was presiding was likely behind the black curtain at the back of the stage, preparing for the big event.

Not wanting to draw attention to herself, she ducked out of the tent and skirted around to the back, looking for another way in when she saw a wooden ramp leading from the back of the tent to the face of the watermill. She climbed up onto the ramp and walked to the mill and opened the door. There was light coming from the other side of the room, casting shadows off of the thick hand-hewn pillars, and the heavy links of chain that hung down from the ceiling. As she stepped around the massive iron cogs of the grinding mill, she saw a woman, unconscious, strapped to a wooden platform held up by two ox-cart-sized wheels. The woman was dressed in a black, ankle length dress, her wrists and ankles tied with leather straps to the four corners of the platform. Holly recognized the woman from her photograph. Lana Friedman.

On the floor next to one of the large wheels was a weathered gray casket. Its lid had been removed, and it contained what appeared to be a skeleton.

A man was standing next to the wooden platform with his back to Holly. He turned when she entered. He had on a long, white gown with a short hooded cape that draped over his shoulders, a black skullcap on his head and a large gold cross on a chain around his neck. Red shoes poked out from under his gown, and a large hunting knife was in his hand.

"Ahh hell," Holly said, recognizing the man. "Lyle, what are you doing?"

Lyle stared at the intruder for a moment before a look of recognition registered on his face.

"You've finally come, Holly? I've been wondering when you'd show." His voice was soft, as though he was completely at ease with the situation.

"Would've come earlier too, but you've done a good job of hiding yourself, Lyle. Changing your name, not to mention all this." Holly held her arms open. "But I have to say, you *do* look different. The years have been unkind to you."

Lyle gave her a loving smile. "I didn't change my name, Holly. God gave it to me. 'Father Paul'. It's a righteous name, don't you think?"

"If you say so," Holly said. From the corner of her eye, she saw Lana take a breath.

"God has called upon me, Holly," Lyle said, his voice rising. "And I have answered his call. There is salvation waiting for all of us. For you too, all you have to do—is believe."

Holly cleared her throat and huffed. "So, what are we doing here Lyle, and why is that woman strapped to an ox cart? And why, Lyle, are you holding that knife in your hand?"

Lyle cocked his head as though he didn't understand. "It's all right, Holly, we can't all be believers. Which is sad, because only God's children will be allowed into the next life." His eyebrows knitted closer together. "Oh, you don't understand. Nobody does, only God. But you'll see."

"See what Lyle?"

"My miracle. Megan is coming home," he said, his eyes glowing.

"A Miracle? Uh huh, and God told you Megan's coming home, did he?"

Lyle's grip tightened on the knife as he cut into the dress covering Lana's ribcage.

"Now, hold on, Lyle. You don't want to be doing that. It's just going to get you in deeper trouble."

Lyle tilted his head. "You don't understand."

"You keep saying that, but what exactly are we talking about here, Lyle? What is it that I don't understand?"

"God, he understands. For he sacrificed his son for us, and only through sacrifice can God be sure of our love for him."

Holly rested her hand on her .38. "That is a load of horseshit, Lyle. You *are* insane, you know that—don't you?" Holly watched the knife. "Look, I don't have time for this, Lyle. You're living in a fantasy world, can't you see that? You're a sick man, and you need help."

"You're wrong! Those who took her away from me, their sacrifice will bring her back to me!" He gave his head a hard jerk as if trying to shake off an unwanted thought. "God understands me! No one else does, but you'll see. I am right! God will deliver Megan back to me!"

"Ohh, Lyle." Holly sighed. "How can I make you understand?" She took a few steps toward him, doing her best to give him a reassuring smile. "You see, Myrna and Doris and the others? They didn't take Megan away from you—*I did*."

Lyle's brow knitted tight across his forehead, a bewildered look filling his face.

"What you saw in that little slut, frankly, I could never figure out."

"You're lying—you're trying to—"

"Slit your girl's neck like she was a Sunday hen. Thing is, she bled out so fast, I had to jump out of the way or she would've ruined my dress. I mean, how would've I explained that?"

"You! You're lying! You just don't want to witness my miracle!"

Holly smiled and drew her .38. *"Ohh Lyle,* you never had a chance. The cards were all stacked against you. Daddy wasn't going to see his little angel fry. But *you . . .* trash like you? Yeah, that'd be okay. But hell, if he'd known you'd deflowered his little girl? Well Lyle, there wouldn't have been a trial, now would there? I guess you could say, in a way, I saved your life." She frowned and her eyes went cold. "But I gotta say, it has stuck in my craw something awful, the thought of you still sucking air all these years."

Lyle tilted his head as though he still didn't get it.

"What, Lyle? You thought you could *fuck me* then *forget me?* You were my first love Lyle, don't you understand?"

Lyle's eyes darkened and he lunged for her. Holly stepped back and a tremendous boom rang out as a slug pierced his chest, severing his spine and dropping him to the floor.

The chanting died down, then rose back up again—louder than before.

Holly holstered her gun and sat down beside Lyle, resting his head on her lap. Reaching over, she picked up the knife. "You know, I should've done this from the get go." She placed the edge of the blade on his throat and slid it gently across his neck, cutting the skin. A thin red line oozed behind the blade's path, blood trickling out and running down his neck. "Sure, your little whore was out of the picture. But knowing you were still alive, well, it bothered me something awful. I know, I know, it's weird to think that way, but it did Lyle, just the same—" Holly stopped and turned her head.

Josh was calling her name . . .

She slipped the knife under her thigh and looked down at Lyle. He was trying to tell her something. She lowered her ear to his mouth, but heard only a gurgle as blood filled his lungs. She kissed his forehead, then placed her hand over his mouth and pinched his nostrils closed. He lay there motionless, his eyes wide, as the screams buried deep inside him faded.

Then Holly pushed him off her lap, raising her head as Josh entered.

"Holly, are you all right? I heard a gunshot."

"Josh, thank God you're here! Lyle, the crazy bastard, he went insane, tried to kill himself—then he lunged at me."

"What?" Josh asked, then saw the shallow cut on Lyle's throat, his body twisted over, his head turned sideways, blood splattered on his white robe. Crossing the room he checked Lana's neck for a pulse. Her skin was warm, her pulse slow, but strong.

He turned back to Holly. "Is he dead?"

Holly sighed. "I . . . I'm afraid he is."

Josh grabbed Holly's hand and helped her to her feet. "Why didn't you wait for me? And where's Rachael? She was with you. And Mary, where's she?"

Holly shrugged and looked down at Lyle. "Poor mixed up soul. Such a sad, sad, boy."

"What're you talking about? *Where* is Rachael?"

"I guess his troubles are all over now." Her tone was growing more distant.

"Answer me! *Where* are they?"

Holly looked him in the eye. "You love her, don't you? It's all right, a woman knows these things."

"What?"

"No, really. It's okay, you can tell me. I won't be mad."

"Holly. Tell me, where is Rachael? Something happen to her?"

"Funny really. One minute she was there, and the next, well—she wasn't. *Gosh,* you know, you're right, something must've happened to her."

Josh studied her for a second. "Rachael, she is okay, right?"

Holly started to laugh. "Oh, she's got her hooks in you good, doesn't she Lover Boy? I have to say, I am surprised. Never would've pegged you for being such a pussy." Holly drew her gun. "But you're whipped, aren't ya, stud!" She raised the gun, pointing it at his chest.

Josh stood there saying nothing.

"Am I lucky or what? Get to finish off two of you bastards in one day. You're all alike—fuck 'em and forget 'em . . . The good ol' boy's badge of honor, huh?"

Josh remained silent, staring at her, his breathing calm.

"What?" She smiled. "Oh, yes you did . . . you thought you could *fuck* me then *forget* me! Then you'd just go on with your life. Well, sorry to break it to you." Tears began welling in her eyes. "Oh, that's right, I've seen how you've been looking at her, like I don't matter. Like the two of you finally found each other. How special. You thought you're gonna throw me away, didn't you? Like I'm nothing . . . like I'm used meat!"

"Ahh man . . . it was you. You shot me. You made the boots prints outside the hotel." He paused as another thought struck him. "And the gun—the .22 caliber—it's the same gun that shot the student coming home for Christmas. The student that bled out."

"Oh, good for you!" Holly said, wiping a tear away. "I have to say, you're smarter than you look. But you know, this time, I'm thinking I won't be missing the target."

Josh raised his hands. "Holly. Put down the gun, okay? You're not thinking straight."

"Uh-uh, you are so wrong. I'm thinking just fine. Because I've seen how you look at her." She shook her head. "So, you can just . . . go . . . fuck yourself!"

Chapter 63

Mary turned off the road, crossed a cattle gate, and drove another hundred yards before the watermill came into view. That's when she heard it, the faint, distinct echo of a gunshot. "Ahh, no!" she cried and hit the gas, the front wheels spinning on loose gravel and spraying stones into the air. As the car careened into the parking area the passenger-side wheel caught a crater-sized pothole, swerving the rental sideways before it came to an abrupt halt behind Holly's Jeep.

Mary scrambled out of the car, sprinting between the Jeep and the white panel van and ran straight into a giant tub of a man backing out, ass-first, from the van's side door. She rebounded hard and hit the ground on her back, the wind knocked out of her. She was shaking it off when a large, plump hand with sausage-like fingers came into view. She grabbed the man's hand, and as she rose, his hairy belly grazed her cheek. The man began telling her that she should be more careful and watch where she was going.

"Shut it!" she growled, giving him *the look*. The big man took a step back and Mary raced for the tent.

The congregation was on its feet, chanting, their trance-like gaze fixed on the stage. Mary shouldered her way through the faithful, zigzagging, and almost tripped on an incense pot before making it to the stage.

She stopped at the black curtain, taking a second to gather her thoughts, then drew the .45 from her waistband and pulled back the curtain. The space was empty. Then she saw an open flap at the back of the tent and stepped through it. She walked across a wooden ramp to the watermill, entered, and quickly maneuvered around some large wooden pillars. As she stepped out from behind a huge iron cog, she saw Holly pointing a gun directly at Josh, her finger squeezing down on the trigger as she cried, "So, you can just . . . go . . . fuck yourself!"

"Drop it!" Mary shouted.

A single gunshot rang out . . . and Holly dropped.

Chapter 64

The ER was quiet, just as it had been the last time Josh was there. The same admitting clerk was at her station, sipping her tea, the chairs in the waiting area empty. Josh was about to step up to the clerk when the doctor who had taken care of him earlier came around the corner. She paused then smiled, acknowledging him.

"I'm looking for a patient named, Rachael Tanner?"

The doctor thought for a moment, then pointed down the hall. "Miss Tanner was moved to Unit two. Third room to the right."

"How is she?"

"She should be okay. Mild concussion and a cracked rib. We'll be keeping her here overnight for observation."

"So, she'll be all right?"

The doctor nodded. "Gave her a sedative, expect she'll be ready to leave in the morning." Then the doctor checked her pager and walked away.

Josh headed down the hall to Nursing Station 2. No one was around, so he continued to the third room on the right. The door was partially open, he knocked and then entered. There was an unoccupied bed closest to the door, and a curtain drawn around another bed by the window.

Josh drew back the curtain and saw a man holding Rachael's hand. He had a phone to his ear and a sullen look on his face. The man looked up to see Josh, frowned, and raised his index finger, indicating he'd be a minute.

You must be Thomas, Josh thought.

Twenty seconds later, the man ended his call.

"How is she?" Josh asked.

"Sleeping. Doc says she'll be okay."

An awkward silence took over as Josh stared at Rachael, watching her sleep. She had a bandage above her right eye, but looked comfortable, peaceful and somehow content. *You're so beautiful,* he thought, then leaned over and kissed her forehead. A full minute passed before Josh turned to the man. "Tell her Josh dropped by. Okay?"

The man scowled. "I'm Thomas Berenson. Wait a minute, do I know you?"

"No . . . no you don't." Josh turned and walked out of the room.

Chapter 65

Judge Higgins knew it was time to go. All the others had left some time ago. Vehicle after vehicle, turning out of the cemetery and onto the main road, their taillights dissolving into the flow of traffic. They'd all gone back to their lives, off to their next scheduled meeting, their next event, their next luncheon. Another busy day ahead of them. He knew it was time to go, time to move on, but he wasn't ready to leave. How could he be?

He sat in the backseat of the limousine looking out through the tinted side window, his gaze fixed on the headstone near the top of the hill. *I . . . I don't know how to say goodbye. How can I leave you there, so cold and so very alone?* All he wanted, all he needed, was to hold her one last time. To feel her heart beat against his skin, see her lovely face smiling up at him. But he knew that would never be the case. He would never hold her again.

Looking up, he saw the driver watching him in the rearview mirror, waiting for the signal. The signal to drive on. He ignored the driver, turning his attention back to the gravesite, when the throwaway phone in his breast pocket began to vibrate. His heart rate picked up a beat. Only one person had this number.

He fished the phone out of his pocket. There was one new text message.

We got him. He's dead.

The judge clutched the phone tight in his hand and took one last, long look at the tombstone. Then he tapped the window with his wedding ring and said, "Drive on."

Chapter 66

The morning sun had just breached the horizon, its fiery round mass hovering over the Gulf of Mexico. A wide swath of brilliant colors rippled across the water, flooding the cirrus clouds with red and orange. The air was cool and calm, and the tide was on its way out as a couple of fishing trawlers edged past the marina breakers. The boardwalk smelled of fish and seaweed, with a ribbon of diesel in the air.

Tyler stood at the edge of the pier in front of Josh's place and cast his line out, then turned to Josh.

"I'm gettin' better aren't I, Mr. I?"

"You're doing good, Tyler," Josh said, and then took a sip of his coffee. He leaned back in his chair, letting the sun warm his face as he listened to the putt-putt of the diesels heading out to sea.

"Gran told me to ask if you're still coming for Christmas dinner?"

"You bet I am. Looking forward to it."

"And Gran wants to know if you're bringing someone this year?"

"No, not this time around, kid. Maybe next year."

Tyler smiled. "Don't worry, Mr. I, you'll find someone."

Josh looked at Tyler. "How about you, Tyler—you bringing someone?"

"Ah Jeez, Mr. I," he said, his face red. "I'm only thirteen."

"Well, maybe next year?"

Tyler grinned. "Yeah, maybe." And he started to giggle.

Chapter 67

It was Christmas Eve. Crawlies had shut down for the holiday season and wouldn't re-open until the New Year. The staff had said their goodbyes, and the place was dark except for the turret overlooking the marina. Josh, Mary, and Hollister were sharing a last drink before heading out.

"You'd better dress warm," Josh told Mary. "It can be cold in the mountains."

"Not to worry," Hollister replied. "The cabin's got a fine fireplace, we'll be warm as toast."

Mary smiled. "You know, I haven't been cross country skiing since I was a kid. Be nice to have a taste of winter again, kinda balance things out." She paused and a concerned look crossed her face. "Any word on Lana Friedman?"

"Yeah, actually she called me this morning," Josh said. "Wished me a Merry Christmas. She's staying with her sister in Wichita. Said she figures she should be ready to go home soon, maybe in the New Year."

"And how about that young girl, Hanna?" Hollister asked. "How's she doing?"

"I hear she's getting better, starting to talk more. She's living with her aunt on her mother's side. Word is, it'll take some time . . . but at least she's safe."

Mary glanced at Hollister then turned to Josh. "And how about Rachael? Any word from her?"

Josh didn't answer.

"Didn't she get married last week?" Hollister asked.

Again, Josh remained quiet.

"Maybe it's not my place," Hollister said, "but she'd probably like to hear from you. You two have been through a lot together."

"I can't do that."

"Well, that certainly explains it, Josh," Mary said, a layer of sarcasm coating her words.

"Hey, c'mon. She's better off this way. I'm damaged goods—let's leave it at that, okay?"

"Son, we're all damaged goods," Hollister said.

Josh got out of his chair and grabbed his jacket. "Yeah, you're probably right." He paused for a second. "I guess I'd better get back to Eddie, he's been alone for most of the day."

Mary gave Hollister a look that said they should be heading out as well. Standing up, she wrapped her arms around Josh and gave him a warm hug. "Merry Christmas, Josh."

"Merry Christmas, Mary."

"We'll see you in the new year," Hollister said, and shook Josh's hand.

Josh smiled and gave Hollister a pat on the shoulder, then left the restaurant.

Chapter 68

The marina was quiet except for a few seagulls crying overhead. The fishing trawlers had returned and were tied down for the holiday season, as were the sailboats and the diesel power yachts. The boardwalk was empty and dark except where the pier lights flooded the deck surface. Everyone had gone home for the holidays.

Josh came to a stop where Lily's cabin would be built, trying to visualize how it would look when it was finished. *She should be comfortable,* he thought, and was going over how the construction process would unfold when the wind picked up and the water around the boardwalk began to ripple. Then the seagulls' squawking rose and the boats began rocking in their slips. Josh gathered his jacket about his neck and turned toward his place, and was surprised to see Tyler coming out of his door.

"Just finished walking and feeding Eddie for ya, Mr. I."

"Hey, thanks a lot, Tyler." The rain started to pelt down and bounce off the boardwalk deck.

"You're still coming for dinner tomorrow, right Mr. I?"

"Yeah, I'll be there. Getting hungry just thinking about it. Oh, and make sure you remind Lily I'm bringing the pie."

"Will do."

Josh glanced back toward the Tackle Shop. "So, where is Lily?"

"Oh Gran, she's in the car, waiting."

"You'd better get a move on then, you know how she doesn't like to wait."

Tyler nodded, turned, and hurried down the board-walk toward the parking lot.

Josh went inside and was greeted by Eddie, his big tail wagging, his body twisting. He gave Eddie a hug and patted his side, then made a fire, poured himself a brandy and eased into his leather chair. Eddie did his 'Eddie move' and flopped over, plopping down across Josh's feet, and let out a tired groan.

Josh took a long pull on the brandy, laid his head back, and was about to drift off when a knock came at the door. Eddie raised his head and looked at the door for a moment, then dropped back down—far too comfortable to investigate.

Another knock followed, then another.

Josh slid his feet from under Eddie and they both got up.

He opened the door. Rachael was standing in the rain, a bottle of red wine in one hand and a small present, wrapped with a blue bow, in the other.

"Merry Christmas, Josh."

He hesitated for a second, his heart pounding. "Ahh, Merry Christmas, Rachael."

"May I come in?" She looked down. "Oh, and you must be Eddie. I've heard so much about you." Eddie's tail went into overdrive.

"Yeah sure, of course, come in. Um, sorry, I, I wasn't, you know . . ."

"No, I'm not sure I do know," she said as she stepped up close to him. "I just dropped by to give you this." She handed him the bottle and the gift. "Christmas, *you know*—a present—it's what people do."

He put the gift and the bottle on the table by his leather chair. "Sorry, I . . . I didn't get you anything." He paused. "But, shouldn't you be on your honeymoon?"

Rachael shrugged. "Things didn't quite work out. Didn't turn out as I thought they would."

"What are you saying, Rachael?"

"It, it just didn't feel right."

"What didn't feel right?"

"Jesus, Josh, do I have to spell everything out for you?"

"Oh, okay then." He couldn't think of anything else to say.

She studied him for a few seconds. "You doing okay?"

"Yeah, yeah sure, doing good, great in fact. And you?"

"I guess so," she said, her eyes filling with hurt. "And, um. Mary, how's she?"

"Still talks about you all the time."

"Oh, I bet she does." Rachael half-smiled, looking as though she was trying to make up her mind about something. Then she began buttoning up her raincoat. "Well, it's been good to see you again, Josh. But, I'd better be going. I can still make the last flight, if I hurry." She reached down and scratched Eddie's ears and gave him a hug. "Bye Eddie. You take good care of him, okay?"

"It was good to see you too," Josh said, the words barely making it out, followed by an awkward moment that seemed to fill the room.

As they walked to the door, neither said a word. She turned and touched his cheek with her hand. "I guess . . . this is goodbye?"

He didn't respond, he just looked at her.

She closed her eyes and gave her head a shake, then turned and walked out the door.

As the door closed behind her, Josh felt a sadness so hard and deep, he thought his heart would stop. He knew he should do something, anything, but instead he just stood there, staring at the door, listening to the rainwater overflowing the gutters and splash onto the boardwalk. *Ah man, what's wrong with me? How can I let her walk away?* It was at that moment he realized he would never see her again. She was gone and she wasn't coming back.

And that was something he could not live with. He opened the door.

Rachael was standing there, water dripping off the hood of her raincoat, her hands in the coat pockets, tears running down her face. She looked up at him. "I've got nowhere to go . . ."

Josh stepped forward and leaned in toward her, softly kissing her lips.

Holding her tight in his arms, he whispered, "Please stay . . ."

About the Author

t.g. brown grew up in Edmonton, Alberta and attended the University of Alberta.

He and his wife live in British Columbia.

80999219R00217

Made in the USA
Columbia, SC
24 November 2017